Red, White & Cue

by Polly Meek

Copyright © 2025 Polly Meek
All rights reserved

RED, WHITE & CUE

First published in Great Britain in 2025 by Kindle Direct Publishing.

Copyright © Polly Meek 2025

The right of Polly Meek to be identified as the Author of the Work has been asserted by her in accordance with the Copyright, Designs and Patents Act 1988.

All rights reserved. No part of this publication may be reproduced, stored in a retrieval system, or transmitted, in any form or by any means without prior written permission of the publisher, nor be otherwise circulated in any form of binding or cover other than that in which it is published and without a similar condition being imposed on the subsequent purchaser.

All characters in this publication are fictitious and any resemblance to real persons, living or dead, is purely coincidental.

ISBN: 979-8-34330-266-0

POLLY MEEK

For Mum
Thank you for a lifetime
of unconditional love.

RED, WHITE & CUE

1. Boom

Cassie Forde smiled to herself, relieved to have reached the gates of Camford Rugby Stadium on schedule. Throughout her sports journalism internship with Hystar, she'd made a point of punctuality and the first day of her Outside Broadcast secondment was no different. Early was on-time, and on-time was late. Swept by the early September breeze, she'd hot-footed off the 6am train from King's Cross, and successfully navigated the twisting, cobblestoned route using a screenshot of the town map she'd taken last night. Cambridgeshire's notoriously patchy data signal nil, Cassie, one. Or five, if you counted in rugby tries, which today, she would be.

Whatever the sport, the special silence of an empty stadium never failed to heighten her anticipation. Though tempted to take a peek inside Camford's historic ground, she headed directly through the open-air carpark towards a trio of long white Hystar Media trailers. In six hours' time, turnstiles would be giddy with twelve thousand supporters for the first match of the season, but almost a million viewers across the country would rely on Hystar's televised feed.

Cassie raked her fingers down her ever-present block fringe, and smoothed the flyaways of her dark bob. It was a miracle how the break-up induced, DIY hair trim a few months back had held its shape. Quid pro quo for her lack of love life, perhaps. Today would be spent fetching and carrying, not exactly her dream job, but first impressions were a one-time gig; the community of sports journalism, in whatever form, shockingly tight.

Hoping for an indication as to the whereabouts of her contact, Izzy Fitch, she smiled at two technicians who were unreeling cables from industrial-sized tool chests, but they mustn't have seen her. Likewise another pair stood on the roof of the furthest trailer, cranking up tall aerials and a satellite dish. Just as she noticed that the side doors of the trailers had been labelled, a blonde, pixie-haired woman, wearing a lumberjack shirt and hiking boots exited the one marked 'Production'.

Hystar's fastest rising outside broadcast producer scrutinised a computer tablet, scanned the area and strode towards Cassie. 'Hello there, are you Cassandra Forde, our latest help?' Questioning brows above blue eyes even paler than Cassie's own, marked a fair reaction to meeting a soon-to-be thirty-year-old intern on a programme designed for twenty-two-year-olds.

'Cassie, nice to meet you,' she replied, retracting her hand when Izzy waved it away.

'Welcome to OB, I'm Izzy Fitch, producer for today's live coverage. So, you've been writing digital content for the Sports News Desk for three months? Bet you're glad to breathe some fresh air.'

Not about to admit to her ambition of securing a sought-after journalist role in Sports News once the internship was over – nor to the impending financial disaster if she didn't – Cassie hedged her bets. 'I'm looking forward to understanding more about outside broadcast, for sure.'

'Good, although today might be more brutal than usual – two crew members have called in with flu, so stay sharp and try to learn fast. You'll be at the pitchside commentary area that's currently being set up inside the stadium. Your main role will be to provide our presenter, Griff Hughes, with any stats from last season's club and player performances, and to relay production info from me, when he's off-camera. He should arrive before lunchtime. Stay with him, and fetch whatever he asks for. He's very knowledgeable but chock your tablet full of as much background and detail as you can on both teams, just in case. You do have a tablet with you?' Izzy held out her hand expectantly.

Cassie hustled to retrieve the tablet from her shoulder-bag and opened the screen to the correct pages.

Izzy nodded as she scrolled through. 'These are extensive, well done.'

'Thanks, rugby is one of my three preferred sports to report on, so it helped knowing what to look for.'

'Indeed. What are your others?'

'Hockey and volleyball.'

'I see why – team sports have more elements to report on. Perhaps consider some individual ones – that will help keep your options open when projects are being allocated.'

'OK, I will. Been writing up golf all summer.'

'Oof, you poor thing.' Izzy grimaced. 'Golf's widely regarded among sports producers as the snoozefest to beat all others. Maybe volunteer for something more exciting – in the aquatics arena, for example. Swimming, diving, even kayak? Those are worth considering because they'll add to your reporting repertoire, whether in front of the camera or from a desk.'

'I'm open to anything.'

'Really? Excellent attitude.'

Cassie felt her chest puff; the late nights of gathering statistics had already paid off.

'Two things before that; head to Trailer 1 for headphones and a talk-back mike, then go and see whichever camera man will be recording the team arrivals. In a couple of hours' time, he'll need help with the sound boom. Other than that, generally listen-in to the order of events and for my direction.'

'Got it.' Cassie patted her ear in solemn acknowledgement.

'Lastly, you'll find that OB works closely with the media management of whatever club are hosting us. In this case, it's Patricia Murphy, Camford Rugby's media and marketing manager – people seem to call her Trish. She works from offices here at the stadium, and at their media centre in The Manor, the club's training centre you've probably seen in the media. She's one of the best – experienced, organised and helpful. Introduce yourself when you see her; curly dark hair, older than me, early fifties maybe, usually wearing a red club hoodie and attached to her phone.'

Cassie pulled out her own phone and made a note of the name. 'Will do.'

'This leads me to another last thing,' said Izzy, smothering a smile. 'Catering vendors won't set up in the grounds for staff or ticket holders for another three hours or so, and we all need coffee. Unfortunately the nearest coffee shop is at the station; best write down everyone's order – we're too busy to keep being asked. There'll probably be a couple of rounds to fetch this morning.'

Cassie nodded, but any smugness from having chosen to wear comfortable Chelsea boots was replaced by immediate concern at the cost of twenty coffees on her straining overdraft.

'Oh, here, use this card and keep a note of expenses. There'll be a team debrief at around 6.30pm. After that, if you're serious about your future with Hystar, wait around for some individual feedback on your performance. I'll be gathering notes on you throughout the day.'

Cassie disguised her gulp of fear with a nod.

'Izzy?' A gruff voice yelled from the roof of the furthest trailer. 'Problem.'

'Coming,' she shouted and jogged off, leaving Cassie puffing her cheeks. 'And mine's white, two sugars, by the way. Why are you still standing there? Time's a ticking!' she called over her shoulder.

Stood in a queue at the nearest burger van, Cassie had a moment to herself. The morning had been a whirlwind of memorising the names of riggers, camera operators and sound desk engineers, and running around after Griff. Outside Broadcast was her least preferred option once the internship finished, but during run-through it had been fascinating to watch the technicians tweak their set-ups and test their feed to the OB trailers. Griff had rehearsed deftly in an easy-going style, reading from an autocue when necessary. It seemed unlikely that the diligently gathered information on her tablet would be needed.

Of course, being Welsh, Griff had quickly picked up on Cassie's South Valleys accent, greeting her in a strong dialect with '*helo fy ffrind o gymru*'. Hopefully she'd remembered it correctly from primary school as meaning 'hello my Welsh friend'. His smile in response to her stumbling '*rwy'n iach a chi?*' seemed like it had been correctly received as 'I am well, thanks, and you?'.

In a parallel queue, at a falafel stall, Camford's Trish Murphy waved across at Cassie and waggled a questioning thumbs up. She'd been of enormous help, during the camera set-up run-through, in identifying which players would be live interviewed by Griff during the match warm-up and the protocol for Hystar's selection of post-match interview candidates. Unsurprisingly, that seemed to rest mostly on performance merit. Under Griff's direction, it would be Cassie's job to secure agreement for those interviews at the end of the game. All she would need to do was intercept the relevant players before the team's post-match walk around the pitch, when they thanked and chatted with fans, friends and family, and before leaving for their showers. Otherwise, as Trish had put it, 'you and I will have to enter the den of filthy, sweating men, to retrieve two of them – preferably before they've stripped or plunged into ice-baths.' Surely she'd been joking. Cassie smiled across at her with a thumbs up.

When Cassie returned to the pitch-side commentary area with Griff's burger, she found the presenter in the company of three similarly aged men, busy greeting him with dummy shoulder barges and the suggestion of an early pint in the members bar before the match. Griff chomped into his burger, declining the invite, insisting he'd need a clear head for the programme introduction, the audio commentary and subsequent match interviews. His friends doubled down on their tactics by revealing that a former teammate of his was already in the bar waiting for him. Cassie had been about to back him up when a voice beside her cut in.

'Are you the intern? Let's go, the away team are delayed but the Camford team bus will be here shortly, Izzy said you'd help.' Before she could reply, Matt, or possibly Mark, dumped a large backpack by her feet and stalked off towards the main entrance, a portable camera in one hand, and a sound boom in the other.

Cassie eyed the bag, then Griff. 'Do you need anything else at the moment? I've got to help film Camford's arrival.'

'No, I'll probably be back before you. It'll only be a quick half pint. Don't worry. I can see what you're thinking, but it's a useful way of picking up some inside info for the broadcast.'

Even having a 'quick half' seemed like a bad idea to her. Slurred TV and audio commentary was not on Izzy's running order. Cassie hefted the backpack onto her shoulders and would have tipped over, had Griff not blocked her backwards momentum. She staggered forwards, arms akimbo. 'Thanks, I'll see you later, then.'

At the main entrance, around a hundred home supporters and some local media had positioned themselves on either side of a cordoned channel. Matt or Mark was all pinched irritation when Cassie shrugged the bag onto the ground next to him.

'Get a battery pack ready and try not to speak,' he muttered, apparently devoid of basic manners.

Still catching her breath, she unzipped the bag and discovered two grey blocks. 'So they weren't solid gold bars, then?'

Matt or Mark ignored her attempt at humour and extended the long handle of a microphone boom before passing it to her. 'The players don't usually stop to talk; they're headed straight to the changing rooms. Most of them can't hear anything through their headphones anyway, they're getting pumped up by their playlists. Occasionally, head coaches might acknowledge the cameras with a quick sound bite, or one of the supporters might say something interesting, so be ready to pick up any conversation. Keep the boom above their head, out of my shot line. The camera's built-in mic will pick up everything needed for the wider angled clips.'

'Sure.' She rested the base of the handle on the toe of her boot, while the fluffy-headed boom wavered above her.

'Here's the bus,' someone at the entrance announced. Adorned with Camford's crimson and white-striped livery, prominent sponsorship logos along its length, and superstar blacked-out windows, the bus's arrival immediately enlivened the atmosphere. Small kids were lifted onto shoulders, people's phones removed from pockets. Matt or Mark adopted a steady stance, switched on his equipment and muttered, 'Ready?'

'Ready.' Cassie hoisted the boom above her head, angling it towards the action, ready if needed. She groaned inwardly at the immediate burn in her biceps.

'Recording.'

A pneumatic swish of the bus doors revealed Camford's head coach with the team's captain. They waved, disembarked and smiled as they passed through the channel of waiting supporters. Both of them verbally acknowledged the good wishes, carefully within shot of Hystar's camera. Media training had clearly reached Premiership Rugby. Behind them, the team disembarked in single file, wearing pale grey club tracksuits.

Cassie challenged her research by attempting to identify each passing player, recalling his position and some specific facts. Anything to distract from the muscle pain shooting through her arms.

The battle-scarred, front-row players grinned and waddled past, and taller, formidable second-row players followed with brief smiles, but eyes facing forwards. Cassie's reporter-brain would describe their hungry postures as 'oozing power'. Next came some of the backs, more handsome, hair styled, their low-bodyfat-percentages revealing muscle-honed limbs that would cover the field with pace and precision passes. There was plenty to admire. One of Camford's new signings, Connor Wilson, filed through, eyeballing media representatives as he passed. Near Hystar's camera, he veered towards the crowd and high-fived some of the youngest children. Anticipating a need for the boom, Cassie angled nearer and was immediately rewarded when a supporter asked if he was ready for the day's friendly match. Cassie locked her arms above her head.

Even Connor, the shortest player in the side was a comfortable 5'10.

'Definitely,' he responded, then did an obvious double take at Cassie, batted her a slow wink and walked on without awaiting her reaction. Just as well – it was non-existent. Even if she wasn't on a self-imposed boyfriend ban, salacious winks were an utter turnoff. After him, seven of the eight substitute players for the bench passed, keeping their focus on the man in front as they filed through.

Matt or Mark reached a hand over his camera and pressed the buttons to power it down.

'Hold on, isn't there a debut player, up from the Academy?' Cassie whispered. 'Danny something – he's on the bench, but this is his big moment. Izzy will want that, won't she?'

'Don't bother, she usually crops this footage to ten seconds anyway. You never see the whole team arriving, viewers aren't interested,' he retorted, sliding the camera from his shoulder.

The player in question exited the team bus and paused, scanning the scene. Immediately, Cassie picked up on his discomfort, perhaps at the undivided attention he was about to face. As he stood at the head of the cordon, she noted hair even darker than hers, styled into a recent taper fade, a glint of product through the front lengths. If he'd been aiming for decent hair on his debut, he'd succeeded, and for a ridiculously unprofessional moment, Cassie imagined running her fingers through it.

'Who's that, Dad?' a nearby voice piped up.

'I think that's Danny Reed, he's from Camford's Academy. It's like rugby boarding school. This is his first match for the senior squad.'

Cassie knew this to be accurate, but she recalled finding very little information about him when researching his key statistics, except for his unusually long stint as an Academy player.

The boy called out meekly, 'Good luck on your first match!' and Cassie tracked the look between him and a now smiling Danny, wishing that the camera had caught the lovely moment. Viewers would certainly have been interested in that.

Partly in recognition of Danny's decision to walk over to the boy, and partly in frustration at her colleague's attitude, Cassie held the sound boom high in place as the player drew level with them. To avoid it bopping his head, she raised herself onto unsteady tiptoes. Barely shy of six feet tall, with a strong jaw and nose, Danny held undeniable appeal, though not in a traditional, film-star sense – more a security-forces vibe, if anything. Though most definitely untimely, she couldn't recall ever experiencing such a strong reaction to a man's physicality. The prospect of having to enter the post-match changing room suddenly didn't seem so unappealing. With her brain momentarily fizzing, an adjective to best describe his appearance escaped Cassie's usually broad vocabulary. But it would be a sexy one.

Much to the relief of Cassie's calf muscles, Danny crouched down in front of the boy. 'What's your name?'

She didn't miss his effort to soften a gravelly voice.

The boy recoiled, hiding his face in the legs of the man beside him.

'Arlo,' said the man. 'My son's name is Arlo. And I'm James, his dad.'

A rivulet of sweat trickled from Cassie's temple towards her cheekbone, betraying the effort needed to keep the weight of the now quivering boom under control, even at this height. To her embarrassment, Danny switched his focus up to her. Above intensely dark eyes, an eyebrow lifted. He was probably wondering if she was about to clock the poor kid.

'All good,' she mouthed down at him, fixing a smile in place. 'Carry on.'

Something in the lingering, tight smile of his acknowledgement suggested interest, perhaps beyond the welfare of her arms. While her journalist instinct mused, she noticed how sun-exposed skin and the lines bracketing his mouth had aged the serious-looking face beyond its years. Danny blinked slowly at her a few times, as if gathering himself, a heady combination of softness and masculinity. Boy, the difference between a blink and a wink.

He cleared his throat and returned his attention to the boy. 'Thank you, er, Arlo, that means a lot. How about, the first time a kick of mine goes through the posts, I draw a little "A" in the air?'

The boy's eyes widened.

'That's good of you, thanks.' Arlo's father reached down to shake Danny's hand.

'No prob—'

'What the hell are you doing?' blurted Cassie's irritant colleague. 'Why are you still holding the boom when you know I've stopped rolling? The lead's not even connected, look.' The end of the boom's jack dangled glaringly in front of her face.

Heat flushed across her cheeks, a combination of exertion and embarrassment. 'I know,' she hissed, 'but it's this player's debut, and that kid will remember this interaction all his life.' Any second now her quaking arms were going to flop.

Danny unbent himself and while looking directly at Cassie, grasped the boom handle to tilt the fluffy microphone head towards his mouth. 'Thank you,' he spoke into it, then gently twisted the handle free from her grip. Though he handed the boom back to the cameraman as if he were lending a pen, the disgust on his face did the talking.

'Enjoy the match.' Danny said to the lad, before continuing on his way.

'Can we bring a shirt for him to sign, next time, Dad?'

Emotion pricked at Cassie's throat, regretting that Danny hadn't heard him.

'You're new at this,' said the cameraman frostily, disassembling the boom, 'but take my advice: don't be doing extra work; you won't get thanked for it. Izzy knows what she wants and expects to get it.' He rammed the final pole into its carry case and picked up his camera. 'Back to the trailers. I'll let you know when we do the same again for the opposition's arrival. Let's go.'

Cassie might not have known much about outside sports broadcast, nor about Izzy's methods of success, but she knew about sport – and her bullshit radar was match-fit. After rolling her shoulders, she hooked the heavy pack through her arms and onto her back. As she trudged back to Hystar's trailers, a word to describe Danny Reed's brand of appealing masculinity came to her. Rugged.

2. Handsome Dan

'Finally. Where the hell have you been?' Head Coach Alex fired from a stool in the changing room.

Danny mumbled his apology for the delay, pushing the encounter with a ballsy sound engineer with pretty blue eyes to the back of his mind. This wasn't the time to reflect on how her smile had lit him up, either. He quickly took his place on the bench where a shirt numbered '20' hung with team shorts, socks and a warm-up kit.

'Protein bars here, bananas, nuts and pre-game drinks,' Kicking Coach Jim called out, but Danny shook his head. Earlier, at The Manor, the team had attacked a high energy breakfast, confident in its micronutrient, carbohydrate and protein credentials. Danny had been unsure whether his stomach would welcome it, and still wasn't, but that wasn't a reflection on the food. Throughout his Academy residency, the fully catered meals had been superb. Even so, he wasn't about to admit he'd almost puked while putting his socks on.

Conversation in the changing room was limited to basic chatter and, like him, a few players kept to themselves. He respected their choices; preparation was personal. If your whole week was going to be judged on eighty minutes of match play, then your head had better be ready. He swallowed the knot of nerves reminding him that after four long years, his ball handling, tackling and, most of all, goal kicking were about to be scrutinised.

'OK, settle down I want a few words before you get into warm-up kit,' said Coach Alex. 'Camford ended last season three from the bottom, something we not only want to improve upon but smash. We've had three weeks of training for this friendly match, and I'd like to acknowledge the new faces in this changing room: our Academy player, Danny Reed…'

Half-hearted claps rippled around the room, and someone patted him on the back.

'Connor Wilson, who, as you know, transferred from Axminster.'

Danny watched players continue their lukewarm clapping but share deadpan looks with one another. No doubt they were as wary of Connor's rocky reputation in the media as he was. The guy played with flair and, though short in stature, was known as much for scrappy nightclub brawls and gobby interviews as his rugby.

'And of course, our respected international hooker who's joined us all the way from Cape Town, South Africa, Rynhardt Koch.'

In unison, the squad whooped their ongoing appreciation of the signing. Training with Ryn had already shown that Camford's forwards pack could be truly dominant this season, and the line-out throws would be more consistently on target.

Ryn raised a hand. 'Thanks, you blokes. I'd like to add my appreciation for making me and Heather welcome, so cheers, let's do this,' he said, his distinctive blonde viking-esque mane grazing his shoulders.

'Yeah, let's hear it for Thor!' quipped Josh Webber, one of Camford's stalwart forwards.

Everyone laughed until Coach Alex pulled the attention back with a brief raise of his hand. 'Alright, settle down. This is a good moment to remind you that the club will be having the usual new season fish and chips afternoon on The Manor's lawn this Sunday, so bring your families, kids of course are welcome, we can provide suitable equipment and balls.'

'Recruiting them early, Coach?' said Lewis, the multi-year team captain, who was once again tipped for England duty in the upcoming Six Nations tournament against Scotland, Ireland, Wales, France and Italy.

'If it's in the DNA…' Coach Alex grinned.

Danny clamped down on a flicker of insecurity about his background, determined as ever to focus on his game. Maybe he'd make his excuses for Sunday.

'And in case any of you were thinking otherwise, club functions are mandatory. Right, I know it's mild, but bodies are cold. Get yourselves into warm-up kit and be out on the pitch in fifteen. Half the stadium will be in their seats early to watch your prep, so I want spot-on clockwise perimeter jogs and the usual breakout drills for forwards and backs and for goal kickers, including you, Danny, in case we bring you on. Practise all the angles with Jim. Go.' At the sharp pip of Coach Alex's whistle, the squad busied themselves with changing into their kit.

Pre-season training had initially been about reuniting senior players from their ten-week summer break, joking and backslapping, sharing family news of babies, barbecues and beach holidays. Like all teams, the players were a mix of experience and personalities, but Danny preferred to remain on the edges, socially. No one would have wanted to hear that, unusually, he lived at The Manor year-round, so had spent the summer working weights, resistance strengthening in the gym and going on stamina runs in the countryside. Nor would they be interested that when he wasn't drilling hours of kicking practice, he'd be helping Head Groundsman Norm with the gardens. Instead, when necessary, he'd occasionally recount tales from some of the legendary Academy clubbing socials to London and Cambridge that he'd sometimes attended. Less often, as the years rolled on, truth be told. Drinking and hooking up behind nightclubs had lost its appeal.

In the past three weeks, Danny had identified who to keep at arm's length and a couple to befriend. It was true that rugby was a team game, but it was also an individual competition that fuelled selfishness and egos. Young players up from the Academy might inject energy and pace, but they also threatened an existing position-holder's grip as first pick. Shirts were a hard-earned honour that no one wanted to give up. A strong slap on his shoulder made Danny turn.

'How are you doing, bra?' asked Ryn, scanning Danny's face. 'You got this today, ya know.'

'Thanks, settling the nerves. Hoping I'll get off the bench, though obviously I don't wish Crofty ill. I know he's nailed his name on the number 10 shirt. Your first match for a UK club, are you ready?'

'Born ready, maybe missing the weather though.'

'Late August in Camford not comparing to sunny South Africa?'

'Nah, summers over there are constant braai weather, flame-cooked food outdoors – lekka. I'll tell you though, England's so green. Nothing like the Veldt – completely brown over there at the moment, ground like rock.'

Danny smiled to himself at Ryn's topic of conversation, unusually bland compared to their often-long discussions over beers back at The Manor's bar. 'Yeah, well, the ground is pretty hard here too, for Britain anyway.'

Ryn shook his head to himself. 'Sure, sure. Look, so you know, I don't usually chat shit about the weather on match days, it's just first day nerves. I'll leave you be and go bother some other fella with my awesome conversation.'

Danny nodded and punched his friend softly in the chest, just as Josh came over to talk to them. 'Don't worry, Brits love talking about the weather, don't we Josh?'

'Definitely. How are you guys feeling?'

Josh was one of the few who ever waited for a response to questions such as those, not that many asked at all. Danny gestured for Ryn to answer first.

'Good, Heather's looking forward to cheering everyone on from the friends and family seats. Do your wife and kids come to watch?'

'Last season she came occasionally. She's been terrified of seeing any injuries, but now, thanks to you and Handsome Dan here, she tells me she'll definitely be at home matches this season. Might even travel to some away fixtures. Nothing to do with supporting a husband who displays a striking similarity to Shrek, I suspect.'

'Ag, man,' said Ryn, 'everyone knows that Shrek scored the princess.'

'Hell yes, I did. And you, Danny? Feeling good?'

Danny chuckled through a 'Yep,' fervently hoping that 'Handsome Dan' wouldn't become his team nickname, and set about changing into his warm-up kit. 'Nerves are mostly under control.'

'It's OK, use that adrenaline. I bet you're glad to be wearing senior squad kit at last. Academy quality wasn't great, even when I was there. Whatever happens this afternoon you can remind yourself that at least you're not in a classroom session. We all feel for you Academy sods when we see you through The Manor's lecture-room windows.'

Danny had to chuckle. He'd watched the senior boys jog past the windows so many times, wishing he was with them. 'A fourth year of weekly presentations on nutrition, media skills and first aid does get repetitive.'

'Well, we're all rooting for you. And don't forget, there isn't a man here who didn't make his first professional appearance in a senior squad. Do yourself and your family proud.'

Ryn shot a brief wince of sympathy at Danny.

'Thanks Josh, I appreciate that. I'll see you out there for warm-up.'

Almost ready to leave the changing room, Danny delved a hand into his holdall, fingers meeting the envelope he'd found pushed under the door of his room in the Academy's accommodation annexe. To his surprise, a good luck card had been signed by all the catering and grounds staff, many of whom he'd known since arriving as a moody and distrusting twenty-year-old. After the match he'd stand it on his small, built-in desk, where he kept a special mug, an old wind-up torch and a celebratory photograph of himself at fifteen. Thinking of that occasion, when he'd held a candle-lit cake with his new adoptive mother and her two nephews, he rued for the thousandth time the cruel ravages of dementia. Unless he had a disastrous outing that afternoon, he'd finally be offered a senior squad player's contract, and his long Academy days would be behind him. Laura would have been proud. That, and the less-than-ideal alternative of labouring on a building site somewhere come spring, fuelled his determination.

As Danny pulled his boots on and stashed a gum shield in his sock, Captain Lewis passed by. 'Wait, which boot did you put on first?' he asked, frowning at Danny.

'Er, the left I think. Maybe it was the right.'

'Try to remember. Things like that might make a difference to a performance streak, you know. I always wear this t-shirt under my warm-up shirt. Kelly knows my whole game could be in jeopardy if I don't have it. I even took it to the Six Nations matches in February. Not a similar one, this exact one.' He tugged out the hem of a worn white t-shirt from beneath his club top to show him.

'Let's see how I do, assuming I even get on the pitch. But thanks for the tip.'

'I'm not the only one. When you're out there in a minute, notice how Josh insists that he touches all four corners of the turf during warm-up – hoping that he'll score tries there during the game – and Crofty, even during kicking practice with Jim, will use the same signal in the air with his fingers when he's kicked a ball successfully through the posts as he'll do during the match.'

'I hear you. Good luck today, Lewis.'

People surprised Danny sometimes, but in a way, his own ritual of gathering calming mental images to call upon when kicking had become something he depended on. He reached for his phone and searched for the set of photographs he'd prepared for the match and warm-up. The latest image was of a bowl of green apples in a wheelbarrow. Much earlier that morning he'd left his small ensuite room in the annexe and strolled up to The Manor's orchard, finding Head Groundsman Norm harvesting apples. Conversation had been light, exactly what Danny had needed.

'No rain, cool breeze but still mild. Good conditions for later,' Norm had greeted him, without looking away from his long-handled fruit picker.

'Hope so. The stadium pitch gave good grip earlier in the week at practice.'

'As it should. Me and the crew have already been up there at dawn watering it to give you lads the best chance.' He handed Danny the picker, perhaps recalling from the previous year how he'd enjoyed taking a turn with it.

'What, a chance that we won't shred the pitch to bits, you mean?' Danny had smirked.

The groundsmen were very protective of their turf. Even The Manor's training pitches were competition standard. Danny swore as a third apple fell to the ground. He attempted to correct the angle of the net, keeping it directly beneath the blades.

'We don't have long in the off-season to work miracles with the turf, I'll tell you that much,' said Norm, adjusting the handle slightly in Danny's hands. Norm's role was primarily concerned with pitch management, but he also oversaw the gardens and orchard at The Manor, some of which supplied the kitchen. Danny didn't know Norm's official hours, but the man was always there. He'd retired from the army, though only ever referred to it in passing. Danny rarely mentioned challenges of his own past to him; perhaps they both knew not to ask. That the past should stay where it was. The only time he ever saw Norm caught off balance was the occasional tongue-tie when speaking with Trish, the club's media and marketing manager, who for some reason he always called Patricia.

Danny studied the photograph of the apples in Norm's wheelbarrow, ready to draw calm when he was kicking for the posts, to help block out other distractions. In recent Academy matches, Danny had used images of views across the Cambridgeshire hills, and of newly emerging flower bulbs, to help him settle and ready himself for his set-up process. He scrolled back to another picture, of the topiary bushes outside the front of The Manor's main entrance, recalling Norm's frustration at how he 'seemed to make the peacock-shaped sculpture worse each year he trimmed it'. Danny hadn't had the heart to say it was supposed to be the club's shield.

As several of the team congregated at the door, ready to file out for warm-up, one of the team physios called from across the changing room where he was taping sponge lifting blocks onto the thighs of one of Camford's back row players. 'I bet this feels a long way since your days of mini and junior rugby, eh? Good luck, Danny.'

'Thanks.' The gesture had been well-intended and Danny smiled like he understood, but in truth, he hadn't been a mini or a junior, which he expected the majority of the squad had been. As had everyone at the Academy. You had to be someone's son, for that. Have someone take you to and collect you from training and matches, maybe stay to watch. Few players at the club knew he'd never given rugby a thought until he was sixteen. Yes, he might have fudged vague stories over the years about his pre-Academy experience as being mainly from casual community teams 'in London', yet in reality he'd attacked two years of college rugby like the lifeline it had been. A player with nothing to lose.

'Ready fellas?' Coach Alex called out to a chorus of positive responses. Danny stowed his phone away and headed for the back of the queue at the door, trying to shake off unwanted demons of his past. Despite the odds, he was about to warm up for Camford Rugby's senior team. Perhaps the best day of his life so far. As his boot studs clacked across the concrete floor, his inner voice served a piercing reality check; the fact that several thousand pairs of eyes were about to be on him wouldn't matter – because in truth, when it came to him, nobody was there.

3. Tunnel Vision

Near the pitch-side commentary area, Cassie perched on an empty seat, gobbling down a very average cold burger. In a brief respite between tasks, she soaked up the stadium's classical 1950s architecture, marvelling at the decades of fixtures it must have hosted. From the neat red and white rows of flip-up seats, people had watched hundreds of careers launch. After filming the team arrival earlier, she'd certainly be on the lookout for Danny Reed, who would be earning that honour today. Despite being a little younger than her, he made the few men she'd dated look like boys.

In an hour, the TV programme's running order would commence. Sport broadcast was already more stressful than copy journalism and they hadn't even gone live yet. Attending, then writing up, was more Cassie's comfort zone. During her first stint at university, she'd tagged along with her then boyfriend when he undertook pitch-side first aid duties for various team sport matches. Though on a creative writing degree, she'd volunteered to write up match reports for the relevant university societies, because writing was writing. She'd also developed a knack for getting to grips with complicated rules within the various disciplines and relished the buzz of competitive occasions. Little had she known that those experiences would help convince interview panels for a second degree that Sports Journalism was within her capability.

Swallowing down the last of her burger, she sighed to herself; without having anyone to fall back on, she'd busted her gut during the News Desk secondment, earning a much-coveted recommendation for hire from the Chief Editor. Just three months of this OB secondment to go and she'd be doing everything she could to secure herself a job.

'Cassie, where's Griff?' Izzy's authoritative tone filled everyone's headsets. *'We need to politely remind him of the Television Code for standards and practices, please. Don't want any swearing and penalties from Ofcom on my watch.'*

A shiver ran through Cassie as she pressed the coms button on her headset. *'He's, erm, somewhere in the grounds with three friends. Should be back soon.'*

'PLEASE don't tell me he's anywhere near alcohol,' Izzy roared, making Cassie's ears ring.

'He's gone to the members bar – but he's only been gone…' She checked her phone. Oh no. He'd been gone almost an hour. *'A short while – I can go and get him?'*

'Yes, for God's sake, use some common sense. No presenter should be drinking before live television.'

'His intention was to pick up some useful information for the commentary, I think.' Or maybe it was to steady his nerves? Right at that moment, Cassie could use the calming effects of a stiff margarita, even though she rarely drank.

'Trust me, it's never a good idea. Is everything else ready for him?'

'Yes.'

'Water, spare battery packs, the camera powder polish?'

'Yes, and the cameras looked clean during rehearsal.'

Something indecipherable fed into Cassie's headset. *'Cassie, the powder polish is for Griff's face, didn't you use it on him earlier? It's the warm-coloured buffing talc that prevents sweat from shining on camera, so presenters don't look washed out?'*

'Oh yes, of course.' Cassie shoved the burger wrapper into her pocket, debating whether to mention that Griff hadn't worn any powder in the rehearsal. Fortunately, what looked like a recent holiday tan and today's mild weather had probably negated the need.

'You've got a key supporting role today, Cassie. We can only do so much with the sound and images mix, and by coordinating the timing of periodic breaks for adverts. Ensuring Griff keeps to his cues, performs his pre- and post-match pieces to camera flawlessly and delivers efficient audio commentary throughout the match is critical.'

'Yes, I'm on it.'

'I hope so, is your tablet completely ready?'

'Yes, I've picked up a few bits and pieces here today – some talk about Camford's kicking coach, Jim Williams, possibly being tipped for a position with England's Six Nations staff, and chatter about the academy debut player, Danny Reed being the best goal kicker ever trained through their academy.' That had been an especially great thing to overhear two support staff discussing in the burger van queue.

'Hmm, pressure on him today then. Right, find Griff – and switch off your screensaver by the way, you don't want him stumbling mid-sentence if he decides to read anything from your notes.'

'Thanks, will do. And, sorry, where would the spare powder be, in case I need it?'

'There should be some in the box near you marked 'Presenters'. Slip a pot into your pocket, then go and fetch him,

please. The teams will be on the pitch for warm-up shortly. Everyone needs to be in position to capture some of that.'

Cassie couldn't help but be impressed – she'd expected to spend the day on planet testosterone, yet here was Izzy, a seriously impressive female professional, kicking ass. A pump of adrenaline ramped up Cassie's focus. It was time to do her best, whatever task she'd been asked to do. First on her list: locate the presenter.

Naturally, Camford's club bar was situated at the furthest point within the complex. By jogging most of the way, Cassie had made rapid progress, weaving between early arriving ticket holders as they meandered within the stadium's internal concourse. Ahead of her, four security guards had stretched a pair of ropes across the walkway, blocking everyone's path in both directions. Players from the visiting team streamed between the rope cordons, from their changing rooms towards the concrete tunnel that would take them through to the pitch beyond. Cassie noted their steely expressions, preparing themselves for less ticket-holder support, even during warm-up.

She waggled her Hystar media lanyard at the guards. 'Any chance I could zip through? I'm up against it.'

'No, love. Camford players are coming through, hold on please.'

'Couldn't I please—'

'No. Here they come,' he barked, flashing 'told you so' eyes.

Muttering at the delay, Cassie took note of each player's body language as they passed her – information potentially of use to Griff, assuming he was *compos mentis* when she found him. Some players jogged, others sauntered, a few stretched their necks as they walked. The sound of tape being ripped from reels and wound around heads and wrists accompanied Velcro band-fastening of scrum hats. Others slipped gum shields into their mouths when their boots hit the rubber mats at the entrance of the tunnel. Bringing up the rear of the players came Camford's support staff, carrying training and medical kits. Finally, two teenage water boys lugged pairs of carriers, loaded with Camford-logo water bottles. Cassie checked her phone again, frustrated by the extended hold up. She glared at the security guard. Surely that was everyone?

He blanked her and chose to crack a joke with his colleague instead.

Seizing her chance, she ducked beneath the nearest rope and dashed towards the other side.

'WATCH OUT!'

A slow-motion blur of rolling water bottles hit Cassie's awareness before her feet could avoid tripping over them. She staggered, arms flailing into the path of the team's videographer, who had clashed with one of the water boys. Pinned face-down to the rough concrete, beneath at least one person, Cassie could hear muffled voices above her, asking whether she was OK. In what seemed like minutes, but was really mere seconds, the weight was mercifully yanked away. Someone propped her up into a sitting position.

'Oh my God, are you alright?' a worried teenaged face asked.

Cassie blinked at the boy, registering the name 'Gene' on his Camford photo lanyard. You didn't meet many people with that name, she thought vaguely. Or Arlo, come to that. She tested her shoulders and neck. 'Erm, a little fuzzy, but yes, I'm fine. I think someone bumped into me.'

'Jeez, yeah, I'm sorry,' said the videographer, who scrabbled to his feet, holding his camera aloft. 'Bottles came from nowhere. Hope my camera isn't broken.'

Gene, the panicking water boy, scurried after his bottles, shaking his head to himself as he slotted a pair at a time back into his carrier. 'My fault, everyone, but sorry, gotta go, players need their drinks during warm-up.'

Watching him dash towards the tunnel jolted Cassie into action and she pushed herself up to standing. 'I've got to go, too.' Only while attempting to steady herself did she discover that the contents of the pot of camera powder in her pocket had splattered artfully down the length of her black jeans. She started to pat them down, hoping that Griff looked neither too pale nor too shiny when she eventually caught up with him.

'What's happened?' said a deep voice from behind her. She turned to meet the collarbones of a player in Camford warm-up kit. She tipped her chin, meeting the concerned eyes of Danny Reed.

'Oh shit, your cheek's grazed,' said the videographer beside her. 'Not surprising, everything took a real thump when we collided.'

Cassie prodded her cheekbone. Now that attention had been drawn to it, she noticed it was throbbing. She swiped two fingers across the area, but there was no sign of blood, so she continued to pat herself down, accepting that any attention to her cheek could wait until she was able to check it in a mirror later. 'All good,' she replied, feeling herself suddenly sway. 'But I need to be somewhere.'

The videographer nodded in agreement. 'Me too. Main thing is my camera is undamaged.'

Danny thrust out a hand to steady Cassie by the shoulder. 'Seems like you bring out the best in cameramen, don't you? Hold on, you're not "All good". Get that graze cleaned, at least. There's a decent scuff along your cheekbone. You don't want it to scar.'

'I know how to cover scars, and honestly I do need to go.'

From the way he cocked his head, she suspected that further questions were forming. 'I won't ask what you mean by that, but you do look pale.'

Cassie dismissed his concern with a wave. 'I'm always pale. And now I'm also late.'

'A team member will pass through here in a second. I'll ask them to get a message to the medics. You're definitely paler than before.'

'I was holding a six-foot boom above my head before. I was a red, sweaty mess before' – she held up her arms to demonstrate – 'and now you're stopping me from being somewhere I need to be urgently, so I'm pale and stressed. Which will no doubt increase my chances of irritating even more cameramen when I get to the pitch-side commentary area.'

The heat of Danny's dark-eyed scrutiny prompted Cassie to self-consciously straighten her fringe. Wait, now he looked as if…'Are you *smirking*? This isn't funny, you know. Not at all.' She brushed down her jacket, aiming to demonstrate her disgruntlement, which wasn't easy when faced with such a disarming smile. He wasn't even trying to disguise it now.

'You're right, it's not funny. Not at all.'

'Griff is in position for his final soundcheck, where are you, Cassie?' The edge to Izzy's tone was more than compensated for by Cassie's swell of relief at Griff having safely returned on time. Which was better than she herself had managed.

'Be right there.' She released the talk back button on her headset. 'I'm off. Thank you, Danny, for your concern and the side-dose of sarcasm.' She tried to swerve past him but he easily blocked her way, even with his arms folded. Side-stepping a professional rugby player was never going to be easy.

'A small injury can mask another thing entirely. My Academy first aid lectures had to be good for something. Before I let you go, tell me how hard you banged your head.'

'Not hard at all, I don't think. Look, I appreciate the gesture, so I forgive the sarcasm, but seriously, it's a light scuff. I can even walk in a straight line.' She took a deep breath and focused hard on taking six steps away, then returned without deviation from an imaginary straight line. 'See? Also, it's the third Saturday in August, and I'm at Camford Rugby's stadium. I've passed your head injury assessment, if that's what you're worried about.'

'What's your full name?' He smothered the half-smile threatening one side of his mouth.

Cassie cocked her head, eyeing a way out of this macho display of over-protectiveness. 'Oh, I see. Well, if what you wanted was my name and number, you could have just asked.'

'Funny. Name, or you're not going anywhere.'

'Seriously? Why are you wasting time and overreacting like this? You're supposed to be warming up.'

Danny looked at the tunnel and sighed, 'I don't mind the brief delay, if I'm honest.'

If she were being equally honest, and were not under enormous pressure to be elsewhere, she wasn't exactly hating the delay, either. 'If I'd forgotten my name, I could have looked on my lanyard for the details, couldn't I? But fine, if it gets me on my way, and you out on the pitch for warm-up, it's Cassandra Rhoswen Forde, Sports Journalism intern with Hystar. Everyone calls me Cassie.'

'Well, the name sounds…long…but you're not a journalist, you're a sound technician or some kind of engineer.'

'No, I am a sports journalist. MA City University, London, to be precise.'

Danny took an almost comical step away from her, as if she were emitting a dreadful smell. 'Shit, now I'm trying to replay everything I've said to you,' he muttered to himself.

'Save yourself the bother. This little incident is hardly newsworthy, Danny. Compared to say…now, what do I know about you? This is your *debut,* for example. That's what's newsworthy. So get yourself through that bloody tunnel instead of delaying me.'

'Hold on, you've researched me?'

'Yes, of course. I've done a little.'

Danny widened his stance. 'Let's hear it.'

'For…alright – Danny Reed, er…almost twenty-five, fourth year Camford Academy graduate, after…I can't be sure, Business Studies, I think it was, at college and two years of something else. I don't remember what. Probably PE or sports. I don't recall any youth club history; you have no family connections. Think there was a line on the club's bio about you being a *competitive perfectionist* which, by the way, is such utter—'

'*Cassie? You'd better be almost there? Griff's dry-mouthed and asking for some extra bottled water.*'

'*On my way, Izzy, will do.*'

'Utter what? Finish what you were going to say.' Danny frowned.

She shrugged. 'Nothing, and now I've got even less time because I need to find some bottled water.'

Danny toyed at a loose pebble with the studs of his boots.

What the hell was going through this guy's head? He should be out there running sprints or something, not concerning himself with the detail of his media bio. His reluctance to get out there piqued her professional interest, but on a personal level, intuition suggested that all might not be well.

She calmed her tone. 'Look, I'll be fired if I'm not at the commentary area with water in hand in the next minute, but is there something quick you want to tell me, if my facts aren't straight?'

'No comment,' he mumbled and shook his head.

Before Cassie could assure him that she hadn't been after a juicy story, another of the club's support team passed through the cordon, juggling a pack of bottled water and a heap of dry robes.

Danny grabbed his arm. 'Mate, can you ask one of the medics to drop some antiseptic wipes over to the media commentary team please? Also, can I nab a couple of those?' He took two bottles and handed them straight to Cassie.

'Will do, but you should be through there by now,' said the staff member, looking at his watch. 'You're likely to be called off the bench today, aren't you?'

'Yes, I know that,' Danny called out to his colleague, who'd scurried away. Danny didn't follow him, but instead, rested his hands on his hips, staring alternately at the tunnel and down at his boots. Something was off, but everyone was out of time.

'Thank you, for these, and for checking on me,' Cassie said, making as if about to walk away.

It was almost as if he hadn't heard her.

'Right. Well, I'll be off. Hope your debut goes well.'

To her amazement, Danny bent his head towards Cassie's ear. 'Could you, I mean, without broadcasting it…' He sighed to himself.

She pitched her voice to an almost whisper. 'What's up? Oh, you're nervous? That would be understandable.'

'No, it's not that. I'm ready, been waiting years for this day, it's just…'

Cassie clocked the exact moment some kind of inspiration came to him.

'…just that I'm sorry to delay you. Why not come through the tunnel with me? It'll definitely be quicker. This way.'

'What? No, the seats will be half full by now,' she scoffed, but Danny had already set off. She didn't feel able to do anything other than rush to catch up, and speed walk in silence beside him. Too quickly, the concrete beneath her feet gave way to springy rubber matting inside the tunnel.

When they met the edge of the turf, Danny paused and took three slow deep breaths, giving Cassie a moment to register her horror at the number of spectators already in their seats. The stadium was almost full. 'God, there are thousands of people watching,' she muttered.

'Yes and no,' he spoke into the air, before cricking his neck and lifting each knee to circle wide hip rotations. His hands jerked towards his warm-up shorts and tugged at the hems.

'What do you mean by that?'

'Nothing...but Cassie?' he said gruffly.

'Yes?'

'Thank you, that helped.'

"S'OK.'

'And you won't say—'

'No. I won't. Now go and warm-up, then show them what you can do.'

He nodded then sprinted forwards, raising his hand to meet a ripple of welcoming applause.

With a bottle of water in each hand, and her rucksack bouncing on her back, Cassie jogged along the perimeter, headed to where the cameras, portable lights and presenting equipment were positioned, opposite the tunnel. As she pivoted around the first corner, some of Camford's forwards thundered into practice tackle bags beside her, under the watchful eye of their defence coach. Further along, the backs executed drills of sprint shuttles. At the next corner, the flat-capped figure of Coach Jim Williams was unloading balls and tees ready for his kickers to attempt their angles. He raised his hands in frustration, 'Finally. When you're ready, Danny,' he shouted.

Cassie turned to see Danny jogging towards his coach.

'Sorry. Be with you after my warm-up jog,' he called out.

'Easy does it, don't want an injury on your first outing.'

Perhaps Cassie had knocked her head after all, because she almost walked past her colleagues. Danny's perplexing behaviour in the tunnel may have played its part; admiring the flex of his leg muscles as he ran, hadn't helped.

RED, WHITE & CUE

4. Breathe

Cassie pressed her fingers to her headset, struggling to hear Izzy's directives over an excitable crowd that anticipated the referee's imminent half-time whistle.

'Ten seconds until commercials, seven, six, five, four, three, two, one, roll commercials, and we're out. Thanks everyone. Stand by, Griff, for half-time analysis to camera in three minutes.'

Cassie joined the cameramen, sound technicians, lighting crew and Griff in releasing a collective breath of relief. Three minutes would allow time to roll shoulders and grab a sip of something. She couldn't believe how fast forty minutes of commentary had whizzed by. And so far, dare she say it, so good. During Griff's pre-match live-to-camera pieces, she'd managed to stay quiet and not mess up, even if her knees had shaken the entire time. Throughout the match audio commentary, she'd sat beside him, impressed by his free-flowing account of the game, and with herself for being able to keep up with the technicalities. To her very great relief, his earlier visit to the bar hadn't hindered his delivery at all. Griff's tendency to fill gaps of stoppage time with interesting and relevant facts had kept her and her tablet notes alert to occasionally being called upon. Learning fast, she readied herself with options as soon as pauses in play arose, and she'd adjusted to the flow. Protracted queries by the referees underway over whether a try could be awarded? Get some facts up on her screen about try rates. Player hobbles off with an ankle issue? Pull up his medical stats or the club's replacement strategy for that position.

So far, the teams had been evenly matched, the visitors taking an early lead before Camford went into the fifteen-minute, half-time break two points ahead. Throughout the first half, the wall of crimson and white-striped home supporters chanting and out-singing those of the green and black visiting ones had been entertaining and more of the same would come in the second half. In a tight match like this, every one of them would know that the result could go either way, but that was the way she liked it.

Griff returned to his seat after a few seconds' stretching, and Cassie passed him some water, saying 'I can't call it, can you?'

'Nope, excellent opener for the season; glad this one's being televised. Thanks for your info on Camford's goal-kicking percentages; did you see Crofty flinch after that last kick?'

'No, but hopefully that's not a hamstring.'

'Griff one minute until your half-time roundup, live to camera.'

'OK, Izzy,' Griff responded, then lined himself up in front of the camera, his back to the pitch once again. 'Cassie, do I look OK?'

'Yep, still no powder needed.' Fortunately.

'Griff, ten seconds until live…'

Out of shot, Griff waggled his hand at Cassie. 'Maybe prep extra info on Reed?' he whispered.

Cassie raised a thumbs up and pulled out her phone. During warm-up she'd watched Danny practise his kicking, setting and re-setting the ball on its tee, then line himself up, one step back, two, then one to the side, position himself correctly for a forty-five-degree strike. It was intriguing how kickers varied in their final moments before striking the ball. Danny seemed to take a deep breath each time, stand stock still and carve out a trajectory between the ball and the goal. Another breath, a final look at the ball, a back swing of his arms, a right step, left step and a straight sweep of his right foot through the ball. Good Lord, the man had skills. She really hoped he would come off the bench in the second half.

'Cue Griff.'

'Welcome back to Camford stadium, where the half-time score is seven to the hosts, five for the visitors from Northampton. Home supporters have enthusiastically welcomed South African international Rynhardt Koch to their fold and been rewarded with his 100% successful throw-ins to Camford's line outs. In the second half, fans will be eager to see whether Head Coach Alex Johns will give his other new signing, former Axminster scrum half Connor Wilson, a run out, and eyes might also be on Academy graduate Danny Reed to make his debut. Supporters will want to watch Reed in action for the first time and get to know more about this relative unknown to the pitch.'

In Griff's line of sight, Cassie waggled a thumbs down. She had nothing supplementary to offer him yet. Not for a second would she reveal that something odd had spooked Danny in the tunnel on his way through to warm-up. Whatever the cause had been, he'd got it under control by the time he and the team ran through the tunnel and onto the pitch for the beginning of match. Integrity in journalism was essential, but more than that, she wanted to keep her personal ethics intact. Instead, she pulled together a related sentence about the number of debut players used last season and propped her tablet in Griff's line of sight. A flash of red-and-white shirts caught her eye as Camford's players returned to the pitch. A ripple of encouraging applause continued as the opposition appeared next, from the tunnel. No half-time substitutions appeared to have been made by either team. Cassie updated her tablet.

'Griff, twenty seconds to wrap up.'

'Players have returned to the pitch after their half-time breaks, with substitutions' – Griff flicked his eyes to Cassie's tablet – 'yet to be made by either team. Let's hope the second half here at Camford stadium gives us the same quality of passing and kicking as the first. All eyes will be on the coaching decisions for substitutions, with players eager for their first run-out of the season, and in the case of Danny Reed, his debut. Camford introduced six Academy players last season; he'll want to be this season's first.'

Griff tapered his final seconds perfectly, to coincide with the referee's whistle that signalled play.

'Griff, cue switch to audio commentary in five, four, three, two one.'

To Cassie's secret delight, after twenty-five minutes of second-half play, Coach Alex Johns opted to rest Ben Croft, their main kicker and bring on Danny. She watched intently, hoping he would have long enough to make his mark. If you had to appear for the first time in front of such a large crowd, not to mention the vast television audience, you'd surely want that performance to be remembered.

Almost in front of the commentary team, Camford's captain Lewis Banks wrestled the ball from the opposition and attempted to clear it by firing a powerful box kick up into the air. The ball sailed high but oncoming wind prevented it from gaining any distance. Lewis positioned himself for a standing jump to gather it, but as he sprang up, his head crashed with force into the temple of an opposition player, who was trying fairly to snatch the ball.

Cassie scrunched her face; at least one head injury seemed likely, but it was the sickening crunch and horrendous scream from Lewis as he landed that stunned the nearest spectators, including Griff, into shocked silence. Cassie sucked in her breath, wanting to look away, but unable to.

At university, she had watched copious games of low-standard rugby and hockey matches, some of which saw injuries – often caused by inexperienced players who failed to tackle properly. Bloody cuts, a few dislocated fingers, the occasional concussion. She had never seen a bone protruding from a player's calf – nor the leg in question bending at such a horrific angle. Right in front of her. Blood seeped onto Lewis's white shorts as he lay motionless. The opposition player he'd collided with immediately curled into a ball and thumped the ground in obvious agony.

'Christ! Cue commercials in five, four, three, two, one.'

All Cassie could do was stare. Players around the injured pair clamoured, then shot backwards, holding their mouths and urgently beckoning the medics from further up the touchline.

At Lewis's head, Danny Reed and one of the opposition players argued.

'Gotta stop the bleeding!' the latter shouted at Danny.

'No, first check he's breathing.'

'Wait for the medics,' said another.

'No time,' said Danny, swiping his fingers into Lewis's mouth. He removed the mouthguard and peered inside.

A scream came from the other injured player.

'Help's almost here,' Danny shouted over to him.

'So much blood,' someone mumbled.

'Fuck, now his tongue's tipped back,' said Danny, re-hooking his fingers into Lewis's mouth to release it. 'Is his chest rising?'

'I don't know…no…yes…no, it isn't.'

Several pitch-side medics and Camford's team doctor skidded onto the grass next to them.

'Airway is clear, haven't confirmed pulse,' said Danny.

'OK, move away.'

Cassie held her breath as Danny stood up and staggered backwards. For a second, he looked towards the media crew, his eyes immediately connecting with hers. She stared back at him, aware that her mouth probably hung loose. Everything about Danny's body language read 'serious', but then she realised he was pointing at her.

'Me?' she mouthed.

He shook his head and motioned to her right. Beside her, Griff had fainted, slumped to one side.

'Griff, thirty seconds until live to camera, fill until play resumes.'

Cassie depressed her mic button. '*Izzy, he's out cold, it was right in front of us.*'

'*Does he need a medic?*'

In Cassie's peripheral vision, a couple of St John Ambulance cadets were approaching, beckoned by a Hystar lighting technician. Only a few feet in front of her, an electric cart had now been driven onto the pitch, presumably ready to transfer Lewis once the doctor had stabilised him. The other player was sitting upright, breathing from an oxygen mask while an inflatable splint was strapped to his leg. Compared to those, Griff's condition seemed minor.

'*No, I think he'll be OK, help's almost here. Honestly, the game might be abandoned, Izzy.*'

'*OK, roll athletics trailer. Cassie, we've got sixty seconds. Can you take over presenting until we know either way? Talk to the camera about the match, rugby life, stuff you'd want to hear, and make it interesting. Once play resumes there's only ten minutes of audio commentary left, a post-match to-camera piece and player interviews.*'

'*What do you mean "only"? No! No, no, no, no, no, I can't do it.*'

'*You can. You've got this.*'

In the absence of any viable alternative, Cassie accepted that she was their only option. Microphone. She needed a microphone. There it was, on the ground, beside Griff. '*Is this working?*' she asked, tapping the foam head.

'*Yes, it is, I hear you, Cassie. Thirty seconds. Position yourself facing the pitch, so viewers can't see the scene, please.*'

Out of nowhere, Camford's Trish Murphy appeared, puffing heavily. 'Here, let me help you. Hold it this way round.' She swivelled the microphone in

Cassie's hands to angle the Hystar logo forwards. 'What's happened to your cheek?'

'Eh? Oh, argument with the ground by the players' tunnel.'

'We'll discuss that later.'

As the media technicians scurried around her to reverse their transmission angles, she felt sick.

Trish offered an encouraging smile. 'You'll be OK Cassie. Talk to the camera as if it was one single person.'

A red light appeared on the main camera.

'Alright, just listen for my direction. I'll count you in.'

She was definitely going to be sick.

'Breathe…' said Trish, inhaling and exhaling deeply, as if coaxing Cassie into a better state.

'Maybe puff some camera polish over your face, when you've time. You're reading very pale.'

No chance of that, Cassie thought with a sigh. She shook her head.

'Ready in ten seconds, nine, eight, seven, six, five, four, three, two, one, cue Cassie.'

From somewhere, words left her mouth that she hoped would sound professional. 'Welcome back to a sombre mood at Camford, where the game has been suspended at seventy-two minutes. If you've been watching, you'll know that two players collided mid-air for a high catch. An awkward landing has caused a devastating injury to one, who is still on the pitch, surrounded by team medics, and a nasty, but less serious-looking injury to the other, who has been stretchered off. We are awaiting a decision from the referee as to whether play will recommence.' Within Cassie's blurry line of sight, a nodding Trish motioned 'keep going' with her hands. Cassie stared into the camera, trying to keep focus. And to not be sick.

'Maybe say why you're there, that Griff is unwell.'

Cassie nodded, then realised she shouldn't have. 'For those of you at home wondering who I am, my name is Cassie Forde. I'm a Sports Journalism graduate interning with Hystar and I've stepped in front of the camera for my first and probably last time, to cover for Griff, who is feeling unwell. At university, I wrote match reports and website articles for rugby union and super rugby competitions among other sports. So, if this match restarts, at least you shouldn't hear me muddling rucks from a maul. Erm, and for those of you still learning about the game, perhaps it might help you to know the difference between those...' Cassie swallowed and took a breath, before giving her best explanation and risking a smile. 'All clear? Don't worry if not, it took me months to understand how rugby works. Learning the rules isn't a one-time thing either, because we have to keep up with the changes to them, don't we? All the same, given that I'm your short-notice presenter, go gently on me please.'

'Excellent, really good, Cassie. Keep going. But try not to fidget with your hair so much.'

Cassie clenched her other hand to prevent herself from nodding a response, or from patting her fringe again. Concentrate, she just had to concentrate, it could only be for a few minutes more. 'Alright, I'm seeing the cart carrying Lewis Banks being driven away so we'll have news shortly on whether play will restart. In the meantime, let's have a recap of the match so far...'

RED, WHITE & CUE

5. Step Up

Danny wiped his shaking, blood-smeared hands down his shorts, monitoring the linesmen and referee for their signal. Surely the game would be abandoned. In every direction, faces wore masks of shock; other players on the pitch, worried subs on the bench, and friends and family in the seats behind them watched as Lewis was driven off the pitch. Stewards were using litter-pickers to place stray debris from the emergency first aid supplies into special plastic sacks. A concerned hush had fallen over Camford's stadium, but few had left their seats. Everyone knew the incident had been serious.

The space in Danny's head that would ordinarily be occupied at this stage of the game by tactical thinking lay silent. Instead, the sound of a lone voice, drifting from the nearby commentary area filled it.

'…the question of whether accurate ball handling would be a challenge for these players, let alone kicking, with the adrenaline from witnessing such an incident. As it stands, Camford would lose their opening match of the season…'

The voice was not Griff's. Wait, was that Cassie presenting? His eyes strained to confirm that yes, it was her. Facing the pitch and even more pale-faced than before, except for that swollen pink scuff on her cheek, her eyes were fixed on a camera. Somehow, she was delivering a stream of update and assessment for Hystar's viewers. Even from where he stood, Danny could see that the microphone she held in a white-knuckled grip was quivering. She couldn't be immune from the aftershocks either, let alone presenting live television. Trish was pacing the media area, on the phone, as usual, concerned eyes switching between the players and Cassie. Griff had been laid out on the floor; his legs raised on a seat. A couple of first aid cadets were chatting with him.

A sudden blast from the referee's whistle beckoned the players from both teams over to the centre. Danny jogged over, draping his arms over his teammates' shoulders as they formed one circle with others from the opposition. The referee gave a little cough, 'Right, fellas. The decision is to play on for the final ten minutes, unless anyone has objections?' He cast his eye around the men. 'Does anyone feel they definitely can't continue?' Silence. 'OK, Reed, wash off that blood quick.' He blew his whistle. 'Three minutes until we resume play, everyone.'

Danny scanned the touchline for one of the ever-present buckets of water and sponges. The referee was insane; three minutes was not even enough time to get to the changing rooms, let alone wash and come back. He dashed over to the nearest bucket, by the commentary team, too late realising that the TV cameras were switching around for pitch-direction recording. Cassie had sat down, the microphone still to her mouth. She must now be on audio-only duty.

'...And we are hearing that play will resume in a minute or so. Academy graduate Danny Reed, who has briefly made his debut this afternoon is quickly washing off his hands. Home fans and viewers supporting from afar are no doubt sending their heartfelt thanks to him after his swift action directly after the dreadful incident with his captain, Lewis Banks…'

Danny rubbed and swished his hands, watching the cool water turn pink, but curiously comforted by the sound of Cassie's voice. Despite her being a journalist – four years of media training had pummelled into him the necessary precautions when dealing with any form of media, let alone the fact that he didn't want *anyone* poking around his background – he was compelled to seek her face. An inconvenient sizzle of heat spread through his body when she noticed him looking. She showed a thumbs up, a cute smile lifting her cheeks, just for him. He acknowledged it with a discreet nod then plunged his hands back into the bucket to refocus.

'Ah, yes, for those of you on social media who have been suggesting it, no I wasn't caught up in the incident. Me and my cheek had a clumsy accident right before the match, no time to use what we call in the biz "camera powder polish" before taking over the presenting helm, either. Thought I'd got away with it, without anyone noticing. Perhaps you eagle-eyed viewers also saw the death grip I actually still have on my microphone and will bear with me through the final few minutes of play.' Danny tucked the beautiful sound of Cassie's chuckle deep inside himself, safely away from the hard business at hand.

'So, here we go,' she said. 'Stay with us here at Hystar and maybe cut me a little slack because the referee is poised with his whistle, ready to resume this eventful match. Players from both teams are almost in position, the referee's checking his watch...'

Danny flicked the water from his hands and blotted them down his shirt, in the hope it was cleaner than his shorts. One last look towards Cassie was rewarded by her cheekily mouthing 'Go!' at him. An entirely new, almost magnetic force made him wish he could stay where he was, but he bobbed his head, retrieved the gum shield stashed in his sock and sprinted into position. Later, he would unpick just how Cassie had fuelled the sudden surge of exhilaration coursing through him, but for now, his mind had to be on the remainder of the match.

Though both teams committed to the same professional-level effort as before the stoppage, the rate of handling errors rocketed, including, to Danny's embarrassment, his direct pass to a fast-paced opposition player, who then went on to score. Hearing the vast proportion of supporters groan their frustration and the rest of them jeer wasn't great, but Danny's well of resilience was deep.

Moments later, the referee penalised the opposition, and Danny was handed an opportunity to add his first points with a kick at goal.

Breathing steadily to calm himself, he lined up in his usual way. The image of freshly picked green apples calmed him for a few seconds but his legs were wobbling like never before. He was certain that spectators could tell; they were shaking even more than Cassie's hands had been. He swore silently at the distraction of thinking of her and began his set up process again. Breathe. Just breathe. Filter out the noise, focus. As the timer for the kicking stopwatch ticked down, his legs still trembled. No way was he was going to be one of those kickers who couldn't hold his nerve. No. Way. In desperation, he closed his eyes for a second and an image of Cassie, stood behind the camera, bolstered his composure. Get a grip, he told himself. If she'd stepped up, so could he.

Luck, and the Cambridgeshire wind, were on his side and his first professional kick for Camford Rugby flew squarely through the posts. He picked up his kicking tee, tossed it off the pitch and recalled his promise from earlier. While the home crowd still clapped their appreciation for the much-needed boost, Danny steepled his fingers and thumbs into a capital A, for the young supporter Arlo. Kids had an inbuilt faith in humanity. Adults breaking promises to them was unforgivable – and he wasn't going to be one of them.

The clock suspended high up in the West Stand read five minutes until the final whistle. Both teams found an extra gear, desperate to chalk up their first win of the season. Between them, Danny and new signing Connor successfully deployed the set piece moves, culminating in popular forward Josh Webber heaving himself over the line for a try – in one of the corners he had indeed visited during warm-up. Danny's boot did the honours to equal the score, but after the final whistle blew, he crouched to the ground, eyes on the turf. Aside from the horror of the incident, neither team would be satisfied with a draw and nor, it seemed, were the supporters. Low-level muttering and head shaking mirrored his own and other players' body-language. He sucked in a deep breath and pushed himself upright, ready to follow the etiquette of shaking hands with each player, then with the referee and linesmen. Many from the opposition mumbled a sympathetic 'Sorry about Lewis' as they passed along the line. One congratulated Danny on his debut, and another, the player he'd mistakenly passed to, jokingly thanked him for the gift.

Coach Jim came over, cupping a hand onto Danny's shoulder. 'Tough outing, that one, but you didn't miss the kicks. Even with all the practice we put in, it's hard to replicate the level of adrenaline you must have had to contend with. It's ridiculous that the match played on.'

'Legs like jelly, never felt anything like it. Have I done enough though? Couple of kicks, a stupid pass to the opposition; the club might reconsider giving me a senior contract.'

'Well, the physios just told us that a couple of the boys have muscle strains so it looks like you'll be first pick at least until Christmas, I should think. Anyway, look lively, the cameras are still rolling and Coach Alex will call you over to a central huddle debrief any second now.'

All Danny wanted to do was head to the changing room, wait for the stadium to empty, then drill some post-match kicks.

At the centre huddle, Coach Alex opened his debrief with news that Lewis was being treated in hospital, and thanked Danny for his potentially life-saving action before the medics had arrived. Several of the players voiced a request to bring forward their next first aid course. After Coach delivered some general encouragement, he congratulated Connor, Ryn and Danny for their debut appearances.

Connor immediately raised his hand to interrupt. 'I'm glad that my experience can be made full use of, especially as I'll be first pick for the rest of the season while Lewis is out.'

Danny balled his fists, imagining a square jab onto Connor's arrogant nose, but his shoulders felt the tell-tale sympathy squeeze from similarly angry players either side of him.

'I want to say I'm sorry about Lewis,' said Ryn. 'Seen a few injuries during my career, and that was a shocker. Otherwise, thanks for my first match, fellas. Your line-out jumps for my throw-ins were great.'

'Thanks Ryn. And Danny, anything you'd like to add, being new to the squad?'

'I'm also sorry about Lewis, especially as he was tipped for international duty again. As for going forwards, we all know that individuals can make a difference in this game, and I hope to bring my best. I guess we've all got to support each other, if we're to hit winning form in the Premiership this season.'

'Well said.' Coach Alex nodded. 'Alright, quick walkabout of the perimeter, hit the changing rooms then the team bus back up to The Manor will leave in forty minutes. Hands in.' All the players stretched their right arms into the centre. 'One two three Camford!' they shouted in unison, lifting their arms upwards and into three sharp claps.

The circle disbanded, and many of the players headed to where family and friends were still waiting in their seats in the specially designated area. Others, including Danny, began a tour of the perimeter, clapping their thanks to the straggle of supporters that had lingered. He was heading for a bottle from one of the water boys, when Ryn passed across the pitch in front of him, like a man on an urgent mission. Seconds later, he shoulder-bumped an unsuspecting Connor.

Danny jogged after him.

'No, don't turn away from me, you arrogant cock,' Ryn was spluttering in Connor's face. 'At least try to hide your glee that Lewis will likely be out the rest of the season, if not longer.'

Connor stabbed a finger at Ryn's chest. 'You and I are here for the same reason, buddy, don't give me that high and mighty crap. This club needs our experience, or they'll be *relegated* at the end of the season.'

Ryn walked away, shaking his head. 'Better keep that fuckwit away from me,' he muttered to Danny, who wouldn't have needed asking twice if Ryn requested help in landing a 'stray' punch in Connor's direction – carefully out of sight, of course. To make a bad situation worse, for some reason the obnoxious git's face had suddenly lit up, all smiles in his direction.

'Hi!' came a cheerful female voice behind Danny. Immediately recognising that it belonged to Cassie, he turned to find her holding a tablet and dangling a microphone beside her leg. 'Danny, Trish and I have got three minutes while the ads are running to secure two people for the post-match, live-to-camera interviews. She's grabbing the opposition's captain, and my producer would like you to be the other.'

Seconds passed while he processed the words she'd delivered in double-time.

'Why not me?' asked Connor, pitching her a godawful grin.

She blanked him and kept her eyes trained on Danny. 'Please?'

'I'd rather not.'

'Oh c'mon, viewers would like to hear from you about your debut, and the-incident-with-Lewis-and-get-to-know-more-about-their-new-kicker,' she gabbled. The adrenaline of live broadcast must have strung out her nerves.

'Guess I'm surplus to requirements,' said Connor, cuffing Danny's arm way too hard before walking off towards an opposition player he'd played with at yet another former club.

Cassie pulled her phone from the back pocket of her jeans, but he doubted she'd be able to read anything on it, her hand was shaking that hard.

'I hardly even kicked today, Cassie, and anyway, kicking is only the final thing in a chain of events, it's the speed of the backs to get the ball over the line, and before that, it was only in their hands because the forwards got it there.'

She brought a hand to her chest. 'God, that would be such a *perfect* quote for camera, just say that.'

The way she fluttered her eyes on the word 'perfect' almost undid his resolve. 'Sorry, I was just headed for the changing room.'

She closed the gap between them. 'You don't want me coming in there to get you, not with all those other half-naked, sweaty – or should I say *hot* players I'd have to squeeze past, do you? Because I would.'

Bloody hell, no. He could think of at least three players who brazenly 'air-dried' after showers, whose bodies would have her eyes on cartoon stalks. He cast around, looking at who was still on the pitch, hoping for a fast alternative. 'Ask Ryn. Get his first take on UK club rugby, maybe?' he floundered, hoping his teammate had calmed down.

'We'd prefer you, Danny.' She looked at her phone again and swore to herself. 'Look, this will only take five minutes, you'll be in the showers and back home in no time.'

Home. His room in the Academy annexe was not worth rushing back to, except maybe to catch up on the results of other warm-up matches in the Premiership. He'd planned to skip the team bus back and hang around at the Stadium to practise some kicking instead.

Pools of silvery grey, framed by thick black lashes, stared at him. One second became three, then six, then her frown and a brief slump of disappointment in her shoulders was immediately replaced by a shrug, seemingly pulling herself together. He was cracking. If she asked again, he might actually agree to the interview, risk the awkward question about himself that he didn't want to answer.

'Sorry, Danny, I know I'm hassling. You've had one hell of an afternoon, don't worry. I've got to go.'

He raised some kind of appreciative smile and watched as she ran in Ryn's direction.

She suddenly stopped and turned back. 'By the way, I noticed the "A".'

It surprised Danny how quickly several thousand spectators could empty from a rugby stadium's ground. Within fifty minutes, he was stood back on the pitch almost alone, save for Norm and some of his groundsmen, and the last few stewards collecting litter from the seating, row by laborious row. At the media area, tech guys joked with one another, loading cumbersome black cases onto a trolley. As they wheeled their kit down one of the exit tunnels, guilt pricked at Danny's conscience at not having helped Cassie earlier. It had been a pressurised day for her too, and selfishly, even if unintentionally, he'd probably added to it.

'What are you still doing here, Danny?' said Jim. 'That's enough for today. You've missed the team bus and still haven't showered.'

'I know. I meant to stay back. How's Lewis?'

'Double fracture, concussion. Out for the season.'

'Poor sod. That'll be a long recovery, and a harder shift for us without him.'

'Yep, and with Connor in as first pick in his place, everyone's going to have to swallow the crap that comes out his mouth and get along. He's a good player and, unfortunately, we need him.'

Danny nodded. 'He's made that clear, trust me. Any chance you can arrange for me to have another hour or two here? I'm buzzed and won't sleep. The training pitches can't replicate this.'

Jim checked his watch. 'Alright, let's drill the usual angles, shall we?' It's 6pm, security won't lock up until 8pm, I shouldn't think. You've got me for an hour. If I'm not home by 7.30, my dinner will be in the bin, again.'

RED, WHITE & CUE

6. The Ball

The longest day ever was still rolling. After the team debrief had concluded and Cassie had helped technicians to pack the media centre's broadcast paraphernalia into the trailers, she waited outside the production trailer for her individual feedback from Izzy. Still trembling from the adrenaline surge, she wolfed down a chicken sandwich she'd purchased hours earlier. That, and the Mars bar she'd packed this morning, would probably be dinner.

The door of the production trailer snapped open and Izzy beckoned Cassie inside. As they propped themselves against opposing sides of the galleried rows of screens, she braced herself for feedback.

'Right, let me airdrop you this,' Izzy said, angling her tablet. 'Among other things, it contains basic pointers to consider regarding the fundamentals of OB presentation, based on my limited observations so far. Grooming, speaking voice, preparation, that sort of thing.'

Cassie studied her tablet with unease. Appearance was one thing, but she'd be annoyed if Izzy suggested her effort today had been lacking.

'I give this sort of information to every intern, many of whom are after the sole role available in our department after your programme ends. You're no doubt aware there's huge competition for it.'

Cassie nodded; it was the same for the coveted News Desk role. 'Thanks for today, Izzy. I've learned a whole lot more than I expected to, particularly from you but also the crew, and from Griff, who passes on his best, by the way. He's gone for a meal with his friends.'

'Thanks, yes, he doesn't usually hang around. You did very well, exceptionally so, and I know he thought so too.' Coming from someone whose trajectory was surely headed for management, Izzy's praise felt meaningful. 'How flexible are you, location and format-wise?'

'Very. If I'm lucky, I'd expect to be on-call to write up sports events from across the country, and hopefully in time, overseas.'

'I see there's a recommendation for hire on your file, after your stint writing news copy for the website, but from what I've seen today, I think you've got serious potential as a presenter in broadcast journalism.'

'I hadn't—'

'And if you were interested, even for a few years, I'd recommend you for hire in January. We have a sharp-suited young presenter called Fox Cavalier waiting in the wings from last year's internship programme. I think you two would make quite the dynamic presenting duo.'

Cassie blinked at Izzy, lost for words. The concept of presenting televised sport for a living was almost too unlikely to imagine.

'Of course you'd both have to take the graveyard shifts for a while, TV studio sports roundups, that sort of thing, but the Olympics next year will need twenty-four-hour coverage and as many presenters willing to travel there for it as possible. High salary but high commitment, and though you'd bounce between hotels instead of being home, it would be a huge career step.'

Paris. She'd finally get to travel abroad somewhere, use the passport that Hystar had requested all interns have ready…'Can I think about it?' she mumbled, already processing the potential upsides of clearing double-stacked tuition debts, saving money on rent and getting herself known in key sports journalism circles.

Izzy began to pack up her bag and check that equipment was secure. 'Of course. My mobile's on the sheet I've just sent you. Call me either way. You've got screen presence, Cassie, and that's something relatively rare. You'd probably need to upgrade your grooming, learn to control a few ticks, especially with that fringe of yours, but today showed that you're knowledgeable, adaptable and that you don't crumble under pressure. Quite the audition tape, had you sent it in. I'm not on the hiring panel but could influence it for the right candidate. If you want it, I'd be confident in assuming the job's yours.'

Confidence seemed to be Izzy's middle name. Cassie could use a slice of that. Having an impressive force like Izzy as a mentor might provide the decent female role model she been without for…had it been *eleven* years? 'You've certainly given me a lot to think about.'

'Good. How are you getting home?' Izzy said, gesturing at the door and switching off the light.

'Train, back to King's Cross.'

'Your boots will know their way to the station, that's for sure,' Izzy joked. 'And now you've seen how important that coffee was to everyone this morning.'

'It's a long day, glad I could help.'

As they descended the trailer steps, a whole other future than the one Cassie had imagined – or reimagined, if you counted her original novel-writing dream, lay before her. Questions of role, location, even hairstyle fought for attention as she watched Izzy call a five-minute warning for departure to her crew. Cigarettes were stubbed out, drinks and food were finished, rubbish carefully added to a plastic sack.

'This needs to be tied up and put into the big green bins around the side of the stadium,' someone called out, to no one in particular. 'We always try to leave venues as we find them, if not better. Reputations, and all that,' he added. When nobody moved, Cassie took it to mean the explanation had been for her.

Izzy reappeared, heaving a rucksack onto her shoulder. 'I just need to find Trish and tell her we're off back to Essex. She wanted to run an idea by me, too.'

Groans echoed through the crew. To be fair, they must have put in sixteen hours already; and it would be a couple of hours yet until they'd reach Hystar's engineering depot.

Cassie saw the solution. 'I'm headed back towards the stadium to get to the station, and the bins are on my way, so I can take the rubbish sack and pass Trish a message saying you wanted to get away, that maybe you'll touch base with her next week?'

All heads turned to Izzy, who absorbed her team's unspoken eagerness to hit the road with a wry smile. 'That would be great, thanks Cassie. Have a think about what we discussed.'

Safe in the cast of the stadium's floodlights, Cassie diverted towards the rear entrance to sling the bag of rubbish into a rather foul-smelling, industrial-sized bin. When dialling Trish, she heard a phone immediately ring nearby and followed the sound to the players' tunnel.

Trish had changed into an elegant black cocktail dress, blazer and heels, and carried a laptop bag over one arm and a large bottle of champagne in the other. She greeted Cassie with a smile. 'Hello there, I was just going to answer your call. I thought Hystar had all gone by now?'

'I'm on my way, but Izzy asked me to thank you for today. The team left a few minutes ago but she hasn't forgotten you wanted to talk through an idea. She'll contact you during the week.'

'That's good, thanks. You're driving back now, too?'

'I'm taking a train, no need for a car in central London.' Not that she could afford one. Cassie checked a screenshot she'd taken earlier of the return train times. 'There's one in about forty minutes, others after that. I love your dress, by the way.'

Trish nodded, then brushed down her jacket. 'I'm due at a dinner with two of the club's sponsors shortly, but if you have a spare minute, there's an enjoyable task you can join me for first?'

'OK.' Cassie followed Trish inside the stadium.

At one end of the pitch, pigeons were launching themselves from the roofline, swooping freely before touching down – but at the other end, the air was far from calm.

'FUCK that fucking…fuck!' came the trailing echo of Danny Reed's expletives as he sliced a ball wide of the post. With mud smears, grass stains and the bloody evidence of the accident still evident on his kit, it was clear that the man had yet to use the changing rooms. And furthermore, having used the changing rooms as an excuse, he must definitely not have wanted to give her that interview earlier.

'It's Danny I'm after,' Trish explained. 'Jim messaged after having had an hour of practice with him, told me he'd probably still be here.' She slipped off her shoes and dangled them by their spindly heels as she walked onto the pitch. A groundsman with an aerating fork stopped mid stab of the turf and hurried over to meet them. Trish gave him a little wave.

'Hi Norm, this is Cassie. She's a journalist with Hystar, on her way home.'

'Hello Cassie, I heard your commentary in my earphones – quite enjoyed the "back to basics" explanations on the latest rules the RFU brought in over the summer.'

'Thanks, I was scrambling to fill time. Luckily, I'd done my homework. Excellent grass conditions by the way, hardly a divot.'

'That's kind of you. Part of me never wants rugby boots on it, if I'm honest,' he revealed, though his attention had already turned to Trish. 'It's gone 8pm, Patricia, you're putting in another long shift.' He eyed her shoes. 'If you're not about to help spike the pitch, do those mean that someone special is taking you out after a busy day?'

'God, no.'

Unmistakable relief relaxed Norm's face. 'In that case, can you wait until Danny's finished? I'd then only have to tweak the last of the repairs. Fancy a table at Ruby's, nice bottle of red, over a bowl of their slow-cooked ragu?' From the heightened colour on Norm's face, he was invested in the idea.

Cassie discreetly side-stepped away. Another thud of boot on ball diverted her eyes to Danny, whose demeanour screamed wired-but-exhausted. Oblivious to anyone around him, he sagged to a crouch and set up another ball on its tee.

'Thank you, but no,' she could hear Trish telling Norm. 'I don't have time for anything else, certainly not during the season.'

'There's always time to eat, Patricia,' he replied. You had to admire his persistence.

'I'm working through dinner and there's something I need to do first or I'll be late, sorry.' She padded barefoot in Danny's direction.

Cassie flashed Norm a sympathetic smile before following her.

'Danny?' Trish called. 'Got a minute, please?'

Danny stilled, midway through his back-then-sidestep. He turned, then did a double take of Cassie. 'I'd rather you didn't bring me a media interview right now, Trish.'

'It's not for that. Would you just come over?'

Danny picked up the ball, gripping it easily in one hand, and gestured at Cassie with it. 'I don't know why you're still here then, if there's nothing to report.' Walking towards them, he tossed the ball between his hands, irritably, as if caught off guard. Weirdly, the intensity of his stare did not affect his appeal; to the contrary, this tired and dishevelled version of Danny was, quite frankly, even hotter. A frisson of attraction sizzled through her again. She could be wrong, but did the way he adjusted his stance mean she wasn't alone in feeling it?

She tossed an imaginary ball to him, testing his reaction: 'I'm off duty, Danny, just killing time before a train, but I can leave now if you'd rather?'

Danny looked at Norm and Trish before returning a silent shrug. The metaphorical ball, dropped.

'Fine, it was good to meet you today, Trish. I hope our paths cross another time. And…congratulations on your debut Danny. Good luck with the rest of your season. Norm, nice to meet you.' She turned to walk away.

'Wait.' Danny stepped nearer, squinting, whether from the lights, or the toll of the day she couldn't tell. 'You don't…have to go. I'm sorry. You did a great job today, stepping up like that.'

'She did,' said Trish, sharing a brief look with Norm. 'I've been wanting to ask, what happened to your cheek? It still looks sore.'

Before Cassie could respond, words blurted out of Danny's mouth. 'She was flattened under a couple of jerks in the tunnel before warm-up. I asked one of the staff to take some antiseptic wipes over to the media station for her.' The ball jolted to life and bounced back.

'Jerks, were they?' Norm echoed, with a bemused expression. Danny tutted.

'The wipes arrived, thank you. It was just a small incident compared to what happened on the pitch. Honestly, after seeing that accident, even my hair was shaking. It might still be.'

For some reason, Trish put her arm around Cassie's shoulders and gave her a squeeze. 'I'm sure it didn't show. It's been a long day, look after yourself please.' Trish's motherly tone hit the spot Cassie hadn't known she needed.

'Thanks, I will, though I could say the same about all of you – don't you want to get home or go out after the match?'

'If it wasn't for the sponsorship potential, I'd be heading home myself,' Trish admitted. 'But in the case of players, well, they find their own way of dealing with the post-match highs.'

Everyone looked at Danny, who was picking at the valve on his rugby ball.

Trish held up the bottle of champagne. 'Well, between the pair of you, I guess today was a double debut of sorts, pity I don't have one of these for you, Cassie. Danny, congratulations from the club management.'

'Thanks. I suppose you want a picture?'

'I'm afraid so, but maybe tidy your hair a bit, you look like you've been in a war zone.' Trish waited while Danny did what he could, then handed the bottle over. Cassie gave a little clap that Norm joined in with. A faint bloom of pink appeared above Danny's stubbly beard-line.

'And smile, yep, turn the label of the bottle towards me, yep, a little to your left so I can see the shirt sponsors – perfect.' Trish checked the shots. 'All good. Right, there's a cider representative waiting to be wined and dined.'

'Presumably not on their own product.' Cassie chuckled.

'Not in the expensive French restaurant they've booked, no.' She cocked her head at Danny. 'Maybe call it a night, eh? Been a bit of day, all round. Oh, the French thing reminds me, I need your passport details, please. Vannes Rugby in Brittany have invited the senior squad over for a friendly before Christmas. How fantastic is that? Anyway, I have to sort the flights. Count yourself lucky I talked the board out of putting you boys on a ten-hour ferry to Saint-Malo.'

Danny's face froze.

'Danny, did you hear me? Ping me your details sometime in the next few days, please.'

Call it intuition, but Cassie knew his problem wasn't a lack of sea legs. 'If he's like me, he's probably trying to remember where his passport is.'

'Ah. Right, I'd better go. Looks like Norm is almost finished, too. Cassie you'll be OK getting back to the station? Don't let these lights fool you, it's dark out there now.' The unsubtle way she shot Danny a meaningful look forced Cassie to hide a grin.

'It's alright, I've been there a few times today.'

Trish grabbed her hand and shook it with feeling. 'Congratulations again on today, from what I can see on the socials, our viewers lapped up your presentation style. It could help open up our matches to the female demographic and to all those less familiar with rugby. I'll be feeding my thoughts and ideas back to Hystar, but it would be good to work with you again sometime.'

'Thank you, and you too.'

'Danny, I'll see you for Tuesday's media briefing back at The Manor?'

'Will do.'

Cassie waited beside Danny and Norm, watching Trish disappear through the tunnel. 'Do either of you mind if I hold on here a few minutes, before heading to the station?'

'Of course not. Probably safer and definitely more tranquil,' Norm said, before casting an amused glance at Danny. 'Usually, anyway.'

'I might slot a couple more balls, while I can, then,' said Danny, as he headed back towards his kicking tee.

As they watched Danny set up and strike the ball, then curse as it hit the bar, Cassie couldn't help but admire his impressive physique as much as his skill. A whole-body movement; and a whole lot of body. But though he'd been calm under pressure, the extent of his post-match practice intrigued her.

'Adrenaline's taking a while to leave his body, so it's messing with his kicking practice,' Norm said – she'd really need to manage her facial expression more carefully – 'Likely he'll need a few consecutive good strikes before stopping. Mind if I crack on, Cassie?'

'Of course not. I'll take a seat for a minute or two then head off.'

Cassie climbed the nearest concrete steps and settled herself a few rows up from the pitch. The regular thud of Danny's boot on a ball was soothing, even if the sporadic shouts at himself were not. Every fifth ball or so, he cast glance in her direction. From this distance, his expression was difficult to decipher, seeming to alternate between making sure she was still there and being suspicious that she was.

After a few minutes, he jogged over and called up to her, 'Think I'm done here, you're going to the station?'

Cassie trotted down the steps to meet him. 'I am, but I can hold on for you if you're going that way. Think I saw a photo booth there this morning.'

'What do you mean?'

'I mean, you'll find it useful, given the urgency for a passport application.' She was playing a hunch, but he'd looked embarrassed when Trish asked for his details. 'Look, I'm not judging you. I've been short of all sorts of things, especially in the past five years, so I recognise a reaction to people who assume you have something that you can't or haven't ever needed to pay for.'

Danny rolled his eyes, but didn't deny the conclusion she'd drawn. 'Five years is nothing.'

'To some, maybe. All I'm saying is, if you want some company, I'll hang on for you to change or whatever. Preferably to shower.' That wariness in his eyes had returned, prompting her to offer him an out. 'Or not, it's up to you. I'll wait at the main turnstiles for fifteen minutes, after that I'll assume you've other plans.'

He landed a ball with a pile of others, without even looking. 'Are you properly off the clock? I don't want anything I say to be hashed into an article for someone's amusement.'

How many more times? 'You don't know me, but I'd like to think that I'd never "hash" anything, nor break a promise.'

Danny scooped the pile of balls into a capacious carrying net and tugged at the drawstring rope. 'That's admirable, and believe me, I'm all about trust, but that doesn't answer my question.'

'Yes! I'm off the sodding clock, and who's going to be interested in you not having a passport for goodness' sake?'

'You're not that naive, surely? You must know bits of information are stored up for future reference, ready for a different context or conversation?' He launched the huge bag onto his shoulder and waited, one hand on his hip.

Perhaps he had a point there, and she'd get similar reactions from now on, once a sportsperson knew her trade? 'Well, nothing from this point onwards will be reported by me, OK? And…you've missed a ball over there.' She pointed over his shoulder.

Danny blinked slowly to himself, as if weighing his next move. 'I'll meet you at the turnstiles.'

The metaphorical ball was in her net.

RED, WHITE & CUE

7. Alternative Route

'You waited, then?' Danny's words accompanied a sudden waft of coconut shower gel.

Cassie mustered an equally *laissez-faire* response. 'It's what I said I'd do, though I wasn't sure you'd turn up either, you're harder to read than most.'

He nodded as if he'd heard it said before.

She ran her eyes up the length of his grey Camford tracksuit, wrestling an unaffected expression into place, while admiring the way the taut fabric clung across his broad shoulders, arms and thighs. Despite its gaudy sponsor logos, it flattered every inch of his physique.

He started to shake his head. 'You don't have to hide it – this season's kit is a shocker. We're grateful for the cider company's sponsorship, but are the cartoon apple trees really necessary?' he mocked, pointing at the offending images across his chest. 'The supporters don't want to see us in these any more than we want to wear them.'

Cassie begged to differ. 'I like it, actually,' she mumbled, hoping the poor light hid the heat surging to her face.

'Oh. Well, good, then.'

The way a drip of water splatted from Danny's hair onto his nose made Cassie's throat feel dry. 'We'd better get going then, if you still want to go?'

'I do.' Danny let her through the turnstile ahead of him, but she struggled with swiping her media pass on the scanner.

'Are you cold?' he glanced at her obviously fumbling hands. 'The only things in my holdall are my boots, mouthguard and the champagne.' Adorably, his fingers had half unzipped his tracksuit top.

'No, my leather jacket's warm enough. It's still the adrenaline flowing, I think. Perhaps I should try kicking balls, too?'

He smiled, zipping his top back up and indicating their direction across the stadium's external concourse. 'Have you ever tried kicking a rugby ball?'

'Yes, it's hellish. They have a mind of their own.'

'They do, and despite being machine made, they all fly slightly different, which is why I practise with all the match-day balls earmarked for any given game. They're numbered beforehand and I try to remember the subtle differences in the way my boot has to connect.'

'That's the sort of thing people would want to hear about. I'd keep that in your locker for an interview if I were you.'

Danny shrugged the suggestion away.

'Before anything else, I'm so sorry about Lewis, I heard it's a double fracture.'

'I can't comment on that,' he said, ushering her across the road on a blind corner with the briefest touch of his hand in the small of her back.

'I wasn't after a quote, Danny, I'm just telling you I'm sad about it, for him and the team. It's lucky freak accidents like that rarely happen.'

'It is, though there isn't a player that secretly doesn't fear them. Lewis will be alright; he has a strong mindset.'

He'd need it if he was to return, mental strength made such a difference in sport. She pondered Danny's resilience. 'Mind telling me why you practised for so long after the match?'

'As long as I'm not being psychoanalysed now?' A half-smile curled the side of his mouth, and Cassie nodded. 'Fine, it's mainly because Academy players don't get as much time in the stadium as the seniors, and I just like it in there, I guess.'

'It's kind of a happy place for me, too. I got into watching sport in a big way at university, but it really started when my dad was alive, and he sometimes took me to local matches. We were often in our seats early, feeling the excitement build during warm-up as the stadium filled.' She smiled at the thought of it, then realised that Danny was watching her as they walked.

'Sorry about your dad. What other things bring that smile to your face?' His subtle compliment made her stumble on the cobbles, but he caught her arm in a flash and steadied her.

'Er, thanks, workwise? I guess, praise and recognition for a good piece of work. Otherwise it's something simple like a refreshingly good sleep. I haven't had much relationship stuff going on for a while, been focused on this internship.'

'Same. Look, if we head over to that crossing, it's a faster route to the station.' He pointed out a turning between roads.

'Wish I'd known about that earlier. Seriously, you try bringing ten hot drinks back across these cobbles.

Scrap that, I've seen the size of your hands.' It had been one of the points in her audio commentary, how securely he'd held the ball as he ran, fending off tackles before offloading it.

Danny chuckled. 'Maybe, but I'd probably get the orders wrong. When I'm walking back from the station to The Manor, I'm only ever carrying the one, for myself.'

Single, then. Loud and clear. 'After nights out, you mean?'

'Yeah, mainly to Cambridge or Ipswich and sometimes London. Camford's very quiet.'

'Got to blow off steam somewhere, right?'

'Sometimes. Not so often these days, it's been the same old nightclub routine with the Academy lads. Socially, it's been a very quiet summer, and last season I wasn't out much. They're all younger and sometimes their immaturity gets to me.'

'God, I hear you. My fellow interns are straight out of university and drive me nuts at times.'

At the pedestrian crossing, Danny pressed the button. 'Didn't you say you've come from studying Sports Journalism at university?'

'Yes, I did, and I have, but that was my second degree – my first one didn't lead where I needed it to.'

Danny peered down at her face. 'So…you're not in your early twenties, then?'

Despite laughing at his error, for a fleeting moment Cassie considered fibbing. 'Well hopefully that's a compliment, but no I'm…' No, she couldn't say the number she'd be turning in March. 'Late twenties, actually.' As the traffic lights turned red, they crossed over.

'You're joking?'

'Sometimes I wish I were.'

'You don't seem like you're almost *thirty*.'

Cassie thwacked his arm, and he burst into laughter. It was the first time she'd heard it, and the delicious boom echoed around the empty streets. 'Not "almost", there are seven months to go yet, but thanks, good to know I don't look decrepit. Luckily, I don't feel it, either, despite the last ten years having been…let's say, *testing*, being without parental support,' she said, wondering why on earth she was spilling such personal information.

Now he was observing her again. 'You don't have your mother, either?'

'We don't speak.'

'Surely it's worth—'

'It isn't.' She almost missed it, the sympathy-graze of his knuckles along her hand.

'I'm sorry,' he said quietly, as if he meant it.

After a silent minute of following the winding shortcut, they caught up with a pair of middle-aged men walking on the other side of the road, and wearing the afternoon's opposition replica shirts. Given the hours since the match had finished, and their uncertain direction of travel across the pavement, several post-match beers had been sunk somewhere in town.

'Hey, big man, pass us the ball, go on!' the one with a beer-belly taunted Danny. The other man sniggered as he held out his hands, ready to replicate the accidental pass made during the match.

Danny acknowledged them both with a polite smile and a brief raise of his hand. 'No thanks, fellas. Once is a mistake, twice is a choice. Safe journey home.'

He turned to Cassie, and discreetly thumbed towards a side road ahead. 'Mind if we take an alternative path to the station?' he whispered. 'It'll only add a minute.'

She nodded, but the men were keen to engage with them.

'How's Lewis doing?' the taller man called out.

Danny turned to respond. 'He's with the medical team. Getting good care.'

'Career ending injury, do you reckon?'

'Couldn't say, even if I knew. Hope not. Thanks for asking after him.' In the streetlight, Danny's eyes flashed at Cassie.

She understood the need for caution in the circumstances, and his desire to conclude the interaction as quickly as possible.

'You 'is missus, love? Better look after your Danny after witnessing that collision. Post-traumatic something.'

Cassie registered a slight stiffening of Danny's posture, but he just smiled at the men.

'Ah, early days, is it? Good luck to you – and fair's fair, mate, balls of steel to have carried on. You did good with the emergency stuff.'

That was rugby for you, banter galore, and decency shone when it mattered, priorities were straight. All the same, Danny had now positioned himself between her and the men, and curved a hand lightly around her elbow, ready to turn her towards the path.

'Guess we'll never know, but have a really good night,' beer-bellied guy sniggered, chuckling and bumping shoulders with his friend as they continued up their road.

'You, too,' Danny called.

A few feet down the path, he removed his hand; Cassie immediately missed the connection.

'Sorry about that,' he said. 'If I haven't messed up my debut, then as a regular senior squad player, this might be the type of thing I'll have to deal with.'

'Don't suppose you'd usually be walking around town at this time after a match, though, would you? Not unless you're accompanying your "missus" somewhere, obviously.'

'Yeah, sorry about that, too. Guess they assumed.'

'Relax, I've heard plenty of ribbing, and merrily shovelled a fair bit back too, if I'm honest. And don't worry, I wouldn't have said anything. I have my own position to think about, too.'

'I hope Coach's memory of that pass is short, that it won't come back to haunt me – that's off the record, right?'

'God, your media training has done a real number on you. Yes, as I said before, we are off the record. You can trust me. No need to ask me again.' She hitched up her bag and cleared her throat. Maybe she'd struck a nerve about position insecurity at the club? 'It's competitive there, then? Bit at odds with the "one team" ethos?'

'Very much, but I've been with Camford a while, and know most of the Academy players, so a team atmosphere should come easily.' The word hung in the air, too tempting to ignore.

'Should?'

'Not sure you can completely rely on someone who'd step over you to take your spot in the team,' he sighed.

'But you've kind of got to work together, haven't you? Rugby is such a team game; it's dangerous if there's one broken link.'

For some reason, Danny hesitated. 'Exactly, except people would probably say I'm…I don't know.' He stretched his neck before changing the subject. 'You're good with words, by the way, on camera too. Every media outlet is going to be after you after that performance.' He pointed to the entrance of a narrow alleyway behind two metal pedestrian bars. 'After you.'

The alleyway's lack of lighting, and the curve in the path ahead, would normally have screamed 'avoid'.

'Looks a bit risky and it sometimes freaks me out, people walking behind me in the dark. Is there an alternative?'

'Not if you want to make your train. It's straight ahead after that bend. You'll be safe with me, don't worry.'

Her gut agreed. Danny Reed emitted a distinctly bodyguard vibe.

'Wait, what if it's *you* that might be trouble, what would I do then?' she smirked.

'I'm not.'

'Not even in private?' she teased, cocking him a suggestive glance.

'I'm going to shoulder-carry you the rest of the way to the station if you don't stop.'

Thrilled by his engagement, she switched to walking backwards. 'No, I can't let you do that, today's battering and everything. Better not risk carrying me,

I've only eaten fatty carbs today, there's probably a dead weight circling my middle.'

He appeared to size her up, more slowly than strictly necessary. 'I lift heavier weights than you at the gym.'

Half of her wanted him to pin her to the side of the alley wall, let him feel what his eyes had been lingering on, but the other half was resigned to the fast-disappearing time. Instead, she soft-pinched his ribs and sprinted off up the alleyway. 'Doesn't mean you're as light on your feet as me though,' she called. 'Last one to the end is a loser!'

'Wait, you don't know where you're going!'

'I can't hear you,' she laughed into the cooling air.

'What?' his voice trailed from behind, but she pelted on, one hand trying to minimise boob-bounce, the other pinning her bag tightly against her hip. On she ran, just able to make out another set of pedestrian safety bars at the brow of the steep hill. Almost there, the sound of Danny's heavy breaths closed in behind her and he bundled past, only to position himself against the bars, waiting. When she caught up with him, he pulled up his sleeve and pretended to consult an imaginary watch.

'It was surprisingly close, though, you've got to admit,' she puffed, doubling over and resting her hands on her knees. She should incorporate more cardio into her routines. And arms days. Maybe leg days too. That would, of course, necessitate joining a gym, something her finances were still too thin to allow.

'It was only close because I waited ten seconds before setting off, and then only jogged at my slowest warm-up pace,' Danny chuckled.

'These spindly legs can't possibly compete with your inhuman ones, plus I'm not wearing my sports bra.'

'Nothing wrong with those – your legs, I mean not your…not that there's anything wrong with…the opposite, in fact…' he trailed off, forcibly studying his trainers. 'Fuck,' he muttered to himself and when his eyes lifted, the light was too poor to properly distinguish the look he was giving her.

Cassie wasn't sure what to say next and grasped an easy topic to get them along the last stretch. 'After today, I might look up what to eat to make my muscles grow. I'm hoping for plain chocolate.'

'Congratulations, you're going to be happy, then,' he said huskily.

'I was half joking.'

He cleared his throat. 'The Mediterranean diet includes some plain chocolate. That regime forms the basis of our menus at the Academy. Trust me, I've completed a fourth round of the programme's nutrition training, so I know how to replenish glycogen storage efficiently and which foods contain the antioxidants that soothe inflammation and oxidative stress.'

'Sound more like biology lessons. Does the Academy make their players eat those meals then?'

'Why wouldn't we? They know the science and we want to be peak athletes. And it's included as part of the package.'

'Meaning?'

'I don't pay for it, nor for my room in 3A at The Manor, which is the Academy Accommodation Annexe. Not as glamorous as it sounds; it's basically a long corridor with single ensuite rooms on both sides.'

'Like uni halls?' she said, and immediately regretted the comparison, since he clearly hadn't enrolled at one.

'I don't know, maybe.'

'And you've been there for four years? Bet you're happy the season's only eight months long. Nine, I guess, with pre-season. Time off for good behaviour, to get home, eh?' She smiled.

'If you want it.' He shrugged, all serious again.

'Don't you?'

'You ask a lot of questions.'

'Do I?' she grinned, knowing it full well.

He raised his eyebrows.

'OK, maybe I do. Sorry, I'm just trying to understand your reasoning, I guess.'

'Fine,' he sighed. 'The Manor's grounds staff like some help off-season. I enjoy it and find the exercise a good way to keep my conditioning up, not like the others who head home or go away on holiday, losing their tone. Gym's available twenty-four hours, even in middle of the night when I need it. A few kitchen staff are permanent residents, so there's always food.'

So he had nothing to go home for, either? Something in his tone suggested it wasn't as simple as that. She'd been about to ask more, when he pointed ahead.

'There's the station, see? We've come in from the other side of the carpark.'

'I see it. That was quick.' Bloody shortcuts.

RED, WHITE & CUE

8. You Started It

Being the topic of conversation with anyone, especially a girl – correction, a woman – as beautiful and smart as Cassie, made Danny nervous. In this case it diverted at least a few brain cells away from the rocketing desire to discover how kissing her would feel. Every time he glanced at her lips, or caught the moon's reflection in her eyes, he considered taking her mouth with his. She seemed to have no bloody idea how close he'd been to giving in to it when they were in the alleyway.

With time against them, they began to navigate the dark car park. 'Where's home for you Cassie? Careful, there are potholes here.'

'I rent a studio apartment in Clapham. It's tiny, but at least I don't have to share a fridge, although I wouldn't mind splitting the utility bills, you know?' She caught him studying her face and he quickly turned his head.

Don't look at her mouth. Do *not* look at her mouth. 'No, not really. I came to the Academy from college after resitting my A levels for a couple of years first. No bills there.'

'You're lucky then. My credit rating's in tatters over late paid utilities, but with maxed out overdrafts I've had little choice.'

'Don't think I've got a credit rating to worry about.'

'Well, we all have but – never mind. By the way, I know what your next question's going to be, I saw you screwing your eyes at my mouth.'

He stopped walking and turned to face her. There was no one around, no one would see them. He leaned in towards her. 'Cassie—'

'It's why don't I sound like a Londoner, isn't it? It's because my childhood home was the Valleys of Mid Glamorgan in Wales, Merthyr Tydfil to be specific. It's north of Cardiff.'

He eased backwards. 'Yeah, I...I thought your accent sounded different. The way you say your "r"s is sometimes—'

'Mmhmm, it's a Welsh thing. They're rolled when my tongue vibrates.'

Jesus, now he couldn't save himself from staring at her mouth, up to her eyes, then back to her mouth. He felt his Adam's apple bob on a slow swallow and muttered something ridiculous like 'I thought maybe it was a lisp or something.'

Cassie bumped playfully into his side, and she was there, *right there*, if he'd wanted to take her face in his hands but she chatted on, apparently oblivious.

'To be fair, both times I was at university, people asked if I were Irish, or Scottish, "from somewhere up North" and even if I were Australian. Very few realised I'm Welsh.'

'I don't think I'll forget.' He'd be thinking about her later tonight, long after she'd got on her train.

'Yeah right, except I'm rather forgettable.'

'What? Who's told you that?'

'Sorry, that slipped out, ignore me.' She started walking again, the station lights ahead of them.

Danny caught the arm of her jacket and pulled her to a stop. 'I don't want to. Tell me, who said that to you?'

She waved her hand in vague manner. 'Publisher reactions to my writing pitches, boys I've fancied, the usual crap. I don't know, perhaps it's my fault. I'm just not unique enough, I guess. As it turns out, I actually don't like standing out, anyway.' She trailed her fingers up and down her mostly black clothing. 'I much prefer observing, weighing people up, finding the story, you know?' Her tenacity in the face of criticism was impressive, and he'd have asked more had she not pulled out her phone and checked the time. 'We've got to keep walking, Danny, I'm sorry.'

'It's alright. Where's that photo booth?'

As they climbed the steps of the station's outer concourse, Cassie pointed over to an illuminated photo booth. 'I've got five minutes, but kind of wish I had more though.'

'Me too.' Meeting someone like Cassie had been new to him. She wasn't the sort of girl he'd have picked up in nightclubs, or the hook-ups he'd agree to via an app for some mutually quick relief. Within the space of a seriously eventful day, and a fifteen-minute walk, she already knew more about him than any of them, and he admired so much about her.

At the booth, Danny wrinkled his nose. 'It smells like cat piss in there, even before I'm behind the curtain.'

'You're lucky, this photo booth is an improvement from the last one that I used. Try concentrating on posing for your headshot when there's a dead mouse in the corner.'

He peered under the curtain, eyeing an instruction guide. He didn't want Cassie's last impression of him to be of stupidity, but he'd never used one of these machines before. He ran a finger down the picture formats available.

Cassie pointed at the second option, six single prints, giving eight photograph attempts to choose from.

'Right, let's get this over with,' he muttered, folding himself into the booth, finding that he needed to hunch almost double to sit on the small metal stool.

'I'm going to check on the platform for my train, be one sec,' she called from outside the curtain.

The Passport Office wasn't about to accept a picture of a cider logo. Danny reached beneath the seat, hoping for some kind of height-reducing lever. Nothing. 'Cassie?' he called. 'You there? I can't even crouch down low enough for the stupid shot.'

Her boots returned at speed outside the booth. 'Yeah, coming, hold on.' She ducked her head under the curtain, bringing her cheek within a breath of his. It was lucky her train was imminent, otherwise he'd be pulling her onto his lap.

'I think you can wind the stool up and down from the seat.'

Danny quickly reversed out, reduced the height of the stool, then repositioned himself back inside the booth, satisfied that his face was at least now within the booth's guidelines. He selected the option he wanted and posed for the shot. 'Here we go then...'

The first flash lit up the booth, pinging white stars into his eyes.

'Shit, I was speaking.'

Flash.
'Think I blinked.'
Flash.
'Chrissakes...I...'
Flash.
'Nope.' He could hear Cassie giggling outside.
Flash.
Flash.

After his penultimate photo, a grinning Cassie bobbed under the curtain and squashed her body between his legs so that her face was also in the frame for the final shot.

Flash.

Danny grabbed at her hips to stop her from toppling out of the booth.

'This is like the anti-Tardis, way smaller than it looks on the outside.' Her legs shook from the effort of her held squat, so he hitched her upwards and, with a quick twist, had sat her sideways on his lap, letting her legs dangle out beneath the curtain. The harsh lighting had reduced her pupils to pinpricks, floating in coins of liquid silver. Danny's pulse picked up speed.

'How'd it go?' she asked, her warm breath meeting his throat.

'Guess I'll find out in five minutes, but you'll be long gone down...the track by then.' God, her thick, black eyelashes as she blinked were so mesmerising, he almost forgot what he was saying.

'About that,' she mumbled. 'Something's happened between here and London. The information board says the last two trains of the night have been cancelled. So it looks as if I'll be sleeping on the platform until the 5.35am tomorrow morning.'

Relief, and other thoughts, flooded his head.

'So…any ideas Danny?'

Yeah, he had plenty of them. He'd start with the responsible ones. 'Maybe take an Uber into Cambridge? Then a bus? I think there are a couple of companies than run that route.'

'I'll check.' Phone in hand, she shuffled on his lap. He couldn't help a soft grunt escaping his lips. 'Sorry, I'm too heavy, I—'

'No, you're not.' He tugged her a little closer. Only, he told himself, so she wouldn't slip.

'Nope, those companies are already booked out. At least it's not cold tonight. Is it safe, staying here for…' – she counted the hours on her fingers – 'eight hours, on the platform?'

The words fell out of his mouth before he'd even thought them. 'I can hang around if you like, see you onto the early train.'

'You don't have to do that, I'm sure you've other plans back at The Manor, celebrating with your team.'

Now the smell of her hair was messing with his head. He was in trouble here. 'I don't. The senior team will have had a drink and gone home by now, and I think the Academy boys were headed to Oasis in Ipswich in one of the minibuses.'

'You've time to get back and be ready for that, surely?'

'They have different ideas to me on what passes for a good night.'

'I doubt they'd think much of having a cougar on their lap, inside a dingy station photo booth, that's for sure,' she chuckled.

'They don't know what they're missing,' he said, failing at an attempt at humour when his fingers twitched against her waist, finding soft, warm skin. The mood inside the booth shifted.

'Are you sure? You don't want to miss the chance of bedding some young woman from Ipswich or wherever?'

'That wouldn't have happened.'

'Bedding a gorgeous man?'

'I wouldn't have been bedding either, exactly.'

'Ah, oh I see, you're holding out? Good for you. If it makes your confession any better, I'll admit to not having slept with anyone for several months and – this will shock you – although I don't usually drink more than one, I've rarely ever had sex sober.'

So many thoughts collided, he didn't know which to deal with first.

'Sorry, sorry, that was a ridiculous over share.' She placed a hand on the wall of the booth, ready to leave, but he tightened his hold on her.

'Stop, Cassie. I only meant…I've never had sex in a bed.'

She screwed her eyes at the unfortunate misunderstanding. 'Really? That's pretty much the only place I've ever had it.'

'Seriously?'

She tilted her head. 'Yes, seriously. Oh and on sofas, too, although that was a sofa bed, to be fair. But you've used…?'

He nodded. 'Other places, yes.'

'Not photo booths?' she said, jostling on his lap.

'No,' he hissed, 'might be a bit tight for that.' He needed one more signal from her, just one more to be sure.

'So…cars are fine?' Her voice was huskier now, and the warmth of her legs was seeping into his thighs. His body twitched its appreciation.

'As long as they aren't tiny ones, but, as they're always the girl's, they often are.'

'So far, it's just been casual, then?' she murmured into his neck, and a throb pulsed through him.

'I haven't wanted anything more.' A feeling in his gut told him that someone like Cassie Forde could change that.

'You might need to be careful, you know, with being recognised, now you're in the big time Premiership. Even someone you don't suspect might be thinking about taking advantage of you, in one way or another. Someone *right* under your nose.'

Danny swept his thumb across her undamaged cheek and tucked some strands of hair behind her ear. He bent his face towards hers. 'Someone like who?'

She tilted her face into his hand. 'A fan, someone who saw you in action on the pitch, maybe.'

'Nah, could be a stalker.'

'How about a photo booth assistant?' she murmured.

'Those, I think, might be a bit different. I'd hold out for one of those.'

Her lips parted as she stared at his mouth. 'Do.'

As always, he needed to be sure. 'Kiss me?' He tugged the curtain fully across and angled his head, waiting.

Cassie kissed him once, softly, then again. On the third, he engaged, and soon pressure from his lips gave way to tentative tasting, then sweet, probing exploration. He hoisted her up and swivelled her around to face him. Both of them giggled as legs and elbows bumped the sides of the booth, before she straddled his lap. The way she settled herself triggered an urgency in him; within seconds, they had escalated to crazy, breathless kissing. He ran his hands jerkily through her hair, swept them down her neck, inside the collar of her jacket.

Suddenly, she pulled away, gasping. 'Whoa, slow down, slow down,' she panted, covering his hands with hers.

He stilled, chest heaving. 'Shit, didn't you want this? I should have asked more clearly, I thought—'

She took his face in both hands, giving herself a second to catch her own breath. 'I do, Danny, I really, *really* do. What I meant was to literally slow it down, like this.' She pulled his mouth onto hers and kissed him ultra slowly, purposefully taking her time over his bottom lip, then his top, caressing the corners, before sealing a lingering, seductive kiss across his mouth.

He couldn't even open his eyes, but nodded his understanding, and curved a hand behind her head to follow her lead.

For a few glorious minutes they were lost in the thrill of shared desire. His lips located a sensitive area beneath her jaw that unlocked soft, encouraging moans, and when he tilted his pelvis up to meet the apex of her jeans, Cassie began to rock back and forth, back and forth. So many things he wanted to do, too little space to manage them in. 'Fuck, you're gorgeous,' he muttered, his fingers finding the opening of her shirt. As he cupped the weight of an utterly perfect-sized breast, a growl of frustration left his lips at his inability to manoeuvre himself sufficiently to taste it.

'Don't stop,' she urged, leaning into the contact. 'Please.'

'I don't want to stop, but we'll have to,' he breathed. 'I want more than this tin box will let us have.' One of them had to keep control of things; they were in a public place with only a useless half-curtain as a barrier. He held her still, and tried to pull away from the way she was sensuously grazing his neck with her teeth. 'This is also…too risky…and the photos will be ready.' Without giving her the opportunity to resist, he snatched opened the curtain, twisted her over the agonising strain in his tracksuit bottoms and onto her feet, outside.

'Fine,' Cassie snapped, then flicked her fringe back into place, picked up her bag and strode off.

Frustration kicked through him as he cooled his face against the metal door frame, watching as she jammed her ticket into the turnstile's slot and pushed through to the platform.

After a couple of minutes to calm himself, he hurdled the turnstile to Platform 1. Two people were already sat in the shadows of the furthest away bench. He'd definitely done the right thing in stopping something that could easily have escalated inside the booth. He hoped that whoever the people on the bench were hadn't seen or heard him and Cassie on their way in.

She was sat on the nearest bench, her arms folded, eyes closed.

'It was too risky, Cassie, you know it was.'

'Christ, don't sneak up on someone like that!' she hissed, forcing Danny to step into her line of sight.

He gestured at the space beside her. 'Can I sit for a minute?'

She nodded, but clutched her chest. 'Seriously, don't ever do that, you scared the crap out me. Promise me!'

He sat down and squeezed her hand. 'I promise, I'm sorry.'

'I thought you might have gone.'

'No, had to wait in the booth. Took an imaginary cold shower.'

She smiled then, and nodded. 'I was sat here doing much the same, if I'm honest.'

He doubled over and dropped his forehead onto propped up palms. 'Please don't put an image of you in a shower into my head.'

'Hey, I was just as fired up as you, though for the unofficial record, you started it.'

'Maybe, but it was talk of your vibrating tongue that tipped me over.' As he sat back up, she met him with a sexy smile.

'Who knew an explanation of Welsh accents could be such a turn on?'

'Well it is for me. And slow kissing you was…'

His eyes darted between her mouth and her eyes. 'So bloody good.'

'It was.' Cassie scooched herself nearer to him, the whites of her eyes glinting in the platform's light.

He rested an arm around her shoulders, and she snuggled into his chest. As his hand stroked her hair, he reconciled himself to a few hours sat there until morning.

'Danny? Danny, mate! Is that you again?' Two familiar profiles emerged from the shadows, one rotund, the other taller.

'See, I told you that was his girl, it's the same one we saw him with up the road,' the other called along the platform.

Hell no. Danny murmured into Cassie's ear, 'There are at least seven hours until your train. It's not too cold, how about we go for a walk?'

'Where to? It's almost ten.'

'I guess we'll find out, but I'm not keen on waiting here for a night of interrogation by those two.'

One of men had almost reached them, and held out his phone. 'Hey, would you mind a quick selfie?'

Danny was quick to his feet, he didn't want the men near Cassie. 'Sure, I'll come over to you and your mate, wait there.'

After a quick chat and a couple of pictures he returned to Cassie's bench. 'What's the verdict?'

'You're right. A walk sounds best.'

He picked up her bag and hooked it over his shoulder with his holdall. 'We'll start with a tour of the town.'

'It's going to need to be a long one.'

9. The Long Walk

Cassie strolled the quiet streets of Camford with Danny, their comfortable silence interspersed by light conversation, mention of pretty thatched cottages, and her being startled by foxes crying out to one another. After passing a third high street takeaway, she could no longer ignore her growling stomach.

'Is this place any good?' She lingered near a Turkish kebab shop that had attracted a short queue.

Danny shrugged. 'I guess so, it's busier than the others.'

'Something from there would tide me over until morning. Do you want one?' she asked, joining the queue at the doorway.

'God no, those are full of crap.'

She raised her eyebrows at his immediate dismissal. 'Yes, but delicious crap. Maybe tuck one in your bag for the morning – everyone knows they're as good cold.'

'Not unless it transforms into breakfast muesli, or an egg white omelette with ham and veg, between now and then.'

Athletes. 'Maybe a drink, then?'

'Thanks, but I'm OK,' he said, but shuffled along with her as they joined the queue.

While they waited, Cassie pointed out a film poster in the shop's colourful wall display. 'I loved the

Enola Holmes movies, it's good to see feisty women characters.'

'It is. Nothing to do with Henry Cavill being in them, then?'

Sprung. 'He's a brilliant actor, actually.'

Danny flicked his head back and laughed. 'Yeah, that's what everyone's looking at, his acting.'

'Body envy, have we?'

'Spot on journalist nose. Yes, you guessed it, me and all the other players working hard in the gym look at ourselves in the mirrors and say, "if *only* we looked more like Henry Cavill". The coaches have locked onto it and put a Superman poster up, for motivational purposes.'

Cassie grinned. 'Ha-ha, obviously I'm joking. He'd definitely come off worse when compared with you lot of peak physical specimens. But…you do look a bit like him, though.'

'So it's not just your nose, those kiss-me eyes don't work properly either,' he breathed, dropping the briefest kiss onto her nose.

'Just saying what I see. What sort of movies do you like?' she asked, as they moved forwards a space.

'Thrillers, spy movies, that sort of thing.'

'OK, how about *Mission: Impossible – Fallout*?'

'Yes but – oh, right, that's the one Henry Cavill stars in, isn't it?'

'Is it?' She fluttered her eyelashes innocently then whooped as Danny enfolded her into a big hug. Since he didn't seem bothered about low key PDA, she slung her hands around his neck and nuzzled his jawline. He held her there, releasing the softest groan into her hair, before someone behind them tapped her on the shoulder. A tired-looking server at the counter rolled his eyes, waiting to take her order.

Danny nudged her forwards. 'See that old water pump over the road? I'll wait there for you.'

While her kebab was being wrapped, Cassie peered periodically over to where Danny stood. He'd remained facing the shop, arms crossed, eyes trained on her as if Henry Cavill himself might suddenly whisk her away. And she was so here for it.

'Mind if I eat as we walk?' she asked, extracting a strip of the deliciously aromatic meat from her wrapper, as she sauntered over to him.

'If you're happy to?'

'Yep. So, is this Camford's town water pump, then?' she eyed the long handle and cast-iron plaque behind him.

'The original one, I think, and it still works.' He lifted the handle and a gush of water fell from a bell-shaped spout into a drain below. 'Locals call this Pump Corner; supposedly the supply is full of minerals from the Gog Magog Hills.'

'Sounds more like Wales than Cambridgeshire. Does it taste good? My dad used to swear by Cardiff's tap water. "Corporation Finest" he used to call it. He could never understand it when people bought bottled.'

Danny stared at the water as it trickled away. 'I wouldn't know.'

He'd never tried it? Cassie shoved her kebab bag into his hands and retrieved her empty water bottle from the bag on Danny's shoulder. Raising the pump lever was far harder than Danny had made it look, but she held her bottle patiently beneath the dribbled flow, then tested it. 'Nice. Cold. Try some?'

Before he had a chance to decline, she'd switched the bottle for her kebab. Danny stared at the bottle, then at her. 'No, I'm good, but thanks.'

'You're joking. We were full on kissing earlier, drinking from my bottle is no different.'

He tutted. 'It's not that. I'm careful what goes into my body.' Still, he lifted the bottle to his lips and took a sip. His throat bobbed sexily and the way he provocatively swiped his tongue over his lips made her swallow hard. 'Delicious.' He winked.

Cassie snapped her drooling mouth closed; Danny had known full well what he was doing. 'Of course, it's no Diet Coke.'

He paused the bottle mid-way to his mouth. 'Please, that's one of the worst drinks on your body, even used as a mixer.'

'Well first of all, I'd never put alcohol in my Coke, and secondly, I limit myself to one or two a day.'

'So only the fourteen weekly cans of chemicals contributing to poor blood sugar, heart disease and cholesterol, then?'

'Ugh, please don't spoil it – Diet Coke is my daily pick-me-up. What would I do without it?'

'I don't know, but I can tell you what you can do with it – I saw a video clip once of Diet Coke being used to rid a shower head of limescale. If it could do that, imagine what it's doing to your intestines.' He looked too pleased with himself, so she bit off another mouthful of kebab then wafted the wrapper under his nose.

'Mm, this is so greasy, so full of bad, bad things. And I love it. Which way shall we walk now?'

A sparkle of humour danced in his eyes. 'Bad, bad, things, eh? I'd better watch myself. Well, assuming you haven't poisoned *yourself*, would you like a tour of The Manor's grounds? I wish you could see inside the main building because it's amazing, but it will be locked. The gardens are great though, and night views from the high ridge will look superb in this light.'

'I'd like that, there's this blueish tinge to the moonlight.'

'It's a Blue Moon, the last full moon of summer and the only blue one this year. Norm, who you met earlier, told me about them when we had one last year. You might get some good pictures.'

Cassie wiped her lips after finishing her kebab. 'Isn't the thing about blue moons that it can make people do crazy things?'

Danny took the empty wrapper from her and scrunched it into a ball. 'Norm didn't mention that, but I can't promise crazy things won't happen. By the way, the price for my tour was going to be a big mouthful of your disgusting looking kebab.'

She slapped a hand on his arm. 'Why didn't you say something, then?'

'I had no idea you'd eat it that fast and I admit, it smelled fantastic. Who knows, I might have needed the fuel if the woman on my tour is going to turn into a crazy person.'

'I *knew* you wanted one, wait here.' Before he could say anything, she strode back to the mercifully quiet kebab shop and returned with a bottle of Diet Coke, one of water and another kebab. 'Here you go.

From now on, say what you mean, and when you're off Camford's clock, maybe consider doing a little of what you want?'

'I do.'

'Like what?'

He took the kebab and water from her and ushered her along the road. 'You'll see. How much do I owe you?'

'The price is you continuing to carry my bag, giving me a tour of The Manor and getting me back to the station in plenty of time for the 5.35am tomorrow morning.'

'Deal. It's a couples of miles this way.'

A mile later, down a country lane, Cassie was regretting her culinary choices, and rubbed her tummy to relieve her discomfort.

'Are you alright?' Danny slowed. 'I'm walking too fast, again, sorry.'

'No, this is self-inflicted, from bolting down that kebab and washing it down with Coke. Though I will say, the godawful smell in these fields isn't helping.'

'Try sipping the water,' he said, passing her his bottle. 'The farmer must have been muck-spreading earlier, they don't usually do it in the evenings or at weekends; the weather must be about to turn.'

'Getting the full sensory experience, aren't we? I've only just got the smell from the photo booth out of my nose.'

'Surely the farmers in the Welsh Valleys muck-spread?'

'You know, I can't remember, but if it's for crops then probably not. Their fields are usually full of sheep.'

'When did you last go back?'

The question knocked her, so she took an extra breath, made a couple of stalling stretches as they walked. 'I don't know. A while ago.'

Danny stopped walking and scrutinised her face by gently tilting it towards the moon. 'Sorry, too painful. I should have remembered.'

She found herself being brought into his chest, and her back rubbed. The feeling was good on many levels.

'Are you OK to keep going? We'll see headlights if anything's coming but if we do, tuck in behind me,' he said, 'and that way I won't make you jump, either.'

Cassie nodded and they continued on, tired footsteps relieved by rugby talk, Camford's history and, to her surprise, the trees and shrubs they were passing. The way Danny could identify a sycamore from an oak under moonlight impressed her.

'And those are hawthorns, I think, mostly for hedging…am I boring you? I've never walked with girls, like this.'

'No, aside from the heartburn, this is lovely. I don't often walk in the countryside these days.'

'Good, but tell me if I start talking about things that make you think of Wales.' He might be a strapping big guy, but his thoughts were surprisingly tender.

The space felt safe enough to give a little of herself, it was only fair. 'It's OK. I'll tell you a little about it, if you like.' Danny nodded. 'Well, I grew up in a pub in rural Merthyr, called Stumble Inn. It was always busy.'

'Great name for a pub.'

'It was, and my parents made a success of it despite my mother's family turning their back on her when she fell pregnant with me. There were weekend students to help, of course. I did too, once I was fifteen, and they had a regular bar manager when Dad got sick…' Cassie's thoughts drifted to places she tried to avoid, though she kept one foot in front of the other, on automatic.

'Stop a second,' said Danny, and carefully avoiding her graze, swiped away a tear she hadn't realised had fallen. 'Take a breath.'

She once again leaned into the warm wall of comfort. 'It's alright, occasionally I'm reminded it's me against the world, that's all.'

'God, Cassie, I know how that feels.'

'Do you? What about your family, Danny?' She took a deep breath and motioned that they should walk on, but the hesitation in his response concerned her. 'Sorry, we can change the subject entirely, if you want?'

'I don't want this talked about anywhere else, Cassie,' he said quietly.

She slipped her hand into his. 'You can trust me.'

Danny paused before sighing, 'I don't have much experience with family, either.'

'As in, you don't have a good relationship with your family?'

'No, as in, I haven't had a proper family to have a relationship with.' His words trailed into the night air.

Her heart broke a little for him and she squeezed his hand tightly.

'I had a good couple of years with a foster mother who adopted me. Many others don't even get that.'

Well, shit, now she felt dreadful. No wonder he was so dedicated to rugby – wait, was that all he had? She studied his face, gauging whether he wanted to elaborate, but his expression was guarded. Something told her he rarely spoke about his background, so she tested the theory with another question. 'What was she like, your adoptive mother?'

'Kind, generous. Patient.' He cleared his throat, twice. 'And yours?'

Cassie stopped walking and silently brought him into a tight hug. This rugged guy needed to know it was alright to be vulnerable with her. His arms came around her shoulders and the weight of his head dropped onto the top of hers. He mumbled something unintelligible into her hair, and she pulled him closer.

'I read somewhere that hugging for eight seconds or more lowers blood pressure and raises serotonin levels,' she said into his chest.

'You're good at them, it's been a long time since I've had one.'

'Same.' She held position, letting the emotional intimacy flow between them. Eventually, he pulled them apart and urged her forwards. They continued on, but to her surprise he maintained the clasp of his hand around hers.

'Do you want to tell me about your mother?' he asked, 'Is it something fixable?'

'Would you mind, if I don't? But I just want to add, I'm sorry for your loss.'

'Oh, Laura's alive, but unwell. She's in a dementia care home. Sadly she only recognises her sister now, anyone else seems to trigger distress.'

'God, that's rough, I'm sorry. So you don't visit?'

'I stopped going eighteen months ago, because of the upset it caused. She lost understanding of my adoption; even photographic evidence confused her.'

Cassie wanted to hug him again, she could only imagine the pain for Danny. 'And your adoptive father?'

'Unfortunately, Laura was a widow when I was placed with her at fourteen but, you know, she was the kindest foster carer I'd had. Kids in care dream of being placed with someone like that. My fifteenth birthday, when she officially adopted me, was the only time I've ever cried.' Now it was him, gripping her hand tightly. 'Jesus, what's got into me tonight? I can't seem to stop. Don't tell anyone…I feel stupid, ignore me.'

'Of course I won't, Danny, and it's not stupid, you were still a child. You've an aunt through her? Anyone else?'

'Another Aunt. Both of them have a son, one's an airline pilot, Nathan, and the other is a theatre performer, Jake.'

'Do you reach out to them at all?'

'Rarely. I hadn't known them all for very long. I got a message from Nathan today, congratulating me on my debut.'

'That was nice of him.'

'It was, but I'd reminded him and Jake that I was playing. To be honest, I don't expect anything from either of them – I went off the rails a bit during my run at A levels, so I don't blame them.'

Cassie wondered at exactly what 'off the rails' meant, but skipped over it. 'Still, he bothered, and it sounds like your adoptive mother wanted you to be part of the Reed family. Do you have a middle name?'

'No, just Danny. Well, Danny Smith was my given name, when I was found as a baby. It sounds ridiculous, but as a kid, I often wished I'd had one. Something tough, like Damon, a character in an adventure book I'd read.' He kicked at something in the road, then turned them onto a small footpath. 'Fucksake, sorry Cassie, I don't share this stuff with anyone.'

He'd been abandoned? A hundred questions flashed through Cassie's mind, but she appreciated that he'd been open with her, and that was enough. She tugged him nearer, silent reassurance that his secrets were safe. 'I'm glad that you enjoyed reading, I did a lot at that age, still do. It's an escape, isn't it? I remember a book about a girl called Story, once, based somewhere exotic in South America. I wished I'd been given that name instead of my embarrassing middle name, Rhoswen.' She giggled.

'I recall it from earlier, when you banged your head.'

'When did I bang my head?' she said, pretending to be shocked, but when his stride faltered, she quickly added, 'Only joking! Cassandra was my parents' joint choice, but my mother insisted on including something properly Welsh – Rhoswen means white rose – because obviously I'm hooked into Dad's Irish ancestry with Forde.'

'Cassie suits you, though. Celtic Cassie.'

'As opposed to your English blood?' Too late, Cassie regretted the question, but Danny shrugged his shoulders.

'It's all in the DNA, isn't it? I don't know whose blood is in my veins.'

'I wasn't thinking. Well, I can tell you, wherever they're from, you've inherited stupidly handsome genetics.'

'Back at you. Be careful here, it's dark and there's a stile to climb over, but we're only about fifteen minutes away now.' Danny negotiated them over the rickety wood, holding Cassie's waist while she clambered.

'I'm looking forward to getting to The Manor, I've seen it on television a few times.'

'Yep, it's just as well it's impressive; it'll turn your night around, after me unloading on you.'

'Don't be silly, I'm happy that you could talk to me. I expect sharing can be hard, especially in your environment, but just so you know, not everyone is out to take advantage of you, Danny. You could try giving a little of yourself, see how people respond.'

'I'll think about it.'

'And by the way, I'm having a lovely evening, best for a very long time.'

He ran his thumb back and forth along her hand as they walked, smiling to himself.

Despite Danny's family revelations, and unwanted recollections of her own, Cassie's conversation with Izzy wasn't far from her mind. On a scale of big decisions, it was nearing the top end. 'Could I talk through something about my work? It's just that

I've been asked to consider a major change in direction.'

'Of course, happy to.'

Cassie outlined the opportunity Izzy had offered, and Danny helped her to weigh up the pros and cons.

'It sounds interesting, though I've got to ask, what sort of a name is Fox Cavalier? Is he an actor or something?'

'No, he's British, a former England youth cricketer who busted his knee, apparently. Izzy thinks he's got what it takes to be a sports presenter.'

'Knees are the worst.' Danny nodded sympathetically. 'They end a lot of rugby careers, too. As it is, we know we'll have to give up the game sometime in our early thirties and find something else. It sounds like that Izzy person is giving you some options that could be long term, though?'

'She has, but in my case, I can't make another wrong move. I don't have the money or time for that, especially after having one false start already.'

'False start?' he asked, as the path at last brought them out onto a tarmac road. They thumped their feet into the ground, clearing debris from their soles.

'My first stint at university was to study literature and creative writing, ready to launch myself as a romance author. Tried to make it for a year, but nothing. I still write in my downtime but it's hard not to feel I wasted time and money. Sport reporting has been interesting, though, apart from the extra student debt and suffering another four years of student life, at least I now have a degree that opens doors.'

'Romance and sport, not the usual combination.' He smiled down at her.

'Depends on the people, I guess.'

He pulled her in for a quick kiss. 'If anyone can find a way to make a sweet romantic story fit with some sweaty sport or other, I hope it's you.'

'Ooh that's good,' she mused, making a note on her phone. 'Sweet and Sweaty, no Sweet and Salty, from the sweat…that could work as a promotional quote on something,' she mumbled to herself, but stopped to admire a pair of old iron gates, set within a fir hedge. 'Wow, those are beautiful.'

Danny flipped down the cover on a plastic box affixed to the gate post. 'They are. And luckily there's pin-pad entry, because the locks are a bit rusted. Might have needed to splash some of your Coke on it otherwise.'

10. Moonlit

'Danny, this is amazing,' Cassie gasped, as she followed him along the gravel path that encircled the exterior of the building.

He had to admit, the way The Manor was base lit at night showed off its sandstone architecture.

'It's much bigger than it looks on TV.'

'England Rugby sometimes use us for media announcements if their facilities are out of action, but the cameras don't show half of it.'

'I can see why they'd choose here. Are all the facilities in this old building?' Her wide-eyed attempt to take it all in reminded him of the first day he'd arrived.

'The conference hall, a media centre and other things are in there. The rest is in the annexe, down this way.' As they wandered along, he enjoyed the familiar building anew, through her eyes, as she commented on features like the sash windows, smart stonework archways and block edging.

She gasped again as they turned the corner, seeing the club's contemporary, glass-roofed annexe.

'That's the conditioning suite – our gyms, pools, clinic and treatment rooms, all that.'

'The other premiership teams must be green with envy,' she said, walking up to the tinted windows and squinting into the prized space. 'Obviously there's no one in there at this time on a match day?'

'No, although it's technically open for us, if we want. I find this is a good time to use it, as most of the staff and Academy residents are out, or away on Saturday night until Monday morning. See that long two-storey block over there? That's our accommodation. Something like forty of us live here the moment; there's lots of pressure in our talent pipeline, trust me.'

Cassie cocked her head. 'And where's your room located? I guess since you've been here a while, you've had your pick?'

'Mine's right around the back, at the end of the ground floor corridor, next to an emergency exit that's rarely used. I like it because there are steps outside that lead to a bench in a quiet, leafy space that's rarely used by others.'

'And…personal guests?'

'Unfortunately aren't allowed in the annexe, and that's a rule everyone sticks to.'

'Ah, hence never-in-a-bed?'

'Partly, although I've not brought anyone here at all, before you.'

'Really? I feel extra special, now,' she said, and wrapped her arms around his middle.

A swell of happiness choked at his throat. 'Want to see the gardens?' he said, through a sudden husk in his voice.

'Love to. Didn't The Manor's grounds win some award a couple of years back, beating a National Trust property, or something like that?'

Danny recovered his voice as they walked. 'It did. Norm and the grounds staff maintain six training pitches which we churn up pretty hard, and then there are the formal gardens; the ones you've probably seen pictures of, all manicured topiary and year-round flowerbeds.'

'That's right, it was an award for flowers, wasn't it?'

'Yes, for our rose gardens. The original owners of The Manor, a Lord and Lady Winthrop, had a passion for collecting species, so the gardens own the rootstock of some of the rarest in the country. Shame you weren't here in June, the colour and smell is fantastic.' He turned to find her staring at him.

'You surprise me, when you're talking about gardens and plants, Danny.'

'In a bad way?'

'Not at all, it's lovely to hear and quite the contrast to your day job. I don't even have a window box; you get to enjoy all this.'

'Thanks. Maybe you could start with a pot? You'll notice loads of them here full of red and white flowers – I helped to plant them.'

'I was about to ask whether you have an opportunity to help out, while it's…quiet.' The care with which she avoided mention of other players going home was just one of the ways in which Cassie's personality called to him. Her acceptance and encouragement felt unbelievably freeing.

'Over Easter breaks, during our summer downtime and for a couple of days of Christmas break. Norm has taught me a few skills, and I sometimes use the ride-on, turn the compost, that sort of thing. I enjoy it.'

'It's in your voice. It makes me happy to hear it.'

Their feet crunched on further until the gravel path changed to old, smooth paving bordered by solar lights.

'This goes down to the orchard, my favourite area. Want to see it?'

She slipped her hand into his. 'Lead the way.'

As they arrived at the nearest apple trees, Danny tugged at some of the lower hanging fruit, testing its readiness, and twisted one away from its stem. After rubbing it down his tracksuit sleeve, he offered it to Cassie.

'Our very own Adam and Eve moment,' she joked, 'although I'm not sure who'd be the sinner in this version.' She took a bite and closed her eyes as she tasted then swallowed. The effect of her soulful moan of satisfaction oozed through him.

'God, that is so hot,' he muttered, 'I'm never going to look at these apples in the same way again. Come on, the ridge with the view is behind those Bramleys.'

Even he wasn't prepared for the sight of the enormous, blue-tinged moon hanging low in the sky.

They stood there, gawping at it.

'Could we stay here for a moment, so that I can take some pictures?' she asked him, crouching to the ground. 'Although the grass is a bit damp, so I'll be quick.'

'Night dew. I could jog back to my room, and grab something for us to sit on?'

She held his gaze and nodded. 'I'd like that.'

'Alright, won't be long, you're safe here.'

Despite stiffening legs from insufficient post-match kicking stretches, and the cold shower afterwards as all the hot water had gone, Danny doubted he'd ever made the round trip via his room as fast as he'd just managed. With dry robes and a rucksack of hastily gathered objects in his arms, he stopped for a moment right before reaching Cassie. Instinct told him that her silhouette against the blue-black sky would be something to remember. He'd been about to call out that he was approaching, but she must have caught his movement in the shadows. Even in the dark, he saw her feet leave the ground when she shrieked. He dropped everything and dashed towards her. 'Shit, I'm sorry,' he said, and brought her into his arms, both of their hearts hammering. 'You're OK.'

With trembling fingers, she fussed that thick fringe of hers back into place. He'd already seen the long, silvery scar near her hairline, first at the incident with the water bottles in the tunnel, later under the floodlights when a gust of wind ruffled her hair. But this wasn't the moment to ask about that.

'It's the dark — made me extra jumpy or something,' she offered, not quite meeting his eyes.

It was more than that, he'd bet on it, but the strong need to comfort her overtook his need for answers. 'Not right now, but I'd like to ask you more about that why that is. Do you still want to sit here for a while?'

'Yes, I do,' she said, a brief shiver rocking her upper body.

He held one of the robes out while she fed her arms into it, then spread the other over the ground for them to sit on. As he bent his knees to join her, tightness in his quads made him flinch.

'Are you OK?'

'Yes, only post-match soreness.' He didn't add that a cold sprint wasn't the wisest thing to have done, and instead unloaded two mugs from his rucksack. 'But I have the bottle of champagne in my other bag, if you were interested?'

'I'll only have a little. I'm not a massive drinker – and that is a huge bottle.'

'I'm not big into it either, give me a beer any day. Maybe I'll put it behind the bar, share it with the boys.' He pulled out a large bottle of water and a pair of mugs, one of which he handed to Cassie.

She held it up to the moonlight. 'I love this – "O Scrum All Ye Faithful".'

'From my old PE teacher at college, Mr Hayes, who also taught religious education. It was his parting gift to me, when I left. I keep it on my desk to store gum shields in.' He caught her grimace as she passed it back to him.

'Quite glad I didn't say yes to the champagne, now.'

So was he, but when he'd packed, rinsing it out had been the last thing on a mind several steps ahead.

They stretched out onto the grass and laid back to admire the blue moon. The pattern of clouds passing in front of it gave the sky a marbled effect.

'It's unbelievably stunning,' Cassie murmured beside him.

'I'm glad you're here to see it.'

'Thank you, I won't forget it.'

His fingers found hers and squeezed them. 'Me either.'

For a few moments, they gazed at the stunning night sky, both in awe. Then Cassie turned on her side to face him. 'I don't think any teacher of mine gave me a farewell gift.'

'No? Well, this teacher was the one who got me into rugby. At school we'd been taught by an IT teacher and I didn't enjoy it as much, but Mr Hayes persuaded me to join the college rugby club. After Laura got sick, going to rugby practice and playing in matches gave me somewhere to go. Otherwise I'd have end up in serious trouble.' He'd park that conversation there. Cassie didn't need to know that Mr Hayes had been the adult to rock up at the police station in the middle of the night after Danny had been given a behaviour warning. Twice. Somehow, she was reading his mind.

'Bit of a bad boy, were you? Tearing around town on a noisy moped?'

'You'll never see me on two wheels, one of the boys in our class lost a leg. Bikes are one of the few things that terrify me.'

'Me too, actually. I notice you didn't disagree with my bad boy tag though, so I'm glad that teacher helped you. They say people come into your lives when you need them,' she murmured. 'Sounds like he was one of those.'

He turned to her, then, asking himself if maybe she was one, too. The thought scared him a little, but he was distracted by sight of the dark scuff on her cheek. 'Does that graze hurt? The club has every imaginable injury product in the clinic, I can run and get something.'

'It's fine, nothing to worry about.' When she placed her hand on his chest, he closed his own over it. 'Danny, what was on your mind in the players' tunnel, when I walked through with you to warm-ups? It wasn't just nerves, was it?'

It was tempting to echo her own response with a glib 'nothing to worry about', but he owed her more. 'The nerves were there, but I'd expected that, and the thousands of supporters weren't the issue. What I wasn't ready for was how it took me back to being a school kid, still living in care. For years, I'd perform in school plays, compete at sports days or participate in assemblies without even a foster parent to cheer me on, or to go over to and meet afterwards. In the tunnel earlier, I wasn't prepared for that feeling again.'

'I'm sorry, that must have felt rough.'

'It was manageable, having you there.'

Cassie leaned over and kissed him tenderly. 'Thank you for sharing that. I'm glad it was me that could help.'

'Me too. And can I ask you something about earlier? What were you going to say to me, about my bio, back in the tunnel? Before you were interrupted, you hadn't sounded very impressed with the phrase "competitive perfectionist".'

'Probably because being one isn't necessarily a good thing. I suppose it brings to mind borderline obsessives that can't handle defeat. You know, black-and-white thinkers who can't handle the reality of grey. It might be good for rugby, but it's awful for life, surely?'

'Not really. I practise hard so that I can believe in myself. Belief is everything because we are out there to win. My job is to win. If I don't believe we can win, then more times than not, we won't. It's all consuming, and it's my life.' He grimaced to himself. That had sounded way too defensive. But she wasn't right, was she?

'I see that, I do, but surely there's a way for rugby to be your life without it also becoming the way you avoid life?'

'I'm not avoiding life.'

'No, you're right, that was the wrong word, but hiding from it a little bit, maybe?' She pinched her fingers in the air, and he threaded them with his own. This woman had an uncanny knack for drilling down to the facts, however hard they were to reach. Cassie Forde was way more streetwise than him; another one of the reasons he felt drawn to her. She swept her hand along his jaw and smiled.

There was that feeling again, in his stomach, like he'd swallowed something fizzy, full of caffeine. 'How is it that you're so easy to be with?'

'Ah, you see, I have special ways with asking questions.' She grinned and rolled on top of him to plant a line of kisses near his mouth.

In response, he tumbled them over so she lay on her back, his weight suspended on his elbows. 'That's interesting, because I have special way of answering them.'

'Shit…Cassie? Cassie, wake up, what time is it?' he spluttered into cooler air. With no response, he patted the ground beside him with his free hand, seeking his phone. Much to his relief, it had only just gone 2am. On his chest, Cassie was breathing heavily, the dry robe over them both, her blouse and jacket still open, her exposed breasts pressed into him. A new swell of need punched through him, desperate for another chance to bury his face in their pillowy softness, and to experience the maddening combination of Cassie's fingers raking through his hair as her nipples hardened in his mouth.

He pulled her closer, wanting a moment to himself before he woke her. Outdoor sex would never be the same again. The smell of her shampoo, mingled with the damp grass, triggered a play-by-play flashback of the simple yet deeply satisfying experience they'd shared. Magnified for the first time in his life by an intense emotional connection, Cassie's instructive pleas had helped him to enthusiastically satisfy her needs. That, and the way she'd slowly explored his body, had blown his mind.

The memory of his professional debut would be with him forever, but he'd remember this day just as much as being the day he met Cassie. Unfortunately, she was leaving in three hours, and however tempting it was to influence her looming career decision, her talent was obvious, the potential for a high-profile career of international travel within sight. Even if she rejected that producer's offer, he would spend nine months of the year on the Premiership circuit. Trying to ignore the odds against them, he gently tapped her shoulder and waited for her to stir.

'What time is it?' she grumbled, lifting her head to look around.

'Just gone 2am.'

As she sat up, Danny helped her to fasten her clothing, the first step of a slow-peeled farewell.

'Are you sure we can't get into your room? I could do with using the facilities. You said most people are away at weekends?'

Though the club's fish-and-chips family gathering later that afternoon might have prompted overnight guests in the main building, the annexe would most likely be its usual ghost town. He pretended to debate the dilemma, but he wasn't thinking about the rules. 'I guess if we're very quick, no one will see us. I could open the emergency exit door, let you in that way?'

He couldn't tell you how quickly they'd walked up to the annexe, but neither of them exactly lingered. After he'd let himself through the front door, he sped down the corridor to let Cassie inside.

'So it's a whole corridor of rooms like this?' she whispered, while his arms tensed in an attempt to close the emergency exit without its usual bang.

He nodded and gestured at his room's door, and once inside, indicated his ensuite. Danny kept his room orderly – it was the only way with such a small space. Even so, while Cassie was busy, he straightened his set of dumbbells then shook out his duvet. He was replacing his stack of gum shields into his mug when she came out.

'Not as grim in there as I feared,' she said, pitching him a cheeky smile.

He put the mug back in its special place. 'I'll admit, we have cleaners.'

'Lucky you.' Cassie scanned the other objects on the shelf, eyes coming to rest on the photograph. 'That's Laura, your adoptive mother, and your two cousins?'

'Yes.'

'She has a caring face. Look at how big your smile is.'

'That was a good day.'

'I'm sorry she didn't see your debut.' Cassie circled her arms around his waist and pressed her cheek into his shoulder. 'I'm sure she'd have been proud.'

Danny was momentarily choked for words.

'But I was thinking,' she said, 'now that we're in, couldn't we hang out here for a while? As long as we turn the photograph around, no one's going to see what might happen.'

Without letting go of her, he reversed the photograph's position and pulled down his window blind. 'You are going to get me into trouble,' he predicted, eagerly toeing off his trainers. 'We have to be very, very quiet.'

'Shh, save your breath, we're heading into extra time.'

Another hour later, and way too soon, they tiptoed from his room and out the emergency exit. With an overabundance of caution, Danny suggested that they wait until they were back through The Manor's side gate, and into the lane, before they spoke. As the gate clicked shut, the prospect of coming back through it again in a few hours, alone, felt like a low-grade body tackle. The prospect of polite conversation over fish and chips at the club social also loomed. Maybe Cassie's suggestion to trust others, open up a little about his background, would make it bearable? He pulled her in for a hug, squeezing her tight, anything to delay setting off on their return walk.

'Hey, are you alright?' she whispered. 'This is like a quadruple hug, our blood pressure's going to bottom out.'

'A bit longer,' he muttered into her hair, feeling suspiciously needy.

Her hands twisted the material at the back of his tracksuit jacket. 'I can't believe you shushed me in the corridor,' she complained, as she eased out of his hold, 'I wasn't even talking that loudly. And you gave me sound warnings in your bedroom, when your sex groans probably woke people up.'

He slung an arm around her shoulders and kissed her the top of her head. 'Well if I did, hopefully it sounded more like I was using my weights.'

'If they think it's normal to call your dumbbells "Cassie" or exclaim that you're "going to come so fucking hard" while doing some reps, you've got bigger problems that noise disruption, my friend.'

Now that he replayed it, he did vaguely recall Cassie's fingers covering his mouth a few times. She, on the other hand, had wisely muffled the sound of her own deliciously long moans with his pillow. Maybe his room would still smell of her, when he got back there after walking her to the station. Bed sex had been whole other level of enjoyment.

Cassie Forde was a whole other level of everything.

RED, WHITE & CUE

11. Opportunity Knocks

Two Years Later

'Ten seconds until credits, medium close-up Fox/Forde, cue Fox.'
'And that's a Hystar High Five for tonight's Sports News Roundup.'
'Close-up on Cassie.'
'I'm Cassie Forde.'
'Close-up on Fox.'
'And I'm Fox Cavalier.'
'Medium close-up.'
'Thank you for joining us.'
'Until next time, goodbye.'
'Goodbye.'
'Roll credits.'
'Wide studio angle.'
'Fade to black.'
'Well done everyone, that's this evening's episode in the can.'

On a long exhale, Cassie disconnected her earpiece from the battery pack at the rear of her belt. 'Good show today, apart from the Formula 1 piece, it will keep our ratings up.'

Beside her, Fox loosened his tie. 'Ratings, shmatings. That's all Izzy talks about too, can't get her off the subject. At least the satellite link to Belgium held, it shreds my nerves when we lose contact, even on our tape delay.'

'I know it does, but that team boss was a tricky interview, wasn't he? Formula 1 media training needs to ease up on making them think we're trying to catch them out all the time. What were the one-word answers all about? The autocue was set up with excellent open questions but somehow he managed to close them all. Thank goodness for beta blockers because with all that dead air he left us with, my heart rate would have otherwise made my words dry up.'

Someone's polite cough interrupted her adrenalized flow. 'Sorry to disturb. Before you leave, Boss wants to see you both upstairs.'

'Thanks, Ella, no problem,' said Cassie, hoping that a warm smile of acknowledgement might relieve the tension on the runner's face, before watching her scuttle away.

'This won't take long,' Fox predicted, dropping his earpiece and pack onto the studio's presenter desk. 'I have tickets for Hamilton at 7.30pm.'

A digital ceiling clock displayed a green neon time check to within tenths of a second. Cassie glanced at it and sighed.

'I don't know how you've got the stamina to be out every night when we're in London,' said Cassie, already relishing the exact moment she would be shutting herself inside the sanctuary of her little-used but mercifully peaceful studio apartment.

Fox simply returned one of his famously flirtatious grins that his thousands of admirers had come to know. 'Not forgetting stamina for what comes afterwards,' he smirked, straightening the lapels of his charcoal suit and running a hand through his trademark dirty-blonde hair. 'Knock for you in ten?'

'In ten.'

Sat at her dressing room's desk, Cassie packed up the designer tote she'd bought herself last Christmas, when presenting Hystar's coverage of European cycling from Paris. A delayed-gratification gift for almost two years of non-stop graft and dedication to her broadcasting career. Beside her, the non-negotiable coffee machine pinged, delivering a mug of steaming hot mocha latte, her current post-recording favourite. She brought the mug to her nose and inhaled the sweet, comforting smell, knowing that as soon as it were cool enough, each sip would bring her down from the nervous high. It should probably be green tea, or something less stimulating, but after a rabbit-food brunch bowl, then taping through lunch, the sugar would help get her home without fainting on the Tube.

She cocked a head at her reflection in her bulb-lit mirror and sighed. Beneath the layers of broadcast-grade make up and – her breath hitched at it, even now – camera powder polish, she read as 'tired'. The plethora of strategically placed highlights in her hair weren't doing their job. In years past, she'd sometimes been told that she looked younger than her age; now Cassie suspected that she looked every one of her thirty-two years, maybe more.

She'd just twisted the cap off of her bottle of eye drops when Fox knocked on the door. After a second or two, he poked his head inside. 'Ready?'

'Almost, do you think I need drops?' She widened her eyes and blinked at him.

He joined her at the mirror. 'Yeah, maybe. Want me to do it? Your hands are still shaking.'

'Yes please.'

'OK, head back.' With his usual ease, he added a couple of drops into her eyes. 'Might just top mine up too.'

The pair of them froze for a moment, smarting at the sting.

Fox slipped the bottle into her tote bag. 'We should have shares in the company that make these. Alright, let's see what our Big Bad Producer wants upstairs.'

'Just don't call her that to her face.'

'She'd secretly love it.'

Upstairs, in the management offices, Cassie knocked on the door marked 'Head of Production' and waited, but Fox opened the door anyway and led them inside.

'Izzy, good to see you, I didn't realise you were in this afternoon,' he said, switching on his easy charm. 'You look well.'

Izzy batted away the compliment by waving her hand at the empty chairs. 'Come in, you two. Another good week for Fox/Forde, I was watching from the gallery.'

Cassie accepted the praise; she and Fox had carefully honed their style to deliver effortlessly engaging programmes.

'I wanted to speak to you about the next six months and run by you both some ideas we're considering for ways to extend your exposure.'

Cassie groaned inwardly; she'd followed Izzy's advice faithfully over the past two years, but ideally there would be less exposure in the pipeline after the series finished recording next month, not more. Though she kept her smile in place, Fox, who'd yet to realise his cricket-presenting dream, long-dangled by Izzy, was unable to hide his scepticism.

'What sort of things are you thinking about?' He frowned.

'It's not cricket, *yet*, but we've been approached by two organisations whose proposals would fit between the Fox/Forde commitments you both already have locked in with' – she pulled up an alarmingly congested-looking planner onto the room's interactive whiteboard – 'Aquatics GB's Open Water series throughout September and October, and the European diving championships through November and December. But, it would mean working separately on projects again. Firstly, Cassie, are you still willing to cover cycling over Christmas? I see it's in Berlin this time?'

'Out of the country again this year?' Fox interjected.

'I am. I still prefer to be away over Christmas.'

Izzy nodded, 'Alright then, so for you, Cassie, something between those bookings – probably September through to January, a more hands-on opportunity has arisen for you. It's been a couple of years, but how would you feel about writing and filming a sport-specific three-part docuseries?'

'Open to it,' Cassie confirmed, perking up. For the chance to create content, she'd have cheerfully attach herself to most sports.

'Fantastic. Well, as you'll be aware, there's a rising female interest in rugby union, possibly off the back of the World Cup coverage. It might be the game itself, or it could be more superficial, given famous popstars dating athletes of similar build to our rugby players, but either way, I feel there's a moment to ride the wave.'

'Absolutely,' Cassie nodded, but a trickle of suspicion ran down her back.

'Excellent. You'll be delighted to know that Camford Rugby are the Premiership club in question, where of course we first met, and didn't I tell you that there'd be a bright future ahead if you followed my advice? Keep doing it, and Hystar will serve you well.'

Cassie wasn't so sure about that. Privately, she and Fox felt that Izzy hadn't always had their best interests at heart and they had often borne the exhausting, over-high-exposure consequences of her determination to exceed ratings targets. Cassie wouldn't be surprised if Izzy had been fanning the perpetual 'Fox/Forde – are they or aren't they a couple?' rumours in the media, just to keep the show on people's radars. Whenever Cassie was asked, she'd awkwardly trot out the same, completely true line that she and Fox were simply good friends, and there for one another. But right at that moment, her mind was in Cambridgeshire, envisioning an awkward reunion.

A double click of someone's fingers pulled her attention back to the meeting. 'Cassie?'

'Sorry, Izzy, you were saying?'

'You remember Trish Murphy, the media and marketing manager at Camford? In media circles, she still has an excellent reputation. This is her brainchild, something she's been sitting on for a couple of seasons, hoping we could all make it work. She's right in believing this would continue to raise her club's profile and continue the success she and the management have seen. I know you've been out of the rugby loop since then, but you'll remember a few players from before.'

Some more than others. Cassie finally found her voice. 'How do you envisage my schedule looking?'

'The broad outline would involve two home matches and two aways between September to January. You'll observe some team training, attend a couple of the club's Tuesday media briefings and accompany Trish when players are on community outreach projects. Overall you'll report into me monthly, and we want it edited and ready for airing during February as part of the Six Nations tournament.'

'Mind if I pour myself some water?' Cassie mumbled, reaching for the carafe and a glass in the centre of Izzy's table.

'Only if you say yes to the project,' Izzy chuckled. 'Joking, fill your boots. It would be a busy few months, because you'd still have Fox/Forde Sports News Roundup to deliver on Monday and Friday evenings, at least until the new year. But think of your career. Trish tells me she'll identify which rugby matches could fit with your existing bookings, and even offered use of The Manor's facilities.'

Warmth crept up Cassie's neck. 'Is there another option on the table?'

Izzy didn't try to disguise her disappointment. 'I guess we could send Kelly D. up to Camford. Her ratings are as good as yours and she'd be a hit with the players. I will say that Trish specifically asked whether you'd be available. I'd have to check whether she'd still want to go ahead with someone else.'

'What's your concern, Cass?' Fox said quietly, 'Remember you can say no to it.'

Though she hadn't ever given him any details of the night she and Danny shared, her and Fox's easy ability to read one-another's expressions and body language was a cornerstone of their on-air shorthand.

He turned to Izzy. 'How about you talk through what's coming up for me, while she thinks about it?'

Cassie tuned out a discussion about Hystar's coverage of England Hockey League fixtures in the upcoming months, giving her some space to debate her decision. If she declined the Camford gig, Izzy would most likely allocate her to ad-hoc presenter features, none of which would offer an opportunity to gather and write her own content for filming. Forsaking the chance, simply on the basis that she couldn't face a former one-night stand, wasn't acceptable. Cassie quashed the uncomfortable twist in her tummy, knowing all too well that Danny had meant something more than that, and forced herself to engage with the conversation in the room about hockey's Adult Super 6s. 'I covered a Super 6 tournament during my university hockey reporting, lots of fun but they're frantic, they play and party hard, those guys,' she said, giving Fox a cautionary glance.

The pair of them knew the toll that live television took and it did not mix well with a party lifestyle. As it was, she and Fox were running on fumes.

Fox nodded, picking at a thumbnail. 'OK, Izzy, how about I cover the hockey, if it means you'll look favourably on me presenting cricket next year?'

'I would certainly keep you in mind for it, but it might mean further dial-down in our Fox/Forde output.'

Fox turned himself towards Cassie. 'What do you want to do, Cass? I'd cover hockey if you want to film the docuseries at Camford. If not, we can take our chances. No offence, Izzy.'

'None taken. It's entirely up to you. You're not unique, there are others we can approach, I just wanted to give you first refusals. If you're not up to it, I can't force ambition on you.'

Cassie recoiled on both of their behalf. Izzy really didn't like it if you showed weakness.

Fox rolled his eyes.

'Alright,' said Cassie, 'I will if you will.'

'Great!' Izzy, jumped to her feet before Fox had agreed, then started to tidy her desk. 'We'll sort the details. I have to go, places to be,' and with that, she powered down her tech and left the room.

'As have I,' said Fox, pouring himself a dribble of water and knocking it back. 'Talk about it on Monday, Cass?'

'Monday.'

Fox air-kissed her cheek and dashed out of the room, leaving a trail of the distinctive cologne that seemed to drive every woman, except her, wild.

Dozing on the sofa, inside the studio flat she still rented in Clapham, Cassie was transported to a Sunday morning two years earlier. When she'd been roused by a melodic blackbird, only to find herself lying on a station bench, her head on the sizeable thighs of Danny Reed's lap. She remembered the weight of his protective arm curved over her waist, and the way his lips pursed as he slept. Her hand twitched, recalling how she'd swept her fingers through the dark, dangling strands of his hair and how his overnight bristles had prickled against her palm when she'd cupped the side of his slackened jaw.

The intensity of those whirlwind twenty-four hours had taken some getting over. Truthfully, however hard she might have tried to convince herself otherwise, no relationship or late-night drinks at hotel bars since then had matched the chemistry she and Danny had shared. No one, in the array of sportsmen or support staff or colleagues in the media, had held the appeal of his tough, talented yet tender character. And now she'd have to face him again, this time in a capacity that carried professional expectation and career opportunity. She'd kept tabs on him, of course she had. Been pleased when he'd nailed his name to the number 10 shirt at Camford, concerned enough whenever his name was missing from the team sheet to seek out the club's media briefing on medical updates; a muscle strain here and there, an episode of concussion, nothing too serious. Unsurprisingly, his social media presence was still lacking; she recalled his understandable reluctance to draw attention to his personal life. Had he found someone special, that could see his qualities, soothe his fears, give him someone to belong to? Maybe that could have been her, had she made different decisions?

Just as she'd been then, lying on that station bench, Cassie was struck by a useless pang of longing for her family home. Perhaps remembering that blackbird had triggered it, hawking memories of a childhood waking to Welsh Valleys birdsong. It had been a crazy couple of years and now, like then, she could really have done with some sound, parental advice. As a career mentor, Izzy had enabled Cassie's international success, but as a role model and a confidant...no.

Cassie stirred, thinking about the final moments when she and Danny had pushed themselves upright from that bench, rolling shoulders to ease sore muscles. How she'd fervently manifested another train delay, despite knowing it would only prolong the inevitable goodbye.

Danny hadn't tried to sway which fork in career road she would take, but she'd never forgotten their last conversation.

'We both know things don't always go the way we want,' he'd murmured into her hair. 'The kicker is, now I know what I was missing.'

She had grasped at levity, something to stem the building well of tears behind her eyes, and said, 'Bed sex?'

But Danny hadn't laughed. Instead, he'd taken her face in his hands and choked, 'No. Someone like you.' The way he'd kissed her on the station platform, slowly, thoroughly, then hugged her tight had been unforgettable.

Maybe they'd keep in touch, from time to time, they'd said, though neither offered their contact details.

She'd boarded the train and found a seat by the window to wave from, but he'd already gone.

RED, WHITE & CUE

12. Drumroll

At Coach Alex's request, the entire senior squad and the club's support staff had congregated in The Manor's 100-seat media centre for the first Tuesday briefing of the season. Principally a weekly meeting for publicity-related matters, today's would also feature the announcement of this year's senior captain. In front of the small, raised stage, a technician was setting up a serious-looking film camera facing a backdrop screen of club sponsors. Another sound-checked microphones and tested a projector.

It seemed excessive, to Danny, as he descended the shallow steps towards the front rows, but in Trish's domain no one, including him, doubted the set-up.

Five chairs were placed behind the on-stage presenter desk, while the cinema-layout seats facing them slowly filled up. The players occupied the first four rows; Danny sat with Ryn and Josh, who had become his best friends at the club, along with others he'd found ways to get along with. A sea of happy, energetic faces generated a deep hum of camaraderie. It had been a long summer break, without hearing it.

Over the past two seasons, Danny had learned to go out of his way to include fellow players in conversations, and to find common ground, even if it was purely rugby related. He'd also made time to help bring new recruits into the fold, whether from the

Academy or from other clubs. Certain individuals, however, occasionally tested patience. Behind him, Connor Wilson guffawed over videos on his phone while slurping noisily from a water bottle. Off the pitch, the two of them still tended to avoid each other, but on it, their communication had settled, and the team's results had improved accordingly. Lewis Banks, last year's captain, had only played in a handful of matches, a legacy of the horrific injury from two years ago, which had needed numerous operations and a full year off for recovery. Connor had retaken Lewis' position as first pick scrum half with thinly disguised relish.

At ten o'clock precisely, Coach Alex arrived to take the first seat on the stage, along with Trish next to him and Lewis beside her. He picked up the microphone, tapped it twice and addressed the room. 'Good to see you all, after our first training session yesterday and welcome to the support staff, I hope you had a good summer break. As you know, I'll be announcing the senior team captain and explaining my reasons for his selection. First, I'll handover to Trish, who has news of an exciting project that has the management and coaching staff's fullest support. It will affect us all, so listen up.'

Trish stood up, thanking Coach as she picked up the microphone. 'Hello everyone, I hope you're all doing OK. For those newbies I've yet to introduce myself to, my name is Trish Murphy, I am Camford's media and marketing manager. I also work alongside management in handling team sponsorships and seeking new revenue streams with local businesses and national brands. I'll tell you more about that next week, but please come and see me if you have suggestions or new contacts, and of course I'll try to hook you up with individual sponsorships, depending on your needs and interests. I see you're all wearing the updated training tracksuits, looking very smart with the Aspire Homes logo. I'm relieved to tell you that they have signed a two-year extension to their top-tier sponsorship, so we can keep the lights on for a bit longer!'

A rumble of appreciative laughter bounced around the room. Danny was not alone in recognising Trish's dedication to her role. Yet another club had gone under at the end of last season.

'So, on to the news Coach Alex mentioned. Between now and January, I'm thrilled to say that Camford's senior squad is going to be the subject of an exciting, three-part, fly-on-the-wall documentary-series – a docuseries that will air on Hystar in February. It will raise our profile and bring in a serious sum of money that will help us to secure the upkeep of these tremendous facilities.'

Danny's heart began to race. Surely not. Surely it wouldn't be—

'To tell you more about it, I am delighted to welcome the lead on this project, one half of Hystar's popular due, Fox/Forde, Cassie Forde.'

It surely was. Whoops and whistles filled the air as Cassie strolled onto the platform in a tailored trouser suit remarkably close to Camford Crimson in colour. She waved to everyone, picked up a microphone, and focused on the midpoint of the raised seating. 'Hi, hi, thanks for the welcome,' she said in her on-screen, friendly manner, 'lovely to be here. Yes, as you've heard, I'll be with you for a few months with Hystar. The series intends to give viewers insight into the professional lives of rugby players, so my plan is to attend two home matches, to travel with you to two away ones, and to incorporate some of your community work. We'll also be filming some pitch-training sessions and gym-work, that type of content. There are more details to come, and if you have time after this meeting, I'm happy to talk them over with any of you. I'll be outside in the foyer for a short while before filming an interview with your new captain, then back here in Camford for your first home match. For the moment, though, does anyone have a question?'

Danny had questions. Lots of them, starting with why the hell no one had mentioned this to him? Why hadn't she?

'Will you be interviewing us?' one of the physios called out.

'Yes, if the support staff are happy to be involved, I'd love to include you, although I won't be appearing on camera for this project – except of course to introduce and roundup each episode. I'll be writing and performing the episode's voice-overs, back in the studio.'

'Will you be staying here?' Connor asked, prompting a few sniggers.

Cassie pulled a humorous sad face. 'Rarely, although Trish has kindly offered rooms for me and the two crew in front of me here – give them a wave, guys. Everyone, this is Fynn and Zac – they won't mind me telling you that they're huge rugby fans and begged to be on this project.'

Two heavy-set men turned to acknowledge the audience. They might be out of condition, but by the looks of them, they'd played a bit of rugby in their past.

'I'll be back and forth to various other Fox/Forde commitments throughout filming, so don't worry, I won't be under your feet.'

'Shame,' said Connor.

Danny sat motionless, but a part of him imagined Connor choking on whatever was in his bottle. The grinning mugs of Fynn and Zac smiling up at Cassie weren't exactly filling him with the warm and fuzzies, either.

Coach Alex sprang up from his chair and without a microphone, projected his voice in the way everyone in the room knew he could. 'That's enough, Connor. Cassie, welcome to Camford, we are delighted to have you with us over the production period.'

Another round of clapping spread through the rows.

'Thank you.' Cassie smiled. She replaced the microphone in its holder and took a seat next to Trish, who signalled a conspiratorial thumbs up in her direction.

Coach Alex picked up the mic and stepped forwards. 'Alright, settle down, settle down. Now for the captain announcement.'

Danny adjusted his posture, aware of the imminent reveal. His long conversation with management yesterday evening had only just convinced him that Coach Alex's rationale was sound.

Suddenly, Cassie clicked her fingers at the Hystar crew, then murmured something to Trish, who passed mention of whatever it was to Coach Alex. They both nodded and the video cameras powered up.

Fynn – or Zac – held up his hand and signalled a silent five second countdown with his fingers, before pointing at Cassie.

'Go for it, Coach Alex.' She grinned.

Like a starstruck kid, Camford's grown man of a head coach blushed when acknowledging her with a polite bob of his head.

Cassie's posture was ram-rod straight, her shoulders back as she began to systematically cast her twinkling eyes through the audience, row by row. When her gaze found his, he couldn't pull away. Two seconds became five, five became ten, then their attention was dragged back to the announcement, when it was explained to everyone that Lewis Banks had decided to step down from the additional responsibilities of captaincy, and that this year, someone new would be given the role. The microphone was passed to Lewis, who stood to address the room.

While Lewis recounted some of his highlights from his four-year tenure as captain, Danny discreetly observed Cassie. Like millions of others, he had seen her on television, of course, so the blonde streaks in what to his memory had been silky, dark brown hair, were not a surprise. The longer length now bounced off her shoulders and her fringe, though still heavy, was swept to one side, drawing even more attention to her eyes. Large, grey-blue and still beautiful, just as before. Hadn't she once said that she'd been referred to as 'forgettable'? No one could say that about her now, not that he'd ever thought it.

For a moment, his mind cast back to the night he and Cassie had shared that long walk to The Manor, their deep conversations and unexpected chemistry. For months afterwards he'd thought of her, fantasising how their relationship might have developed if they'd overcome the challenges of distance and time. In bed or in his shower, and hot with need, he'd imagine her with him, her hands, her mouth, her gasps and moans. He'd admit, part of him had been relieved that things he'd revealed to her in confidence had never appeared on a media platform; he'd felt guilty for suspecting they might, because Cassie Forde had shown herself to be trustworthy. She couldn't be aware how fundamentally he'd adjusted his approach to life after being inspired by her own. She'd kept going, had made bold choices and hadn't looked back. He'd been close to contacting her a hundred times, wanting to hear her voice or to talk something over, knowing she'd keep his confidence, but Fox/Forde commitments seemed to take her to Florida, Birmingham, Madrid, sometimes in the same month.

Guilt nudged at Danny's conscience, for the local trainee sports masseuse he'd ended things with earlier this summer. It hadn't been her fault that she couldn't understand his deep-rooted issues, that sometimes he craved the peace of The Manor's gardens rather than clubbing, nor had she known how it was to be without parents. She was also not to blame that any urge to protect her, or desire to spend time with her beyond the bedroom, had been missing.

Lewis sat back down after a tremendous reaction from everyone in the room. He would be a hard act to follow.

Danny took a breath, steadying himself while Alex talked about the new captain having a quiet strength and steadiness, of how popular he'd become amongst players and the club's support staff. An embarrassing compilation of video clips began to play on a projector screen.

'You all know it's important to win matches,' Coach Alex narrated as the film played. 'This year's captain wins but is smart with it. He holds steady in challenging atmospheres – those of you who were with us at the time will remember this being the case right from his debut. His internal drive is to be admired, as is his physical and mental endurance. So, please give this year's captain a big cheer as he joins us on the stage, a third season senior player, seven season homegrown club member, this year's senior squad captain, Danny Reed.'

On his way to the stage, Danny struggled through an assault of congratulatory back slaps, aware in the corner of his eye that Cassie had sprung to her feet and was clapping animatedly. When he climbed the steps, the only available spot to stand on the stage was next to her. He took his place, acknowledging well wishes from the audience.

High heels brought Cassie's eyes nearer to his than he remembered, and her perfume smelled more expensive. Only now could he see that the sparkle in her eyes didn't mask pink rims of tiredness, and that her frame had slimmed. When she held the microphone towards him, a whispered word of 'congratulations' puffed from her red lips, his task of delivering thanks for the captaincy intercepted by clouds of attraction that whispered something like 'it's-still-there', in his ears.

He took the microphone carefully, so as not to make contact with her fingers, aware that one hundred pairs of eyes were on him. He took a deep breath and turned to the audience, many of whom were on their feet. 'Thanks, everyone, please sit down. Coach Alex, Jim and all the other staff, I'll do my best to be the link between you and us players. I'm proud to wear the captain's armband and will try to represent us all. We know that a rugby career is short, sometimes shorter than we'd want, so I'd like to thank Lewis for the great job he's done as captain and I'm sure I speak for everyone here when I say we hope to have more game time with you yet.'

More cheers of agreement gave Danny a moment to collect himself.

'I wanted to say this: a handful of people have helped to give me direction in life, some have shown dedication, others bravery or openness and whether they realised it or not, have kept me moving towards being the man I've needed to become. Lewis, you are one of them, Coach Alex, Jim and others in this room, I hope you know who you are, too. Thank you. My teammates, the support staff, let's all have a fantastic season.'

RED, WHITE & CUE

13. Non-verbal

Everyone decanted into the bright sunshine of the media centre's glass foyer and pockets of upbeat chatter filled the air. Meanwhile, the world of sports news waited for no one. Cassie scrolled through the usual sources on her phone, squinting against dazzling reflections while she screened for announcements, rumours or results that she might have missed while in Coach Alex's presentation. Anything and everything could pop up, at any time of the day or night; she mustn't miss it, when it did. Hystar expected no less, especially when helming a project.

Trish was stood beside her, scrutinising her own phone with similar focus.

'That went well,' Cassie said, while making a note about a GB springboard champion just having announced his engagement to a celebrated Canadian platform diver. Something as back-up for her or Fox to mention on Friday's programme, perhaps.

'Yep, a good start to the season. And I'm particularly pleased about the captaincy. You remember Danny, of course?' Trish suspended her own typing and glanced up, apparently awaiting Cassie's response.

'Yes, and many of the others.' Cassie scanned the players' faces, ready to give examples and divert the conversation away from anything personal.

But Trish was not finished. 'He's matured, don't you think?'

Cassie nodded, keeping her expression neutral. When Danny had stared back at her from his seat in the meeting, she'd barely taken a breath as memories rippled between them. Stood next to her on the stage, he was broader than she'd remembered, his face a little fuller, but what had struck her most was the increase in his confidence. As if the man couldn't get any sexier. 'They've all changed, in two years.'

'Mmhmm. Did you get the footage you wanted?'

'I might collect some supportive reactions on the captaincy, while we're all stood here.'

'Go for it. I'm sure you'll have plenty of volunteers.'

With Fynn and Zac beside her, Cassie gathered the thoughts of the catering manager, who mentioned how Danny had instigated whip-rounds for The Manor's kitchen staff and ground staff at Christmas. Then Cassie chatted with one of the club's newer signings, who revealed that when his daughter had been sick, he'd been blown away when the team had funded her treatment. Danny hadn't wanted it known, apparently, that he had been behind the initiative. Her favourite footage was from a conversation with Josh Webber, who'd shown sentimental appreciation for having joined Camford as an Academy player, for its facilities, while admitting to having stayed because he belonged with people like Danny. He also provided a hilarious anecdote about having put Deep Heat in Danny's pants on his debut away match.

A gentle tap on her shoulder made her jump. 'Hello Cassie, how are you?'

'Norm! Lovely to see you again,' she said, clutching her lapels until her heart rate settled. 'The grounds are looking wonderful, I hadn't seen them in the daylight be…' She stopped herself in time and smothered the error by waving away her crew away, and mouthing 'take five' at their grateful faces.

'Thank you. We try our best, and I wouldn't want to be anywhere else; this is home.'

'I don't blame you at all. Most days I wake up needing to remind myself where I am, sometimes even what country.'

A smiley, shorter man of a similar age to Norm, wearing rimless glasses, joined them. 'Norm, sorry to butt in – I've got to head off – but could you introduce us?'

'Of course, Cassie, this is Doctor Andrew Harrison, Camford Rugby's head of medical and rehabilitation services.'

'Hello, pleased to meet you, Doctor. Is there an acronym for all of that?' she teased.

'I've often wished there was. Everyone calls me Doc and as for the department, you'll most often hear either "Clinic" or "Rehab".'

'And he's too modest to say that his clinic here is like a mini hospital, and that the rehab rooms have sports physios clamouring for a job with us,' Norm added, seeming rightly proud of the club's facility.

Cassie smiled at them both. 'The Manor's reputation continues to be well-founded, then?'

Doc puffed his chest. 'I believe so. While you're here, if there's anything you need, please let me know.'

For a split second, Cassie wondered whether he might somehow be able to provide her with stronger sleeping tablets, but dismissed the idea, remembering her professional responsibilities. 'Thank you, and please be assured that privacy and respect with regards to medical confidentiality will be observed during filming.'

'I appreciate that, thank you. Apologies, but I do need to go, I'm afraid. Have to sign for a delivery of flu vaccines that are about to arrive. They have to remain in a cold chain and cost a small fortune. It's hard enough persuading some of the players to have the jabs, without having to rearrange dates in the diary again because I've rendered a lukewarm batch of vaccine ineffective. I'll see you soon.'

Cassie smiled and tracked the direction of Doc's exit, only to clash eyes with Danny, who had positioned himself facing her, while speaking to another group. To her dismay, he immediately concluded his conversation and came striding towards her.

'So…they give everyone flu jabs here?' Cassie scrambled to extend her discussion with Norm.

'On a rota, even for us support staff. The players are split into groups, too, just in case there is a reaction. Wouldn't look good if everyone playing a particular position has a sore arm or fever, all at the same time. Danny! Chuffed for you, man, I really am.' Norm hugged him, and the two men shared a moment that Cassie wished she'd caught on camera.

'Yes, congratulations,' she said, holding out her hand.

Danny wrapped his fingers around hers and shook it. Had she imagined the extra squeeze before he'd released them?

'I'm sure the captaincy is well deserved,' she added, monitoring her tone so that it didn't flicker with emotion. Back on the stage, when his name had been announced, she'd hidden the sniff of a tear by adjusting her fringe, something Izzy had still not managed to fully drum out of her.

Danny drew his eyebrows together. 'You weren't spilling secrets about the flu jabs were you, Norm?'

'I was about to. I thought Cassie here would like to know that several of our biggest, most feared players are terrified of a needle prick. One of them fainted last year, even before the nurse had got a syringe near him.' He began to chuckle.

'I don't suppose whoever it was would admit to that on camera?' Cassie giggled, and Norm shook his head.

'I wouldn't think so. Oh, but it still makes me smile.' He dabbed at his eyes with the sleeve of his tartan shirt. 'Anyway, I'll leave you two to it. Might see you later, Danny.'

'Might do.'

Cassie and Danny's laughs dwindled to silence as they watched Norm walk away. There was no avoiding their first conversation alone, now. She debated whether to open with an apology for not having forewarned him about Hystar's project. Perhaps she'd compliment him on how well he looked or elaborate on the opportunities the docuseries was giving her? Then, he might understand that she couldn't mix business and pleasure, however much she might want to…assuming he had any interest in doing so. Perhaps she should stop over-thinking? Perhaps she should—

'It was me,' Danny said, with a glint in his eye.

'It was you?'

'That fainted.'

Cassie covered her mouth to conceal her laugh.

'Yep, I'm in a sweat even thinking about it. I know it's ridiculous – and don't ask me to own up to it officially, the flack I'd get for it from opposing teams would be even worse than I've taken from everyone here.'

'I seem to remember you saying something about never wanting to get a tattoo – and you definitely gave the impression it was because of its permanence, not your exposure to needles.'

'It was both.'

'Well, needle phobia might humanise rugby players for viewers, keep it real. Everyone has vulnerabilities that we try to keep hidden.'

Danny's eyes flicked to her forehead. So he'd seen it, back then, yet asked nothing.

'It's faded, but still there,' she said. 'I've learned a trick or two from Hystar's make-up artists.'

Danny simply nodded. 'The graze on your cheek healed though. I wouldn't want you having bad memories made on my watch.'

It was as if they were the only two people standing in the foyer. She cast her eyes down, pretending to avoid the sun's glare. 'I don't. Only good ones.'

'I'm glad. Me too. How are you, still living in – Clapham, wasn't it?'

'Yes, still in the same apartment as before. Not that I'm hardly ever there.'

Danny nodded, then asked quietly, 'Are you happy?'

Cassie didn't really know. Was she? She babbled an obscure response, hoping to distract from his deeper meaning. 'It's super convenient for the studios and getting to Heathrow, but do you mean work?'

'Either, both.' He smiled, slipping his hands into his tracksuit pockets.

'Work is crazy. Sometimes I think it's making me crazy too.' She was definitely off-kilter now. How hadn't she remembered the gold flecks in his dark brown irises, when those eyes were the first thing she'd noticed about him two years ago? One thing was for sure; had she been meeting him for the first time today, her reaction would have been the same. He blinked slowly, staring back at her. Nonverbal communication swirled around them, and for a few, very unprofessional seconds, she imagined how a sizzling reunion might feel.

With a half-smile, he stepped closer. 'Is there a way to avoid eye contact while we're filming the captain's interview, do you think?' His husky tone sent a delicious shiver through her body.

The interview. She was working. 'Shit, I forgot we've still got to get that done. Where should we shoot it?'

'Maybe outside – where it's cooler? I'll meet you there in a few minutes.'

At Trish's request, Danny had changed into senior squad formal wear for the interview. Like her, Cassie knew the programme's demographic would appreciate the tradition and the implied respect to the role. And for those interested in more than the game's competition, if they weren't already swooning over well-honed rugby-types, this would clinch it. With the

Cambridgeshire chalk hills behind him, Danny sat in his dark grey wool suit, with its Camford Crimson lining, a white shirt and striped crimson, grey and white logo club tie, with matching silk pocket square. He looked every inch the man you'd want to represent you. Or, Cassie mused, to call yours. Although they would film a one-shot over her shoulder, she had to dig into the mental techniques she used to control her on-air delivery. She didn't want her interviewee being distracted by evidence of her nerves. 'Ready, Danny?'

'Yes, I've gone over the main points of what I'll say with Trish. It's still just the four main questions?'

'It might roll naturally into follow-up ones, but I won't be trying to catch you out.'

One side of his mouth lifted, disarmingly.

Cassie checked the questions on her tablet, pulse hopping. She needed a little extra help. 'Actually, I just want a sip of water, hold on a sec.' She raided the workbag that she'd stowed at her feet, discreetly popped a tablet into mouth and swallowed it down with a glug from her water bottle. When she looked up, Danny was frowning. 'Oh, sorry – do you need a sip of water?' she said, tilting her bottle at him.

'No. Headache?'

She batted away his question with a shake of her head. 'Alright, are we good to roll, guys?' Cassie waited for Fynn to verbally confirm that the light and sound equipment was ready. 'Danny?'

'I'm still ready. Are you?'

'Definitely. Zac, if you could do the honours.'

As he counted her in, she took a deep breath.

'Congratulations, Danny, on this morning's announcement. Captain of Camford Rugby's senior squad. How do you feel?'

'Thank you. I'm proud to represent the boys and grateful that management have faith in me.'

'You've been with the club since your Academy days. How do you think that adds to your commitment to the role?'

'Personally, I owe the club so much and it's part of the reason I train hard. Coming up through the Academy gives a different perspective, but we've had great captains who joined us from highly respected clubs – Lewis originally came from Bath, for example.'

'What was it that got you into rugby in the first place, Danny?' At the last moment, Cassie, altered the wording of her pre-approved question that had originally asked 'when' he started playing. Unless he wanted to do so himself, there was no need to draw attention to the lack of childhood exposure to the game, which most other professional players had enjoyed. His additional blinks before answering seemed to transmit his thanks, but then he leaned nearer and took deep breath.

'This isn't something I talk about often, but I know that captains should lead by example and my experience might help others. I came to rugby very late – at sixteen, thanks to a college teacher. My childhood had been, let's say, challenging, and I was probably on the wrong path. But he saw that rugby could be my outlet – both physical and mental. It was more than I could have imagined.' Danny studied his hands.

'Break?' Cassie murmured, knowing that her voice could be erased, in the edit.

Danny returned his intense, dark gaze to hers and held steady. 'The thing is, everyone needs a family, a support system. Rugby became mine. If people watching this don't have that, I'd encourage them to keep looking – one's waiting for you to find it. Rugby itself is an inclusive sport – all shapes and sizes of players form a team. But it might not be a sport you discover – it could be a hobby or faith, but you'll be grateful when you find it. You'll belong to something.'

Cassie's slow swallow of emotion told her that Hystar's viewers would react similarly to Danny's unexpected openness, even if they hadn't faced the family turmoil, he – and, unbeknown to anyone there, she, too – had.

She nodded her encouragement to Danny and moved the conversation on. 'What is it that you love most about playing the game, and what do you find the hardest?'

'Well, I've just said about the family the game gives you, but it can also help you to develop decent values, to learn about leadership and respect, and how to work as a team. I could go on. What do I find the hardest? If I'm honest, every player understands what constantly having to prove yourself feels like.'

'In what respect?'

'For selection, fitness checks and, I'm sorry to say it, sometimes it's media scrutiny. Those are the hardest to deal with. Things like that can be worse than the risks of playing the game.'

Cassie smiled at his effortless link to the question he knew was coming next. His media skills had really come on. 'How much do you worry about injuries, or something worse, happening?' she asked.

'There are risks, there's no getting away from it. But rugby isn't alone in that – think of hockey players being hit in the head by a deflected ball or some of the fielding positions in cricket. Most players know the risks we face, but we train hard and play safely. Rules are updated regularly to help, and though not always consistently refereed, we don't want those rules to change rugby too much.'

Cassie moved Danny on. Lingering over the contentious subject of refereeing or rule changes might lead to unfavourable media courage for him, and the club, however strongly he felt about them. 'Thank you, Danny, and finally, how do you rate Camford's chances this season?'

'We have a special group of people here. Coaches will be doing everything they can to prepare us, and I'll do my best to lead us to a better table position than last year. This could be our season to achieve a final four spot for the Premiership play-offs.'

'Thank you, Danny. Good luck.'

'Thank you, Cassie.'

Cassie nodded at Zac, who called, 'Cut.'

Trish hovered nearby. 'Great job, Danny, a really strong start. My phone is going to blow up once this airs. I don't think you realise the influence professional sportspeople like yourself have on youngsters. Oh, and speaking of, are you still planning another visit to the hospital in a couple of weeks' time?'

Danny unbuttoned his collar. 'Yes, can you get some merch for me?'

'Will do. Cassie, are you happy with how that went?'

She was more than happy, she'd been impressed, not just by what Danny had said, but the way his tone had developed over the past two years and how it gave weight to his words. 'Yes, and thank you both, I understand that you're busy people.'

Trish checked her phone. 'So, just to lock the match details in, you'll be here for our home match against Bristol, then you'll come with us to…' She scrolled lower. 'Newcastle, then another home match before Christmas, against…who is it? Sale, who'll come down from Manchester, and finally we are away in January to Cardiff.'

'Cardiff?' Cassie whipped her neck round.

'Yes, why, did you fancy a trip home while you're with us?'

She definitely did not, but calmed the rising panic by reassuring herself that January was four months away, that perhaps they'd have enough footage by then anyway. She would make every effort to ensure they did.

Fortunately, Danny interrupted their conversation. 'Are we all done for now, because I'm sweating like mad in this gear, and need to get changed for training.'

'I'm done,' said Trish.

'Me too, I'll be leaving in the next hour, for some Fox/Forde pre-recording in London.'

Zac interrupted, holding out his phone, 'Er, Cass, transport's arriving in five. Fox messaged to say that the M25 is blocked by the Dartford Bridge. We'll have to head through London. He's also asked what colour tie he should wear today.'

'Right, I'll get in the car as soon as it's here and tell him I'm wearing Camford Crimson.'

'Got it.'

'Do you need anything for the journey? Water, a fruit bar?' said Trish, making little effort to disguise her reaction to the weight Cassie had deliberately lost. It was true that cameras added ten pounds to your appearance.

'No, I don't usually eat until after filming, it's bad for phlegm. I'll see you both a week on Saturday, though?'

'That's to film us at the home match against Bristol on Saturday?' Danny asked, rolling his tie up and stuffing it into his trouser pocket.

'Yes, and some before and after frames, too.'

Zac began to laugh. 'Fox says, "Damn cuuute, baby" with lots of "u"s.'

'And that's my cue,' said Danny. 'See you next week, Cassie. Trish, no doubt you'll still be here after training has finished.'

'Where else would I be?' She grinned, then turned her attention back to her phone.

RED, WHITE & CUE

14. Appeal

'Cheers everyone, first match, and first home win, a fantastic start.' Danny raised a pint glass to his teammates, who had gathered at The Manor's club bar. One of his intentions as captain was to begin a new tradition; after a home win, he'd buy everyone a drink. Thanks to Bristol Rugby, who'd handed them an easy contest, he surveyed the happy-faced turnout. Several players were swollen and bruised, and a couple had seen Doc for an eyebrow stitch, but no one was injured beyond what a six-day healing window could fix. The feeling of community almost outweighed his restlessness at having skipped the extended version of his usual post-match kicking practice.

Towards the other end of the bar, Cassie had her head together with Trish, comparing phones.

Since the docuseries announcement visit, he'd made time to watch the Fox/Forde TV coverage of a swimming competition, and the evening sports roundup which Hystar aired twice a week. She was good, very good, and her smile had beamed at him through his screen. Fox's not so much, the easy manner between the two of them irritating him after a while. Danny had then fallen into an internet hole that seemed obsessed with Fox/Forde 'Are they or aren't they?' rumours pedalling a soppy 'real-life' love story.

At the stadium earlier, while the team changed from warm-up kit into match colours, Hystar's Zac and Fynn had entered the changing room to set up and check if the coast was clear for Trish and Cassie to pop in for some quick footage.

Danny had refused until all the lads had made themselves decent; though Josh Webber, for one, never batted an eyelid at strutting his sizeable bulk, even he'd drawn the line at it appearing in a fly-on-the-wall docuseries.

Locking eyes with Cassie again had then necessitated some determined focus. He'd been polite, offered a few words of welcome, but the priority had been his players, and the game they were about to play.

Across the bar, Zac and Fynn had now joined Cassie and Trish. Danny caught the men's eyes, raised his glass, and, as he expected, they beckoned him over.

'Good, you all have a drink,' he said to them.

'Thank you, Danny, just the one for me,' said Trish. 'I'm still posting photographs to our channels.'

Danny flicked his eyes at Cassie's glass of brown saccharine fizz, but she shot him a warning look.

'Don't. It's keeping me going,' she groaned, with far less sparkle than her Coke.

'I'll try to resist. How did filming go today?'

'It was an OK start. What do you think, boys?' She turned to her crew.

'We got some good baseline clips in the can,' said Zac, necking the dregs of his pint. 'All good, I'll upload tomorrow but, sorry, Fynn and I need to get going back to London.'

'He recently put a ring on some poor girl's finger, and my other half is waiting for me too,' Fynn added, but glanced expectantly at Trish.

'Oh yes, right then, boys, I'll walk you out. You wanted to see the trophy cupboards before you go? Most of the silverware is decades old, but it's next to my office and I'm heading there now. Saturday evenings are prime slots for sports news, there's plenty for me to do before I can go.'

'Can you have a look at filming angles, while you're there please, boys?' Cassie asked, the project clearly still on her mind.

'Will do. Just checking the sheet for next week,' Fynn said, pulling his phone out. 'So, team media briefing here on Tuesday, then a community visit, and some filming in club rehab, is that still correct?'

Cassie waited for Trish's smile, then nodded her confirmation. 'Meet you over in the media centre on Tuesday at 8.30, then.'

'Yep. When's your car coming? You could come back to London in the equipment van with us if you wanted?'

Danny shifted his weight from one foot to the other; there was never a moment for him and Cassie to talk alone.

'Thanks, but there's no need, Hystar's car is on standby for me. I just have to give the driver a call.'

As Trish and the boys walked away, Cassie sipped her drink, apparently lost in thought.

Danny had been about to ask about her week when Ryn's wife arrived and gave him a kiss on the cheek.

'Well done, Handsome, proud of you.'

Since he'd moved out of The Manor, into his apartment in town, he'd lost count of the number of meals he'd eaten at Heather and Ryn's home. Despite being thousands of miles from their Cape Town families, her and Ryn's place had a warm, settled feeling, and the pair of them often included him in their plans. Neither seemed to mind if he sometimes stayed the night on their sofa, after they'd all sunk too many beers watching sports or listening to Heather mix dance tracks from her vast collection of music.

Danny wanted to introduce Cassie, but she'd turned away from him, and perched herself on a stool, studying the bar's TV screen.

Heather said something about the depth of scuff that an opposition player's boot had left on Ryn's head, but 90% of Danny's attention was consumed by Connor, who had pulled up a bar stool next to Cassie.

'I knew you'd come back for me, beautiful,' Connor oozed.

'Yes, you guessed it, that's exactly why I took this gig,' Cassie replied evenly.

'Danny, are you *listening* to me?' Heather asked.

'Yes, sorry. But Ryn's OK?'

'He's…'

Dammit, Connor was not easily deterred, he was leaning towards Cassie now. 'Checking out scores from the other matches?' he asked her.

'If you're about to say that I've scored, please don't,' Cassie said, poker-faced.

'You've read my mind, but come on, tell me what I was going to say after that, then.'

'It's been a while, but doesn't that line go something like, "you've scored, get your bag"?' A smile toyed with her lips. Watching Cassie being entertained by someone else's jokes felt the opposite of funny to Danny.

Heather, unfortunately, was also not amused. '...so if you're really listening, tell me what I just said, Danny.'

He turned back, his hand raised. 'Sorry.'

'Oh, now I see, someone's caught your eye, have they?'

He forced himself to lock onto Heather's face. 'No.'

'Hmm, well, I wanted to meet Cassie Forde anyway, so I'll do you a favour,' she said, stepping round him before he could stop her. 'Hi, sorry to interrupt you, I just wanted to introduce myself. I'm Heather Koch, married to Ryn.'

Cassie shook her hand, all smiles at Heather. 'You're not interrupting at all, I think Connor was just leaving. Good to meet you.'

To Danny's and possibly Cassie's relief, Connor slunk off his bar stool, picked up his pint and went to join another group.

Now it was time to do Heather a favour. 'You and Cassie have similar careers, don't you, Heather?'

'Oh?' Cassie came to stand with him and Heather.

'Yes, of sorts. Back home in Cape Town I was a radio DJ. I had a weekday drive time slot.'

'Sounds like fun. Do you miss it?'

'I miss the routine of it. I love music and had some authority over what I played. But conversation beyond concert tour dates or album launches rarely happened, which was a waste because my original background is in journalism.'

'Really? That's interesting, if you have a minute, can I run an idea about the project at Camford by you?'

'Me? Sure thing.'

Danny couldn't tell which of the two women's smiles were bigger.

Cassie didn't waste any time. 'Great. For a fuller picture of rugby life, I'm thinking of asking whether I could interview the senior squad's wives and girlfriends. Would you or any of the girls be up for that?'

'It's a good idea, I see it would help to give viewers a balanced view of life away from the club.'

'That's what I thought.'

'God, the things you might hear, though!' Heather giggled.

'I'm kind of hoping for something special, as long as it could be aired. What do you think about a group interview, and some footage of you all supporting the next home match? Then perhaps a longer, off-camera chat between just you and I, for deeper context?' Cassie's face as she proposed the ideas to Heather gave Danny a glimpse of her professional side. Her enthusiasm and ambition were infectious.

'I'd love that, I really would, but let me speak to Ryn, to see if he'd be comfortable with the idea.'

Danny stepped in. 'Come off it, Heather, the man would do anything you ask, though this might need a courtesy mention to Coach Alex, as well as Trish.'

'Presumably the captain needs to give his approval, too?' Heather cocked an eyebrow.

'You have it.'

Colour bloomed in Cassie's cheeks in a way that made him want to hold them in his hands, reacquaint himself with what he remembered as smooth softness.

'Thank you,' she murmured.

Heather removed her car keys from her bag. 'Right, I think it's time I took my man home. Don't get to enjoy my Saturday night G&T until I've completed taxi duties and Ryn is soaking his muscles.' She gave Danny another kiss on the cheek, then leaned in towards Cassie. 'I might have a few things to say about this one, too,' she said, winking in Danny's direction. 'I'll get your number from him, to let you know about the interviews?'

Cassie flicked her eyes at Danny awkwardly, which Heather astutely pounced on.

'Jeez, ignore that, my stupid assumption that you've got each other's details – how about I share my contact details with you now instead?' She waggled her mobile at Cassie.

'That would be great.' Cassie pulled out her phone. 'Let me know.'

Once they were alone, Danny asked Cassie if she wanted another drink, but she looked uncertain.

'My car will be here in thirty minutes; I contacted the driver while I was talking with Connor.'

'I can see why he might trigger that.'

'Yep, although I'd planned to leave around now anyway, my sleep's severely lacking after a couple of days away in Rome. I guess I could squeeze in another Coke, before I go, if you're free?'

Danny surveyed the dwindling numbers in the bar, and for once, no one was lingering to speak with him. 'I'll order, then shall we sit over there?' He pointed to the more secluded corner of the room, where empty velvet sofas were angled towards a display of club memorabilia.

'Or we could just drink here, at the bar? Eyes are on us, Danny, I have to behave professionally.'

'So do I, but just because we're having a drink, it doesn't automatically follow that I'm bedding Hystar's talent.'

Cassie levelled her gaze at him. 'You've preferred beds in the last two years, then?' she teased, then immediately closed her eyes. 'Wow, that was completely inappropriate, ignore me.'

'You aren't making it easy, and yes.'

'Yes?'

'As in yes, I have, though I've been single for a few months. You?'

Cassie pinched the inner corners of her eyes and hopped back up onto a stool. 'This conversation is already straying to places we shouldn't go. Can we get back to less personal talk, please?'

'If you want. Tell me more about how you're doing. You seem happy at work.'

She gave a long exhale before responding. 'I don't know – are any of us?'

'I am.'

'That's great. Me, I'm functioning with semi-permanent fatigue. I have a kick-ass boss whose apron strings I've hung onto, and I've met some inspiring people, in all sorts of sport, but broadcast reporting on them is harder than I imagined.'

'I don't doubt its harder than it looks. The public has little idea of what professional sport is like, other than what they see on television or on game days.'

'Exactly. We are presenting to inform, and entertain, sometimes to persuade, but management are always pushing us to acquire some extra, unique soundbite. What isn't shown to the public, is that I'll have sat through six hours straight of speaking to players in whatever sport I'm covering, hearing them all stick to the same lines they're given by their media managers. No one wants to stir the shit.'

'Come on, Cassie, see it from our side. You know how tightly Trish manages our media relations, there are reputations at stake.'

The bartender placed their drinks on the mat in front of them, and Danny tipped his chin at him for the cost to go on his tab.

'I know, but there's a balance to be had, isn't there? I've been so under pressure that lately that I've taken to sweetly antagonising the odd player – I've even asked whether they were tired, just to see if that fires them up.'

'That's risky, how do they react?'

'Usually, it's "I or we didn't lose because we were tired, it was because of xyz" but that small titbit opens up a conversation. Gives me some freedom to create something interesting, different from our competitors.'

'Noted, if you ever interview me again.' He took a sip from his drink. 'I still regret turning your interview down on my debut match, by the way. I realised pretty quickly that I'd made things worse for you, that day.'

'It's forgotten and forgiven. If I'd known then what was on your mind, I wouldn't have asked you, anyway.' She pulled her glass to her lips and Danny was transported to their long walk to The Manor, two years ago, and reminded how gentle and sympathetic she'd been.

'All the same, I've thought about it a few times. You certainly look different from then.' He smiled, hoping that his face didn't publicly broadcast the strong tug of attraction he still felt for her, no matter how fancy her hair had become.

'Izzy, the mentor and producer I was just referring to, helped me understand the stats on how well certain grooming is received. It's part of the struggle for female sports presenters, although it's lucky I'm not that attractive, because women that are often try too hard and it shows. None of us want to be "fluffy", you know?'

'I understand, but I don't agree.'

'Take it from me, casual sexism still happens, even now.'

Danny couldn't stop himself from shaking his head. 'No, I realise that. I meant, from my perspective at least…do you not see that you're attractive? I wish it wasn't the case, but no woman in the past two years has come close.' He took another gulp of his drink to stifle other words that would reveal how her personality still held his attention.

'Don't, this isn't helping with my stress.' She pulled out her phone and swiped away a couple of messages.

'How are you stressed?'

'Oh, you know, the usual unrelenting competition, comparison, social media trolls, blah, blah, blah – then sports news is just as twenty-four hours as the main news and let's not forget how nerve-shredding and unpredictable live TV is. I don't know, Danny, maybe I should have learned from my first match here and made different decisions.'

Her jaded tone pumped an uneasy feeling through him. Others might believe the upbeat gloss she presented on camera, but he could see beyond that. Her natural optimism had taken a bashing in the last two years and the his desire to make it better urged him into action. What did she need? To know she wasn't alone in feeling overwhelmed, maybe? 'I'm sorry it's been like that for you. There's stress in every job, though, isn't there? Camford's coaches are constantly evaluating and keeping everyone tense, but when you think about it, maybe they're tense too, answering to management? Sundays and Wednesdays are our only downtime, except for me because now I'll spend more of those in meetings and checking up on each player.' He took a breath and jumped. 'Last night, when I was having a confidence crisis, I promised myself I'd use my stress to perform better. You know, tackle it head on.'

'You had a crisis?'

'Off the record, I did.'

'God, Danny, I wish you'd…I wish we'd…' But her words petered out. Perhaps, like him, she'd regretted not having had each other's numbers.

Last night, pacing a circuit of his open plan apartment, in the dark, he'd thought of her more than once. Needed her.

'Yeah, well, I drove up here, turned on the lights at Pitch 1 and kicked a few balls. Went home, scanned over my game notes, and focused on which referee we'd have today—'

'Why on the referee?'

'There's still so much inconsistency, for example, with the number and specific types of penalties they give. Each referee has passion points, and offences against those are more likely to be penalised. It's up to the captain to suss out any trends and brief the team.'

Cassie stared at him for a few seconds, then smiled. 'I hear you. By the way, you're better at talking that you used to be.'

'I guess if something matters enough, you have to do what you think's necessary – like changing your appearance.'

'You're right, but you know what I hadn't realised before?' she said, waggling some strands of her hair at him. 'How often women's hair colour gets mentioned in women's sport – sometimes it's the players', sometimes even mine. What's that about? You don't see mention of Fox's hair but if I get layers cut into mine, everyone has an opinion.'

Danny had seen several 'thirst' articles celebrating Fox's 'Brad Pitt hair', but didn't want to bring that into their conversation. 'It's similar for us with muscles – whether it's our mass, or fat percentages, if we're lean, or stacked, it gets referred to. The boys are more image conscious than you might think, especially the backs players – you can't get them away from the mirror before running onto the pitch on game day.'

'You're technically a back, Danny.'

'I'm thinking of certain wingers and a cocky scrum half that likes his chances with you.'

Cassie laughed discreetly. 'I was glad Heather came up to introduce herself, she helped rescue me and, oh, sorry, I've just had a message to say my car is outside.'

'I'd better let you go, then. I'm sure someone's waiting for you, back in London.' He resisted asking whether it was Fox.

Cassie covered a yawn with her hand. 'The only thing waiting for me is a bubble bath, then bed. I'll see you on Tuesday?'

'I'll be here.'

She squeezed his arm playfully while picking up her bag. 'Oof, great muscles, very lean, I'll be sure to mention their fat percentages in my voice-over of the captain's interview,' she joked.

'Thank you and your lovely hair.' They exchanged grins and walked slowly towards the main entrance.

'Danny, just so you know, this project means a lot to me. It could be my way back to a more creative role, more behind-the-camera writing and production. It's the reason that, on balance, I agreed to do it.'

'I can see that, and I'll do what I can to help it run smoothly. On balance? What was your reluctance…our history?'

At the solid oak front door, Cassie stopped walking and took an extra breath. 'I'm embarrassed that I didn't find a way to keep in touch, so I thought coming back here might feel awkward.'

Danny held the door open for her, taking a few extra seconds to be clear in his mind. 'I'm not feeling awkward, but you know that this thing between us is still here?'

'I do. Being here, especially in the dark, it takes me right back to the night we shared.' She kept her eyes on his and it was all he could do not to pull her into his arms.

'You'd better get in the car,' he said gruffly. 'If I hadn't had a couple of pints, I'd offer to drive you myself, at least no one would see us, then.'

'You'd be sorry, I'll be asleep before even hitting the motorway.'

'Still, I would have.'

He opened the car's back door, but before she slipped inside, she pulled out her phone. 'It feels stupidly late to suggest this, but maybe we should exchange numbers? You know, mostly for work purposes.'

Danny forced himself to slow down the enthusiastic removal of his phone from his pocket. 'It's not too late.'

15. Just Try

Tuesday had arrived both shockingly fast and agonisingly slowly.

'Morning Miss Forde, returning to The Manor at Camford?'

'Yes, please, Martyn, and sorry in advance if I nod off.'

'I'll keep the radio down low.'

Cassie smiled at the Hystar driver's wise eyes in his rearview mirror. These days they seemed to exchange the same words whenever he drove her. It spoke to her lifestyle, as well as his smooth driving style, although on Saturday evening's journey home from The Manor, she hadn't slept at all. Funny how four words from Danny Reed could keep you awake. *It's not too late.*

As she passed Tower Bridge on the route out of the city, she sought her phone again, and scrolled through her brief conversation from three short – and long – days ago.

DR: **Get home safe, sleep well. D**
CF: **Thanks, next 24 hrs zzz + editing, early Mon a.m. @ GB Aquatics in Bath, back to London to record Fox/Forde C**
DR: **Ouch, but will also be in bath (of ice) then back (massage - physio elbows, nothing**

      good), Mon @ match debrief, coach 1:1, then squad training
CF: Busy busy busy
DR: No regrets, all part of the job
CF: Good, don't want you having any of those
DR: Maybe one. Didn't keep in touch with a girl I met
CF: Why not, do you think?
DR: Constant comparison with Henry Cavill
CF: Surely not. Maybe timing was off; probably still is
DR: *probably. #Quits while ahead. Pace yourself, see you Tuesday D
CF: Till Tuesday C

At The Manor's media centre, the air was filled the fragrance of freshly laundered sportswear, and deep-voiced, playful banter, Cassie opted to stand at the back and observe the final few players and staff trickle in. Everyone stopped talking as soon as Trish arrived.

    Without delay, she pulled out her tablet and got down to business. 'Right, everyone, good morning, well done on Saturday's result against Bristol. Media impressions were very encouraging. Let's keep the momentum with next weekend's away match at Gloucester. Please remember the guidelines for players when you are out representing the club, whether on match days or out in the community. Be aware that anything can be recorded or repeated, so keeping to the outlined responses is advised.'

    Cassie glanced down at Danny, who had turned from his position in the front row to make an obvious sweep of the players who were nodding their heads at the media instruction.

Catching sight of her, he raised a rueful eyebrow as if to say, 'See what I mean?'

She acknowledged him with a small smile, their first interaction since Saturday.

Trish held up an official Camford scarf. 'Alrighty, on to promotional items. Most of you will remember from last season, but for those that are new, we have plenty of products for your use in charity links, and for giveaways at your discretion. The company we use can also personalise items with names or initials or whatever's needed within a couple of days, just submit your order directly using the Camford account and the delivery will come to my office for you to collect. OK?'

The murmurs of acknowledgement made Trish smile.

'Good. So, several of you will be out this morning with your chosen charities and local organisations. Hystar are filming some of those. Cassie and her crew tell me that filming so far is going well.' Trish paused to look up at her – quickly followed by the rest of the group turning like meerkats.

Cassie confirmed the progress with a thumbs up.

'Excellent. I will be accompanying Cassie to Danny's usual visit to the Cambridge Children's Hospital, and with Josh to the learning disability school. Also, a date for your diaries, please. In a fortnight's time, this Tuesday slot will be used by Doc, who is bringing sport psychologist Trudy back to see us. They will be talking to the group again about what motivates you, so have a think about how you might contribute. It's a great way for players to know and understand one another better. Super, that's everything. Have a good day, boys, and I'll see you next week.'

The players, including Danny, clapped and filed out of the room.

Cassie waited behind to speak to Trish. 'Can we film the psychology session for the series?'

'I'll check with the two doctors, and the boys. I hope so, it would make interesting viewing. Last year's flip charts were full of words like "money", "glory", "team" and "pride". I remember Ryn and Danny helping things along by being open and a few others followed.'

'What did they say?'

'Off the record until I have the go ahead?'

'Sure.'

'Ryn said "family", Danny said "fear". I'm sure all the players related to not letting their families down, and the fear of losing.'

From what Danny had told her, Cassie was certain his fear ran beyond the result of a match; more likely it reflected how he depended on rugby, and what would happen if he lost it. She made a mental note to tactfully raise the subject with him if an opportunity arose.

'We can take one of the minibuses to the Children's Hospital,' said Trish, 'that way we can all travel together and there'll be room for your crew's filming kit. Leave in ten minutes?'

Trish had excelled in clearing permissions from patient clinical leads for the filming. At the hospital, she also liaised with busy nurses and carefully explained Hystar's filming to some emotionally drained families who were visiting their sick children.

Cassie was impressed and grateful; seeing rows of beds with obviously unwell children was traumatic, all that brave smiling through discomfort and pain. Only by digging her thumbnails into her fingers had she so far held back tears.

'I haven't been here since Danny's first visit, a few months ago,' Trish sniffed, beside her and the crew. 'Usually he comes alone, but you probably noticed he was very quiet on the way over here.'

'Yes, but I couldn't do this every month,' Zac mumbled. 'The guy reminds me not to assume that loud is strong and quiet is weak.'

Cassie swallowed.

Danny spent ten minutes at a time with four children on the junior ward, all of whom had a parent with them. Depending on the children's ages, he gave them signed shirts, programmes and mini Camford rugby balls, and posed for pictures with patients, parents and staff. He left with a cheerful wave, and a brief word with all the adults. After almost an hour, and despite the grim situations, the mood had become surprisingly upbeat. Camford's community programme was undoubtedly worthy.

'I'm going to the adolescent unit next,' Danny said to her and Trish. 'They have a lad in there who's obsessed with rugby. I'll take the crew, but maybe give me ten minutes before you come in?'

They both nodded, but Danny paused before walking away. 'This will be harder; you're both OK?'

Cassie glanced at Trish, then back to Danny. 'We'll be there.'

'I don't know how he visits these poor kids and their families so often,' Trish sniffed again, walking slowly with Cassie along a long corridor, while Danny and the boys went ahead, 'I couldn't, the nurses would be mopping up after me.'

'I know what you mean.'

'I've seen this in many ways, with our squad. They like to play the role of meat-head rugby player but really most of them are soft. They might be unflinching when confronted with tackles or whatever, but some of them – including Danny – are remarkably empathetic and attuned.'

'The way those kids' eyes shone when they saw him,' Cassie squeaked.

'Danny's come on since you first met him, he's very committed to the team. Off the record, now that he lives alone, he doesn't take care of himself as well as I'd like, though I know Ryn's wife, Heather, keeps an eye on him. He carried an injury earlier in the year which meant he was more isolated. It's hard for our single players, quite often they don't have a lot of life going on outside of rugby, and they don't have a partner to lean on.'

'They're pretty resilient, though,' Cassie replied, thinking about Danny's care system background. Perhaps that was how he was strong enough to help kids that were sick or struggling?

'Some more than others. In my time, I've seen upsets triggered by all sorts – homesickness, absence of relationship with family, cultural separation. It's partly why Doc incorporates mental health support for Academy students right from the outset. You saw earlier about the psychologist coming? She's another help – but sometimes behaviour manifests itself as guilt or insecurity, occasionally anger.'

'How does the club handle that?' Cassie asked, pointing out some signage for the Adolescent Unit.

'Mostly it's the coach's job to work it through with them, but more often than you'd think, I've had players in tears in my office, at their wit's end, not knowing who they are, unable to cope.'

'Christ. What do you do then?'

'Some just need to talk, others are young and will mature. Time heals, as we know, but when things aren't going well, you forget that. Quite often, they just want a hug, which I know probably isn't professional, but even the biggest, oldest, gnarliest players need a shoulder sometimes and being old enough to be their mothers, I don't mind if it's me they come to.'

No wonder she was treated with such respect. Every club should have a Trish.

Even Cassie wanted one.

Danny had put on a medical face mask and was sat in a chair beside the bed of an emaciated teenager, who'd lost his hair. Through the door's window, he signalled a thumbs up to Cassie and Trish. They'd been about to enter when a middle-aged man, holding two coffee-machine drinks, walked up.

'Hello, I recognise you. You're Cassie Forde, aren't you?'

'Yes, I'm here with Hystar, filming with Camford Rugby for a docuseries.'

'The nurses and Danny mentioned that there would be cameras today. But I didn't know that it was you. Woody's going to grin from ear to ear. Come on through, there are masks inside. I'm Richard Thurston, his dad.'

'Pleased to meet you.' Cassie felt a squeeze on her shoulder from Trish.

'I'll wait out here.'

Cassie nodded and followed Richard inside. Noting how the room smelled of disinfectant, she took the mask offered to her by a nurse, and internally braced herself.

At the bed, Danny was sympathising with Woody about the process of calculating angles. 'Yeah, same, mate. Me and protractors didn't get on during GCSE maths, so I had to learn fast when it came to the science of kicking for goals.'

'That's also physics,' said Woody in a thin, raspy voice, 'I was studying about forces last week in my workbook, downforce and drag, something called, I forget…gravitational potential, is it, Dad?' He looked up at Richard.

'Yes, that's right, it was in the unit on aerodynamics. Anyway, talk about two surprises in a day, look who else is here!'

Cassie stepped forwards, briefly pulled down her mask to smile, and gave Woody a small wave.

Against wax-white skin, there was no disguising a hint of pink spreading over the boy's face. He opened his mouth, but seemed to have been stunned into silence.

'Don't worry, she has that effect on all of us,' Danny quipped, then beckoned Cassie to take his chair. 'Here, maybe tell Woody about the project while I drink my coffee?' He stood up and accepted one of Richard's cups with a grateful nod.

'I'd love to,' she said, sitting down.

Slowly, Woody found his voice again, and asked about aspects of live television, and which sports personalities she'd most liked working with.

'And Danny, too, you must like working with him?' He grinned at Danny in an adorable, hero-worship way.

'Careful how you answer that, Cassie, don't want my hard-earned reputation tarnished.'

Captivated by the way his eyes crinkled above his mask, she lost her trail of thought, but Woody must have interpreted Danny's caution, and Cassie's hesitation, as a need to supply additional evidence.

'The thing is, he isn't like other visitors, he understands a bit about how I'm feeling. It's my background, from before.'

Cassie didn't ask him to elaborate. 'Yes, he's pretty good, and now club captain, of course.'

'I was made up when that happened.' Woody said to her, smiling shyly,

'I see that. Me too.'

'Me three,' said Richard, squinting at Woody's eyelids, which had noticeably drooped. 'Well, I think we'll leave it there, thanks for coming in, again,' he said, gesturing to everyone at the door. 'Cassie, it was such a bonus to meet you, good luck with your filming.'

'Thank you, Richard, and Woody, lovely to meet you.'

'Would you sign this programme from last week's win, that Danny brought in?' Woody asked.

'Of course.'

While she was writing an autographed message, Danny shook Woody's hand. 'What do we say about keeping positive, one day at a time?'

'Don't promise, just try.'

'That's it.'

Richard walked them out into the corridor, where Trish awaited them. 'My Woody loves that saying, Danny,' he said. 'It's clever getting the rugby "try" into it.'

Cassie hoped to remember it, whether or not the moment made it to the final edit. It seemed a wonderful never-give-up mantra.

'Mind if I just collar you privately, for a moment?' Richard asked him.

Danny sought Cassie's eyes.

'The rest of us will go down to the main reception, wait for you there.'

At the hospital foyer, Trish raised the subject of Cassie interviewing the club's wives and girlfriends. 'The coaches and management think it's a good idea. Heather is keen to write something up about it for our staff newsletter, too, if you're happy with that?'

'I am, and I'm pleased for her. Shall we schedule that for the next home match, the weekend after next?'

'Perfect.' Trish checked her phone, tapped in some responses and turned to brief the crew about the practicalities of their next location for filming, a local special needs school. 'We'll head back to The Manor, drop Danny and after a half hour break, take Josh with us to town.'

From the corner of her eye, Cassie saw Danny slip past everyone and out through the automatic doors.

'OK, sounds good,' she said. 'Mind if I stretch my legs for a few minutes while we're waiting for Danny? I have a couple of calls to make before we get back into the minibus.'

'No problem, oh, good, the promotional merchandise order has just been delivered. Right on time for the school visit.'

Outside, there was no sign of Danny, so Cassie followed the path around the hospital perimeter, passing an alleyway of commercial laundry bins before making way for a family pushing a small boy in a wheelchair. She continued until the carpark, where the Camford's minibus sat empty, so she retraced her route. Following an inkling, she stepped into the alleyway she'd passed and, to her relief, found Danny, hidden from view, crouched on his haunches.

'I need a minute,' he said into the air.

Cassie hovered, uncertain.

'You're watching me.'

She could hardly help it. Professional Cassie was observant, noticing everything. But this, she understood, was private. She crouched beside him and balanced against the wall.

'I've got my eyes closed,' she whispered.

A minute went by.

'Doctors have told Richard that they might have to try something else.' Danny's gruff voice echoed up the alleyway.

Cassie opened her eyes. 'I'm sorry, he seems a lovely lad.'

'He's had it tough, so has Richard.'

'Does he live nearby? He seemed aware of Woody's current schoolwork.'

'Richard stays at a charity's parent support hostel in the hospital grounds, during the week. They're from Colchester, so it saves him a lot of time and money and means he can keep his work going too. I have a lot of respect for him.'

'What was the thought behind "Don't promise, just try"?'

'Because kids like that…maybe had promises betrayed so young that trust has been absent.'

'By his parents?'

'Richard is his adoptive father, four years ago.'

Several pennies dropped.

'Is that how you feel, about trust?'

'This isn't about me.' Danny stood up abruptly and rolled his shoulders.

She did the same, but blocked his path. 'I know, but I'm asking if you're OK.'

'Interviewing me again?' His reaction bore the defensive tactic she'd remembered from before.

'No, just seeing if you wanted to talk. Or not, either's fine.'

'Only a fool confides in a journalist.'

Maybe she was wrong, and he'd feel better left alone. Either way, she was only prepared to put up with so much. She turned to retrace her steps, but his hand caught her arm.

'Not yet,' he said, gruffly, eyebrows pinched, his expression distant.

Whether from instinct or a simple need to give comfort, she didn't know, but Cassie hooked her arms around Danny's waist and back, pressed her cheek into his shoulder and pulled him close. A few seconds later he wrapped his arms around her and dropped his forehead onto the top of her head.

'Eight-second hugs,' she said into his jacket, squeezing hard. 'Remember?'

'Everything.' He planted a kiss into her hair, pulled her closer for a few more seconds, then led them out onto the main path.

As they approached the main doors Danny paused, a look of regret on his face. 'I didn't mean what I said, back there, about confiding in a journalist. Pre-rugby me is nearer the surface than I'd like, sometimes.'

When he was honest, like this, Cassie felt close to him again. The need for physical contact, even if only to hold him, tingled through her. 'It's alright, but I wish we had some time in the schedule. The day's jam-packed; we're filming in the clinic and on the training pitches after these visits.'

'When are you going back to London?'

'As soon as I'm done with today's filming. I'll be at the South Bank studios all day tomorrow; we have a new set to get to grips with before Friday.'

'Dinner, this evening before you leave?'

'Maybe, if it's somewhere nearby and…discreet?' Cassie blinked up at him, and one of his beautiful smiles lifted his mouth.

Trish and the crew appeared through the main doors. 'Hello, you two, you had me worried, but I'm glad to see smiles on those faces. I've bought chocolate for the ride back to base,' she said, handing out bars to everyone.

Cassie opened hers immediately, but Danny shook his head. 'I don't eat—'

'Oh please don't do a Coke on me,' Cassie begged under her breath. 'Chocolate makes me happy – I eat some every day and I'm not gonna lie, sometimes in the bath, and even though I shouldn't, in bed.' She cast him pleading glance, only to see his pupils widen.

He held out his hand. 'Thanks, Trish, think I'll save mine for later.'

16. Knock, knock

In the worst mood for a long time, Danny dialled the number for Luca's, a rustic trattoria that served handmade pizza. He'd suggested it to Cassie when their paths crossed at the club's rehab unit that afternoon. On the basis that it was located in a quiet road, and that a 6.30pm reservation on a Tuesday would be unlikely to draw any unwanted attention, she'd agreed. He'd booked online almost immediately, but now he was ringing to cancel. Sat at home, on his sofa, he glared at his swollen ankle as if it had deliberately sabotaged his plans. Training ground injuries were common, and he was not exempt, but the timing was more frustrating than usual. He finished the call with Luca's, apologising for the late cancellation, then wiggled his toes, frozen from the re-freezable ice-wrap one of the physios had sent him home with. In two or three days' time, she'd review the mobility, but Danny already knew she'd declare him unfit for next weekend's away fixture. Feeling sorry for himself, he messaged a picture of his ankle to Cassie.

DR: Ankle roll, left early, 24 hrs ice
CF: Oh sorry, dinner plans?
DR: Can't, rest, crutches. Shit timing

The three dots of Cassie's imminent reply came and went, came and went.

He flexed his foot and winced. Nope, he wasn't going anywhere, however much he wanted to.

His phoned pinged.

CF: Have checked and Luca's delivers

Danny scanned the state of his apartment – it was clean, but there was little else he could do to improve its appearance in a couple of hours, not in his condition. On the plus side, they'd have privacy.

DR: They do. U sure about coming here?
CF: Man on crutches is no threat ;)
DR: Can't promise (or try). Apartment 10, Watergate, Riverside Walk, CB26 2GE. Intercom at main gates. Come whenever
CF: See you in an hour. Rest up x

Given his frame of mind only moments before texting, a happy buzz of anticipation now flowed through him. He stared at the letter 'x' on his phone, thinking hard about its use.

DR: Will do. Dx

Fifty minutes later, he'd hobbled to the intercom by his front door, buzzed her through the main gates and waited while she found him on the second floor. Her smile as she stepped out of the lift and saw him holding the door hit him like summer sun.

'Hi,' she said, holding a carrier bag from the local supermarket. 'You didn't trade down much from The Manor, then?'

He closed the door behind her, resisting the desire to welcome her with a kiss as she stepped into his hallway.

She slipped off her shoes and paired them neatly, so small against his row of trainers.

'This complex is one of our sponsor's luxury developments; a few of us have apartments here, thankfully they were massively discounted.'

Cassie crooked her head into the bedrooms and bathroom as they passed down the hallway into his open plan living area, then whistled at the view through the floor-to-ceiling windows onto his balcony, and beyond. 'Nice, bet that river is gorgeous in the summer. You haven't been here long, then?' she said, gesturing at the room.

'Just over a year.'

'Oh, I thought – there's only a sofa and TV in here. Where's your stuff?'

'What stuff? So far, I've only bought the basics – sofa, TV, bed, wasn't really sure what next. Don't forget it's my first place on my own.'

'Yeah, I realise that. How about getting a rug? I did that for my place. It killed the echo from the wood floors and cosied it up, not that my whole place wouldn't fit down this end of your room.'

'Not sure I was aiming for cosy.'

'Just an idea. I bought a shaggy one, it's lovely to lie on and watch a film from sometimes.'

Danny stared at his floor, imagining Cassie lying on a rug there, her long legs wrapped around him, while he lost himself exploring her breasts. Trying to quash the thumping visualisation, he cleared his throat. 'I'll think about it. Drink? I'm sorry about having to cancel the restaurant.'

'It's fine, I had a taxi drop me via the 24-hour shop on the corner,' she said, opening the carrier bag on her arm. 'I have red wine, Coke and beers, but I've just realised you might not be drinking if you've taken painkillers?'

'One will be fine, with a beer, or a glass of wine, if you're having one. Which would you prefer?'

'I still rarely drink, but maybe a small glass of wine?' She wandered up to the open kitchen area and started examining the contents of his cupboards. 'But I'll open it, you'd better stay there. Where do you keep your glasses – oh that's sweet, you've still got that funny rugby mug…you might be getting wine in that at this rate.'

'There are tumblers above the sink.' He might add wine glasses to his shopping list.

'Those will do.' She returned to the sofa with two half-filled glasses. 'Why aren't you keeping that ankle up?' She tutted.

Danny hadn't wanted her to sit on the floor. 'It's fine down like this.'

'You know it isn't. Lay your leg along the sofa, I'll fit myself around it.'

'If you're sure. I'm about to ring in an order to Luca's. Any preference?'

'Anything, despite Trish ushering me towards the snack stands in the rehab unit every two minutes, I'm surprisingly hungry.'

Wasn't that just typical of Trish? Danny had been the recipient of several portions of lasagna from her that had been 'going spare' when he first moved in.

'In that case I'll order the extra-large meat-feast.'

Cassie returned to the supermarket bags she'd bought with her. 'Thanks, though I'm surprised you eat processed meat.'

'I was once told by a smart-mouthed, soon-to-be TV presenter to live a little.'

'Wise words. I also got you these to cheer you up,' she said, presenting him with a bunch of three sunflowers, 'but I don't know if you've got anything for them to go in?'

Danny stared at the bright yellow petals. No one had ever bought him flowers before.

'I haven't – just use a pint glass.'

'Good idea.'

Sat together on the sofa, they sipped at their wine, his sunflowers displayed in a glass on the floor, next to the TV. Cassie insisted that Danny keep his ankle raised and had gently rested his foot in her lap. She held the freeze pack in place, through the pulled-down sleeves of her top. 'I'm sorry this happened to you, but at least that impressive rehab unit will get you sorted. Got some interesting footage today of players being treated. It was great, when you dropped in to encourage them.'

'It helped me in the past; you still feel part of the team, that way. How did filming of the training go? I didn't see you there.'

'We were with the forwards up on the furthest pitches, watching the work they were doing on scrums. A powerful pack you have, this season.'

It was one of the many things that appealed about Cassie, how she understood the mechanics and rules of the game. They spent a while talking about varying training techniques according to a player's position, before she explained how cyclists prepared for velodrome competition, and the way divers did as much training out of the pool as in it. Before they knew it, they had finished their wine.

'Another?' he offered, angling his glass towards hers.

'No, I'll hold off, and you've said you need to anyway. Mind if I get myself some water?'

Her request gave him a timely prompt. 'Actually, I have something for you. Out in the hall you'll see my holdall. Inside the top zip there's a white padded envelope for you.'

Cassie padded out of the room silently, in her bare feet. He'd been about to call out, asking if she'd found it, when she returned, blotting her eyes with the heel of her hand.

'I peeked inside,' she croaked. 'A personalised water bottle is one thing, but you remembered something I told you two years ago? That's so, so...'

As a tear trickled down her cheek, Danny doubted himself. Maybe having 'Corporation Finest' printed on her water bottle was too painful a reminder of her father?

'Thank you,' she juddered, 'I haven't explained what happened with my parents. I want to, but it's...'

Danny forced himself up onto one foot, and hopped towards Cassie, horrified to see her tears. He tugged her into his arms and rubbed her back.

'Shh, that can wait,' he said into her hair. It took many eight-second hugs before she recovered and though his ankle throbbed, it was worth it to feel the relief of her mumbling something amusing into his chest about even his sweat smelling good. His fingers found her chin and tipped it upwards. He smeared away the last of her tears and locked onto her watery-grey eyes. Honest and vulnerable in his arms, he'd hold her for as long as she needed.

'You're OK,' he muttered, and brushed her hair away from her temples, carefully tucking damp strands behind her ears. He'd suspected it two years ago, but now he was certain, every part of this woman was beautiful.

Inch by inch she brought her mouth nearer to his, until she pressed a slow soft kiss to his lips. A second kiss, a little firmer, then during her third she wound a hand behind his neck, increasing the pressure and coaxing his own lips to engage. With an unapologetic groan, he kissed her back.

As their tongues danced, hands that had waited two years lost their patience and sought contact with skin. Cassie's throaty moan as his hand slid up her top pulsed through him, and he was about to abandon the promise to himself, of not rushing their reunion, when someone banged on his front door with four loud knocks. He pulled away, breathing deeply.

'Wow,' she puffed, pulling her clothes straight and swiping under her eyes. 'Possibly the worst timing for pizza delivery ever, but I'll get it.'

'Wait, Cassie,' he called, trying to form the words she ought to hear as she ran out into the hallway, but it was too late. He closed his eyes, waiting to ascertain the identity of the voice at his door.

'Heather…and Ryn, er hi,' Cassie was saying.

'Oh, sorry, we were just checking on Danny. Never mind, let's go, Ryn,' said Heather, sounding apologetic.

'Eh?' came Ryn's response. 'I want to see if he's alright, I heard it was a nasty ankle roll.'

'No, babe, we can do that by phone, later – or maybe tomorrow.'

'But it won't take long.' Ryn was either oblivious to or having none of his wife's attempt to postpone coming in to see him.

Cassie regrouped admirably. 'No, of course, come in. He's on the sofa, I think.'

Danny hopped backwards urgently and settled himself into the expected position on the sofa, while Heather said something quietly like 'sorry', and Cassie answered in equally hushed tones. The three of them came through to the living area.

'There he is,' said Ryn. 'Mate, you alright?'

'Better than expected.'

Ryn looked at the two empty glasses then winked at him. 'Reckon so, my friend. How long will you be out for?'

'A week, ten days maybe. I'll miss the away at Gloucester, probably be back to train for the home match against Quins.'

'You're coming to that one, aren't you, Cassie, and interviewing the girls before the game?' said Heather, refusing to come further in than the living room doorway.

'Yes, that's the second of the two home matches Hystar is covering.'

Danny stored the extra motivation to be fit. 'How did your session go this afternoon, Ryn? Cassie tells me she was impressed with the work the forwards are doing.'

'Did you film us doing the scrum drills? Shows off the old hip hinges perfectly.'

'Ryn,' Heather chuckled, 'Not everyone is as interested in your hips as me, babe.'

As expected, Cassie didn't miss a beat. 'More than you'd think, it only took Taylor Swift dating a tight end American Football player, and girls start to realise how handsome these powerful guys are.'

'It's about time,' said Heather.

'Mate, you've never bought sunflowers?' Ryn gasped.

'Er, yes,' Danny mumbled, noticing Cassie and Heather exchange a look of amusement.

'Do you want to stay for a drink? There's wine and some beer, or Coke,' said Cassie.

Ryn's eye lit up, but Heather was already shaking her head. 'Thanks, but I think we'd better go, things to do. I'm starving.'

'What things? Come on Heth, we won't be long and tomorrow's our day off. A beer wouldn't hurt before we go.'

Danny could almost read Cassie's mind when she raised an eyebrow at him. He nodded, making his friends the offer. 'To be honest there's plenty enough pizza arriving shortly, if you want some?'

'Great,' said Ryn, grimacing as he tried to make himself comfortable on the floor. Heather took up a position in front of him, leaning back.

Danny couldn't remember ever feeling happier, even without an injury. For an hour, the four of them laughed and joked their way through pizza, contentment purring through him. It reinforced something he'd felt in the hospital alleyway that morning, about what he needed. And who.

Heather was in deep in conversation with Cassie, explaining how it felt to be a wife or girlfriend of a professional rugby player. 'What people don't see is that players are often ruined for days after a match. Ryn looks invincible, but it's me that knows he can't put his own socks on the following day because bending is too painful for him. After really physical matches, sometimes he can't even lift his arms above his head until Thursday.'

'Aw, Heth, don't tell her that.'

'It's OK,' Cassie assured him, 'but I will say that viewers might like to know the price your body pays. It humanises the game. You guys look tough but you're like anyone – there are times when you need support.'

Ryn studied his fingernails, then glanced at his wife. 'You're right, can't say you're not. Heth gets me through a lot, behind the scenes and not just on match days either. Remember when you slept next to me in hospital?'

"Course I do. There have been amazing moments in your career, especially the internationals, but the lows can be properly low.'

'She didn't leave me the whole time. Couldn't sleep without her.'

Danny had heard the story many times before. He felt Cassie's eyes on him and turned to see their shimmer.

She blinked and cocked a small smile just for him.

How would it feel to have her beside him, like Ryn had Heather? To have someone who knew the difficulty of sleeping on Saturday nights with whole-body soreness and unspent adrenaline surges; someone who would help him shed emotion, share a physical release. And he'd willingly do the same for her, whatever she needed to manage her stress. Unable to help himself, he smiled back, obstacles of geography and incompatible careers forgotten. Images of domesticity and togetherness of the sort he'd never allowed himself to anticipate flashed before his eyes.

Heather set about hastily gathering up the empty pizza boxes. 'We'll stick these in the bins on our way out,' she said. 'Ryn, come on, it's definitely time we were going.'

'That was fun,' said Cassie from the kitchen area, after they'd gone. 'Do you need anything? More painkillers?'

Danny prayed that she wasn't about to add 'before I go' to her question.

She didn't.

'No, thanks, it's sore but I'm OK. If you have time, come and sit for a bit?'

Cassie wandered through and sat herself down with his ankle propped. 'How good is your memory?' she asked him.

'Unless I'm concussed, it's good, I think.'

'Alright, do you remember the psychologist I told you about who reported on the physiology of eight-second hugs, a Dr Holmwood?'

'Not the name. Why?'

'I read another of his reports, it caught my eye because it was called "Try Four-Minute Kisses".'

Danny shuffled himself closer. 'I'm liking this doctor's area of interest, including the word "try". What were the key points?'

'It produces endorphins and lowers cortisol levels, reducing stress. I was thinking it might help with your ankle?'

'I'm feeling happy even talking about it.' Every part of his body was.

'And as it's a two-way thing, and I'm so wired with work, I thought we could—'

Danny had heard enough. Opening his arms, he pulled her over him, curling one hand behind her neck, the other on her shoulder. 'Four minutes,' he muttered against her lips and revelled in the sweet sensation of his mouth upon hers, connecting and exploring. Cassie's gentle moan vibrated through him, urging a faster, deeper rhythm, and as and she raked her fingers through his hair, a new heat pumped.

Four minutes wasn't nearly long enough.

'Phew, yeah, he was bang on with that report.' Cassie breathed, pulling back.

A disconcerting thought occurred to Danny, that he might not be the first person she had tested the theory on. Despite the risk of ruining the moment, he asked, 'Ever told anyone else about Dr Holmwood's findings?'

She cocked her head. 'Yeah, a little, I was seeing a production guy for a few months, but we were rarely in the same country, and not in a proper relationship really. That isn't my style at all. If I'm in, I want to be all in. A handful of snatched dates, hotel room hookups, hardly ever talking, was unfulfilling, then once filming finished, we only saw each other in person once a month or so. It's how it would have been for you and me, only we were smart enough to realise it before we put ourselves through that.'

'I don't know if that was smart, I regretted it for a long time. I thought about you a lot, Cassie. Maybe something would have been better than nothing.' He interlocked his fingers with hers and she clasped her other hand over his.

'I thought about you too, but it wouldn't have worked, trust me. Half the time we wouldn't even have been in the same time zones.'

'It could have been worth messing up our sleep patterns for?'

'And miss out on watching a film together or sharing a bath or just waking up in the morning with a cuddle? Even mundane things like food shopping must be better when you're with the special someone in your life, you know?'

He didn't, but bloody hell he wanted to try it. With her. 'Is this your way of saying you want to watch a film, because this is a Henry Cavill-free zone. And, just so you know, I only have a shower here.' He watched warring thoughts battle their way across her face.

After a few seconds, she planted a gentle kiss on his mouth. 'I didn't fancy a film anyway,' she said, then pointed at his ankle. 'But if you need any help with that in the shower, let me know.'

'Did I mention that it's a walk-in double?'

'I saw it. Is this your way of asking me to stay the night?'

'I have tomorrow off, except for some physio.'

'Unfortunately I have to be in London by 11am so I'd need to get going before 8am. I won't be back here for eleven days, not that I'm already counting or anything.'

Danny kissed the tip of her nose. 'I'll set an alarm in time for a morning cuddle.'

After a few seconds, she stood up and held out her hand. 'We've plenty of time before that.'

17. The Three Hs

Eleven days later, Cassie slid into a blissfully comfortable back seat and closed her eyes. 'How did we get this swanky car this morning, Martyn?'

'The others are in use. This is the Chairman's car and it's free until Monday, so I thought, it's a lovely day for our drive to Cambridgeshire, why not…or *pam lei*, as we'd say back home.'

'Pam lei?'

'That's Welsh for "why not", isn't it?'

'It might be, but— oh, of course, you spell your name with a "y", I've seen it on your Hystar pass.'

'That's right, my father's side are from Anglesey, but I don't get back there much anymore.'

'Me either.' And that was all she wanted to say about it. 'Anyway, from the looks of this limo, our chairman is transported in style.'

'He is, it's very luxurious – though perhaps don't help yourself to his drinks, eh?'

'No risk of that, I had a bit of a day, yesterday.'

'I'll keep the radio down low.'

En-route to match day at Camford's stadium, Cassie tried to stay awake by scrolling through some of the daily, easy-going messages she'd exchanged with Danny since spending the night together. Many of them made her grin, like his suggestion that Dr Holmwood research 'one-hour sex' as the final element of a high-endorphin trilogy.

As foreplay went, undressing a strapping, albeit wobbly rugby player for the shower was up there with the best ever, and the adoration on his face as she'd peeled off her own clothes told her exactly how he felt. Aside from the intense emotional charge, there had been so much of his skin to explore, so many muscles to map. Then, in bed, they'd revelled in each other's bodies, she spurred on by Danny's urgent, erratic mumblings of how beautiful she was, and how he wanted every part of her. No man had ever turned her on in the way Danny's earnest vocalisation did, especially when he'd followed her into an explosive, climatic free-fall, calling out her name.

Since then, Cassie's endorphin high had taken a bashing. As well as Fox and Cassie's solo projects, Fox/Forde had covered four days of diving in Serbia. Teething problems with Hystar's new studio set up back in London then culminated in yesterday's producer getting cross with them about not sitting up straight, and wobbling on stupidly backless, high stools at their new-style presenting desk. Even now, as she stretched out her back against padded leather, she could feel the effects of those bloody stools. But, though they had killed their postures, they were nothing compared to Fox's sudden escalation of on-air anxiety levels, which had bordered on panic. She'd all but carried him on the live segments and once taken over his autocue prompt while attempting to steady his manic, bouncing leg beneath the desk. A first sign that their evening had been about to go downhill.

As Martyn drove them further North, Cassie tried to stay awake by gazing out of the window at the view from the motorway. She had a workday to complete before she could show Danny exactly how much she'd missed him, which would hopefully involve another overnight stay.

As she picked up her phone to continue last minute checks on the visiting team's latest news, it buzzed with an incoming call from Izzy. After last night, the temptation to reject the call was immense, but there was little option.

'Hi Cassie, where are you?' The typical lack of pleasantries made it easier for Cassie to do the same.

'Thirty minutes from Camford's stadium. I'm meeting the senior team's wives and girlfriends.'

'Filming them?'

'No, for my voice-overs, there'll be some clips of them at the game afterwards.'

'You'll need to look for angles, then.'

'I know.'

'So, I've seen the edits, it needs something more. Your hospital and school clips with Danny Reed and Josh Webber were good but lacked depth.'

Cassie balked. 'How much more are you after?'

'The sort you could find yourself, Cassie, and my background's not even journalism. For example, Reed is financially assisting a sick kid's dad, offered to cover all his travel and parking, apparently.'

'What? How did you discover that?'

'A researcher found a willing nurse at the hospital. Come on, you've got to get smarter, however uncomfortable. You imply Webber is the team's "funny man" yet made little mention of documented mental health issues. Go the extra mile. This is how you'll climb the ladder behind me – don't lose momentum now. Investigate each player. An obvious one would be Connor Wilson's media run-ins, why did those happen?'

Go the extra bloody mile into people's private lives, she meant. God, Izzy was brutal.

'I hear you but it's easy to cross the line and become invasive.'

'Well, you know what's at stake. Remember which side of that line we're on. On a more positive note, Fox/Forde is trending at the moment, after last night's episode. Aside from personal guff, which I suggest you ignore, management are happy and viewer feedback on the new studio set is positive, although please watch your hands below the desk, they're in shot now, remember. Got to go, good luck today. Keep pushing, whatever it takes. I'll see you in the studio on Monday.'

Cassie felt herself deflate like a slow-release balloon, though she was angry enough to have punctured it herself.

Fortunately, there was no time to fester, as Martyn announced their imminent arrival at Camford's stadium entrance. 'Do you want dropping off here at the main gates – I can park further inside if you need?'

'Here's fine,' she said, trying to shake off the effects of Izzy's call. 'Is it OK if I confirm return arrangement later? Not sure if I'll need you.'

'Of course.'

Before leaving the car, she willed her shaking fingers to ping off a quick message to Danny.

CF: Good luck vs Quins. Sorry didn't call last night. Can't wait to see you. Yours, Cx

She waited a few seconds, without expectation of a reply. Almost certainly Danny would be at the stadium, fully focused on the game ahead. After swallowing down a couple of tablets, she opened her compact to touch up her makeup. Unsurprisingly, more under-eye concealer was required.

Up in the hospitality suite, Heather beckoned Cassie towards an assembled group of women. 'Hello Cassie,' she said, voice confusingly chilly, as if they hadn't enjoyed pizza and a fun evening at Danny's apartment just eleven days before.

At a large oval table, with picture window views across the pitch, ten or so women were chatting over hot drinks and assorted pastries.

'Girls, this is Cassie Forde, the Hystar journalist you'll know from television and the fellas. This will only take ten minutes but remember just say things you wouldn't mind being repeated, and think about the contents of Camford's media guidelines that Trish sent us all last night.'

Since Heather's 'reminder' could have been issued beforehand, Cassie assumed it had been unnecessarily aimed at her. But with a journalism background, surely Heather understood the need for angles?

Some of the women smiled or nodded, a handful stood up and shook Cassie's hand.

As she poured herself a black coffee, and took an empty chair at the end of the table, pairs of eyes stared at her, some cautious, others welcoming, all expectant. 'Hi everyone, thanks for coming, you're helping me out by talking through what it's like being the home support to professional rugby players. Just to clarify, I won't be naming names, in fact I'll be careful to summarise and generalise, but viewers will benefit from understanding the responsibilities you undertake, the parts you play in keeping the guys going. Is that alright with everyone?'

A hesitant murmur of acceptance circled the table.

'OK, I'm going to record this on my phone, too, as I won't have an opportunity to work on the material until tomorrow, back in the studio. Is that alright?'

Everyone nodded.

'Great. So, would anyone like to get us started? For example, how do you weather media scrutiny of your partners, or even yourselves?'

'No offence, it's nice to meet you and everything, but media stuff gets in the way sometimes,' said one of the women.

'How so, er – sorry, I'm not sure of your name?'

'Kit, I'm Owen Taylor's wife. I mean, their game should do the talking, shouldn't it? Owen loathes some of the cringey stunts that Camford and a few of the sponsors demand, although he does them. Social media can be dangerous – the guys worry enough about their next skinfold test, or their speed and agility, without it being reported outside of the club. Some of the silly stuff is just distracting and worse than that, inaccurate.'

Cassie nodded, but perhaps unlike some of the women, recognised the financial reality, that without sponsors, Camford would cease to exist.

'Really, if they have spare capacity, our guys should be worrying about the next fifteen years and life after rugby, not their media image.' Kit added.

A couple of the other women nodded their agreement.

'I'm Jo, Ben's girlfriend. Kit's right but players don't dwell on the future while they're fit. It's only if Ben's injured, or not selected, that it even comes up in conversation.'

Cassie could imagine that. Even with just a sprained ankle, Danny had doom-mentioned the looming period of unknown after his career finished.

'Yeah,' another woman agreed, 'that's true. To be honest, rugby comes first, all the time, doesn't it?'

The entire table agreed, though Cassie noted that it was in acceptance, as opposed to regret.

'How does that make you all feel?'

'Personally, I know things won't change until Ben retires. Players are focused on themselves; their regime is tightly scheduled. During the season, they're rarely able to participate in family or social gatherings.'

'No,' added another, 'and nothing can be last minute, either. Conversely, we've had long-planned holidays cancelled or postponed, which obviously causes tension. The important thing is to have your own life. Many of us have children and around the table you've got a lawyer, an estate agent, a caterer and an oncologist. I have my own career, plus I know my value to my husband, privately speaking. He makes that clear.'

A couple of the women sniggered. 'Ashley means sex.' More laughing made Cassie curious.

'OK, sex has a key role, then?' she asked, pulling on the thread.

'Doesn't it always? Looks like your secret's out, by the way, Cassie. He's gorgeous. Well done you.' Everyone stopped talking and stared.

Cassie flicked her eyes to Heather, who completely blanked her. Surely Heather hadn't gossiped to them all about Danny?

'I don't think I should…' Cassie struggled to formulate some kind of vague deflection but was saved by the appearance of another guest at the door.

'Hello?' A petite, long blonde-haired woman entered the room. Cassie put her in her early twenties. 'The man downstairs said this is where the players' wives and girlfriends are meeting? I'm Connor's girlfriend, Naomi. I'm way early for the match, and there's nowhere to go before the stand opens.'

Heather was first to her feet. 'Hi, I'm Heather, Ryn's Koch's wife, and that's no problem at all arriving now, come and join us.'

The woman took the spare seat between Jo and Kit.

'I think we met at the end of last season, didn't we?' said Jo. 'You work at a clothes shop in Ipswich?'

'No, I work at The Copa Cabana club in Cambridge. Officially, this is my first time here, although I've watched Connor play a few times before, when a friend got us tickets. I've fancied him for ages, but we've only been together three months. He dropped me off just now, wants to know I'm there for him in the family seats during the match.'

'Apologies, I've got muddled somehow.' Jo busied herself with choosing another pastry.

Cassie smothered Jo's error with an introduction. 'I'm Cassie Forde, a journalist with Hystar, and I'm talking with the group here about rugby life from their perspective.'

'So maybe just be careful with what you're saying,' Heather cautioned.

Cassie shot her a cool smile, before bringing the conversation back on track. 'Alright everyone, what's been the best part of having a professional rugby player as your partner?'

'Apart from the sex?' Some of them laughed.

Izzy's words of 'advice' bounced on Cassie's shoulder.

'Alright, since the conversation's returned to it, elaborate if you like?'

'Well, sometimes it's sex and booze, sometimes it's sex and tears. Either way they need us,' one of the women in her late thirties offered.

'Being needed is important?'

'Yes, and I'm Kelly, by the way, Lewis Banks's wife. I've a fair few years under my belt, which as you know has included four years of his captaincy, and an England stint. At times you feel helpless and it's hard getting calls from the guys when they're away. Don't attribute this to Lewis please, but you girls already know, I've had my husband on the phone almost breaking down with disappointment and loneliness. On the other hand, when I didn't hear anything from him, I knew he was probably happy.'

'That's tough,' said Cassie, grateful for Kelly's openness.

'It can be, with England he's been away for up to three or four months at a time.'

Boy, these women were a hidden factor in players' success, their contribution needed serious acknowledgement in this project.

'Weirdly, it's similar if they're injured,' said Kit. 'When they're at home more than usual, and you find yourself being their psychologist, reminding them that they're going to get better, that they'll be in with a chance for re-selection.'

'That's true, I've been there several times,' said Heather, finally contributing. 'You have to be prepared to nurse and encourage them through the pain of end of season, off-season, hospitals and rehab too.'

Conversation began to flow and to Cassie's delight, women that had yet to speak were now itching to contribute.

'When Miles ruptured his knee, I had to put parental controls on our Netflix account because he kept jumping ahead on the series we were watching,' said Ashley. Laughter joined the table, and the mood became buoyant.

'Mostly romantic dramas in your house, aren't they, Ash?' said Kit, smiling. 'Miles is a romantic bugger, isn't he?'

'Most of them are,' said another woman.

'Connor is sometimes, but when we met, he told me he wasn't looking for anything serious,' said Naomi, adding her voice. The group felt silent.

'He said that to you? That he wasn't looking for anything serious?' Kelly asked her in a motherly tone. 'Take care, please, sweetheart. Sometimes that can mean they're pretty sure they're going to hurt you.'

'As long as it's only the kinky kind, I don't mind.'

Kelly choked on the mouthful of cookie she'd just bitten into. One of the other women slapped her on the back.

'And we're back to the sex,' said Kit, making everyone snigger.

Naomi's interest appeared to be hooked. '*Well* if it's sex you want to know about—'

'Stop!' said Heather. 'Cassie doesn't want to know any more about that, I'm sure.'

Yes, Cassie would, although how she was going to get any of this into the docuseries, she wasn't yet sure.

'All I was going to say was that I notice something when I watched Connor play.' Naomi had everyone's attention now.

'Which is?' Cassie asked.

'The look on his face when he's tackling someone. Right at that moment, especially if he gets hit hard, it's exactly the same as his come face.'

'Dear God,' said Kelly, hiding her face behind her mug.

'And, by the way, sex before a match is not banned. That's a myth, Connor told me.'

'Here, Naomi, do you want half of my Danish?' said Heather, thrusting some towards her.

'No thanks, watching my figure.'

Jo cleared her throat. 'Maybe we should mention the three Hs to Cassie?'

Kelly and several of the other women nodded.

'Have you heard of them, Cassie?'

'No, I don't think so.'

'Most of the women chimed in unison, 'Hurt, hungry, horny.'

Even Cassie chuckled. 'Oh please, do elaborate?'

Kit cleared her throat. 'It's the state our guys are in once they're home after their matches. Again, don't attribute this specifically to me, but it's a true indication of how I help my husband. Look after any injuries, feed him, and yes, sex is important. Winner's sex is usually fantastic.'

This was an angle of the sort that Izzy would relish, but Cassie wished was for a romance novel.

'Actually,' said Jo, 'when they lose is when our bonds matter most. I can turn Ben's night right around through our connection. It's next level intimacy.' Several of the women hummed their agreement.

Heather waggled her phone, no doubt aghast that her cautionary 'reminder' about what should be discussed had been abandoned. 'On that note, we'll let Cassie get on with her day. Trish mentioned you're doing some filming this afternoon?'

'Yes, which will incorporate a wide sweep of where you'll all be sitting, if that's alright?' A couple of the women grinned; another surreptitiously tidied her hair. 'I'll see the match from the pitch-side commentary area but pop along afterwards to say hello. It was good to meet you all, it's been interesting, and fun, so thank you very much.'

Heather stood up, but Kelly raised her hand.

'Actually, if you have a minute, maybe the girls would like to hear about your life as a sports presenter?'

Several of the women leaned in.

'Sure, I have a few minutes. What would you like to know?'

Heather sat back down with a barely disguised huff.

'Apart from about you-know-who,' Kit smirked, 'which we'd all like the inside track on, you lucky woman.'

Back to her personal life again. 'Er, in the circumstances, with Camford Rugby and everything, I'm not sure it's right to talk about him.'

'Shame. So, do you write your scripts on Fox/Forde or does someone do that for you?' Jo asked.

'A bit of both, but there's not as much of my input as I'd like. This docuseries is exciting for that reason, because I'm creating it.'

'OK, well that's good. And – this might sound shallow – but are you on a diet the whole time? You haven't eaten any of these pastries while you've been here.'

'If I'm on-air or filming I tend not to eat anything containing sugar or milk beforehand because it can clog my palate. Also there's the risk of a sugar crash, and tiredness can ruin a broadcast. My boss says she can tell how tired I am by how my face muscles drag down, even from a slight sigh in my voice.'

'God,' mumbled someone, 'that's harsh.'

'Mm, extinguishes my sparkle, apparently.'

Kelly wrapped two cookies in a napkin and passed them to her with a bottle of water. 'Have these later, then,' she whispered.

Cassie tucked them into her bag, feeling oddly emotional. She'd bet that Kelly was a good mum.

'Oh-my-God, oh my GOD, I just realised where I've seen you – you're the girl that presents alongside Fox Cavalier aren't you?' Naomi blurted.

'Among other programmes, yes.'

Fox, especially after last night, was not someone she was willing to discuss.

'He is so lush. And you're very close, apparently, if today's pictures are anything to go by?'

'I don't know what pictures you're referring to.'

Naomi tapped on her phone with super-pointy nails. 'These – take a look.'

Cassie studied the grainy, zoomed-in pictures of her hand calming Fox during yesterday's high-anxiety moment.

YES, THEY ARE! – THE PROOF WE'VE BEEN WAITING FOR!
Hystar's cutest couple, Fox/Forde, inadvertently confirmed their secret relationship last night when Cassie caressed Fox's leg during their Friday Sports Roundup programme. An anonymous source confirmed that the pair are 'virtually married'. Heat Weekly expected an announcement any day.

Cassie handed the phone back, the reason for Heather's brusqueness now dawning on her. Thank goodness Danny's name hadn't mistakenly left her mouth; the girls didn't know about him at all. She took a breath and slowly eyed each in turn.

'You've all been generous with your time and honesty today, so in return, you can expect mine. Fox/Forde is a professional duo, and a friendship but nothing more; there are reasons for what you've seen, but I can't divulge them. And anonymous sources, or inside quotes like these, are rarely true.'

'Oh I know,' said Naomi, 'Connor's had tons of shit written about him that wasn't true. He says that people jump in for their five minutes of fame, accusing him of all sorts.'

'Well, while others of you are understandably wary of journalists, remember that I'm an ordinary woman, too, with feelings. Gossip articles like these are just clickbait. I'm used to them – it's not the first-time rumours like these have swirled – but I don't like them, and just as you said earlier, they're distracting.'

'So you're not with him, then?' Kit asked. 'You're single?'

'I'm not with him, no, but we are good friends.' She'd stop at that, hoping it would be enough.

'Cassie, watch the time,' said Heather, throwing her a line.

'Thanks, I had better get going, but are there any other questions before I do?'

'I've really enjoyed this,' said Kelly, emphatically. 'Maybe we could all meet up again some time, socially?'

A chorus of interest accompanied several of the women offering their contact details.

'That went well, I appreciate what you did in organising it for me,' said Cassie, as she and Heather reached the stairwell.

'No problem. We can trust you, right?'

'Yes.'

Heather levelled her gaze at Cassie for a few seconds. 'You aren't messing him around, are you?'

'Not that it's anyone's business, but no, of course I'm not. Please tell me this isn't about the stupid Fox/Forde article?'

'Partly, and before you say it, I'm aware of how the business works. But, if you say you and Fox are just friends, well – unless I'm proved otherwise – I'll believe you. Just…don't hurt Danny, please. Ryn says he hasn't seen him this happy before, that training has gone smoothly, and the mood in the changing room is similarly upbeat. You'll be aware that Danny doesn't share much, so me and Ryn feel lucky to be confided in. He likes you, Cassie, we can tell. Maybe reassure him about Fox, before gossip gnaws at his trust in you.'

18. Event 1

The ceiling-hung televisions in The Manor's club bar were running that afternoon's win on a loop. Danny half watched, while making a considerable effort not to be caught staring at Cassie. Tantalisingly near, stood with Heather and Ryn at the bar, her apparent high spirits suited the celebratory atmosphere. But beneath the gloss, in split seconds when attention was off her, he recognised signs of tiredness; a slight dip of the shoulders, a longer exhale, restless shifting from one heeled boot to the other. Unable to resist any longer, he made his excuses to the players he'd been sat with and casually wandered over.

'How about me? What about my physical ticks?' the barman was saying to them, squirting cola into a tall glass. 'How would you describe those?'

Cassie tapped her chin in mock thought. 'Well, you're methodical, you always wipe down the taps with two strokes of your cloth, and you usually set drinks down onto the bar on perfectly lined up coasters. You also wink a lot, at everyone, usually when saying the word "thanks".'

'Bloody hell, you're good,' he said, handing her the drink.

'Told you,' said Heather, 'journalists notice things.'

Cassie clinked her glass with Heather's. 'It's true, I do. It kind of goes with the job.'

Ryn sipped his beer, quieter than usual. Maybe the match had taken more out of him than he'd admitted.

The barman brought Danny into the conversation. 'What about our captain here, what do you notice about him?'

Danny squared his shoulders, pretending to prepare for a verbal onslaught as Cassie sized him up.

'When kicking, you mean? Well, you'll see the same order of preparation as part of his process, and the hair thing, obviously.'

He had a hair thing?

The barman sniggered. 'Definitely, just fixes it the five or six times before the ball goes anywhere,' he chuckled, and Cassie nodded.

'Then there is the way his eyes carve out the trajectory of the ball, back and forth, back and forth, like lasers, until it's locked in. Aside from his kicking technique, he's unusual in that he rarely waits to see whether the ball goes through the posts.'

Danny raised his hand. 'I feel I should defend myself here; that's because unless the wind conditions are difficult, I already know whether it's a successful kick or not from the feel of my boot.'

'Well, those are some of my observations. Can I go now?' Cassie said to the barman, sipping her drink.

'Sure,' he said, with an exaggerated wink. 'Although, first, I think you should fill us in about your gorgeous parcel of a fella, Fox Cavalier. He's your guy, isn't he? What are his ticks?'

Cassie and Heather exchanged a weird look but said nothing.

'Hey,' Danny intervened, 'leave it there, eh?'

'No offence meant, sorry. Yes, Miles, what can I get you?' the barman mumbled, turning away to serve Camford's number 8.

Cassie mouthed a 'thanks' at him. She wasn't going to be bothered by some tired gossip, not on his watch.

Trish approached their group, smiling widely. 'Good result again this afternoon, well done.'

'Thanks,' said Ryn, perking up. 'Fairly easy trot-out as it went, out-powered them in most of the scrums.

'Glad to hear it, keep it up. Cassie, how did you get on with the girls today?'

'Good, I think. I have way more material than I need.'

'She was a hit with the girls,' said Heather. 'Got their trust, so the conversations flowed well. It was a good laugh, actually.'

Trish beamed with delight. 'Excellent, I'm quite sorry that I couldn't make it.'

'Next time,' said Heather, 'or you could join us socially. A few of us girls and Cassie are planning to go for drinks one evening.'

'Definitely.'

Heather removed the empty pint glass from Ryn's hand and placed it on the bar. 'Excuse us, I think we should be heading off, it's already 7pm, I'm starving and my baby promised me a takeaway and a movie if we won this afternoon, so I'm calling him on it.'

Ryn pretended to complain that he didn't want to leave, but Danny knew his friend was besotted with his wife. After the match, the man had sprinted over to where the wives and girlfriends sat in Camford's family seats, and flung his arms around her waist, as usual. As other players followed suit with their respective partners, Danny had stood back, occasionally slapping congratulatory pats on teammates' backs.

Cassie had then come over the pitch, after overseeing Fynn and Zac filming some docuseries footage. On her way, she'd congratulated Man of the Match Connor, who Danny agreed had put in an extraordinary shift and played out of his skin. Before Danny had a chance, several of the women had intercepted Cassie and spent minutes together in friendly-looking chatter. Having just heard from Heather how well their earlier get together went, that now made sense. At the time, for an indulgent moment, Danny had imagined Cassie sat with them regularly, cheering him on through the match, waiting to congratulate or console him afterwards. Beneath his feet, the universe had shifted into a new place of possibility, equal parts thrilling and terrifying. The feeling hadn't left him since.

Heather air-kissed him and hugged Cassie. 'We'll leave you to it. When are you back again, Cassie?'

'I'm travelling with the team to their away match at Newcastle's ground, in three weeks' time – an opportunity to "experience the atmosphere" of team bus travel each way with the team. My boss thinks it's a good idea.'

'Good luck with that.' Heather pulled a face. 'I wouldn't travel in that bus if you paid me. It's our furthest away match so me and a few of the girls are being driven up in one of the club's minibuses. If you change your mind, there'll be space.'

'I'll keep that in mind, but the invite was for a full away experience.'

Trish began to laugh. 'You'll be fine, but speaking of invites, there's something extra for your diary that I wanted to mention. Would you like to join us here for the Premiership Christmas Ball at the beginning of December? It's Camford's turn to host this year.'

Ryn helped Heather into her coat. 'Oh that's a fun night, isn't it Heth? Last year, Axminster hosted and teams from all the clubs went. We all got dressed up but ended up ruining our clothes on their training field at 3am having a giant game of tag rugby.'

'It was, ripped my dress trying to kick a ball if I remember, but it was great meeting everyone. Rugby's a brilliant community, no matter what club you're from.'

Cassie offered what Danny knew to be one of her polite smiles. 'It's a long time since I've been to anything Christmassy. But thank you, I'd love to come.' She might not be as convinced as she'd sounded, but the ball would be so much better with her there. Even if they weren't officially 'together'.

'Good, good,' said Trish. 'I'll reserve you a ticket. Excuse me, I need to speak to Coach Alex.' And she darted between a couple of groups, headed for her mark.

'So after Christmas, you're filming with us until the end of January?' Heather asked, rummaging in her pockets.

'That's the current plan, though we'll review whether there's already enough footage before then.'

'But you won't want to miss our first match of the year, we're away in Wales, to Cardiff, on the second of January. It would give you a chance to visit home, wouldn't it?'

Except for a minute flinch, Cassie maintained a passive expression.

Unlike Ryn, who gawped. 'Why, is that where you're from? I wondered about the weird accent,' he said.

'Ryn!' Heather rolled her eyes.

'What? I bet you didn't know either, did you?'

Heather threw up her hands. 'Fine, I Googled her bio, but her accent isn't "weird", babes.'

Cassie sipped her drink but still hadn't responded.

Danny jumped in. 'No, her accent's soft, and swings with a rhythm when she's speaking – notice how she sometimes rolls her Rs?' he said, aiming to educate his friends, but accidentally casting his mind back to a photo booth.

Ryn grinned at him. 'No, but you clearly have.'

Heather wrestled something twig-like out of her coat pocket, snapped a piece off and put it in her mouth. 'Want some?' she said, chomping down hard as she offered the rest of it around. Danny had tried something similar before at their house. All three of them shook their heads, though Ryn wrestled off a bite-sized chunk and put it in his pocket.

'So Cassie, are you're going to show us round Cardiff, then?' He continued, 'Assuming there's time around the match? Me and Heth haven't been to Wales yet. Bit mad to think it's full of people "rolling their Rs" all the time. Danny won't want to come home.'

'Wait, oh fantastic, it's a Friday night match,' Heather mumbled, after checking her phone. 'Which means we could all stay Friday and Saturday nights, make a weekend of it.'

Everyone paused for Cassie's response.

'I'm sorry,' she said faintly, 'but what is that you're eating?'

'This? Biltong, air cured meat. Mum sent it over, she's good at little surprises, staves off the homesickness. This one's ostrich, I think. We usually prefer game, don't we, babe?'

'Yeah, or beef. What's the speciality in Wales, Cassie?'

Cassie deposited her half-finished drink onto the bar, looking like she wanted to be just about anywhere else. Having lost her father and made no mention of her estranged mother since coming back into his life, he could perhaps understand her discomfort with the conversation. For her sake, Danny had been about to steer a hefty change of subject, but she started to walk away.

'I need to go...to make a call. I'll see you...sometime.'

Two sets of South African eyebrows shot up as Cassie exited through the garden doors, without looking back.

'Maybe she's gone to ring Fox Cavalier,' Ryn muttered.

Heather tutted but threaded her arm around her husband's elbow. 'You can ignore my husband; he's got a weakness for trashy news articles. Cassie's assured me that today's Fox/Forde "revelation" isn't any truer than others before it. But on the off chance you missed the cue, Danny, you might want to think about going after her. Something's seriously spooked her. I'm sorry if it was us.'

Danny caught up with Cassie on the gravel path outside the bar.

She had her phone in her hands and, for one insecure moment, he feared Ryn might be right.

'Cassie, stop.'

'I'm tired and need to get home. Last night was rough, and I'll be editing tomorrow, in the studio anyway, so I'm calling for the car.'

'No, you're not, we need to talk about this. Tell me if I'm wrong, but this is about going to Wales, isn't it?'

Cassie's silence urged him on. 'Right, and you notice I don't ever raise the subject of Wales or your parents, but at some point, you need to trust me, to share why you and your mother don't speak.'

'Please just leave it. She's not worth it.'

'But there must be something you can do to repair whatever you've argued about?'

'Argued about? ARGUED ABOUT? You have no idea—' Cassie began fiddling with her fringe and trying to ascertain which direction she needed to walk.

Danny surveyed the area, hoping nobody else was within earshot. 'Keep your voice down. How could I have any idea, Cassie? Come for a walk with me before you leave, then.'

'I have to get going…'

'Wait, just…wait.' Danny's mind churned through the possibilities – did she think he might not understand because of his background? Maybe that he wouldn't like what heard? Surely it wasn't that she didn't trust him.

'Right, well, if there's nothing else, I'll be going.' Cassie set off at speed in the wrong direction for the main gates.

Once again, he easily caught up with her. This time, he set himself in front of her and he pulled her into a hug, hoping it would bring her some comfort. When she shrugged him off, he couldn't hide his frustration. 'Fine. Where exactly are you going – home, or somewhere else?'

She tipped her chin up, her eyes almost bulging. 'What's that supposed to mean?'

'You know.'

'Sounds like you're implying that I'm headed to Fox's place, which I'm not. As soon as I get hold of my driver, he'll take me straight home where I'm going to bed. Alone.'

Danny rubbed his eyes. 'Don't play games with me, I'm as tired as you, and this isn't how I saw the evening going.'

'ME EITHER,' Cassie screeched. 'Never know what you're gonna get from the fucking daughter of an alcoholic fuck-up, do you? Run, go on, just as I did. And don't look back.'

His head was full of questions, appalled at the revelation, concerned by the way she'd tried to push him away. He'd never even heard her swear before. But not for one second did he consider running. Instead, he carefully rested a hand on her shoulder and steered her down one of the topiary paths. To his relief, she went willingly.

After a few seconds of silence, Cassie leaned into him as they walked.

When they came to a stone bench, he urged her towards it and they sat down. Immediately, the cold surface bit into his legs, so he pulled her onto his lap. 'Do you want to talk about your mother?'

'Not really.'

'Then we won't, not until you're ready. But I'm sorry for what's happened.' He hugged her tightly and she buried her face in his neck.

'I know it's cold, but can we just sit here for a while?' she murmured.

Danny nodded and kissed her hair.

After a few, shivering minutes, Cassie whispered, 'I'm sorry it's spoilt the evening because I've been *really* looking forward to seeing you and I won't be back here for a while.'

'Me too.'

'I even have a countdown app, see?' she said, waggling her phone under his nose.

He squinted at the bright screen.

Event 1 DRxCF

'Only one event? Dr Holmwood would have something to say about that.'

Cassie ran her hand up Danny's arm. 'You've no idea how much I want to be with you right now, and my body is *seriously* needing yours, but the project needs my attention, too. I wasn't exaggerating about that. What I edit tomorrow in the studio needs to improve Izzy's opinion of what I've produced so far. I need to have slept properly.'

'There are problems on the docuseries?'

'Unfortunately, but they're rescuable.'

Danny knew what the project meant to her, and how criticism of it would impact her stress levels.

She'd seemed about to elaborate when her phone rang. 'Won't be a sec,' she mouthed, 'it's my driver...Hey, Martyn, *sori am hyn*, I was going to ring you—'

Danny tapped her hand and murmured, 'How about you ask your driver to be here in thirty minutes? There's something I want to show you first.'

Cassie nodded and made the arrangement.

As soon as she'd hung up, he set her on her feet, saying 'Come on, this way, you're freezing,' and he pulled her by the hand, deeper into the gardens.

'Where are we going?'

'It's down this track, on the right. Norm calls it the Bothy, a little shelter for when the weather turns. It has an oil-fired lamp and heater, some basic furniture, but it's about to be repurposed.'

'Into what?'

'A centre for stress relief, also known as the location for Event 1.'

'How far is it?'

'Just down here,' he said, urging her into an increased pace. 'Sprint training's more useful than I thought; speed and agility on the pitch, whisking the woman I'm falling for to secret dens, the list goes on.'

Cassie skidded to a halt, yanking his arm backwards. She sought his eyes. 'You can't just drop words like that into conversation without warning.'

He tried to steady his breath. 'Couldn't keep them in, sorry. You're on my mind a lot. I mean *a lot*.' He combed his fingers through her hair. 'You are something else, you know that? I don't want you to think you can't trust me, share things with me.'

'I do trust you, and I think about you all the time too.' She circled her arms around his neck. 'Don't know if you've noticed, but I'm really into you, tough guy.'

'Same,' he mumbled, 'though you could probably rip this tough guy to shreds.'

Inside the Bothy, Danny lit the heater and light while Cassie sat on the sofa, outlining her interview with the girls.

'Yep, Hurt, Hungry and Horny, apparently.'

'That isn't a thing.'

'Well, it is from their point of view. If it's not, I'm a bit disappointed, to be honest. I suppose, given today's result, this could technically have been Winner's Sex, but I'm open to discussion.'

'Whatever it is, Event 1 doesn't have much time for conversation, even if it includes some of your sexy Welsh words. Unfortunately, we're on the clock.' Danny knelt on the floor in front of her, tugged her towards him and widened her legs, feeling like a desperate teenager about to lose control of himself. But more than his own release, he wanted to make her forget about her work stress and the history with her mother, to watch her melt, hear her moan. His hands travelled up her calves and traced the inside of her thighs until they reached the top of her trousers. Spurred on by her gasp, he released the zip.

19. Punch and Losey

The four-hour trip in the team bus to the Newcastle Falcons rugby ground had passed without issue, the mood quietly confident as the team leaned into the probability of a successful result. Like the rest of the team, Danny hadn't forgotten their win there last year, as being one of only two the entire season. This season was shaping up nicely, with only the draw at the opening friendly spoiling a run of wins. He and the coaches knew that now wasn't time for complacency, however; you take your eyes off the game plan, the opposition will know it.

Many of the players enjoyed the novelty of having Cassie and her crew on board, a welcome distraction for those who needed it. To coincide with the outside broadcast TV coverage, Hystar had booked her to undertake the pre- and post-match interviews and much of the banter aboard was from guys joking with her about what they might say to her, if picked. One of them even managed to forget about his customary motion sickness. If only gorgeous presenters and chatty cameramen could accompany him everywhere.

For Danny, having Cassie near him easily counteracted the effects of the grey, late October Saturday. When she'd arrived at The Manor, shortly before the team bus was due to depart, he'd been stood talking with Coach Alex and Jim. Radiating enthusiasm, she'd acknowledged the coaches, then him, with a brief hug. His pulse had leapt in response to her subtle squeeze of his shoulders. Nobody knew that she'd only travelled the three miles from his apartment after having driven up late last night.

'Hi, how are you, Danny?' she'd beamed innocently at him, no doubt aware that messages she'd sent him since he left for a light session at The Manor's gym had stirred him up. One had told him that she'd remade the bed (again), another included a link to some light reading for the journey. It was report that 'proved' sex up to two hours before athletic demands on professionals had no adverse impact. The findings had better be right; his surge of need upon waking, and feeling Cassie snuggled into his body that morning, would have overpowered anything.

Unfortunately, after eighty cold, wet minutes on the pitch, it was Camford that had been overpowered. The team's odds had been wrong. Despite Danny's rallying yells, Camford's men went into shock, reacting to play instead of directing it. Frustrations began to niggle with the opposition and within his team, and their general lack of on-field discipline was punished with a sending off. Losing a key player had put too great a pressure on them against a home team with a revenge win in their sights. To make conditions worse, Connor earned them a second sending off after furiously disrespecting the authority of the referee. As twelve thousand Geordies jeered, Danny was grateful that it would be Cassie handling the post-match interviews. As losing captain, it would be him she'd be questioning.

For her, Danny had mustered a few words, hoping she'd allow him to simply trot out the expected 'we'll identify what to work on' lines. To her credit, she'd pushed him on the number of cards his team had incurred. After a few seconds' thought, he acknowledged that those had not been good enough. Had the interviewer been anyone else, he'd have probably given an answer to an entirely different question, just as he'd been trained to do.

Danny slapped a consolation clap on every player's shoulder as they trudged towards the carpark for the team bus, aware that everyone was sore and brooding. The only thing worse than losing a rugby match was talking about it too soon, so he'd wasted no time in rounding everyone up straight after their post-match showers. It was best to get them into their seats, plugged into whatever music they needed to hear through their headphones, and begin the journey home.

As he waited with Ryn to board the bus, the sound of increasingly angry voices from further back in the queue caught Danny's attention. Suddenly identifying them as Connor's and Cassie's, he jogged over.

'With all due respect, Cassie,' Connor was barking at her, 'you don't know the first thing about being a professional rugby player. Go back to Wales or wherever you're from.'

'You can't just say "with all due respect" and then disrespect someone. For God's sake, I literally only asked whether you felt the red card was fair. I don't deserve this abuse, Connor.'

Someone behind them bleated like a sheep.

'Oh funny, yeah, original. Sheep from Wales and oh, wait for it, who's going to mention Welsh daffodils?'

'Daffy Forde!' the same voice joked, but the look on Cassie's face told Danny, and surely everyone else, that she was not amused. 'Caaaaassie Forde!' came the same voice, bleating to a guffawing audience.

Danny had heard enough. The line between banter and abuse was in danger of being crossed, if it hadn't already. 'Shut up, whoever that was,' he hollered.

'Sorry.' One of the young physios showed themselves and walked up behind Cassie.

Before Danny could stop himself, he'd cautioned him, 'And don't approach her from behind without warning, she doesn't like it.'

Pairs of eyes widened in surprise, including Cassie's.

All he could do was change the point of everyone's focus. 'Connor, what's going on?'

'I'm sick of it, Danny, second-rate media trying to second-guess what's going on.'

Talk about an idiot poking a beautiful, angry bear.

'EXCUSE ME?' Cassie closed the space between them.

Danny hadn't seen her this defensive before and was momentarily transfixed by this extra-gutsy version of her.

Connor, it seemed, was less enamoured. 'You heard, don't come at me with your stupid questions and half-baked analysis.' He slammed his bag onto the tarmac.

'Alright, cool down, both of you,' Danny instructed.

Everyone was watching the commotion, including Coach Alex and Jim through the bus windows. Even the driver had momentarily suspended people from boarding, presumably to get a better view himself.

'Right. What's gone on, Cassie? Did you ask Connor about this on live television?'

Cassie shook her head.

That was something, at least.

'Nope, you'd think I had from his reaction, but we were just stood here, waiting to get on the team bus when I asked him. Lucky it wasn't filmed, because he wouldn't have come off well to audiences.'

'Cassie, that's not helping,' he reasoned, doubting that Connor was going to let it drop at this rate. Danny held up his hand, trying to calm his teammate down, but it was pushed away.

'Really? Well YOU try smiling politely when answering questions from writers whose friends are pulling me apart in their columns or blogs. Those people never refer to the game, only a list of kicks I've missed or that my throws were flat. As usual, they'll bang on about my private life which will lead to me being hammered for everything, including being scapegoat for the team's performance, like today. You wait, it'll be there.'

'Yep, OK, Connor, that's enough, on the bus please,' Danny interjected, but Cassie was not done either.

'I've never EVER written or presented any reference to your personal life.'

'But you should know how it feels — from the looks of it, the friggin' paps are on your back as much as mine — those so-called media friends of yours are—'

'NO, IT'S MY turn to speak. You don't help yourself, do you?' Cassie held up her hand to prevent Danny's further attempt at interrupting. 'If you don't want your name in the gossip headlines, don't behave in ridiculous, headline-making ways. It's as simple as that.'

'Oh so easy, Miss Perfect. You do realise you're only here so that Camford gets you onside? Bit of biased reporting here and there, going easy at interviews, journalist in the pocket, congratulations us, job done.'

'Enough.' Danny grabbed Connor by his collar and pulled him aside. 'The rest of you get on the fucking bus. Now.'

Cassie opened her mouth to add something, but with coaches still staring from the window, Danny had reached his limit.

'Including you.'

She probably surprised everyone by picking up Connor's holdall and shoving it into him. 'Don't forget your bag.'

'OK, let's get going,' Danny said to the driver, bringing up the rear. Even in the late-afternoon darkness, he could see why there were empty seats on both sides through the mid-section of the bus. Cassie had sat herself there, next to a window. At the back, players had paired up and were already on their phones, or had settled back with their eyes closed. Even Fynn and Zac, he noted, had sat with them. Towards the front, Camford's support and coaching staff were chatting.

Coach Alex caught Danny as he walked along the aisle. 'What was all that, outside?'

'A stupid spat, I'll handle it,' he replied, which appeared to appease him.

Clinging to the headrests as the bus swung around a corner, Danny made his way past Cassie to check on the team. 'All good?' he asked, raising an eyebrow at the boys. One or two nodded. Most didn't bother. He staggered back towards the mid-section and paused beside where Cassie had sat. 'Are you alright?'

She stared out of the window.

'Cassie?'

She turned briefly, shrugged at him, then returned her attention to the lights of Newcastle. It was long enough for Danny to catch sight of moisture on her cheeks.

To his knowledge, he'd never made a girl so unhappy she'd cried, but indirectly, he'd just let it happen to Cassie. For a moment, old habits clenched his fists, but instead he took a steadying breath and mumbled, 'Stay behind me.' He slid into the seat directly in front of her and in the safety of darkness, wedged an arm behind, through the gap between his seat and the window. Finding one of her ankles, he stroked the heated skin, needing to soothe her; she kicked his fingers away but seconds later interlocked her own fingers with his for a brief squeeze. He clutched hers harder and then released, pulling his arm back through to retrieve his buzzing phone from his pocket. She had already messaged him.

CF: Be honest, does it look like Camford is buying my bias?

Danny sighed as he typed his reply; his role at the club demanded leadership and diplomacy, but Cassie also needed him.

DR: Depends who's looking. R u ok? Dx
CF: No. Connor was out of order
DR: He was Dxx
CF: I've never been that type of journalist. EVER

In his experience of Cassie so far, Danny had found that if she used capitals in her messages, it signified 'handle with care'. She wasn't a woman who'd tolerate meaningless platitudes, either.

DR: I know, but some are. Even your boss? It's not players' job to sell papers, or docuseries Dxxx

Three dots of her imminent reply blinked. He could sense a debate about whether to take issue over his point was raging in the seat behind him.

CF: Let's discuss later. Sorry you lost the game, crowd hostile. Liking the increasing kisses, by the way, keep them coming Cxxxx
DR: Sometimes hostile is good, as are mass punch-ups. Connor obvs wrong to hit him, but easily worst ref on the circuit. Appalling decisions. Wish I could have said what I really thought about that in your interview Dxxxxx

CF: Could tell that but didn't push. Was **NOT** bias though, just fairness. Are you sore? Cx
DR: Back is tight again, and have suspected finger fracture, medic strapped it to next one. Dx
CF: Sorry :(And…how hungry are you? Cx

Danny chuckled, following her line of thought, then adjusted his joggers.

DR: Very. And same answer to your next question Dx
CF: Good news is – something new tonight. Loser's sex. It'll turn your day right around, you'll see Cx
DR: Was going to nap, can't now. Dx
CF: Thinking of all the pitiful begging?
DR: Yours? I am now. Remember the Bothy? Hold that thought, baby…
CF: No, yours. You looked seriously hot on the pitch Mr Reed. H.O.T.
DR: Stop or I'll come and sit next to you
CF: You wouldn't dare. Sit next to me and you'll come, I promise you.

Danny unzipped his jacket, feeling the heat. Behind him, the beautiful sound of Cassie's soft chuckle made him shake his head. She had his measure, alright.

DR: Seriously, stop
CF: Only joking, you'd give yourself away. I love it when you cry out
DR: Last warning

CF: What, then I get a yellow card?
DR: Straight to a red for you. This is seriously reckless behaviour
CF: Too late. Don't think I can turn off now, might have to discreetly enjoy the journey by myself
DR: JUST TRY. Only person who gets to pleasure your beautiful body is in front of you

Cassie's hand appeared beside his hip, and she squeezed him. He caught her fingers between his and raised it high enough to meet his mouth. He kissed the tips, and though tempted to tease her with a gentle suckle, he was nearing his limits, and already thinking of plausible excuses for why he might need to go and discuss something with Hystar's on-board journalist.

CF: Sleep, will leave you in peace Cx
DR: Think I can sleep with this going on? Won't be able to get off the coach at this rate
CF: Just try. Can't wait for later, baby Cx
DR: You try to sleep too. Going deep into extra time tonight Dx
CF: Almost looking forward to tomorrow morning more. Waking up with you on Sunday morning will be heaven. Want to make the most of it, won't be back until Christmas Ball
DR: Know what you mean. You look peaceful when you're sleeping Dx
CF: Can't say the same, your legs twitch when you sleep, think you dream-kick. Guess I'm lucky you weren't practicing your passing, or

I'd be on the floor. Virtual hug. Happy snoozing Cx
DR: Feels good, hug coming back your way See you in a few hours Dx

Danny lasted ten minutes before checking whether she was asleep. After casting a look in every direction of the bus, ostensibly to check on the welfare of others first, his eyes lingered as discreetly as possible on Cassie, who had slumped against the window, eyes clamped shut, her lovely lips slightly parted. He had re-settled himself less than two minutes when his phone vibrated. It was a message from Ryn, who despite putting in a hard-fought performance during the match, had somehow not succumbed to sleep.

RK: Mate, you seen this?

Danny took a weary breath before clicking on the attached picture, then wished he'd taken a few more.

A headline in *The Daily News* titled 'Fox/Forde Affair' offered several angles of Cassie stood at a window, embracing Fox Cavalier tightly, in what could easily be interpreted as a romantic embrace. Very little information supported the pictures, other than that they were taken 'recently' at Fox's home. Danny dropped the phone in his lap, unable to take comfort that the timeframe of the pictures was pre-him; before the visited to cover the last match, she'd surprised him by having had some of the blonde removed from her hair, knowing he preferred her original colour. Exactly as it was in the photograph.

DR: Thanks, leave it with me
RK: Watch your back

He'd been about to reply that he trusted Cassie 100% but settled for a thumbs up. What percentage did he trust her? It can't have been 100% because he was now scrolling through their flirty messaging since he'd been on the bus looking for reassurance that she was genuine. A chill shivered through him – if those reached the media, he'd have something to say about it. A lot of people would. 99% trust, he decided, closing his eyes and attempting rest. But the miles gobbled up the certainty percentage points, the nearer to Camford he came.

20. Rosy

After some pre-arranged choreography, designed to put everyone disembarking the bus off their scent, Cassie stepped out of the lift at Danny's apartment knowing that she was only ten minutes behind her man. Rested and ready, having woken only when the bus came to a halt in The Manor's carpark, she smiled as he buzzed her in at around 10.45pm. The long day, and especially her spat with Connor, now behind her, she couldn't have been keener to get what remained of the night off to a flying start.

As Danny opened his front door, she flung her arms around him, thrilled to be caught by the waist and have her overnight case pulled inside.

'Can I interest you in my special offer-of-the-week, from the three-Hs menu?' she said, greeting him in the hallway with what she hoped was sexy huskiness. Being swept straight into his bedroom would suit what she had planned perfectly.

'Maybe a coffee?' he replied, unclasping her hands from his neck and turning towards the kitchen area. 'Want one?'

'Er, yes, if you are,' she said, trailing after him. 'You didn't manage to sleep, then?'

'Not much.'

'Guilty as charged, it was me, officer.'

'It was.' Danny fussed with the coffee machine then handed her a steaming mug; a quick smell identified the contents as her favourite Italiano flavour. He placed his own drink on the granite breakfast bar and sagged against one end. The way he was running his fingers through his hair was another tell-tale sign of tiredness.

'How about a nice hot shower then a snuggle, maybe raincheck anything energetic until tomorrow?'

Danny frowned at his drink, looked up at her, but said nothing. Maybe it wasn't tiredness, his demeanour had turned distinctly frosty.

She'd overstepped somehow – maybe she'd wound him up too tightly on the bus? 'Alright, I'm sorry, I shouldn't have done it,' she conceded. 'It wasn't fair.'

'What wasn't?'

'Text-flirting on the bus.'

'Oh, no, it wasn't that.'

'But there is something? What else have I done?'

'You tell me.'

Cassie put down her mug and went over to him. 'It's too late to be skirting around an issue, just tell me.'

Danny stared at his coffee.

'Do you want me to go, is that it? Because I can.'

'No…no, I don't.' Danny pulled his phone from his pocket and showed her the photographs and article he'd received from Ryn.

'What the hell? What time is it? I'm going to bloody kill whichever pseudo-journalist at *The Daily News* published this.'

As if that trashy picture in *Heat Weekly* wasn't shabby enough. Now this.

Cassie scrolled through the brief article, incredulous at the invasion of privacy, especially for Fox. In his vulnerable state, this was the last thing he needed. 'Those pictures were taken without permission and were clearly on private property. That's Fox's living room…' She paced up and down the kitchen area, shaking her head, imagining the strongly worded email she'd send in the morning. 'I could obtain rights over that picture, or even sue them. Oh-my-God and it's in the "Showbiz" section? Fox and I aren't in "showbiz" we're in sports!' She turned to Danny, looking for sympathy, but he was back to staring at his mug. 'What do you think?' she asked him.

'What do you want me to think?'

Her gut twisted, uneasy at his tone. 'There's nothing in those pictures, baby, I mention there'd been a difficult evening. Granted, these photos look like something else, but that was a hug of friendship, nothing more.'

Danny folded his arms. 'I hate myself for asking this, but I'm going to need you to elaborate.'

'To be honest, I can't believe you were on *The Daily News* website in the first place, you can't trust that rubbish.'

'Ryn tipped me off.'

Cassie stored the information away. 'I see. Well, it's not my secret to tell, but you know that you can trust me, right? That's enough?'

'I want it to be, but the thought of you with someone else, and him specifically, I don't know…'

'But you do know. Please look at me.'

Danny huffed but lifted his gaze.

'All I can say is that despite Fox still being at work, privately he's struggling. He's had a bad breakup.'

'So he needs to cry on your shoulder?'

'It's more than that—'

'How much more?'

'I can't say.'

'Cassie, put yourself in my shoes please. I'm not after his deepest darkest secrets, just the basic facts.'

She tried to imagine it and acknowledged a pang of jealousy at the prospect, were their roles reversed. 'Fine, it turns out – and I can hardly believe I'm saying it – that he'd been having an affair with Izzy for the past few months.' She took a slurp of her coffee. Saying it out loud made her head spin.

'And you didn't know about it?'

'No, and now she's being extra tough. In her eyes he can't do anything right at the moment. He's convinced his career is at stake. One word from Izzy and he can kiss goodbye to presenting for Hystar or any other broadcaster.'

'And she's taking it out on you as well?' It was characteristic of Danny to put her needs before others'.

'I can't be sure; she wants the docuseries to be a success, for Hystar's ratings, so maybe not. Fox's mental state has since picked up a bit, but he'd spiralled the day this photo was taken, and I knew he'd had mental health issues in the past, after his cricketing injury. I was worried sick.'

'Does he have support now?'

'Yes, his older sister's arrived and is staying with him for a while. It's a relief that he has someone to talk to, otherwise the toll of keeping things buried can catch up with you.' She stopped speaking, fearing she'd shared too much about Fox, and potentially re-opened a conversation with Danny about her own past.

But he nodded, put their coffee mugs into the sink and brought her into his arms. 'Ignore my green-eyed stupidity, I'm sorry that all happened, for him and you. We can talk about it more tomorrow, if you want, but let's go to bed.'

Relieved to have worked through the issue, she took his hand in hers, turned out the light and led him to the bedroom.

A few hours later, she stirred, waking on Danny's chest. As a fidgety sleeper, his light-breathing stillness gave him away. 'Baby, have you slept?'

'Yeah, just woke, and was thinking about Laura, wishing she could have met you.' He placed a hand on her head and twirled her hair in his fingers.

'Me too.'

'You don't have to, but can you tell me a story from your childhood? Something from before you were fourteen?'

Cassie's heart broke a little, knowing the specific age came from him being without any family memories of his own, before he was fostered. She cast her mind through childhood events, carefully ignoring the troubles once her dad had become sick. 'I guess it was unusual for a kid from school to live above a pub, and my parents didn't really do mornings – one of the teachers knocked for me on her way into school each day and walked me back afterwards. At weekends and during school holidays I was on my own much of the time, so by around the age of eight I'd already fallen in love with reading. You are never alone if you're engrossed in a good story, and we had a good community library.'

'I remember us saying before, about the escape of reading adventure books.'

'Definitely – though not all the books were fiction. I'd be thumbing through extra information about dinosaur excavation, or castles or whatever topic we were studying at school. I guess I always wanted to know "why".'

'So, the beginning of journalism?' he suggested.

'Possibly, although the dream of writing a novel came before that. In fact, I can think of a good memory to tell you about. One of the rooms above Stumble Inn was used as an office, and what with my parents working or busy maintaining the pub, at least at that time anyway, I'd sit in there at the desk my mother used for admin. I'd raid supplies of paper from the printer and write little stories, sometimes while watching Dad work on the gardens.'

'Was your mum struggling with alcohol at that time or only after your dad was diagnosed?'

Nope, she wasn't going there. 'I thought you wanted a happy memory?'

'Yes, I do, carry on.' He caressed her back, tracing a random pattern.

'I haven't thought about that desk in a long time, but two things come to mind: that my dad spent hours tending the pub garden's rose beds, and that my mother kept an old cardigan on the back of her office chair. I only remember that because I'd check the pockets for sweets and I'd help myself to two or three, hoping she wouldn't notice. Cherry Colas were my absolute favourite.'

'I'm not surprised about that. Tell me a bit more,' he slurred, but before she could think of anything else, the finger tracing halted, and a low snore rumbled through his chest. As she reached up and smoothed his hair, he murmured 'thank you'.

She lay awake, debating how to even begin to tell Danny about the horrendous years before she'd left home. The timing and terms for that conversation had to be right, for her, and for him.

It was light when she woke again, finding Danny's body tightly curved around her back.

'Good, you're awake,' he said, kissing her shoulder. 'I'm sorry I feel asleep. Tell me more about the gardens.'

'The gardens?'

'Yes, you said something about watching your dad in them, at the pub?'

She turned over to face him and hooked a leg over his, 'Oh, yes, he developed the pub garden from a rough area of turf. He especially enjoyed growing roses. I see now that he probably needed the quiet outlet, because running a pub was full on, but then it was always my mum's ambition, not his, to be a landlord.'

Danny kissed her neck. 'Don't worry, I'm not going to push you on your mum. But I'll tell you one thing, he must have been patient, because roses take a lot of work.' He rolled onto his back, bringing her over into a full-contact body hug.

'Norm's taught you something about roses, then?' Cassie said, giving Danny's nipple special attention in kind.

Danny grunted softly, 'Yes, he did, and…'

Cassie paused. 'And what?'

'And I offered to help him with them, in exchange for a bunch.'

'Oh? And who were they for?' She nipped at his shoulders in mock jealously.

'To congratulate the girl I'd never forgotten after a whirlwind weekend. She'd told me her middle name meant "white rose".'

Cassie untangled her legs from his and pushed herself upright. 'What? When?' But she reached for her phone, already forming the answer to the question herself.

'After your first presenter job aired on TV, I struck the deal with Norm.'

She flicked through the photos on her phone and pulled up a picture of herself surrounded by bunches and vases of flowers, sat in her dressing room at Hystar. 'I don't remember a note.'

'There wasn't a note, I stupidly thought you might know they were from me, and anyway, I just wanted you to have them.'

Cassie pointed at a bouquet on the edge of the photograph. 'Oh my God, Danny, they were those white ones, weren't they? Why didn't you at least tell me, when I first came back to film the docuseries?'

'Partly because those weren't the ones you received. In the end there wasn't a way to get the Winthrop roses from The Manor to you, unless I couriered them or drove them to London myself. I ordered some from a London florist instead, kept mine in a pint glass.'

She launched herself back onto him, kissing his neck. 'Thank you. I'm sorry I didn't respond to them, it was such a hectic time but if I'd given it more thought, I'd have realised.'

He turned her phone towards him. 'It's alright. Look how excited you are in that picture.'

Cassie managed a half-smile. 'I had no idea what was coming, though. By the way, the roses were an exception, but I do notice the things you do for me, for the players and the community, especially for the kids at the hospital. Why didn't you mention that you financially support Woody's dad?'

Danny stilled. 'How did you find out about that?'

'Izzy has her ways. Hauled me up for not having done my job. You pay for all Richard's parking and travel, that must add up?'

'It does. I saw them this week and Woody wasn't doing so well, but you know, he was still smiling, still ploughing through his studies. Richard is under enough strain, being away from home all week, trying to manage his business from the hospital or the charity's parent accommodation. It helps not to have extortionate hospital parking fees to stump up for, on top of everything else.'

'You're a good man.'

'No, adoptive parents like Richard are good men. I just see those kids struggling yet being on their best behaviour; scared stiff, yet being brave and still minding their manners – when I'm there at least. It often reminds me of my time in the children's home, when we'd be ready to meet prospective parents. You're kind of hopeful, yet know the situation isn't. You'd probably say it damaged me, I suppose.'

'It's bound to have affected you – it's sad for so many kids. I'm glad that Laura gave you a home, even if only for a few years.'

'It took someone special to see through my rough edges, teach me what caring looked like – and felt like. Of course, it all went to shit for a year or two after she was diagnosed, until I found rugby.'

Really, it was a miracle that Danny had become the man he was. Somewhere out there, his real mother and father should be very proud of him. 'The way that you show you care is one of the reasons you're the most important person in my life, you know that?'

Danny hugged her as if she were about to blow away, but stayed quiet.

'Baby? Are you OK' she whispered into his neck.

He relaxed his hold on her and pressed his lips into her hair. 'Don't laugh but having you back in my life scares me a bit. Outside of rugby, I've trained myself not to want things. Most of all, I've taught myself to live without…this.'

'Danny—'

He propped himself up onto an elbow and caught her face gently in his other hand. 'We're beginning to share a life with each other, trusting each other to open up, being honest. You're on my mind all the time and I miss you, whether we've been apart for an hour or two weeks. Last night, with the Fox thing, the possibility of you walking out was horrendous. We can't know where exactly this is going, but I don't want it to stop. I think…I must be in love with you – I feel it, here.' He patted his chest. 'I've never said that to anyone before but that's what this feeling is, isn't it? I love you.'

Cassie's slow blink burst the dam of tears she'd been holding back. 'I love you too, baby.'

The following few hours were everything a couple newly in love would want from a relaxed Sunday morning; eggs for brunch, talking and making love, all from their bed. While Danny took his turn in the shower, Cassie reluctantly pulled together her bag, knowing she'd need to head back to London before too long. The next four weeks of work would require extra heavy lifting on her part to help Fox limp through their twice-weekly on-air commitments and she'd agreed to cover three sets of hockey tournaments that would take her to every corner of the country.

Unfortunately, Cassie made the mistake of checking her work phone for the morning's studio arrangements, and found a message from Izzy, sent twenty minutes earlier.

IF: Am at studio reviewing your latest docuseries edits. Better, but still gaps. Still need a hook. Viewers like sick kid stories – especially that adopted one. Did you know Danny Reed also adopted? Something to think about

Cassie slammed the phone onto the duvet and continued folding the blouse she'd worn yesterday. No, she couldn't help herself, she typed in a reply.

CF: Thanks re improvement. Disagree D Reed adoption anything to do with rugby

There was no way, *no way* she'd bring that into it.

Unfortunately, Izzy responded immediately.

IF: He's being touted for England, isn't he? Is he English or not? Why not test his DNA somehow? Be mad if he was French or something (and great for viewing figures).

That fucking, fucking woman. Cassie wasn't about to admit she'd already bought Danny a DNA testing kit as a Christmas gift, thinking it might help with his identity struggles, perhaps even connect him with family. No, she was going to push back, stand her ground.

CF: Uncomfortable with that. Will pursue other avenues. See you later

Giving herself no chance to read a response, Cassie turned the phone off and stowed it in her bag. How on earth had she ever wanted to become like Izzy?

Angry and miserable as she made one final sweep of Danny's wardrobe for any missed clothes, a neat row of rugby shirts with 'Camford 10 Reed' on the back caught Cassie's eye. Her spirits lifted. Hearing the bathroom door open, she quickly slipped one of the shirts over her body. She'd been about to judge her reflection in the mirror when Danny walked in, a towel around his hips.

'Just when I thought Sunday was a rest day,' he said, leaning against the doorframe with an appreciative smile and a glint in his eyes. Loved-up Danny was the hottest version yet.

'Might take this home with me, wear it a few times on calls with you, till I'm back for the Christmas Ball.'

'Definitely. Looking forward to it already,' he said huskily, and dropped his towel, 'but let's test out the in-person version, first.'

RED, WHITE & CUE

21. The Other Rugby Ball

At The Manor's entrance hall, Trish had joined Danny to form a welcoming party for attendees to the Premiership Christmas Ball. Beside him, a towering fir tree twinkled with gold lights and the club's inevitable red and white baubles. It was identical every year. He rubbed some of the greenery between his fingers, testing its authenticity. Real, much like his four weeks of anticipation. Though only the first week of December, this would be his and Cassie's official Christmas weekend, before she headed to Berlin to cover cycling and he would focus on the end of year fixtures. With a home match three days before Christmas and an away fixture in Manchester on Boxing Day, he and the team would also have very little downtime.

He checked his phone for an update from Cassie. A late-running Hystar meeting, the subject of which she'd been reluctant to discuss by text with him, had delayed her arrival. Nothing, yet. Though he had positioned himself at the foot of the wide-sweeping staircase to shake hands with arriving players from other clubs, he was mostly watching for Cassie's face. They'd agreed to keep their relationship private, at least until the docuseries had aired, but simply knowing she'd be there added a frisson of excitement.

'There are enough handsome men in dinner suits here to make a supposedly intelligent woman make stupid decisions,' Trish said, sipping from something with an olive floating in it. 'Unfortunately, most of them are young enough to be my sons. It's lovely to see all the support staff here, too.'

On cue, Danny used his height to scan the entrance hall for Norm, who he knew would be attending and who still had an obvious soft spot for Trish. The space was buzzing with well-groomed Premiership players, transformed by black tie attire, and women in jewel-coloured, full-length dresses. With no sign of Norm, he returned his attention to the job at hand.

'Danny, good to see you,' said the captain of Bedford Tigers as he arrived.

'Marcus, glad you could make it. Is your shoulder recovered after our visit?'

'Not in time for last week's fixture, but I'll be good for the next one. Thanks for asking. This is my wife, Bea.'

Danny shook the hand of the smiley, auburn-haired woman. 'Nice to meet you. This is Trish Murphy, Camford's media and marketing manager. Trish, this is Marcus Stanway, Bedford's captain, and his wife Bea.'

'Welcome, both of you,' Trish said. 'The bar is through to the left, follow the sound of the band for the dance floor.'

Marcus hesitated. 'Be good to speak with you later, Danny. Looking forward to tomorrow's International Selection announcements, eh?'

'I think a lot of people are. You're a certain for Scotland again, surely?'

'Aye, hope so. Think England will give you a spot in the training squad?'

It would be a dream come true, if they did.

'Not expecting it yet, but I'm staying ready. Solid choices already ahead of me, and expected to hold their places, so I'm biding my time.'

'Best glue our bleary eyes to the news conferences in the morning, just in case. See you in a bit.' Marcus shook Danny's hand again and escorted his wife in the direction of the bar.

For the next twenty minutes, Danny and Trish welcomed carload after carload of attendees. With his tank of small talk running low, and Cassie yet to arrive, he waited for a gap between conversations to once again check his phone. Similarly, Trish retrieved hers from a glittery gold evening bag.

CF: 5 minutes, queue of cars up the lane to get in Cx
DR: Can't wait Dx

Trish's phone began to ring and, seeing the identity of the caller, she made her apologies. But even stood several steps up the staircase above him, Danny was certain the news she was receiving was unexpected. Whatever it was, in her typically capable fashion, she ended the call with an assurance that the problem could be 'left with her'. She returned to her position beside him.

'Bang goes my night of abandon. England Rugby's media hub at Twickenham has flooded and fried all the electrics. "Someone" helpfully suggested they hold tomorrow morning's announcement here, instead.'

'They've used our media centre before, haven't they – their tech team know the ropes?'

'Yes,' she said, while tapping something into her phone, 'but I'll have to brief security and the parking attendants, oh and check that the background screens from last time have the current England logos on…'

'What time will they be here?'

'Unfortunately their crew is coming at 8am, journalists and other media representatives will start to arrive around 10am. Think I'll be on constant caffeine by then.'

With last year's dawn party antics on Axminster's training field in mind, Danny would also have to ensure everyone was clear of The Manor well before any evidence could be captured by the media. 'I'll be around, so let me know if there's anything I can help with.'

'Maybe a soft drink,' she said, flicking her eyes along the corridor towards the bar, 'I'm not risking a hangover.'

Ten minutes later, with drink in hand, and moving against the tide of arriving guests, he'd almost returned to Trish back at the entrance hall when Cassie walked through the door and greeted her. Transfixed, he paused while she removed a long, black coat, and handed it to one of the cloakroom attendants.

She smoothed her hand down the length of her strapless dress that hugged the familiar curves he loved. With shining hair bouncing just above her shoulders, she was an utter dream.

A throb of longing punched through him, remembering how she'd 'let it slip' that she'd bought underwear to match her dress. How he'd wait until they were at his apartment, he had no idea. She sizzled in red.

'Ah, here he is,' Trish said to Cassie as he approached them.

When Cassie turned and smiled, he almost drooled. Red lips, as she well knew, were his undoing when she wore them.

'I was just telling her how gorgeous she looks, don't you think, Danny?'

Danny's mouth wouldn't work.

Cassie hid a smirk with a sweeping survey of the foyer. 'Everyone has scrubbed up well,' she said, 'including both of you. Love the tree.'

'It's real,' Danny blurted, to both women's bemusement.

'Right…well, guess what's happened?' Trish said to Cassie.

'I already know. Hystar's News Desk just rang me. Of course, they're feeling smug because they know they already have a journalist on hand, whereas other broadcasters will be scrambling here from wherever.'

'I already reserved you a spare room in the accommodation annexe. I wasn't sure whether you'd need it, but it's there.'

Danny watched Cassie nod her gratitude, suspecting she, like him, felt no guilt at the duplicity for the sake of their privacy. Not when his apartment was a ten-minute drive away.

'How have the last few weeks been, since you were with us for the Newcastle trip?' he asked her, hoping the question didn't sound staged.

'Excuse me a minute,' Trish murmured, 'I'll slip outside to make a couple of calls.'

Once Trish had gone, Cassie maintained the body language of a colleague, but spoke sufficiently softly that only Danny could hear her.

'You are sinfully delicious in that dinner suit. Knowing what's underneath is making me squirm.'

'And you are the most beautiful woman here,' he said, wishing just for a moment that everyone knew they were together. 'There will be players with their sights set on you tonight.'

'They don't have a chance. For one thing, I'll be on Cokes, and for another, I have a really, really serious thing for Camford's captain.'

'Glad to hear it. They wouldn't mess with him; he was a bit punchy in his youth, bit of a reputation now for guarding what's his.'

She innocently fluttered her eyelids. 'Oh? Am I "his", do you think?'

'As much as he's yours.'

'Phew,' she whistled, fanning herself with her bag, 'that's a lot, then.'

Danny sighed as a group of players from Gloucester appeared at the entrance doors. 'Sorry, but I need to stay here and welcome people for a while longer yet.'

'Not a problem, I'll go and circulate, maybe have a dance. The band sounds great.'

'Danny, you lucky bugger!' said Gus Bailey, one of Gloucester's flankers.

Cassie stilled, seeking Danny's eyes.

'We were just nosing at your training facilities, they're easily the best in the Premiership. Know if Coach Alex is looking for contract transfers for next season yet?'

'Excuse me,' Cassie whispered, mock swiping her forehead and headed off into the throng of guests making their way towards the bar.

'He's inside, I'll let him know you've asked me,' Danny assured the player, before welcoming yet more arrivals.

By eleven o'clock, Danny had circulated the bar area numerous times, ensuring he'd spent time with each of the club captains. The mood, as always, was lively, everyone making the most of the mid-season weekend break from fixtures. Players didn't need telling twice to enjoy a celebration. Occasionally a flash of red had caught his attention, and when he'd established it as Cassie's dress, the comfort of knowing her whereabouts, that she was laughing or dancing, was strangely settling.

She, too, could do with some respite from her stressful job. Once or twice during the evening, their eyes had met across the room. He hoped she'd read the same message in his expression as what he'd felt from hers. What had begun as a simple attraction had now deepened into a connection that went beyond anything he'd known before.

After a conversation with Bath Rugby's captain, Danny scanned the room for Cassie. She was at the bar, smiling and chatting with some of Camford's players and their wives and girlfriends. Just for a moment he envisaged that next Christmas, he'd be able to saunter over there with the intention of a PDA kiss dropped onto her head, maybe settle a comfortable arm around her waist. While holding a conversation with others, she might then run a hand up his spine and do that thing she did with her fingers at the nape of his neck. He'd stand there, pretending it didn't drive him crazy. The sound of Trish's raised voice made him jump.

'Danny, did you hear me? I said Marcus and Bea Stanway are leaving. He's looking for you at the entrance hall, come on.'

He nodded and she led the way, weaving a path between increasingly relaxed guests.

Out in the comparatively quiet entrance foyer, Danny's ears buzzed as he and Trish waved off the Stanways with brief farewells. He checked his watch. 'Not even midnight, a surprisingly early exit from him.'

'She's pregnant, expecting in May.'

'I didn't know that.'

'Poor thing looks shattered, told me she only stopped all-day retching a few days ago. Impressively, they planned the baby's arrival to coincide with the end of season. Marcus is in full-on dad-to-be mode, apparently. Has bought a pair of mini Scotland boots already.'

It was alien to Danny, any talk of babies, fatherhood, even family, really. The brief few years of being parented by Laura was his only reference. It seemed a huge leap of faith to bring a child into the world, even if you did know what being a parent looked like.

'Everything is set for tomorrow's press conference,' Trish was saying, as he wondered whether Cassie wanted children.

They'd yet to discuss it. Perhaps the issue of her mother's alcoholism had put her off motherhood. It was tragic, to have a mother but not a relationship with her. Any mother at all was a gift as far as he was concerned, whatever form she took. Surely there'd be some kind of help available, something that could be done to repair things? His mind ran with the idea, casting idyllic visions of mini Cassies and young, junior-rugby versions of himself visiting their grandmother in Wales. Maybe even fostering. Quite how, he didn't know, but curiously the idea didn't scare him. They'd do it together; he and Cassie would help each other. They'd have a house, he'd make sure she had somewhere she could write, work on the novel she'd dreamed of…They'd have friends from the club and further afield. Maybe he could get to know Marcus a bit better…

'Danny, are you drunk or are you simply ignoring me?'

He blinked at Trish and shook his head. 'Not drunk, sorry, mind was somewhere.' Somewhere so fantastic, he almost couldn't contain himself. 'So…er, tomorrow?'

Trish sighed. 'Yes, all sorted. It's a relief to be – oh, here comes Cassie, I'll wait and update her at the same time.'

The exact second he saw her; Danny knew something was wrong. Her unfocused gaze, one outstretched arm in front, feeling her way as she staggered along the corridor. He rushed towards her, barging a couple of guests clear from his path. 'Cassie, what's happened?'

'Feel odd,' she said faintly.

Danny clamped an arm around her shoulder and guided her to the doors.

'What's happened to her?' said Trish, following them outside. 'Too much to drink?'

'No, it wouldn't be that. Cassie, Cassie?' Danny tried, but to his complete panic she slumped against him.

'Erm, we could…take her into the room I reserved for her?' Trish offered.

'Dizz…feel dizzy, Danny?'

Heart pounding in his ears, Danny scooped Cassie into his arms. 'I'm taking her straight round to the clinic. Can you go and find Doc?'

As Trish sped off towards the bar, Danny tightened his hold on Cassie and set off along the path.

When her limbs went limp, he broke into a jog. 'It's OK baby, we're going to get you some help. Can you hold your arms around my neck?'

She didn't respond.

Danny punched in the access code at the clinic's door and took Cassie into the nearest exam room. After carefully placing her onto a bed, he dashed back to switch on more lights, his dress shoes tapping on the white tiled floor of the empty unit.

'OK, Doc's on his way,' he said, as much to reassure himself as to soothe her.

'Feel so…weird,' she mumbled, and Danny picked up her wrist.

After counting for almost a minute, it was obvious that her pulse was way too high. At least it was strong; he'd been mentally recapping a well-ingrained process of how to perform CPR, just in case. He was contemplating placing her into the recovery position when the sound of voices from the clinic entrance reached him. 'In here,' he shouted, poking his head outside the room.

Doc and Trish rushed in.

'Alright, Danny, Trish tells me Cassie has taken unwell?' Doc said, shaking out of his dinner jacket and sanitising his hands with some gel.

'Yes, suddenly, and she seems disorientated. Pulse is strong but around 130.'

Doc wheeled over a monitor and clipped a tracker onto her finger. 'OK, Cassie, this is Doc, and you're in Camford's clinic at The Manor. Remember, we met when you filmed here?'

Cassie rolled her head towards Doc, her eyes crinkled in confusion.

Doc studied her face. 'Have you taken anything tonight, Cassie?'

She shook her head vaguely.

'Trish, check her bag, please,' Doc ordered, indicating the clutch bag dangling across Cassie's body.

'I'm not sure, we should.'

'Just do it, please.'

Trish sought Danny's eyes; he nodded. There was no time to think twice.

'God, well, let's see, there's nothing in – no, wait, there's a little pouch. Oh, there are some tablet strips, looks like maybe three or four different types?'

'Call out the names on them,' Doc said, while flashing a light into Cassie's eyes.

'So, aten-ol-ol.'

'That's a beta-blocker.'

Danny had seen Cassie swallow one of those before and had asked her about it. 'She takes those to calm herself before live presenting sometimes,' he explained.

'Er, oh, that's paracetamol, sertraline is the next one.'

'That's an anti-anxiety drug. I'm guessing the last one is sleeping tablets?' Doc asked.

'It's called, erm, the writing is so tiny, I think it says Zimovane.'

'That's a brand name of zopiclone, it's used for insomnia. Do either of you know how her mental health is?'

Trish shook her head and looked expectantly at Danny.

His head sought answers; there was nothing wrong with needing help, hell some of the players relied on medications like those, but why hadn't Cassie mentioned them to him? 'She's stressed out from her workload, especially live television. Her boss is making life difficult for her.'

'Not Izzy at Hystar? She's lovely,' said Trish, cocking her head.

'I think she might be different as a colleague.'

Doc finished his checks and looked at him. 'Alright, so maybe she mixed them with alcohol tonight?' Doc asked, but Trish was quick to doubt it.

'No, I wouldn't think so, she told me she'd stick to Coke, we have a press conference here in the morning.'

'But she still may have drunk some, whether knowingly or not,' Doc suggested.

Danny darted around to the other side of the bed, patted Cassie's hand and gently stroked her face. 'Baby, have you drunk anything alcoholic?'

'I'm scared.'

He brushed her fringe forwards in the way he thought might comfort her. 'I won't leave you, I promise, and Doc's here.' He glanced up to see Doc and Trish exchange a look of understanding. Danny was past caring about keeping his relationship with Cassie secret.

Doc cleared his throat. 'You two are…?'

'Yes.' Danny straightened up. 'And I can't smell any alcohol on her breath. What should we do?'

Doc checked Cassie's pupils again. 'I'm concerned she might have been spiked with Rohypnol or a similar drug, either in her drink or from a needle.'

'What! Call a fucking ambulance then, and ring the police, Trish.'

Doc held up a hand, attempting to calm Danny's rising panic. 'Hold on, hold on, she's not unconscious, and there's no treatment except rehydration and needing to sleep it off.'

'Also, if we could avoid having the police here…there are hundreds of players and partners still around. How would that go down?' said Trish.

'I really don't give a shit, just – tell me she's going to be alright.' Danny pleaded, taking Cassie's floppy hand in his and refusing to let go of it as Doc checked each of her arms and examined her skin.

'Calm down, yes, she'll be alright though of course cannot be left alone overnight in case she vomits. I can't see any blood spots from a needle puncture anywhere. Of course, spikes can go through material but it's unlikely, especially as she's wearing that long dress.'

Her colour was worrying.

Danny tried imagining who would do this to her. 'Can you give her something to help with recovery?'

'She needs fluids, which I can give her through an IV to begin with, but we have to consider whether she'd want to give a sample for prosecution purposes, assuming the police would ever be able to find the person who did this. There's a small window for gathering it, time is running out if so.'

'Do you think she'd want to prosecute?' Trish asked Danny.

'I don't know. She cares a lot about justice and she'll want to catch whoever did this to her and make sure they can't do it again … but she's also a very private person, and what with being so recognisable in the media, I don't know if she'd want to risk the potential fallout.' He bent down again. 'Baby, we think you've been spiked, you'll feel better soon but shall we call the police?'

'No police…no police…' She flailed towards him, mumbling, '…gonna get me…'

He brought her fingers to his lips. 'No one's going to get you, and we don't know who did this, but I'm here, don't worry.' He stroked her face. Bloody hell, he'd much rather an injury himself, than seeing her like this.

Doc consulted the monitor readings from Cassie's finger. 'Her oxygen sats are little low, we can give her some help with that.'

'Yes, do it,' said Danny, not taking his eyes from her.

After a few moments, Doc had taken steps to begin IV fluids and had hooked her up to a canister of oxygen. 'Here we are, Cassie, just giving you a little O2, that will improve things,' Doc said in his reassuring tone, and placed a clear mask over her nose and mouth. 'Just breathe normally.'

'I really can't believe this,' said Trish. 'When will she recover? Will there be any lasting effects? Hystar are also expecting her to represent them at the press conference here at ten tomorrow morning, that's nine hours' time. I could get hold of Izzy; I have her details.'

Doc checked his watch. 'Cassie will feel dreadful, but if she wants to, she could probably make it. Every hour between now and then should see an improvement.'

They all observed Cassie as she lay breathing the oxygen, a drip in her arm, eyes closed. Her eyelashes lay dark on her ashen face.

Doc left the room and returned with an iPad. 'I need some information for my records. Do you know her full name?' he looked at Danny expectedly.

'Yes, it's Cassandra Rhoswen Forde, she'll be thirty-two on 5th March. Sorry, my brain can't calculate the year.'

As Doc tapped in the information, Danny felt Trish's hand squeeze his arm. 'She'll be OK. Presumably you'll stay with her?'

The desire to keep Cassie safe from further harm almost overwhelmed him. 'Of course I will, but her bags are in reception, I think.'

'I can fetch those.'

Doc adjusted the rate of flow on Cassie's drip, then nodded his satisfaction. 'I'll come back in an hour and keep my phone on loud. If you need anything, don't hesitate.'

22. Dear Read-err

Something roused Cassie from sleep, returning her to the worst headache ever. She kept her eyes closed, praying for oblivion.

'Yes, of course I am, it goes without saying, but...all I'm asking is, couldn't someone else?' Danny was saying. The voice that had intermittently soothed and reassured her and helped her to pull on a hoodie over her dress.

She sunk her nose into the hood, comforted by the smell of him. It must be the one she'd 'borrowed' from his bedroom and since kept in her case. She drifted off again.

'Baby, are you awake?'

'No,' Cassie groaned.

Danny's low rumble of amusement made her lips curl.

'OK yes, but not I'm functioning.'

'You've done really well. Listen, Coach Alex needs to see me so Heather is coming to take over in a minute, she says she can help you freshen up, see how you feel about doing this press conference thing.'

Cassie cracked opened an eye. 'Oh God, what time is it?'

'Just after 8am. Trish could get hold of Hystar if you're feeling too rough?'

Cassie felt around the bed for her bag. 'No, I can do it, I just need my—'

'Medication?'

She stilled. 'No, I was going to say my phone.'

'Then you were going to take an anti-anxiety tablet, maybe a beta blocker? I wish you'd felt able to talk to me. And sleeping tablets?'

'I hardly use those, and only as a last resort, usually across time zones. Never with you though, and the anxiety med is a very low dose I've been on since...well, for years. The internship at Hystar turned things around, but performing regularly on live TV triggered my nerves again, and I've told you what Fox is like at the moment, having a co-presenter who could melt down at any given second isn't great. Izzy's probably not helping either, but, despite all of that, since reconnecting with you, things have been much better.'

Danny's phone buzzed.

'Heather's at the clinic door, I need to let her in. Let's talk about this later, OK?'

Sharing even this short version of her struggles felt good; she only hoped she hadn't transferred them onto his shoulders. She caught his arm. 'Thank you, for staying with me. I'm sorry all this happened.'

'No, I'm sorry it happened. This scared the crap out of me, but however much I wanted to find the person responsible, there was no way I could leave.'

'I love you,' she whispered.

'No more than I love you. I need to let Heather in.'

Cassie turned her head and saw her case, open on one of the chairs. 'You'd better not have peeked at the Christmas presents in there while I was asleep?'

'Of course not.' He winked and left the room.

A moment later he returned with Heather behind him.

'Hey, hey lovely lady – oh Jeez, you look...'

'Terrible?' Cassie suggested, definitely feeling it.

'Rescuable...if you have another sleep. I'll wake you in plenty of time, hun, don't worry.'

'That's a good idea,' Danny said, 'but I have to go and meet Coach, I'll see you both later.' He kissed Cassie on the forehead and thanked Heather for coming to help.

'I saw there's a coffee machine by the office door back there, I'll just go and fetch one,' said Heather. 'Close your eyes, you need all the shuteye you can get.'

'Thanks, then I might need all the coffee I can get.'

'It's time to get ready, wake up.'

Cassie turned her head away from the sound of Heather's voice. Surely she'd only slept another few minutes. She rubbed her eyes and risked a stretch. Her head still pounded, but only as bad as the jet lag headaches she sometimes suffered with. Not ideal conditions for journalism, but doable.

'You have forty minutes until the conference starts. Trish popped by with a cereal bar and banana for you, and a note from Danny, because your phone is dead apparently, not surprising.'

'Thanks, I'll save the food until I'm certain my stomach's settled.' She unfolded the accompanying piece of paper. Inside was the word 'REFEREES'. 'This was definitely for me?'

'Apparently so. Now, do you want to sit up, then work your way to standing? There's a bathroom through that door apparently, I see there is a wash bag in your case. Doc also popped in and left this sachet. It's to mix with your water, some electrolytes or something.'

Chatter among the reps in Camford's media centre was painfully loud. Cassie squeezed herself along a row of bolshy journalists to the only spare seat, halfway up the tiered seating. 'Hi, Cassie Forde, Hystar,' she said to the man on her left. 'What's the running order?'

'Ross McIntosh, Rugby World, yes I recognise you from Fox/Forde. Why have Hystar got you covering this?'

'I was already in the area, said I didn't mind.' She might feel like death, but she wasn't about to give anyone a scoop.

'Apparently the England squad's names will be projected on the screen, we'll have ten minutes to prepare questions for the England coach who will come out to answer them. The Q&A round is usually a snoozefest, the ritual back and forth of set-piece answers – and those of us selected to ask questions will be granted only two, as usual. I wouldn't bet against you being selected, being the only woman here.'

'Thanks.' She reached under her seat and plugged in her mobile phone, thankful for the excellently equipped media centre.

The lights went dim, and for a moment Cassie thought she was feeling faint.

'Here we go,' said Ross.

Cassie powered up her phone and, ignoring a multitude of backdated notifications, flicked her screen to camera mode. The club's projector shone a shockingly bright image on the screen, throwing daggers of pain into Cassie's eyes. Using her phone's 2% battery, she took shots of the list of thirty-six names, knowing that in the worst case, she could study them from those.

'One or two surprises there, otherwise as expected,' someone behind her murmured. 'Wonder why he's dropped an experienced player for Danny Reed?'

Cassie's head snapped up, making the room spin. What? She scrolled through the alphabetised list and zoomed in. Danny had been named in the England Rugby squad.

As she tried to hide a suspiciously happy grin, England Head Coach Luke Barford arrived on the stage to a generous applause.

'Hello, folks. First of all, thank you all for making it out here to Camford. So, every player on this list has a place on merit, that includes experience, skill level, attitude and current fitness. The squad will train together in January, and I'll make the final team selections only a few days before each match to ensure we have the best possible chances. I'll take some of your questions shortly, but first I wanted to take the opportunity to introduce one of our newly selected players, who fortunately for me just so happened to be in the building.'

Everyone chuckled, but Cassie held her breath as Danny walked onto the stage, raising his hand in polite acknowledgement to the assembled media.

'We're shit out of luck,' said Ross, 'Danny's one of the younger ones that's been media trained to within an inch of his life; he won't give us anything new or interesting. They're all too careful now.'

Danny settled into his seat and Cassie saw the moment he paused his row-by-row scan of the media reps.

She lifted her chin in such a way that no one would have noticed, but his brief nod told her he'd seen her.

'Alright then, questions please,' said Coach Luke, and everyone's hands shot upwards. 'Er yes, Charlie.'

'Thank you, Charlie Davis, *The Sportsman*...'

Cassie pressed record on her phone and listened to Coach Luke, then Danny, respond. Ross had been right; the responses were politically careful. Like every other rep, Cassie then raised her hand.

'And who shall we have next? Yes, Ms Forde.'

Cassie stood up slowly. 'Cassie Forde, Hystar Sport. First of all, I'd like to congratulate Danny on his place in the England squad. Danny, how do you feel?'

All around her, the media press pack exhaled an audible sigh at what they no doubt considered a wasted question.

'Very proud, this is an honour and I'm excited to get going with training so that we gel as a team and improve our chance of success in the tournament.'

Cassie smiled as broadly at him as she dared, despite knowing Izzy would be frustrated with the bland exchange. She suddenly thought of Danny's note.

Did he mean she should raise the subject of refereeing? She tested the idea with her second question.

'Thank you, and what do you see as the greatest barrier to England's achievement, Danny?'

'Good one,' Ross whispered beside her.

'The way I see it, there are two main causes of team failures, obviously inadequate training and fitness is one of them, but inconsistent and sometimes poor refereeing plays its part.'

The media press pack murmured their surprise.

'Can you elaborate on the point about refereeing?'

A younger guy wearing an England Rugby hoodie down at the front leapt from his seat and glared at Cassie. 'Sorry, only two questions per media outlet please.'

Danny waved him away. 'It's only fair that I explain what I meant,' he said. 'Yes, I'm aware this is a taboo subject, but from speaking with other Premiership captains, and what I too have experienced, players are frustrated with referees unfairly penalising a stronger team's scrum, for example, and we see them miss clear forward passes, even make knee-jerk decisions. As players we strive for consistency and excellence. We expect the same in the referees.'

'Thank you, Danny, for explaining that.'

Coach Luke took the microphone. 'Next question. Maybe something more upbeat this time?'

Cassie sat down as hopeful hands once again raised around her.

'Well done for getting that out of him,' Ross said, sitting ever taller. 'Talking about referees is a big no-no for players – I wouldn't mind betting that flak will fly.

Did you see Luke Barford's face? Danny's England boots might never hit the pitch.'

The last of the rival representatives had packed up their equipment and set off for homeward journeys.

After catching up on emails and responding to a message from Fox, Cassie dictated a series of voice notes about the conference, for the writers at Hystar's News Desk; in another life, that would have been her.

On the stage, Trish levered microphones into hard-cased boxes and glanced up at Cassie. 'Woman of the moment,' she called, in a more professional tone than she'd used with her of late. 'The press pack are certainly pleased with you.'

'But in this case, it's not necessarily a good thing.'

'We'll see. Danny's going to have to deal with the consequences. I saw his note to you.' She unhooked a background screen from its holder and laid the material on the floor, ready for rolling up.

Cassie walked down towards the stage. 'Need a hand?'

'You probably shouldn't, after last night.'

Still, Cassie climbed onto the stage and picked up one end of the material. 'Thanks for the cereal bars and banana,' she said, without confessing they were still in her bag.

'I'm relieved to see you here. How are you feeling?' Trish picked up the other end and they began to roll the screen together.

'Washed out.'

'I've mentioned what happened to management, they're keen that I double-check with you about reporting it. Doc and Danny did their best to ask you last night, but—'

'I don't want to bring in the police, or involve Camford management, but I don't want anyone else being in danger either. Can you leave it with me?'

'Yes, if you're absolutely sure?' Trish said, pausing before loading the rolled screen into a storage tube.

Cassie nodded. When she'd touched base briefly with Fox about a work matter, and mentioned the incident, he'd been apoplectic to hear that the police hadn't been notified. But if she knew him as well as she thought she did, he'd have already set some investigative wheels in motion.

To her relief, Trish accepted the decision. 'Alright. Can't say I slept much myself, and from the look of him, Danny slept in a clinic chair.' She didn't quite meet Cassie's eyes.

'Have you got a spare minute, Trish?' She gestured at the chairs still on the stage.

'Yes, though there's more than a minute's worth needed, I suspect, but please sit down before you fall down.'

'I don't know what to talk about first; Danny, Izzy, or today's press conference. Take your pick.'

'Well, Doc was definitely surprised when Danny made it clear what you meant to him, though I had suspected it for a few weeks.'

'You have?'

'Yes, don't forget, I've known Danny a few years now. Let's just say he's never been so attentive of the club's media and marketing activities as he has since the docuseries began filming.'

Cassie smiled. 'We met a couple of years back, on his debut.'

'I remember, the chemistry was immediate – and obvious to me, at least. Norm and I talked about it at the time.'

'Norm's lovely, I'm glad you two…talk.' She flicked a look at Trish.

'Yes, well, I'm glad that you and Danny have got each other. Please don't take this as interference, but after that news conference, I wouldn't want him paying the price for you keeping Izzy happy. Can you tell me what's going on with her? Maybe I can help.'

'It's a constant push-pull, with rugby versus non-rugby content. I'm doing my best to make everything at least relate to the game and have refused a number of requests that delve too deeply into players' personal lives.'

'What sort of things?'

'Mental health in Josh's story, for example, DNA testing and foster care investigations in Danny's, among others.'

'Good grief, that's awful- although I will say that Josh might be willing to explore mental health in sport. Does Izzy have the final say on content or can you go above her head?'

'To the board? There'd need to be a good reason because in ratings terms, she's on the money. Hystar's reach and retention is growing under her watch. I've got nowhere to go with this and I'm up to my eyeballs with worry.' Cassie rested her arms on the desk and dropped her forehead onto them. This was a professional low point, talking to a client like this.

When Trish didn't reply, Cassie looked up, meeting a face etched with concern. 'Sweetheart, if you don't mind me asking, why put yourself through working in that environment if it's affecting your health? You might not remember, but it was me that went through your bag and found the medication when Doc asked.'

To Cassie's distress, the kindness behind the question triggered a build-up of tears behind her eyes. 'At the moment I don't have a choice, Trish. I'm the same as everyone, bills to pay, a career to guard. Between you and me, I never wanted to be on camera; the pressure's immense, and I'm slipping further and further away from writing. Did you know my original degree was in creative writing?'

'No, I didn't. What happened? No luck with getting published?'

'None. I'm thankful that my interest in sports got me into journalism and an entry position with Hystar. I owe them a lot.'

'Do you, though? There are so many media outlets now. You could diversify, stay in sport, but manage content for a club or organisation. Or go freelance and combine projects?'

Despite Trish's well-meaning pep talk, Cassie's spirits continued to sink. 'I'm not experienced enough for that. Don't forget this is only my fourth year with them.' Dear God, she was going to cry.

An arm came around her shoulder as Trish scooted her chair nearer. 'Listen, you're tired and you've had a horrible twenty-four hours. Maybe this isn't the time to be thinking about career plans. I'm sorry for mentioning Danny. I'm protective over all the boys but your relationship is your business. As far as your career is concerned, though, when you're feeling a bit brighter, why not come up and have dinner with me one evening and we'll hash out a few ideas?'

'Really?' Cassie sniffed, swiping her face on the back of her hand.

'Yes, really. If you need me, you have my number.'

'I'm kind of lacking in wise advice, so thank you, that means a lot.'

'You've underestimated your worth; I've seen you cover events all over the world for all manner of sports. Take today for example, your work ethic is incredible. How many others would pitch up after they'd been spiked less than twelve hours earlier?'

Cassie shrugged. 'Not many?'

'None, Cassie. Off the cuff, I'd suggest you approach Aquatics GB or World Cycling, see what they need in terms of content. I wouldn't mind betting that England Rugby themselves have their eyes on your capability now and, ooh, how about directly approaching significant characters in the sport, discussing some biography work? There are lots of avenues we can discuss.'

As Cassie blinked back the last of her tears, she did her best to pull herself together. 'I appreciate what you're saying, but before that, I want this docuseries to be fantastic, for all the right reasons and not for sensational personal revelations.'

'OK, let me know what I can do. If Izzy approaches me about anything, I'll run it by you and if necessary, we can push back on things together.'

'Thank you.' Cassie stood up and tilted into Trish's arms. The hug felt unbelievably reassuring.

A door banging at the top of the tiered auditorium revealed a silhouette that she immediately recognised as Danny's.

'What's happened?' he said, speeding down the steps towards them.

'Nothing, I'm fine, just tired.'

'What did they say?' Trish asked him. 'After the conference, about your comments? The look on Coach's face wasn't ideal.'

'Got a rollocking from Luke, then Alex called me in and accused me of wasting my chance.'

Cassie shook her head in regret. 'I am so sorry, baby, I shouldn't have asked that question.'

'I knew what I was doing, and why, but now that I'm in the squad, I've just got to zip it and be on my best behaviour. From now on, my rugby has to do the talking.'

'That's very sensible,' Trish said, standing up. 'As is everyone heading home to spend the rest of Sunday relaxing. I, for one, have plans for loungewear, a big mug of hot chocolate and a few episodes of *Bridgerton*.'

It was early afternoon when Cassie woke from a much-needed sleep on Danny's sofa. She straightened, finding him sat on the floor, watching television.

'This is a ridiculous programme, there's no way that duke or whatever would have ridden his horse right up to the picnic, and that girl – a Bridgerton I think – she looks frozen, but they're acting like it's the middle of summer.'

'Mmm, if you're not enjoying it, then I'll turn it—'

Danny wrestled the TV remote from Cassie's grasp. 'No, wait, it's almost finished, might as well just keep it on in the background.'

'I knew it, inside that hunky exterior lies a romantic heart. Sport and romance, what did I tell you?'

Danny kissed her softly. 'Don't tell anyone.'

'You'd be surprised, I happen to know that one of your colleagues cries at *The Notebook* quite regularly,' she smirked, tapping her nose at the secret intel from the wives and girlfriends.

'Yeah, but I bet they watch *Rugby Focus* first.'

Cassie pushed herself upright, chuckling at the irony. 'Mind if I make a coffee?'

'Of course, I'll have one too.'

She bent to retrieve the two wrapped Christmas gifts she'd hidden beneath the sofa as soon as they'd arrived. 'Before the next episode starts, maybe you'd like to open these – unless you want to wait for Christmas?'

Danny turned the TV off. 'I would have bought a tree and some decorations, if you'd been here for Christmas,' he said, staring at a space beside the TV. 'It would have gone right there.'

She cupped his face in her hands. 'I like the sound of that.'

In an envelope marked 'To Cassie, love Dx', she was delighted to find two tickets to a West End musical, for a Wednesday evening in March. She'd barely mentioned her interest in theatre. 'Thank you, I haven't seen this show,' she said, giving him a kiss.

'Me either, and just to be clear, there will be something else for your birthday. The show is my cousin Jake's first lead role, after years in choruses.'

'I remember his name, one of Laura's two nephews. So, he's a musical theatre actor?'

'Yes. I contacted him a couple of weeks back, and for the first time in years we had a long chat. He's going to take us backstage to meet the cast and crew, if you'd like that?'

'That would be amazing. What I'm most happy about is that you contacted him in the first place, especially after what we talked about the other night. I know how much you wonder about whether you have blood family members out there somewhere, but having two Reed cousins is great.'

'It is. I just thought, I've got family, I should reach out to them, you know?' He caught her hands in his. 'And if you'd like us to do the same with your mother, get her some help, maybe—'

Cassie pulled her hands away, unwilling to let her past spoil their special moment. 'That door closed years ago. Let's focus on you, shall we? Open one of your presents.'

After exchanging smaller gifts of rugby and travel-related presents, Cassie handed him a box.
'It's a gift I bought a few weeks ago, after that night you spoke about your lack of blood family.' She watched him unwrap the contents.

'So, I wipe this swab around my mouth, send the kit off, and they give me a DNA breakdown of my ethnic origin?' He eyed the kit suspiciously.

'Yes, so you'll know the largest percentage of whichever region you're from and some of the smaller fractions. There's also an opportunity to discover any relatives that have used the same service, even build a family tree.'

Danny studied the explanatory leaflet, still frowning. 'I'll have to think about whether I send it off. A part of me is resisting the prospect of connecting with people who abandoned a baby.'

'That's perfectly alright. In your own time, if at all.'

'It's thoughtful, thank you.' He kissed her softly. 'I'm not used to getting Christmas gifts at all, to be honest. I've kept a couple of books that Laura bought me, and from younger childhood, and there's that wind-up torch a social worker gave me. I can't remember her name, but she knew I read a lot, and didn't like the dark. The wind-up element meant I didn't need new batteries all the time. Thoughtful, just like you.'

She handed him another gift. 'See if you like the thought behind this one.'

Strong fingers ripped away the wrapper. 'His 'n' hers naughty Santa outfits? I can safely say these are an excellent thought.'

'Thought so. Red and white are your favourite colours,' she said huskily, and sauntered towards the bedroom.

'That,' Danny said, scrambling to his feet, 'is my cue.'

23. More Threes

Despite that afternoon's win, of their final match before Christmas, Danny's spirits weren't as high as they should have been. Training had been punishing and community visits to the hospital were always harder at this time of the year. Of course, they were even tougher for the poor kids who were stuck in hospital for Christmas. Woody, in particular, had been withdrawn, and though doing better on the health front, faced Christmas in the adolescent unit. Richard, grateful and doting dad that he was, had accepted Camford shirts for him and his son that Trish had organised to be signed by the entire senior squad.

After the stadium had emptied, Norm and the other groundsmen had curtailed the usual time allocated for post-match kicking practice, claiming that they needed to get to the shops for last-minute gifts. As if they hadn't had all sodding week.

'Cheers mate,' Ryn said, smacking glasses with him in The Manor's bar, 'to a good first half of the season.'

Around them, several of the players were sharing a drink before heading off to loved ones for the Christmas break. 'Here's to the next half.'

'And the hope of seeing you with an England shirt on your back, come February.'

'All being well. Training camp starts 10th January, can't wait.'

Ryn was nodding. 'I remember my first camp for South Africa. Dream come true, mate. You're still coming to me and Heth on Christmas Day? She's bought enough food so you'd better turn up, otherwise come the Boxing Day home match and Cardiff on the 2nd, your bra here's going to be carrying extra kgs of fat.'

'I'll be there,' Danny promised, sinking several mouthfuls of his pint without a breath.

'Thirsty?'

'Looks like it.' The sooner he finished his pint, the sooner Christmas would be over with, then he'd be back there training again. Then Cassie would be back from Berlin. Every day in the two weeks since they'd celebrated their own incredibly sexy early Christmas – after the awful incident at the party – he missed her more. He used to be comfortable being by himself, reading, watching TV, going to the gym, a peaceful way of managing life outside of the game. Now when he did any of those things, he felt alone. Doing them beside her, even if they weren't talking, made a huge difference.

Ryn bent his head nearer. 'She's in Germany, not on the moon. Call her.'

'Can't until later. Her boss at Hystar is cracking the whip – when Cassie's not presenting from the cycling championships, she's networking over there, gathering what she needs for the programmes. Between those, she's working remotely on the docuseries edits.'

Ryn pulled out his phone and began to thumb in a message. 'Reminds me, need to tell Heth something.'

Danny overheard a conversation a few feet away.

'Bought myself a new Kawasaki ZX-6R for Christmas, shit it flies...' someone said.

He rolled his eyes to himself. Anyone who rode motorbikes was stupid.

'Then I'm taking Naomi to Paris on the Eurostar for a couple of nights, did you know it's called the City of Lights?'

'No, I thought that was the City of Love,' said another voice.

Danny smiled to himself. Perhaps he wasn't alone in having romance on his mind.

The voice continued. 'Toured Paris once with an old club, boys were on a huge bender, mad on girls in the Latin Quarter, some of whom were in-cred-i-ble, things were dropped into their drinks, got anything after that...'

Danny barged his way into the assembled group. 'Who said that, about spiking drinks?'

'Me,' said Connor, 'but—'

Connor couldn't finish whatever he'd been about to say, with Danny's hand squeezed around his windpipe. 'WHAT did you do, Connor?'

'When?'

'At our Christmas Ball, was it you that spiked Cassie's drink?'

'I-don't-know-what-you're-talking-about,' Connor wheezed, running short of air, and swinging a desperate fist in the direction of Danny's face. In quick reaction, Danny pinned it behind Connor's back.

'Oh, I geddit, into her, are you?' Connor spat.

'Was it you?'

'What do you care? She's a journalist, wake up.'

All bets were off. Hands shaking, Danny dropped Connor and took aim to pulp the living hell out of him. 'I care, she fucking matters to me.'

Behind him, the strong arms of another player yanked him backwards. Danny swivelled free of their grip, intent on taking a swipe at whoever it was, but met the superior height of Ryn, his hands up in a boxing stance.

He levelled his eyes at Danny's. 'Try it and you'll be sorry. Now calm the fuck down before I drag you out of here,' he cautioned.

'BOYS! What the hell is happening here?'

Everyone in the vicinity froze, including Danny, Connor and Ryn, who puffed on unspent rage. There was only one person outside of the training staff who could stop everyone in their tracks so effectively.

Trish eyeballed each of them in turn, with looks so full of abject disappointment that Danny let his arms hang slack, like a reprimanded schoolchild.

'Ask him,' he snapped, shrugging a shoulder towards the wanker who was very lucky not to have a broken nose.

'Connor?' Trish shifted a large bouquet of Christmas flowers from one arm into her other and raised her eyebrows.

'He's gone, sorry to swear, fucking MENTAL. I was talking about others I'd heard about, I'd personally never spike anyone's drink.'

Trish looked at Danny, understanding arriving on her face. 'I'll deal with this,' she told him. 'Go and calm down.'

Danny didn't want to calm down. He glared at Connor; determined not to walk away first. On the pitch, players like Connor were often scrappy, antagonistic bastards. Right at that moment, he was pushing all of Danny's buttons.

Trish tutted. 'You, over here with me,' she ordered Connor, 'and the rest of you, I had better not hear about this outside of the bar. No mention of it to the coaches, especially not international ones, nor to the media. Are we clear?'

'Yes, Trish,' everyone mumbled.

Danny's phone vibrated in his pocket. He turned away to read its message.

CF: A birdie (aka Heather, via Ryn) tells me you're *officially lovesick. Seems it's contagious. Quick video call later? Guess what outfit I have with me, Mr Claus? Till then, be good. Love you Cx PS Have news re Hystar charity, remind me Cxx

He held the phone to his chest, fighting a contest between anger, self-pity and gratitude.

Ryn shoved a half-finished pint glass at him. 'Drink up, it's definitely time to go.'

'You're a good friend.'

'Based on what I just saw, I wouldn't want to be your enemy.'

Ryn had no idea. There was a time when everyone was Danny's enemy, and the world seemed against him. He didn't want to resurrect that version of himself, having learned to channel aggression for the rugby field, and only then to use it safely and when justified. Even an arsehole like Connor should have been dealt with using words. He swallowed the last of his beer and was about to say goodbye to Ryn when Trish came over. He braced for another reprimand.

'Danny, don't look at me like that, I actually came in here to tell you about something. Little did I expect to find this drama going on.'

'I'm sorry, lost my head and I'm knackered.'

She pulled him aside, so they would not be overheard by anyone. 'And I understand what's triggered it, but you are also the club captain, a role model, so should be leading by example.'

'I know, it's just—'

'Cassie. Yes, I realise. I spoke to her yesterday; she sounded just as tired as you. She's really up against it on our docuseries. It's a ludicrous catch-22, in that the sign-off seems to hinge on whether she agrees to content demands from her boss. I'm sure you're aware, Cassie doesn't want a reputation for that type of exposé.'

'I know, she needs this to be a success. When I first met her, she'd just worked with Izzy and considered her an immediate role model.'

'I remember them meeting, up at the stadium. I'm not defending Izzy but remember that everyone has a boss they report to, and maybe she's facing even greater pressure than anyone realises.

Danny kept knowledge of Izzy's abuse of power in sleeping with subordinates to himself, as Trish continued to offer explanation.

'Perhaps it's being under such pressure that forces Izzy to turn to unscrupulous behaviour like asking Cassie to dig around someone's mental health or gather identity information from DNA checks for the project.'

It was like a bucket of ice had been thrown over his head. Surely Cassie's Christmas gift, given with such care and apparent sincerity, wasn't actually seeking information for the series? For the second time in an hour, rising fury pumped through him. 'I ought to go, sorry Trish.'

'Oh, right, OK then, but just one thing before you go. I wondered if you could run something by her, assuming you're going to speak over Christmas?'

'Of course,' Danny mumbled, his head whirring with doubts.

'The thing is, I may have overstepped with Cassie, the morning after the Christmas Ball. I guess I was mothering her a bit, but I assumed, based on the next of kin information you gave Doc in the clinic…'

Danny exhaled. Surely this could wait. 'And?'

'So I took a phone call, inviting the team for lunch and a drink up, the day after the Friday night Cardiff match on 2nd January. It was from Cassie's Mum, Gwyn, lovely she was, warm and friendly just like her daughter. Owns a pub in Merthyr Tydfil with a fabulous name called—'

'Stumble Inn.'

'Yes, oh, so you know it then. Would you mention the call to Cassie, see if she thinks it's an idea for the series? I know she's been hesitant to firm up whether she'd be coming with us at all, but now her Mum's invited the team, it could pose an opportunity for a some away-team public relations. What do you think?'

'I…don't know what to think.'

'Alright, well, I'll leave it with you, shall I?' Trish raised an eyebrow, waiting for confirmation.

Somehow, he nodded his head.

'Great, you'll be alright, over Christmas? What are your plans?'

'Heather and Ryn's,' he said, monotonic, even to his own ears.

'Good, good, but please have a rest, put your feet up and watch some Christmas TV, too, all of you need it. And thanks for organising these flowers, they're lovely, I know you are behind getting the boys organised for that and for the other staff's gifts.'

On automatic, he pulled Trish in for a brief hug and gave her an air-kiss. 'Have a good Christmas.'

Too many unanswered questions vied for Danny's attention, his imagination headed for overdrive. Hoping a walk would help, he set off towards the orchard, the only sounds cutting through the chilly silence were phrases like 'Cassie's mum Gwyn', 'DNA checks for the project', Connor's 'he's gone fucking mental' and even Norm telling him earlier that time was being curtailed on post-match kicking practice. Added to the mix was Danny's niggling suspicion that he might have blown his chance with the England coach, for Cassie's sake. He pulled the hood of his jacket over his head. The air was still, but inside, he was being tossed around like a tornado. Round and round it went...How many things had she not trusted him with? How many meant he couldn't trust her?

He had to get a grip. He'd withstood testing situations before and despite the hand he'd been dealt, had learned to build relationships, learned to trust. To dream, and plan. Maybe he shouldn't have. One thing was for certain: he needed more time to get his head straight, before he spoke with Cassie. He pulled out his phone from the zipped pocket of his joggers.

DR: Can't do our call tonight, need to crash. Dx

It was the best he could say, and only at the last second did he add the kiss to his sign-off. At that moment, he hated how much he loved her.

There weren't too many pubs called Stumble Inn in Merthyr Tydfil. Shortly before 1.30pm the following day, Danny got out of his car, stretched, then shrugged into his denim jacket. On the off-chance any keen-eyed rugby fans were around, he pulled on a baseball cap. A fretful night of unanswered questions had compelled him into action. He would handle each one head-on. This was the first.

Quashing the hypocrisy of betraying Cassie's trust to discover exactly what she hadn't trusted him with, he pushed through a white picket gate and entered through the building's dark-stained doors. Inside, the low beamed ceilings and framed black and white pictures reminded him of village pubs he and the boys sometimes visited in North Essex. As he wandered further in, a barman greeted him.

'*Shwmae*, hello there, what can I get you?'

'Pint of soda and lime, please.'

'No problem, are you wanting the lunch menu? Might have to be bar food, the Sunday carvery's sold out.'

'I'll see how it goes.'

'OK, we'll put your drink on a tab and leave the menu here, in case you do. Recommend the soup of the day and cheesy bread, the Mrs makes it fresh.' The man, in his forties, filled a glass with ice and prepared the drink. 'So, the soup's spicy tomato today, you don't want to miss that.'

Danny eyed the man. 'Thanks, will let you know. Nice place, worked here long?'

The barman placed Danny's drink onto a Welsh flag mat. 'Been co-owner for ten years, now, but worked here since I left college. Gethin.' He held out his hand, and Danny shook it.

'Danny.' The drink was refreshing, after the four-hour drive.

'Excuse me, need to keep serving. Not many seats free now, are you waiting for someone?'

'No, I'm on my own. My girlfriend's working the next few days.'

'Oh, I get it, bit of freedom. Nice. I'm clocking a London accent, but you can't beat a Welsh Valleys girl. You'd catch some attention, if you've a mind for it.'

Danny levelled his gaze at Gethin. 'Just a seat for myself.'

'Fair enough. Looks like there are a couple by the fireplace nook, if you're quick.'

Danny passed a series of framed newspaper cuttings on his way to a seat. The first was a picture of Gethin and a partially obscured woman stood outside the pub, for an article about his dream of owning Stumble Inn having come true. In another, Gethin was stood beside a football team. Each player bearing 'Stumble Inn' on his chest. Being sponsored by a cider company suddenly didn't seem so bad. He moved to the next picture, expecting more evidence of Gethin being the local 'Mr Big' – ironic, given he'd blow over in a stiff wind. Instead, Danny found a picture of Cassie as a young teen and an older, but strikingly similar-looking woman stood with an arm around her shoulders. 'Bright Future for Award-Winning Merthyr Writer'.

'I know who you are,' a woman's voice said behind him, the tone slightly lower than Cassie's, otherwise it could have been hers.

Danny turned, and found his suspicion confirmed. 'Mrs…Forde?'

'Jones, these days, Gwyn Jones. And you're Danny Reed? I try to keep up with the rugby. Gethin actively dislikes it; rugby was my first husband's thing. He's a football man.'

Danny held out his hand. 'Pleased to meet you.'

'Would you sit with me for a moment?' she asked, positioning herself on one of the two spare seats by the fireplace. 'I know why you're here.'

Danny perched on a chair; legs too large to fit beneath the small table.

'I expect as captain, you're checking out the pub to see if it's suitable for a team event on the 3rd? You needn't have come all this way. As you can see, it would be perfect.'

'It might be.'

'And you're being filmed by Hystar at the moment, I see, from the preview trailers on social media? I said to your PR lady that having their cameras here would be a great opportunity, for publicity – bit of coverage for us while you show that Camford travel well.'

It struck Danny how awkward this conversation must be for Gwyn, but Cassie had been defiant in wanting to keep the link to her closed. No doubt his background had tainted his view, but it had been increasingly difficult to see her miss the chance of having a parent back in her life. Perhaps this was an opportunity to bridge the gap, begin to mend their relationship?

He tested the possibility. 'But in truth, it's mainly to see your daughter?'

Gwyn fussed with the tidiness of some cardboard drinks mats. 'Yes, Cassie is my daughter. I'm sure you recognised her from television, before she joined you at Camford for the project.'

'I've got to know her well, although meeting you—'

'Is a surprise? Let me guess, she doesn't mention me often?'

Danny gave a non-committal shrug and took a sip of his drink.

'For various reasons, we no longer speak. I don't have her mobile number, do you?'

'Presumably the pub's phone number hasn't changed. She could contact you? I could pass her a message. Best I can do.'

'This…might be a lot to ask, but is she happy, and well, do you know?'

'She works hard, is good at what she does.' Was she happy with him? He wasn't as sure as he had been. Maybe he wasn't as important to her as she was to him, if the DNA betrayal was genuine.

'A shame she never made it as a writer. You saw the cutting? That was only one of several awards she won, she got put in a gifted writing programme at school.'

'She'd still like to write, I believe.'

Gwyn peered at Danny in the way that Trish sometimes did, almost seeing through him. Perhaps his tone had given him away.

'You know, there's a special box, tucked away upstairs, with stacks of little storybooks she wrote. It was lucky she enjoyed reading and writing so much, running a pub demanded long hours from me and her dad, rest his soul.'

Danny saw an opportunity. 'Maybe I could take her one, for old times' sake?'

'I'll go fetch one before you go. Some of my best memories are of her being so engrossed in whatever world she was in, she didn't notice I was there. Has she still got a sweet tooth? Something we never had in common, but I'd stuff her favourite sweets near my desk, knowing full well she'd be unable to resist them.'

It was enlightening, listening to the other side of Cassie's story. Gwyn seemed entirely lucid; no trace of alcoholism lingered, as far as he could tell. 'I'm sorry, for your loss, Cassie's father. A rugby man, too?'

'And a keen gardener. Quiet, despite his Irish blood. I've been off the booze for years, but I wasn't too good after he went – alcohol too easy to come by in a pub. I'm afraid Cassie might have taken the brunt of it.'

What did that mean? 'You still have the garden, though, that he set up?'

'Cassie mentioned to you that he set it up? Oh, that's good she has such a nice friend.'

Danny kicked himself, his first obvious slip. 'She did. Something about roses, and spending lots of time out there.'

'His sanctuary, needed it, from this place. Wasn't ever really his dream, was always mine.' Gwyn looked around the room, then over towards the bar. 'Got to be careful, mind, dreams don't always turn out as you'd imagined.'

'Gwyn! Need you back in here,' a woman called from a serving hatch that appeared to lead through to a kitchen.

'I should go, but I'll pop back. Don't leave without saying goodbye.'

'Alright.' Danny finished his drink and headed back to the bar.

'What food did you decide on?' said Gethin, while his staff rapidly unloaded glasses from a dishwasher behind the bar.

'I'll go for the soup and bread, and another pint of soda and lime.'

'Good choice. Some extra bread to go with that? Fella like yourself probably needs the carbs.'

No, Danny needed protein. 'Just the soup and cheesy bread, please. Is it busy like this all the time?'

'Pretty much, weekends especially. Knew it was a goldmine waiting to be properly run. Got my hands on it, one way or another.'

Danny had been about to unpick Gethin's comment when his phone pinged with a message.

CF: Hi baby, hope you slept well. Busy morning, but free in half an hour, if you're somewhere private ;) Miss you Cx

He thumbed in a holding text.

DR: Am out but need to talk. 3pm?
CF: 3pm good. Should I be worried? Where's my kiss? Cx
DR: We'll talk at 3pm
CF: Now officially worried

After getting a message to the kitchen, Danny waited at the bottom of a staircase, marked 'private', for Gwyn. Five minutes later she appeared, looking harassed.

'Sorry, last of the roast vegetables were coming out of the ovens. Can you hold on while I fetch something for Cassie?'

'Definitely.'

Another ten minutes passed, and Gwyn came back down the stairs, her face pink and blotchy. 'Here, a couple of my favourites.' She handed over a pair of booklets that looked exactly as Cassie had described.

'I'll make sure she gets them.'

'Would you tell her there isn't a day I don't think about her? I bet you couldn't imagine a mother telling her daughter never to come back, but it was for her own good.'

He registered the different take on Cassie having 'run away' from her mother, then squeezed Gwyn's hands. 'I will.'

'It was good to meet you, Danny. Hopefully the team can come here on the 3rd, make an occasion of it. We can block off that whole eating area, make it exclusive, like.'

And you could see your daughter.

'I'll speak to Trish, see what she thinks. What Cassie does is up to her.'

Gwyn's shoulders slumped. 'If you have any influence, can you encourage her to come?' A lone tear escaped and slid down the side of her nose. She caught it with a swipe of her finger in such a casual manner that Danny suspected she was used to it.

'These booklets will probably say more than I could.'

'Thank you. I need to go, but hopefully I'll see you all here in the new year. Meantime, have a good Christmas with your own family.'

'Are you closing for the holidays?'

'No chance, £180 per head on Christmas Day, same on Boxing Day. Gethin's favourite time of year.'

'Look after yourself,' he said, meaning it. Only now, in the better light, did the dark circles under her eyes show against unhealthily grey skin.

'You too,' she sniffed, as Danny headed to the garden for some air. After speaking with Cassie, he'd have another long drive ahead of him.

24. Greater Than Love

Cassie peered out of her hotel room at the skyline. Berlin hadn't changed much since the last time she'd visited. Or the time before that. The festive markets had been crammed with tourists buying souvenirs, and the hot glühwein still tasted disgusting. The cycling world had been rocked with doping allegations, and rumours of more had spread around the community, so she'd spent almost every spare minute tracking down and verifying comments, preparing herself for live race commentary each day. After existing on a diet of currywurst hotdogs, potato pancakes and late-night snacking on sweet, gingery lebkuchen, she'd probably need to have a serious reset once back in London. Last Christmas, spent in a similar hotel in Paris, had offered a useful, if exhausting, escape from a UK one. This year, for the first time in as long as she could remember, she really didn't want to be away, at all. Especially from Danny.

At five minutes to three, she slumped onto her hotel bed, anxious to speak to him after the brevity of his messages and the unexpected postponement of last night's video call. Given their lack of opportunity, she'd planned on making it a very naughty experience and would reveal the Mrs Claus outfit she'd already changed into, beneath her suit, at the right moment.

'Hi baby, good to see your face,' she said, squinting to make out the location of his garden background. 'Where are you?'

Danny held up his phone, which bore images of random wooden picnic benches, a rectangle of lawn and borders of bare-stemmed shrubs.

'Is that a pub garden? It must be freezing.'

'Take a closer look,' he said, so she studied harder, but the view was moving too quickly to get a fix on anything.

'No, sorry, I don't know what the pub gardens look like in Camford. Give me a view of the exit from the garden to the pub.' This game was beginning to irritate her, and where was the usual smile that lit her up? She waited while the direction swivelled and then…her blood ran cold.

'Know where I am now, baby?'

'Oh my God…what have you done?' she whispered, trying to gather herself. How in the hell had he come to be at Stumble Inn?

'Your mother rang Trish, inviting the team along the day after our Cardiff match. Quite the friendly chat they had, apparently.'

'She did what?'

'Yes, and that wasn't the only revelation that's got me thinking maybe there's another side to the story, not that you've so far trusted me with whatever happened.'

Cassie stared at Danny's face, his hurt firing through the screen at her.

'And guess what? She's sober, misses you, even keeps bragging newspaper cuttings about you on the pub wall.'

'It's not as simple as that, I can exp—'

'Don't you realise how lucky you are to have a family that cares for you?'

'Stop. You don't know what you're talking about.'

'How can I, if you don't share it? How many other things have you not told me about?'

Memories of events she kept safely locked away flashed before her eyes. Of trauma she'd yet to share with anyone.

'When and what I share has to be on my own terms, Danny, but—'

'Well I'm sorry you didn't feel you could trust me with it. I kind of feel like a fool for having dived head-on into to our relationship, it's like, I'm in the deep end, you're at the shallow, assuming you're actually even in?'

God, if Danny's expression wasn't painful enough, now he was doubting her love?

'I've shared so much, *so much* with you,' he continued, 'maybe that was—'

'You can trust me, Danny; I've never lied to you.'

He shook his head and laughed, and not in a good way. 'I've even admitted to you that I carry the thought that someday, my mother would come looking for me. Or are you waiting for my DNA results to come through on that so you can announce them on the docuseries?'

'What? No, of course not, I'd—'

'Sorry if I don't believe you.' The hitch in his voice brought a lump to her throat. What the hell had been going on in the past few hours?

'Baby, listen to me. My mother is an alcoholic—'

'She was, but she's still your mother. Don't you want to fix things? She seems willing to, from what she's said to me.'

'Oh really, and did she mention she threw a bottle at my head when we had a huge argument before I left for university and she told never to come back?' Cassie lifted her fringe, tears suspiciously close to springing from her eyes.

Danny's eyes widened, 'No, only that she has regrets. Is that where the scar is from?'

'Why, do you think I'm lying about that too? She's the reason why I rarely drink.' For her, alcoholism keyed into one of her biggest fears, that she'd similarly hurt those she loved.

A pair of dark, wary eyes bored through the screen. 'You could have just told me that, why wouldn't I believe you?'

'Because she didn't. And she said nobody would!'

'You aren't making sense. The evidence was there, on your head.'

Cassie put the phone down on the bed and paced the room. This whole conversation was headed towards disaster. Since Danny was still at the pub, goodness only knew what he'd do. She had to think fast.

'You're right. I guess the bottle incident scared me. Things were never the same after Dad died.'

'I can't understand why you haven't told me about this, though. You have *family*...' he stressed, words drifting off.

'There were times, while I was at university, that I'd been close to scraping together the price of a ticket home, but time went on, I was providing for myself, working all hours in between study. The distance became too far, too painful, too risky. I moved on.'

'Well, I'm sorry to tell you that she hasn't,' he said, holding up a few sheets of paper.

Cassie peered into the camera to identify them. The moment she realised what they were, tears chocked in her throat. 'My stories?'

'Only two, she still has more. And just so you know, yours is the exact same reaction she had when she gave these to me.'

Somehow, she'd imagined her mother had thrown away all evidence of having a daughter. The thought that she'd held onto those books was too much to take in. 'Stop it, please.'

'She asked me if you were happy, and whether I could persuade you to come to the pub with Camford.'

'You didn't tell her we're together?'

'No, only that I'd pass her message on. We didn't speak for long, she was busy serving Sunday roast with Gethin, her husband.'

Gethin got what he wanted, then. Cassie guarded her expression carefully.

Unfortunately, Danny knew her better. 'You didn't get along with him – as a replacement after your dad died?'

'Not particularly. And what did you mean about me using your DNA results for the series? You know I would never do that. It was a personal Christmas gift and nothing to do with work.'

'I don't know that anymore. Did Izzy not suggest the idea?'

'Yes, but I'd already thought of it myself, and bought the pack ready to give you.'

'Why can't I believe you?'

This was too much. Cassie sat down on the edge of the bed, struggling to see a way through the conversation that didn't result in Danny getting himself into trouble by turning on Gethin. Her exasperation was her undoing. 'Guess you and my mother have the same problem. I'd tell her over and over again what was happening to me behind her back, but would she believe me? No.'

An ugly silence hung between them. There it was.

'Tell me this isn't to do with Gethin.' Danny screwed his eyes at her, face like thunder as he awaited clarification.

Aghast at having revealed too much, she scrambled to end their conversation. 'Maybe we should speak later, when you're back in Camford?'

'I don't think so.'

'I love you, Danny, and except for this, I've completely trusted you. You know that, right?'

'Completely doesn't have exceptions. I've got to go.'

'Fine, but at least calm down before you drive.'

'I'm not getting in the car yet,' he said and ended the call.

Cassie's ears were ringing. Replaying their conversation worsened her growing suspicion that Danny might add things up correctly and act on them. Facing an impossible decision, she stared unseeingly out of the hotel room window, weighing up what mattered most. After a few, soul-searching minutes, she looked up a telephone number, and pressed the icon marked 'call'.

'Stumble Inn, *Shwmae*, how can I help you?'

Cassie swallowed slowly, uncertain whether the voice was the one she sought. 'Mum?'

Silence.

'Mum, is that you? I'm looking for Mrs Forde, or...Jones?'

'Cassie? I can't believe it...'

A female voice in the background was saying something like 'Gwyn, what's wrong, are you alright?'

'I'm fine, don't fuss,' she murmured, then must have moved the phone nearer to her mouth. 'Danny said he'd pass on my message; I'll thank him in a minute.'

It was odd hearing her mother's clipped tone, it didn't sound like the slurry one Cassie had stored in her memory. 'Danny's still there?'

'Yes, he and Gethin have gone outside to discuss something, Gethin's hoping it's a business opportunity that Danny's got in mind, should have seen his eyes light up.'

Not good, not good at all.

'I think Danny suspects something about Gethin's behaviour.'

'After all these years, you're still on about that, Cassie? Gethin wasn't ever doing anything to you. It was my fault that bottle slipped out of my hands and hit you, and me that sent you away to keep you safe from an alcoholic mother. Don't you think I've replayed it over and over, thousands of times?'

'No, not that, though I still have a scar. I mean Gethin pinning me against the cellar wall at every opportunity, jumping out from dark corners, threatening to ruin us if I didn't sleep with him? He's disgusting, Mum. I had to leave anyway, before something terrible happened and he took what he wanted from me.' Cassie switched her phone to her other hand, only now realising how hard she was shaking.

Her mother was still in denial. 'That whole period was a haze, but from what I remember, he told me you'd had a bit of a crush and exaggerated everything. You didn't realise it then but things like that sometimes happen with teenage girls and men in their thirties—'

'Mum, I swear to God, why do you think I did what you asked and cut communication?'

'Because of my drinking!'

Cassie sat down, feeling nauseous. All these years, and her mother still didn't get it. 'I can't believe you married him. He told me he'd do that, as a last resort if he couldn't get me.'

'No, that's not true, he didn't. And marrying him wasn't all bad, you should see the success he's made of the pub. Maybe not the garden, but that was your father's domain. We're so busy, I'm rarely out of the kitchen.'

'And how is that working for you, Mum? What's he doing while you're in there? Playing the big landlord like he always wanted, chasing teenage skirts?'

The lack of response gave Cassie a moment to take some deep breaths, to steer the conversation back to where it needed to be. 'Danny and I are together. Your call to Camford has shaken our relationship because I should have trusted that he, unlike you, would believe me about Gethin. One of the things I love about him is his protectiveness, he has my back, but it's why I have a feeling that he isn't speaking to Gethin about business. Can you go and check on them, please?'

'You're serious about all this?'

'Yes! Serious about what happened and worried what might be about to happen, if it's not already too late. Danny's opportunity to play for England would be over with an assault charge against him, probably his career at Camford, too. Please, please, if this is the only thing I ever ask for and you ever do for me, go and check.'

'Fine, stay on the line.'

The receiver clanged onto a surface and Cassie waited. And waited. And waited. Eventually she heard footsteps.

'Cassie?' her mother choked.

'I'm still here. Did you find them?'

'Yes, and I overheard some terrible things coming out of Gethin's mouth. It didn't help when he kept taunting Danny, by calling him boyo.'

'Oh my God, you need to get back there, or Danny will do something, I know it.'

'It's alright, they were behind the beer shed, and Danny was squaring up to Gethin when I arrived, but nothing physical happened. I sent Gethin upstairs.'

'He's hurt?'

'No, but he'd have deserved it, if what I overheard just now is true. He's threatening to call the police and get Nicky from the *Merthyr Observer* over to talk about verbal abuse, and suggest that ABH, or even GBH, might have been about to happen.'

That was it, then. Cassie had been the root cause of what could be the end of Danny's career. To think that most players expect their exits to be injury-related, or from aging. Not trial by media, or even worse, the justice system. 'You've got to speak to Gethin, do anything you can to stop him from reporting Danny. If necessary, I will use my media contacts to interview me about what happened when I was sixteen, seventeen, see how Gethin would like that affecting his local reputation.'

'I'll do what I can to calm him down. He doesn't usually listen to me but if it comes to it, I'll mention your media idea. Where are you?'

The personal question felt unfamiliar, but for Danny's sake, Cassie forced herself to answer.

'I'm in Berlin until the 28th, then on-air with Fox/Forde commitments until New Year's Eve.'

'Will you come here with the team on the 3rd of January?'

'I don't think it's appropriate that any of us come, and Danny obviously wouldn't want to see Gethin again.'

The phone went silent.

'Mum, are you still there?'

'Yes. Can we at least keep in touch? I can update you on what he says about Danny?'

Cassie wanted to refuse immediately, but still thinking of Danny's dreams, she read out her mobile number, waiting while it was repeated back.

'OK, got it. I'd better go and check on Gethin. I'm sorry all this happened. I'm sorry for so many things,' her mother whispered.

An ugly thought occurred to Cassie. 'Are you going to be safe?'

'I have my wits about me these days, been sober for three years, now. I'll be in touch, take care of yourself, Cassie.'

The line clicked.

Cassie burst into tears and in a state of panic she fumbled in her handbag and retrieved one of her beta blockers, swallowing it down fast. In a few seconds, she'd begin to feel calmer, but she couldn't wait any longer, before video calling Danny's number.

He answered immediately. 'He was threatening to abuse you?' he rasped, holding his forehead. 'For how long?'

'I'll book a flight home, walk out of my contract.'

Danny slammed his hand onto something hard. 'For fuck's sake, please answer me! How long did this go on for?'

'A year or two.'

He closed his eyes. 'You were a minor…that was coercion, if what he just said about persuading you to, to…If any of it was true – God, that's why you're jumpy sometimes, isn't it? Why couldn't you have just trusted me with this? Even some of it? The thought of someone threatening you or hurting you …Fuck, I'm talking myself down from going back in there.'

Danny's fists were out of shot but she sensed they were priming, ready to punish and dole out repercussions. 'I'll start packing, come home and we'll talk this through. Please don't go back in there, I've asked my mother to smooth over what just happened with Gethin. If nothing else, think about your career and the damage it would cause if this got out.'

'If *nothing else*? Someone harming you matters more than anything, including my career.'

Cassie caught her breath in dismay when Danny's shoulders slumped. After shaking his head to himself, he slowly levelled his eyes at hers, 'Maybe I've read us wrong. Maybe I shared too much, trusted you with my own past and hoped for the same from you. I should have remembered to keep my shield up, ready for this.'

A cold shiver ran through her as Danny seemed to turn inside himself, self-protecting against what he might feel as a haunting rejection of old.

'It's like a scrum, isn't it?' he muttered in a weirdly detached tone, 'if one of you isn't deemed good enough, or you aren't equally committed from both sides it collapses.'

This was sounding way too final. To her, this was a hurdle, not the end. 'I love you very much,' she whispered.

'Don't you know me at all? Trust is more important than love,' he said, 'I need to go.' and cut their call.

25. Fine

'How much longer, Martyn?'

'Since the last time you asked me? I'd say twenty minutes minus three minutes. Are you alright Cassie? We've driven this route to Camford a fair few times now.'

'Yes, I'm fine, sorry. I have a tricky one ahead of me today.'

'Tricky' would have to be the least appropriate adjective in her arsenal. Critical, high stakes, intense – any of those were nearer the mark.

Nine days had passed since Danny visited Stumble Inn. The last text she'd sent him, wishing him a Happy Christmas, had gone unanswered. When she wasn't working, or barely sleeping, Cassie had struggled with regret at having shown insufficient belief in their relationship and guilt over the potential threat to his reputation. But she'd also felt betrayed that Danny had gone to Wales, and distraught that he'd ever believe she would use his DNA results for Hystar's gain. And still she wanted him, to be with him, loved him. The way he'd cut communication had almost broken her, and had it not been for two tremendous women, she might have given up on him.

Heather, balancing the tightrope between loyalty to Ryn and Danny and the firm belief that Cassie shouldn't abandon the relationship, had reported covertly on how Danny was doing. He'd turned up on Christmas Day, stayed for the meal, but left early. Via Trish, Heather had mentioned that Danny was spending time in The Manor's grounds, sometimes with Norm. Ryn had checked in on him a couple of times, reporting moodiness and low spirits. Danny had apparently questioned his own professionalism, after having commented publicly on referees in the press conference and threatened Gethin. He'd also lashed out at Ryn, asking why he hadn't had his back by pointing out he'd never been good enough for Cassie in the first place. Good friend that he was, Ryn had resisted slogging Danny, in favour of suggesting he waited a bit longer before drawing false conclusions. Heather also reported that Danny hadn't wanted to hear her suggestion that the reasons for the way he was feeling was love, and because he'd had something special to lose. Nor could he see the part his action had played in the break-up. Several times, she'd implored him to look.

Trish had, however, given Cassie some good news. At the team briefing for Friday's upcoming fixture in Cardiff, Coach Alex had announced that Josh wanted to address the squad. Stood at the front of the media centre, Josh had apparently revealed that although Christmas had been a hectic but fun time for him and his family, he'd since struggled with his mental health. He'd assured the team that he was getting help, but encouraged everyone to speak to Doc, to the psychologists that Camford provided, or to each other if they were ever feeling low. Apparently, Trish had noted the way Josh and Ryn had concernedly taken Danny aside, and astutely included it in her conversation with Cassie. Mental health in sport, she'd proposed, could be the angle Hystar needed to bring depth to the whole docuseries.

Josh had agreed to an interview with Cassie to discuss the topic in depth, on the promise that it would provide the platform he wanted to build awareness of mental well-being struggles in rugby. And now, Cassie was on her way to The Manor to film it.

'Five minutes and we'll be there,' Martyn said, his usual helpful notice that triggered Cassie's quick check of her notes and a lipstick refresh.

'Thanks, we'll be filming over lunchtime, and I've asked the crew to do some pick-up shots of the grounds and buildings for extra intro and outro footage. I don't know what the plans are after that, but being New Year's Eve, I'm sure you have something organised back home?'

'I'm on the roster until 10pm, so we could say 8pm latest, leaving here? If you're thinking of later than that, remember the trains might be stopping earlier than usual.'

A fresh punch of regret slammed into her. Had she and Danny still been together, the evening ahead would look very different. As it was, she'd loosely agreed to join Fox and his friends for drinks at his local in Islington. 'We'll be off before 8pm, I'm certain, but I'll keep in touch.'

'Right-ho,' he said, being waved through The Manor's main gates by a security guard.

Cassie sought her phone, knowing she was only really looking for one thing. But there was nothing from Danny. He must know that she was on her way. Her stomach churned – maybe they could find some time together, start to pull things back?

What *had* arrived was a message from her mother, a fourth reach-out for general contact, as well as repeated assurance that all was still smoothed out with Gethin. Uppermost in Cassie's mind lay the threat of Gethin impacting Danny's career, but she had to admit, her mother was trying hard. Their brief exchange of messages at Christmas had been surprisingly emotional, when her mother had referred fondly to a particular Christmas play she'd watched at the school. Cassie had appreciated the sentiment, reminded also of Danny never having had that luxury in his own childhood. That he viewed the world through entirely different eyes. Today's message had been one of her dad's hilarious Irish sayings about New Year's Eve. It put a confidence-inducing smile on Cassie's face as she left the car. Today of all days, she really needed it.

At the main reception, Cassie was informed that Trish sent her apologies but would be delayed for fifteen minutes while finishing a conference call. With Fynn and Zac already signed in and gone ahead to set up their cameras in the media centre, now seemed as good a time as any for Cassie to stretch her legs.

The overcast day didn't detract from the buttery warmth of The Manor's stone, both in its building and the perimeter paths. Cassie set off on a route that she knew would be a ten-minute circuit, through the main topiary garden, into the rose garden that skirted the training fields, and back up past the gardening bothy. It was beautiful, and sad, passing the places she'd made memories with Danny.

A sudden whoosh in the gravel behind her made her jump, then turn.

Norm was pushing a barrow piled with garden tools. 'Hello Cassie,' he said, his friendly smile reminding her of the lovely people she'd met since being part of Camford's bubble.

'Hi Norm, need a hand with anything? Guess you're headed to the bothy?'

'No, no, you don't want to dirty those clothes. But I'm about to make a brew, if you'd like to join me?'

Cassie checked her watch. 'I wish I could, but I have to hit the timing of the players' lunch so that an interview with one of them doesn't interfere with training.'

'Next time, maybe?'

'I...don't think I'll be here for a long time, unfortunately.'

Norm shook his head. 'Forgive me if I'm overstepping, but you're also the person who likes "white roses" aren't you?'

Cassie's breath caught, but she managed to mumble, 'Yes, but I messed up.'

'I'm sorry to hear that. There was a spark between you and Danny way back on his debut match, Trish and I both noticed it at the time. Since I've known him, his default has always been self-reliance; it seemed to me that meeting you breathed a bit of light into his life. This season he's shown a different type of drive than previously, more fulfilled, maybe.'

Cassie had to look away.

'Either way, it's been good to meet you, and if you're in the area, pop in. I'll clear it at the front gate.'

'Thanks,' she croaked, then to her dismay heard the distinctive chatter of forty or so low rumbling voices, headed from the training pitches up the path on their way to lunch. 'I've got to get to the media centre to prep, but I hope to see you again, one day.' She took a couple of steps then turned back. 'Norm? Look after him, he thinks he's the tough guy but inside, he's—' She couldn't finish what she'd wanted to say, but his eyes had misted with understanding, anyway.

'Don't worry, we will.'

At the media centre, Trish was her usual multi-tasking self, but still welcomed Cassie with the perfect combination of professionalism and friendliness.

If only Cassie had chosen Trish instead of Izzy as a role model two years ago.

'Hello, Cassie, I won't ask how your Christmas was, same as I haven't directly asked Danny why he's retreating back into his shell.'

'Thanks, how was yours?'

'Better than expected, actually, but I'm also loving being back.'

Hopefully, she and Norm had found some time for each other.

'I'm glad for you. Can I just say again that as far as the series goes, I'm grateful for your quick thinking after Josh's words to the team about mental health. It's exactly what followers of rugby will be interested in, and steered Izzy away from asking for more sensational content that in my opinion crosses privacy lines.'

'Definitely. I'd said to Danny how ridiculous she'd been, even asking you to scope out his DNA. I mean, how was that anything to do with the game? It's a violation.'

A heavy weight clunked into place.

'What have I said?' Trish asked, cocking her head at Cassie.

'I know that was from a good place, it's just – I'd already bought a testing kit for Danny, before Izzy mentioned it. It was one of his Christmas gifts – I thought he'd be interested, to help him with identity and background. Of course, I didn't give Izzy the satisfaction of saying so. Nor would I ever, ever have used it for the series.'

'Oh my goodness, that wasn't my intention, I was just worried about you, as was he.'

'It's done and wasn't the root cause of how things fell apart.' The doors at the back of the room clattered open, saving Cassie from elaboration.

'Well, if it isn't the two most important people in Camford,' Josh chortled as he bounced down the steps towards her and Trish. To everyone's amusement, he veered off to bring Zac then Fynn into tight, bear-hugged greetings. 'Good to see you, boys. And here are two more special people,' he smiled, shaking hands with Cassie then bringing Trish in for an air kiss. 'Cassie, Patricia.'

'Ooh, are you in trouble? He's going for your full name, today,' Cassie mumbled.

'No, we just have an understanding, don't we, Josh?'

He pulled a sheepish face, making Cassie giggle. 'We do. I'm to call her Patricia when we're out of earshot of the rest of the lads, because I'm the one who gave her—'

'Saddled me with—'

'*Saddled* her with the nickname Trish – which, in my defence, only came about because when she joined us, our then head of physio was Pat, and that might have been confusing. You didn't look like a Patty or a Tricia, so I went with Trish. Unfortunately it turned out that wasn't exactly her favourite.'

'I used to hate it, but it's shorter than Patricia, I'll give you that. Everyone uses it now.'

'Except for me.'

'Except for you.'

And Norm, Cassie remembered. She grinned, envious of the history and family that filled Camford's culture.

Josh cleared his throat. 'Time's-a-ticking, let's get this interview filmed, shall we? You've seen my ideas for discussion that I sent to Patricia?'

Cassie nodded. 'Yes, and I'll tie them in with the latest thinking on mental health in athletes that Sport England have published. I'm meeting with a representative from Mind next week, who are interested in contributing, too.'

Josh clapped his hands together. 'Fantastic, where do you want me?'

An hour later, Cassie brought the filming to a close. She immediately recognised the quality of the content; it would facilitate discussion about mental health in rugby and other sports, and it would certainly show off Camford's provision for its players and staff. She and Izzy would hinge Hystar's marketing for the series on the subject.

Everyone, including Zac and Fynn, was chuckling over Josh recounting the chaos of having three kids under seven on Christmas Day in his house. He'd just made everyone holler with an animated retelling of how he might have broken his little toe on his daughter's new 'balance-ball thing', when Danny appeared through the door at the top of the auditorium and trotted down the stairs.

The exact moment Cassie saw him, she held her breath.

'Not a serious interview then?' he said, as his steely face found hers.

She blinked at him, a fusion of regret and attraction consuming her thoughts. Hope was in there too.

'Hello Danny,' said Trish. 'And good morning to you. The interview went well, thank you. Obviously, it's subject to whatever editing Hystar decide on, but it was in-depth and relatable even to non-sportspeople.' She turned to Cassie and discreetly nudged her. 'Is there anything else you need on this?'

Everyone turned, expectant. Nothing came. She sought her crew's faces, willing them to step in.

'Erm, maybe some pick-up shots of Josh, rejoining the training outside by the pitches?' Zac suggested.

Cassie scraped together some professionalism. 'Good, yes, that's a good idea, thanks…but before that, Danny, did you want to add anything for the series about this issue, from a captain's perspective?'

He shrugged his shoulders. 'What do you think, Trish, would it be of value?' he asked.

'Yes, I think so, from the perspective of the club's pastoral care, maybe from your own leadership or personal view, too.'

Danny checked his phone. 'I have a meeting with the coaches in twenty-five minutes, but I could do something now. Then presumably after you've got what you need with Josh up at the pitch, we're finally finished with this whole thing?'

'Oof,' Fynn muttered to Zac, 'thanks for nothing.'

Trish tutted and turned to Cassie. 'It's been a dream working with you and your crew. I'll be saying so to Izzy. Danny, take a seat, best get your "ordeal" over with.'

While Danny shot a look at Trish, Cassie slid a hand into her bag, retrieved a tablet and swallowed it down. She couldn't finish the job with a galloping heart.

When she took her position, ready, he was glaring at her.

'Look, if you'd rather not do this, Danny?'

'Are you okay? Which tablet was that?' He frowned, speaking quietly enough not to draw attention from the others.

She took a steadying breath. 'I'm thinking we could splice this onto Josh's interview, in which case perhaps you could begin by talking about the words he said to you all after Christmas?'

'Cassie, please answer me.'

'And that clip would lead into a mention of the club's perspective and whatever you'd like to add from your own experience?'

Danny sat motionless, ignoring her suggestion.

To avoid answering his, she busied herself with fussing over the angle of the sound equipment, much to Zac's confusion.

'Fine, let's do it,' Danny said, adopting his post-match interview tone.

Pulse rate thankfully returning to normal, Cassie took him through a series of questions and requests for examples. He spoke of Camford's rugby family and the significance of Josh reminding everyone to look out for one another. He referred to his own journey during his academy years, when he hadn't befriended many people, therefore hadn't shared any issues. He'd found it difficult to rely on others back then, but contrasted it with the current season. Since becoming captain, which had necessitated keeping an eye on his teammates, he hoped to become someone they could rely upon and trust.

The hairs on Cassie's neck prickled. This was dynamite footage, but she knew he wasn't only talking about rugby. He was still hurting, still angry. But so was she.

'OK, thank you, that was great. Boys, let's reset up at the training pitches. How long do you need?'

Zac and Fynn conferred. 'Fifteen minutes. It's dry so we can wheel this equipment up there without any problems.'

'Josh, how about you and I show the boys which pitch you're headed to?' said Trish, casting Cassie a meaningful glance.

'Forwards are on two, backs are on three, today,' said Danny, shaking hands contritely with Zac and Fynn. 'Good working with you two.'

Until the crew, Trish and Josh had left, Danny occupied himself with straightening chairs and Cassie slotted her own IT equipment back into her carry case. Eventually, they were alone.

'Your interview will add weight to the subject of mental health in sport, thank you for that. Do you have any questions?'

'Not about work. I guess I wanted to check how you are.'

Cassie was shocked by the cold distance in his voice. 'I'm fine. How are you?' She buttoned her jacket, preparing to head for the training pitch as soon as possible. What she'd have given for one of his big bear hugs. To hear that he'd thought things through and wanted to save their relationship.

'Also fine,' he said, crossing his arms.

She closed her eyes for a few seconds, wondering whether, if given more time, he'd say more and turn the conversation into something more fruitful. She waited an extra beat, but he just stood there.

'Good, well, if that's everything?' she offered, still hoping it wasn't.

'No, it isn't everything. Being apart hasn't stopped me worrying about how stressed you are, what medication you're needing and whether you're safe and happy, Cassie, despite what you might think. You're on my mind the whole fucking time. Even if you weren't, having Norm grab me by the collar on the way up from training, suggesting that I have a "hard think", or Trish serving me cold side-eye every time she sees you and I within twenty metres of each other, is messing with my head.'

Cassie picked up her bags, mustering some calm. Whether against his wishes or not, it seemed she was in his head, as much as he was in hers. But he still needed space to work it out. Maybe the few years of experience she had on him were showing. 'They care about you. As do I.'

Danny sighed, then checked his phone. 'Coach Alex is expecting me.'

'You'd better go then. Have a good New Year's Eve tonight, whatever you're doing.'

'How will you be celebrating?'

'I've said I'll meet F...friends for drinks.'

'You were going to say Fox, weren't you?' Those dark eyes held hers. So he didn't want anyone else having her, then?

'Not that it's your business but yes, Fox and his friends invited me out. I only accepted because the man I really wanted to spend it with can't seem to move forwards.'

Danny studied his trainers and muttered some profanity or other under his breath. 'I suppose Fox knew about...your past?'

'Only that I had a difficult relationship with my mother, nothing else. Less than you know.'

He nodded, but when he added nothing further, she filled the frustrating silence.

'But you know what? He accepts that mothers come in all forms – his older sister has been like a mother to him. Yes, some people are lucky and have a lifetime of unconditional love from theirs, but others have inconsistent, or neglectful care, some might be loved by women who weren't their birth mothers, and a few are tragically abandoned by theirs. Mothers aren't all perfect and guess what? Neither are we. That's the reality of life, I thought you'd understand that.'

For a few seconds they stared at one another, perhaps waiting for the other to make a move. If she'd caught his face in her hands, he'd have kissed her, she was sure of it, but he had to realise her worth, their worth.

Instead of a heartfelt, reconciliatory four-minute kiss, she thrust out her hand for professional goodbye. 'Good luck in January, it will be a busy month, especially training with the England squad.'

He glared at it, then stalked up the stairs, two at a time. The sound of the door slamming echoed around the auditorium.

26. Departure

'Medium close-up Fox/Forde, close up on Cassie, and...cue Cassie.'

'Thank you, and of course Kelly will be giving live updates to Hystar-Sport-dot-com from the province of Gangwon, in the Republic of Korea, during February's curling and bobsleigh competitions. On Friday we will cover the results in our round up of Team GB's performance at the Winter Youth Olympic Games.'

'Close up on Fox.'

'Yes, and we'll also bring you coverage of this week's sport, including the World Darts Championship—'

'Fox, England Rugby's team announcement autocue change.'

'And All-Weather Horse Racing from Lingfield, but before we leave you, there's time for some breaking news from England Rugby. Head Coach Luke Barford has taken the unusual step of announcing his team five days ahead of Saturday 7th February's match against Wales at Twickenham.'

'Team Graphic 1.'

'As we can see, he's retained the expected backbone of experience from England forwards, and several familiar faces in the backs keep their shirts, but he's shaking things up by giving first caps to Camford

Rugby duo Danny Reed for fly-half, wearing 10, and a surprise call-up for Connor Wilson as scrum-half, wearing 9.'

'Medium Close-up Fox/Forde, fill thirty seconds to credits.'

'That's a strong team Luke Barford has named, and there will be celebrations tonight back in Cambridgeshire for the Camford team. Cassie?'

'Er, yes, I'm sure there will be. Congratulations to all players named, and Hystar-Sports-dot-com will of course bring you news of the Wales team once it's announced, as well as those for the Ireland–France fixture taking place in Paris. We'll be discussing the selections here on Friday, ahead of the matches.'

'Until then, that's a Hystar High Five.'

'Close up on Cass.'

'I'm Cassie Forde.'

'Close up on Fox.'

'And I'm Fox Cavalier.'

'Medium close up.'

'Thank you for joining us.'

'Until next time, goodbye.'

'Goodbye.'

'Roll credits.'

'Wide studio angle.'

'Fade to black.'

'Well done everyone.'

Fox removed his earpiece. 'I was giving you an easy-in to promote the second episode of your docuseries airing tomorrow night,' he grumbled. 'Thought you'd realise.'

Cassie knew that was coming. 'I did, but too late. Sorry. There are only six weeks of Fox/Forde left in this contract. Izzy won't pull us off air before that.'

'What is England rugby playing at, releasing the team on a Monday night? Bloody hate last-second changes to the autocue.'

'Me too, but you're very smooth with them, these days.'

'Yeah, it's getting easier, feel like I'm hitting my stride. What are you doing now, dinner with me and a couple of mates if you're free?'

'Can't tonight, I'm fried.'

Someone nearby cleared their throat politely. 'Excuse me, both of you, Izzy would like to see you in her office for a quick meeting,' Ella, the runner, said.

Cassie glanced at Fox. 'Just what we need. See you in ten?'

'I'll knock for you.'

At her dressing room mirror, Cassie's thoughts returned to Danny's news. The team selection had thrown her, choking her usual ability to fill seconds of airtime with Fox, and instead filled her mind with immense joy and pride that Danny would realise his dream on Saturday. She hadn't wrecked his chances, then. And Connor being called up, too. No doubt Camford's winning form and the way he and Danny's playbook had clicked had been at the root of that. How Danny felt about Connor's call-up might be another matter entirely. She pulled out her phone, composed, edited and seriously overthought a text message to him, before hitting the send button.

CF: January went fast, congrats on selection. Good luck on Saturday C

On the off-chance of an immediate reply, she waited for a response to appear, but it did not.

Instead, Fox's knock on her door took them upstairs.

'Come in, sit down, this won't take long,' said Izzy. 'First of all, apologies that I missed this evening's Fox/Forde episode, I was held up talking with the board. All OK?'

Cassie took a seat, noting Izzy's heightened colour when her eyes met Fox's. He, on the other hand, didn't flinch. She was proud of him and how confidently he'd finally emerged from the affair.

'Yes,' he said, 'all was fine, handled some late news from England Rugby. We're back in tomorrow morning to film some segments for Friday's show.'

'Excellent, and speaking of rugby, Cassie, the board is very pleased with the viewing figures and critic reviews of the first episode of *Camford: Inside Rugby*. Congratulations.'

'Thank you, I'm proud of how it turned out, but the crew's contribution is important.'

'Indeed, but it's your content and production that's caught the board's eye. There's talk that it might be nominated for a Broadcast Sport Award, even a BAFTA, given its wider reach to non-traditional audiences for rugby programmes.'

'Congratulations Cass,' said Fox, and, correctly picking up on Cassie's body language, added, 'You should do more of those docuseries, you've often said they hold more appeal to you than live television.'

Izzy shifted in her seat. 'I think we'd be open to more of them, if you're interested. Whether that's full time or not is something we can discuss after the current Fox/Forde contract finishes.'

Cassie's shoulders felt immediately lighter.

'That leads me to you, Fox. Strictly on the QT, I've heard that one of the cricket commentary team will be leaving us in April. Initially, at least, it will leave Hystar one short in the box for the summer series coverage of tests, one day internationals and Twenty20 internationals here in the UK. Am I right in thinking you'd like to be put forward for those?'

Fox didn't immediately respond.

'I think you've temporarily stunned him into silence,' said Cassie, hugely pleased for him.

'No, I mean – yes, I do want to join that team. Definitely.' He beamed.

Izzy leaned back in her chair, her expression not quite coming off as satisfied – more relief, if anything.

No wonder; if her affair with him ever got out, she could be in trouble for abuse of power. She knew it, so did Fox and Cassie.

'I always knew you'd both succeed.'

Fox was no doubt trying equally as hard as Cassie to not react to Izzy taking more credit than she deserved.

Izzy stuttered to fill the silence, 'I-I-I will add, though, that these opportunities are earned solely on merit, there's no favouritism – or anything *else* – on my part.'

'Understood, thank you,' said Fox, wisely stopping at that.

Cassie saw a small window of opportunity. 'When we meet, I'd also like to discuss a different project, something that would run concurrently with producing more docuseries.'

'As long as you're not leaving Hystar, I'll certainly consider it.'

After a morning of filming the following day, Cassie poked some paper towel into the neck of her blouse and jacket and opened up her salad bowl. With one final segment slated for filming, she wouldn't want to cause continuity issues by having to change out of her suit. Even with the material being red, marks would show up on camera. She used her other hand to check her phone. With no reply from Danny, she instead thought of Trish Murphy and how they ought to fix a date to get together.

'Hey stranger, how are you?' Trish answered, her easy tone belying what Cassie knew to be a role resembling a juggling act.

'I'm OK, how are you? It would be good to meet up sometime soon, I'm hoping to have some good news to share on the job front.'

'About time, let me check the diary, see when I'm next in London, and I'll message you – unless you're headed our way for...anything?'

Cassie skipped over the subtle enquiry. 'Most likely London would be better, but have you seen the reviews for the docuseries? It's getting some serious attention within Hystar.'

'I have. My phone's hotter than ever, plus of course we've now lost two players to national duties for England Rugby at the Six Nations.'

'Yes, I saw Connor also got a call-up alongside Danny. It speaks highly of Camford's coaching as well as them as individuals.'

'It does, they're on fire in the Premiership. Have you, er, heard from any of the players?'

Cassie smiled into her phone. 'No, I thought it was good to have some space through January. Luke Barford is probably putting the England squad through their paces as we speak.'

The phone went ominously quiet.

'Trish, did you hear me?'

'I don't want to overstep, but I know for sure that Danny isn't at camp today. He's taken the afternoon off, for a funeral.'

A piece of chicken dropped from Cassie's fork. 'Who's died?' Her first thought was please, *please* make it not be Laura Reed.

'One of the kids at the hospital – Woody, do you remember him? We met his dad, Richard?'

That was just as bad.

'Where is the funeral, do you know?'

'I believe it's in the family's hometown, the Chairman's PA was telling me – Colchester, yes that's it. Awful thing, funerals for children.'

And a funeral for a child of the foster care system, despite having found an adoring adoptive parent, seemed all the more tragic.

Cassie checked the time. 'I need to go, but let me know a date when you're free?'

'Will do, see you.'

Without thinking twice, Cassie tapped into her phone, searching for the information she needed. A brief telephone call to Colchester Crematorium confirmed the funeral for Woody Thurston would be the last of the day, at 4pm. She dialled down to the basement garage.

'Drivers.'

'Martyn? Oh good, are you free this afternoon, and if so, do you think it's doable to get to Colchester by 4pm?'

'Yes, although we've only got the limo available, and yes, but it's a good couple of hours, Cassie, we'd need to leave – well, now really.'

'I'll be down as quickly as possible, thank you.'

'I'll bring the car around the front.'

'Ten minutes, we're going to make it, there's the sign to the crematorium ahead,' said Martyn.

'Can we find somewhere to park that doesn't draw attention to the car? I don't want people thinking we're part of the funeral convoy.'

'Of course.'

Cassie had filled an angst-ridden two-hour journey with back-and-forth messaging with Fox, thanking him for filming that afternoon's segment without her. The decision of leaving him to handle any fallout, compared with her not supporting Danny at the crematorium, had been an easy one.

'Two minutes Cassie, although if you don't mind me saying, there could be a problem,' said Martyn as he pulled into a parking space behind an outbuilding.

'What's the issue?'

'You're wearing a bright red suit.'

'Oh shit, oh shitty shit,' she muttered, racking her head for a solution. White t-shirt under jacket? No, she'd freeze, and her trousers were still red. She even eyed Martyn's suit but realised that couldn't work unless he were prepared to sit in the car in his underwear. 'Coat! Please tell me you have a coat in the boot?'

'I do, I'll fetch it.'

Two minutes later, her suit thankfully covered by an oversized, but almost full length on her, coat, she could have kissed him. 'That will have to do, I can roll up the trousers. Oh, but I can't wear these ridiculous red heels in there, can I?'

'You might not have a choice.'

'There's always a choice,' she said, wincing as her feet, protected only by thin nylon knee-highs, touched cold tarmac.

'I'll be here when you're ready,' he said, taking her shoes.

The crematorium was half full; people had positioned themselves away from one another in couples or sat alone. On the right-hand side, four rows from the front, Cassie spotted Danny's unmistakable shoulders, his upright posture unwavering. She pulled the coat tighter and tiptoed down the aisle, grateful for the carpet beneath her, dreading the reunion, and the funeral itself.

'Hello,' she whispered, standing at the end of his row of chairs.

In slow motion, Danny turned his head, seemed to register her but turned back and continued to focus straight ahead.

Cassie slid into a place on the empty seat beside him, taking care to keep herself covered. 'I'm sorry about Woody, he was a great kid.'

Now, he nodded then briefly bowed his head, as if collecting himself.

Whispers of 'that's Danny Reed' and of her own name swished in the air so, like him, she adopted a carefully composed demeanour. Within a minute or two, piped music began and the congregation were asked to stand. In his smart Camford suit and polished black shoes, standing tall and solid beside her, Danny was the epitome of strength. Inside, she knew, lay a different story.

After the officiant lead the service through readings, Woody's father, Richard, rose to address everyone. His anguished face revealed obvious torture, but he blew his nose and made two attempts before speaking. 'Debs and I thank you for being here. You all know how hard and bravely Woody fought, well, he's at peace now. No more suffering. He had a tough start, in care, and came to us fuelled by distrust and self-preservation, but as soon as we fostered him, we wanted to become his family and, once adopted, have him as our son. There are a lot of dads and a lot of sons in the world, but this lad, my son, was my world. People make mistakes, we're human, and parents aren't exceptions from that. But kids learn what they see, and we hope that Woody saw that as long as you try, and keep showing up, that is the best anyone can do. Erm, some of you I know have brought things to go with him today, thank you.' Richard almost collapsed into his seat.

Around Cassie, many people sniffed, and she too stemmed a flow of hot tears with Martyn's coat sleeve.

Beside her, Danny was stoic, his emotions contained. 'Excuse me,' he muttered, then stood to pass in front of her, ready to join the short queue of people who were placing individual flowers and other small items on Woody's coffin. When he reached the front, he pulled two items out of his suit jacket pockets: a tiny Camford rugby ball and his old plastic torch.

More tears choked at her throat as she recognised its significance.

Danny tapped the casket, uttered a few words and came back to his seat. Only someone sat next to him would have seen that his hands were trembling, and how tense his whole body had become.

She slid her hand into his and squeezed it. He didn't squeeze it back, but he didn't release it either.

As the family led the congregation outside towards the crematorium's gardens, Cassie released Danny's hand but led him past the wreaths and bouquets laid in Woody's name.

At one point, Danny wordlessly tugged her arm, a request to pause at the small red and white arrangement impressively shaped into a rugby ball, from the Chairman of Camford Rugby and its players.

A few moments later, they were in a line waiting to speak to Richard and his family. Her preparation of something to say was distracted by a sharp squeeze of her hand. Through damp lashes, she peered up at Danny's face and realised he was only just holding himself together. But now it was their turn to speak to Richard.

'Danny – and Cassie, thank you both for coming.' He clutched Danny's shoulder. 'You know, Woody loved your visits, they really kept him going. He'd store up things to tell you about for next time.'

Danny cleared his throat. 'I'm very sorry for your loss, he was a brave and positive lad, despite his circumstances.'

'He was, and we've spoken before about your common background. And Cassie, he had massive bragging rights with his friends after you visited. As you're here, can I also thank you for the donation towards the onsite parent support hostel? I have no doubt you had a hand in Hystar's generous commitment. Sadly there are plenty of others behind me that will come to depend on it, just as I did.'

'You're welcome, and I am so sorry for your loss.' She bent forwards to give Richard a brief hug, but a flash of red revealed itself between the edges of the coat. 'Apologies, I hot-footed straight from the studio, and am headed back there now.'

'Don't be, Woody would have loved seeing you in Camford Crimson. Look after yourselves.'

'You too.'

Following a conveyer belt of mourners, Cassie and Danny turned the corner to be met by clusters of people in quiet conversation. Almost immediately, individuals approached them, wanting to shake hands, and ask questions about Camford and England Rugby. For several minutes, they answered politely. While fending off questions about life in front of the camera and concern about what had happened to her shoes, Cassie became aware that beside her, Danny's responses had become almost monosyllabic. Time to make their excuses.

'Who would wear a red suit to a funeral?' someone hissed behind them. 'And no shoes!'

Cassie shrugged off the comment, but Danny must have overheard it too, and turned.

'Someone who wanted to be here *despite* knowing that people might only comment on her clothes,' he said, irritably.

'I think that's our cue, excuse us,' she suggested, gesturing towards a pergola walkway that led to the carpark. Thanks to her presenting skills, Cassie could make small talk last for minutes at a time with strangers, but she sensed that Danny's limits were about to unravel. They walked in silence but hadn't got far when it began to rain.

'Where's your car?' he asked. 'Your feet are getting wet.'

'Behind that building, Martyn's driven me.'

'I'll walk you over.'

'You don't need—'

'Please don't fight me, I'll walk you over. Or I'll carry you.'

'Walking is fine.' She gave him a half-smile as she picked her way around a puddle.

At the car, Martyn jumped out and came towards them holding Cassie's shoes. 'Danny, good to see you, despite the circumstances.'

'Martyn.'

This surely wasn't going to be it? Cassie wanted a few moments with Danny in private, and not for her own sake. She flicked her eyes at her driver.

'Mind if I pop across the road to grab a coffee to go for the journey back?' he said, reading her correctly.

'Thank you, maybe I'll message you?'

'Righto.' He popped up a telescopic umbrella and headed in the direction of the crematorium's exit road. Cassie envisaged he'd be at least thirty minutes, even if he were served straight away.

'Thank you for coming,' Danny said hoarsely, sweeping a hand through his increasingly damp hair.

'I only found out about it at lunchtime, when Trish mentioned you weren't at the England camp.'

'I'll be back there this evening.'

'It's going well, with the squad?'

'Is that an official question? Sorry, that wasn't…I don't know what I'm…Yes, it's going well. I'm rooming with Connor.'

'After the punch-up at The Manor's bar, that can't be comfortable. Heather told me, who'd been told by Ryn.'

Danny merely shrugged. Maybe this wasn't a day for conversation, but he needed to release the valve somehow.

'You know you don't have to be strong all the time?'

He turned his face away.

'For God's sake, come and sit with me for a moment, at least it'll be dry in the car.' She opened the door of the backseat and slid herself well inside, leaving him little choice but to join her. To her relief, he did, and pulled the door closed, but then sat staring through the privacy screen.

Enough. One of them had to make the first move.

'Eight second hug?' she offered.

After a few stilted breaths he crumpled, wrapping his arms around her as she slipped hers inside his jacket. Eight seconds of holding each other went way over time, but when Cassie began to pull away, he kept her close, almost clinging. 'Such a waste,' he croaked.

She squeezed his shoulders. 'Let it out,' she whispered and gently rocked him.

He buried his face into her neck and wept.

Slowly, Danny recovered. Keeping his eyes on hers, he swiped a hand over his face, then stilled. Cassie took her opportunity. 'I've missed you, and I'm sorry about everything,' she said. 'You've no idea how much.'

'Cassie,' he rasped, then, with longing in his eyes, darted a hand around the back of her head and brought her mouth to his. Soft, familiar warmth spilled through her, but deciphering his kiss stunted her reaction, and before she could engage, he pulled back.

'Sorry, not sure what I'm doing. It's the funeral, seeing you.'

'It's alright.'

'No, it isn't.' He leaned back against the seat and straightened the lapels of his jacket. 'And you have to get back to the studio, don't you?'

'Yes, but if you—'

Something flickered across Danny's face. 'Whose coat is that?'

'Not that you'd have the right to say anything, but it's Martyn's. There's no one else in here, believe me,' she said, patting her chest.

He swallowed hard and nodded, looking disappointed with himself. 'I appreciate you coming today, given everything.'

'Well, I wanted to pay my respects, but my first thought was of you. Something to think on; if people turn up for you, there's a reason for it.'

He nodded again, closing his eyes briefly. 'I have to get going, there's a gym session in camp at 6pm.'

'Good luck on Saturday, I'll be at Twickenham, cheering on from the—'

'Not from our friends and family seats?'

Cassie swallowed the sting – only the funeral and the pressure ahead of him prevented her barbed response. 'I'd kind of stick out in my Wales shirt, don't you think? No, I've called in a Hystar perk; although I'm not filming, I have a window seat in the media booth reserved.'

'OK, good. I'd better go, thanks again for…everything, it means…' His tortured look was almost her undoing, but he closed the door behind him and jogged away in the rain.

'That I still love you,' she finished for him.

27. Red v White

'The ball's going to jiggle out of my hands during the match. Why isn't there a toilet on this bus?'

'You'll be fine, Connor, you know we're almost at Twickenham, it's the same thirty-minute journey from the training camp as yesterday when we practised, and the day before,' said Danny. 'Not that I don't feel like chucking up my porridge.'

'West London is a long way from Camford, that's for fucking sure.'

Outside the windows, motorbike escorts accompanied the England team's bus as it approached Twickenham's famous iron gates. Thousands of fans in replica shirts waved and cheered, more than likely unable to make out his or any other players' face through the blacked-out windows. A good number of Wales supporters also watched on, biding their time for when their team's players arrived. Metre by metre, the driver took the bus to its standing point at the beginning of the player's welcome tunnel, which was lined hundreds deep with well-wishers of all ages.

'Ready lads, let's go, new caps Danny and Connor first,' Coach Luke yelled from the front. 'See you all in the changing room for warm-up in fifteen minutes.'

Danny knew the drill. Headphones on, eyes forward, wave and smile, one foot in front of the other.

Today, at least, he didn't have captain duties on his shoulders. 'Ready?' he asked Connor.

'No, you?'

'No.'

They exchanged nervous smiles, unlikely friends in a team made up of players from other clubs within the Premiership. Allocated to share a room during the England camp, the pair of them had to rub along. To Danny's surprise, Connor had dialled down his snarky behaviour, off the pitch at least, and privately, often mentioned his girlfriend Naomi, whom he was determined to introduce to Danny at the end of today's match. Whether she'd played a hand in the change to Connor's attitude, Danny couldn't know. Even so, conversation with Connor had been cautious, any subject that would bring up their drink-spiking altercation carefully avoided. Until, that was, when that morning's media had run a story about Axminster Rugby suspending two of their players, related to historical cases of drink spiking while on tour.

Before they'd boarded the bus, Danny had pulled Connor aside. 'Do you know something about this story?'

'Yes, pair of wankers those two.'

'How exactly did the information get to the coaches?'

'I hadn't wanted to say anything to you, but I got a call from Fox Cavalier, asking for my help. He had a friend of his girlfriend, who works for *The Daily News*, quietly investigate a 'celebrity spiking incident' relating to rugby, and that trail led them to events on tour at Axminster.'

Fox's girlfriend? There'd been someone following this up?

'Anyway, he knew I used to play there and, after your reaction about Cassie's incident, which despite what you think, I hadn't known about, I agreed to draw out information from ex-colleagues on likely culprits and pointed Fox in a certain direction. Eventually he got back to me and off the record, I confirmed what I knew. I understand the police took over after that, got a search warrant.'

'Bloody hell. You've done good.' He'd shaken Connor's hand, and would reach out to Fox, after the match, to thank him personally for chasing down the likely identity of, and consequences for, whoever spiked Cassie's drink.

Cassie. For Danny, January had been a day-at-a-time existence, a diet of rugby, training, nutrition and rest – and thinking of her. How much he missed her, cared about her and regretted some of his behaviour. The words from his team bio, 'a competitive perfectionist', that she'd once teased him with, haunted him; no one was perfect, least of all him. He'd wasted two chances to admit to his stupidity in ending their relationship: Josh's filming on New Year's Eve, then four days ago at the funeral. How many more would he have? Maybe it was already too late; he'd certainly left her with that impression on Tuesday.

Warm-up had gone as planned, the same familiar routines. This was not the time to change anything. Now, the players had five minutes to change into their match kit.

Like everyone else, Danny pulled out his phone and took a picture of their England shirts hung on each individual player's changing peg. He sent a picture of the 'Reed 10' on the back of his shirt to Ryn and Josh, with a quick message wishing them good luck in Camford's match that afternoon in North London. He also sent it to Norm, and to Trish, who responded simultaneously with messages of support, and then to both of his cousins.

As was Danny's standard process, he pulled up some all-essential images to keep in mind when steadying himself for goal kicking. His fingers hovered over a picture of Cassie, taken during their early Christmas weekend. Her face was flushed, her hair dishevelled from his fingers, and he'd taken the picture because of the way she was looking at him. She'd said she felt loved, and safe. Words he now knew carried weight. For a few seconds he was transported to that moment and remembered the way those adoring grey eyes had filled him with contentment like he'd never known. It was the same way she'd looked at him at the funeral.

'Huddle in five,' Coach Luke called out, giving notice to the players for his final team-talk.

Danny rolled his shoulders and took a deep, steadying breath. The moment had come to pull on the shirt he'd dreamed of wearing.

Running onto the hallowed pitch at Twickenham was a full-on fanfare – brass bands, flame blasters and an ear-splitting tsunami of sound from 80,000 rallying cheers. And one of those, he knew, was Cassie's. As well as supporting Wales, she was there for him.

After the rousing national anthem for England filled the stadium, 'Hen Wlad Fy Nhadu' was sung as if the entire population of Wales had travelled to Twickenham. Danny had never felt so fired up. Boots touching painted logos in the grass, he stood in position, waiting for the referee's whistle to begin the match. Taking a last look up at the clock, then through the oval roof to the sky, the symbol he needed for successful kicks came to him. With twenty seconds to go, he shared sideways glances with his nearest teammates that all read the same thing: 'Bring it on'.

At half time, back in the changing room, England's kicking coach pulled him aside. 'Forget missing that one kick out of six, your boot's going well. Not sure what's with the 'W' sign with your fingers after each one, but whatever it's for, keep doing it.'

Danny nodded his understanding, hoping that somehow, somewhere, Woody had seen the tribute.

The first half had been fast and punishing, the only moment of calm when team kickers were preparing to kick for goal. England were ahead by twenty points, outplaying Wales in fitness, set pieces and scrums, but ill-discipline and the number of penalties given against them were notably worse.

'It's ours to lose,' said Connor, taking a seat beside Danny while sipping one of the nutritionist's recommended drinks, 'if I can just keep a lid on losing it with that shit-show of a referee.'

'We've had worse. This one is trying to be fair, at least. We don't want a repeat of your Newcastle red card, much as I sympathised with you at the time.'

Connor stopped drinking. 'What? I wish you'd said that to me afterwards, I could have done with the support. Naomi saw me through a horrible few days, in private. Not for the first time, either.'

Danny slapped him on the shoulder. 'Sorry, I should have. Too caught up with captaincy and personal stuff. Carb gel or banana?'

'The second half is going to need a big push, so both. Is the subject of your "personal stuff" sitting with Naomi and the others?'

Danny fussed with the lace on his boot. 'I'm not expecting her to be, but I won't look over there until the match is finished. Eat your food, keep your head in the game. Coach is about to talk tactics.'

'My head *is* in the game. Naomi motivates me as much anyone in this or the club's changing room. She sees past my flaws, knows what I'm trying to achieve and, win or lose, she's got my back, so mind your own head game, *mate*.'

'Yeah, good advice.' And while swallowing down a sickly, strawberry-flavoured gel, his subconscious answered the question of who, outside of the room, had his back. Who he would most want to celebrate or commiserate with. And who he'd probably blown his chances with.

After listening to Coach's warning that the Welsh side would come back out determined to shock England with quick points, the players drew into ring, arms around shoulders.

'Do yourselves, your families, and the country proud,' Coach demanded.

'ENGLAND,' one of the deep-voiced forwards boomed, and everyone shouted it back.

Coach Luke had been right. Possessed by something England did not have, Wales not only scored a quick try, but their dominant determination racked up more within the following thirty minutes. With ten minutes to go – fifteen exhausted red Welsh shirts versus fifteen equally spent white English ones – the score was even. Songs and chants from the passionate supporters pumped ever more adrenaline into the players, the intense atmosphere adding bite to their physical confrontation.

With two minutes to go, the referee gave a penalty against England for a misdemeanour in the scrum, but Connor, stood right beside the action at the time, immediately protested the call, in a way that Danny recognised as showing the potential to escalate. He and the team captain jogged over to where Connor was then intimidating the referee with the threat of reporting 'obvious favouritism' to the Rugby Football Union.

'Connor, leave it,' Danny barked, yanking him away by the scruff of his shirt while the captain tried to smooth out the kerfuffle. But it was too late, and the three of them watched the referee raise his whistle to his mouth and signal that all England players had to move back ten metres. Within seconds, Wales took the opportunity to pass along ready lines of eager players, to touch down a try in the corner of the field. It was followed up by another successful strike through the posts, by Wales's kicker.

Danny checked the time; England had one minute to score a try that would at least bring them level. With no extra time played in Six Nations matches, it would be the best they could hope for. England refused to fold, and by some miracle, the forwards carried the ball up to the try line and Connor, instead of passing the ball out wide to the wing, dashed inside the opposition's defence and touched the ball down for his first international try. Jubilant English cheers pummelled Twickenham's infrastructure, but all too soon, an eerie hush filled the air as everyone waited to see whether Danny's kick would go through the posts and make the scores even.

With seconds ticking down on the shot clock, Danny stuck to his process, controlling his breathing, snatching a few blades of grass into the air to check for wind changes, lining himself up. His legs trembled as if he were back on his Camford debut, more so, if he were honest, but an image of Woody's smiling face brought the calm he needed. With the clock reading twelve seconds left, Danny took his steps backwards then took his kick, striking firmly.

The ball spun in the air, mercifully on target, and he'd been about to look away, but at the last second a gust must have pushed it to the right. It hit the left post and a mass, communal groan, directed solely at him, swamped his ears.

The referee blew his whistle for the end of the game and as Welsh players began to hug and congratulate one another, Danny stared at the posts, trying to understand how he'd messed up his calculation.

'Well played,' said his opposite number, holding out a hand in the way rugby players always do. 'That was a tight one.'

'Congratulations, hope the rest of the competition is as good,' Danny replied, aware that introspection would have to wait, because a few metres away Connor had crouched to the ground. Careful to check for camera crews that had come onto the pitch, Danny bent down beside him. 'First try for England, well done.'

Connor's face was all dejection. 'Tell me honestly, did we lose because of me?'

'No more than because of my failed kicks. You can't hang this defeat on one moment of the game. Coach won't either, even if he barks at you about the discipline. The whole team gave away too many penalties.'

'Thank God this is only the first match, we can still win the tournament if our other matches go better.'

'Absolutely. Hold onto that thought. Come on, we've got to clap the players through the guard of honour tunnel first.'

'Then I want you to come and meet Naomi, OK?'

'Fine, let's go.'

Ten minutes later, Danny and Connor were finally free from their post-match etiquette.

Connor tugged at his arm. 'There she is, that's Naomi.'

For the first time, Danny allowed himself a hasty scan of the section for an out-of-place Wales shirt; nothing.

Instead, Connor diverted his attention by pointing out the location of a blonde-haired woman waving her arms in the air.

'She looks happy to see you.'

'I'm going to put a ring on that girl's finger, if she'll have me. It's been the best six months of my life. Come and meet her.'

Along the edge of the pitch, his teammates had shaken off their pitch personas, once again husbands, fathers and sons being greeted by loved ones.

Naomi cocked her head as he and Connor neared her. 'There they are, England's two newest caps. What a match, boys,' she said in a smoky voice. Connor circled her waist with his arms; eyes closed, seeking the comfort she offered. Naomi whispered something into his ear, and he nodded, kissed her and stepped back to introduce Danny.

'You've seen Danny at Camford?'

'Yes, of course. Excuse the croaky voice, too much yelling. How are you feeling, Captain?' she asked, giving him a jovial salute.

'Didn't leave anything on the pitch, did we?' He looked at Connor.

'No, I'm absolutely knackered. And hungry.'

'Ooh, trigger – so are you hurt, baby? Wouldn't want to neglect my duties now I know from the others about the three Hs.' Naomi winked.

'What's she talking about?' A bemused Connor mumbled to Danny.

'You'll enjoy finding out.'

Naomi threw her head back in a laugh that spread to Connor.

'I'm heading into the changing rooms,' he told Danny, 'You coming?'

Danny nodded but heard his name being called from the other end of the rows. To his amazement, it was his cousin, Nathan. 'Mate, why didn't you tell me you were coming?' he said, jogging over to him.

'The same reason I didn't, either,' said a voice behind Nathan. His other cousin, Jake, popped his head up, grinning.

'What? Aren't you supposed to be performing a matinee in the West End?'

'I persuaded the director to give my understudy some show time, but I have a cool motorbike taxi booked to get me back for tonight's performance. By the way, whether she forgives me hinges on you signing the back of this shirt – she and her husband are big rugby fans.' Jake held out a pen and an England shirt expectantly.

Danny duly scribbled what he hoped was an intelligible message of gratitude and signed his name.
'Tell her thanks. God, I can't believe you're both here. It means a lot, even if we couldn't get you a win. I can't get over the surprise.'

'There's another one. Come over here,' said Nathan, exchanging a knowing look with Jake.

Danny followed his cousins to the end of the row, then had to check twice that he hadn't mistaken the identity of a familiar, if older, face. 'Mr Hayes?'

'Hello Danny, fantastic to see you, congratulations on your cap. You know, right from college I had faith that you'd make it onto the pitch for England. I'm so proud of your journey.' His old college teacher dabbed at the corner of his eyes.

In a trance, Danny hugged him, choking back his own emotions. Someone help him – he was going to cry for the second time in a week. 'It's great to see you, Mr Hayes, I wish I'd known you were going to be here.'

'I think you can call me David now. Neither me nor your cousins knew for sure it was possible until last night, when your friend Cassie confirmed our tickets. For whatever reason, she'd said that she wouldn't be sitting here, but still wanted there to be people here for you.'

Danny screwed his eyes, gripping onto the last edges of control. Maybe he hadn't blown his chances, after all. 'How did she—'

'I had a message from her passed to me through the theatre,' said Jake, and Nathan nodded.

'Yes, she contacted me via the airline. I guess she found you via the college, David?'

'That's right. I'm so happy you have someone that does things like this for you. I retired at Christmas and might consider a trip to Edinburgh for your match at Murrayfield. I've wanted to explore the Lothian towns, so I can bolt it onto that.'

'I could also see what my flight schedules look like for then,' said Nathan. 'That's a Sunday match, isn't it?'

'I might be able to fly up after my evening performance on the Saturday, we don't have a show on Sundays,' said Jake, 'That's if you'd like us to come?'

Danny couldn't contain his grin as his 'support' group organised itself, overwhelmed by a deep well of gratitude towards them, and even more for Cassie. He had to fix things. 'There's usually a dinner for the players straight after the internationals, but I'd join you straight after that, up in Scotland, if I'm selected. As it is, for this one I'll need to make my excuses. I want to get up to the to the media centre, see if I can find Cassie.'

'Of course,' they all smiled. 'Go, thank her for us and tell her we look forward to meeting her sometime. We'll see you in Scotland.'

Danny embraced each of them in turn, promising to keep in touch in the meantime, then sprinted along the pitch, into the changing room, via the players' tunnel.

'There he is,' said Coach Luke, stood in the middle of the changing room, 'I've been waiting to present you with your official England cap. Not the result we wanted but as I've said to the other boys, we'll remember the pain of losing and channel it into our training on Monday. Today was a lot of pressure, you'll learn from it and your future with England is bright. Here's your cap, congratulations. Now get changed, and either go out with the boys for dinner or go let off some steam, relax or whatever you need. Back to training on Monday.' He shook Danny's hand and handed him an old-style velvet cap decorated with gold tassels, England insignia, his name and the date.

Other players in various state of dress around them clapped enthusiastically and patted him on the shoulder as they passed on their way to and from the showers.

Almost overcome, he placed the cap carefully into his holdall, thinking of Laura, Woody, his Camford friends and his 'family' support group. Most of all, he wanted to share the moment with Cassie. To return her support and love, to protect and encourage whatever made her happy. He saw it now. He might not be good enough for her, but he'd do whatever was needed to get their relationship back on track.

Fuelled by an urgency he'd never known he managed an ultra-rapid shower and changed into his England tracksuit. Next, he messaged Connor, sending apologies for missing the dinner, then coaxed rapidly stiffening legs up several flights of concrete steps to Twickenham's media centre. He peered inside the doors, but unfortunately, the only people there were technicians.

'Hello, I was looking for the Hystar team?'

'Er, they've gone, sorry. Griff and Steve have headed to the bar, Cassie left straight afterwards, said there was some kind of emergency, was headed off to one of the hospitals.'

Maybe Fox or another friend from Hystar had taken ill? Then something dreadful dawned on him. Camford were playing in North London. He messaged Heather, hoping his fear was unfounded.

DR: All ok?
HK: No. Ryn in bad way, in for scans
DR: He's made of tough stuff. Which hospital?
HK: Barnet. I'm worried
DR: Sit tight, on my way

'What's the quickest way to Barnet?' he asked the technicians.

'There isn't one, it's havoc outside, roads are gridlocked. Give it an hour or two, if I were you.'

He jogged back out of the media centre and dialled the number for Jake, who fortunately picked up immediately.

'S'up? Just starting my stage make-up.'

'Yeah, I can't believe I'm asking you this, but I need a motorbike taxi urgently. Who'd you use?'

'I'll ping you the details, they use the Yamaha FJR 1300s, which give an excellent ride.'

'I don't speak bike, but is that fast?'

'Yes and fun.'

Danny doubted that.

'Ask them for pick-up from Gate D, which is the one my rider used.'

In the background, Danny could hear an announcement at the theatre. *'Cast and crew, one hour till first positions please, that's one hour till first positions, thank you.'*

'I've got to go catch up with people after their matinee performance, see you soon?'

'Definitely, and…break a leg.'

'Thanks, but don't you, England need those intact for next time.'

Outside Gate D, Danny waited for a lift from someone on the worst mode of transport in the world, but he was out of options. Around him, spectators were still mingling, those in red Wales shirts wearing the greatest smiles, but the general atmosphere was buoyant.

A noisy, deathtrap of a motorbike drew up beside him, and the driver flipped up his visor.

'Reed to Barnet?'

'Yep.'

'Spare helmet's in the rear box, strap your bag onto your back then we can get going.'

'Thanks, and I'm kind of in a rush.'

'Gotcha.'

RED, WHITE & CUE

28. Losing v Winning

At Barnet hospital, Cassie was directed to a surgical ward and immediately spotted Heather talking to one of the ward nurses. 'Heather, hi, how's he doing?'

Heather immediately sagged into Cassie's arms. 'We just heard. After shoulder surgery he should be fine, but he has a bad concussion and lots of swelling so they're holding off operating until tomorrow.'

'OK, and how are you?'

'A bit calmer, it gave me a fright, seeing him stumble around with his arm dangling. Thanks for coming.'

Cassie squeezed. 'I'm glad you messaged me. Where is he?'

'Along here. They've put him in a side room so that it's darker; bright lights are irritating his eyes. He's on some strong painkillers and his words are a bit muddled, but they're monitoring him closely.'

Inside the half-lit room, Cassie was greeted by Ryn's dopey smile, his body way too big for the bed.

She smiled back at him. 'Considerate of you to be injured in my hometown, certainly makes visiting easier.'

'Heeey stranger, how's you?'

'Sorry to see you bashed up like this.'

'No one's to blame. Committed to the tackle 100% as always, this time I came off worse.'

Heather positioned herself at the head of the bed. 'He did, though that nurse just told me the other player's still down in A&E vomiting with concussion.'

Cassie took in the extent of the strapping around Ryn's right shoulder. 'How's the pain?'

'No pain at all,' he grinned. 'Amazing, this stuff. Really, really good.'

Heather cocked an eyebrow. 'Yes, well, the main thing is, the surgeon doesn't believe Ryn's is a career-ending injury.'

'I'm relieved to hear it.'

Ryn held out his good hand for Heather's and brought it to his lips for a brief kiss. 'It's crazy, when I scored that try a few minutes earlier and looked over to Heth, I thought, this is why I give everything to rugby, but this woman, she's my world and I love her harder.'

'Jeez Louise, don't mind my soppy husband. Why does it take morphine for men to say how they feel?'

''Cos we're shit scared of women's rejection,' he offered, resting his head back onto his pillow and closing his eyes.

'Aw, baby.' Heather climbed onto the bed and carefully laid herself along Ryn's good side. 'This isn't his first injury, but each time it's like it happens to me too. It doesn't get any easier.'

Cassie blinked at the beautiful exchange.

Ryn's eyes suddenly pinged open, making him wince. 'Wait, where's Danny?'

'Probably still at Twickenham, I'm not sure,' said Cassie, vaguely.

Heather smoothed a hand across Ryn's forehead. 'Remember they aren't together at the moment, baby.'

'What? Why not?'

'We've talked about why not; it's probably because Danny's default is to live without love. With Cassie he made compromises, took risks, made mistakes just like we all do in relationships, but after things went wrong it seemed safer to walk away. Don't forget, he lives with the shadow of rejection from his childhood, the boy who wasn't deemed good enough. So, however much he wants to – and we can all see that he does – he hasn't found his way to open himself up again. Sorry,' she grimaced at Cassie, 'am I wrong?'

Cassie was positively squirming. 'I'm not comfortable discussing him like this.'

'You're right, and I don't doubt you had your reasons for whatever happened, but we've seen how you've hung in there, trying to show him the way, haven't we, babes?'

'Have we?'

Heather kissed Ryn's forehead. 'Yes, and don't worry about remembering that now, baby, the point is, for some reason he's hesitating, like he can't get out of his own way.'

Cassie eyed the door. 'Can I maybe get you a coffee? I know I could do with one.'

'Definitely,' said Ryn, his eyes hopeful, until he saw Heather shaking her head at him.

'No, you can have one at eight o'clock if the nurses give the all clear. You're on nil-by-mouth until then, that's partly what your IV drip is for.'

'But that's not fair.'

'No, not fair would be me drinking one in front of you, while you can't. We're both going without. Thank you, Cassie, I might have had one while he was in having his scans, but go, get yourself one. Good luck finding the machine, it's an epic walk.'

'Alright, I'll be back sometime soon, then.' Anything to curtail open discussion about her and Danny's relationship. She'd done just about everything she could to give him space, yet show she was still there, but after today, she might have to give up.

'Love you!' Ryn called as she went for the door.

Heather sighed.

It was a good thing the coffee cups were insulated. Cassie hadn't considered herself as having a poor sense of direction, but twice she'd had to stop hospital staff for directions back to the ward. As she approached Ryn's room she stopped in her tracks, amazed to hear Danny's voice. She positioned herself carefully beside the doorway, out of sight. Ryn, it seemed, was confiding in him.

'Yeah, don't tell Heth, but I was a bit panicked when the pitch medics looked worried, ya know? We put everything into the game and I just thought, don't take rugby away, it's all I have.'

'Hey, you're going to be fine.'

'No, no, I know that, because as soon as Heather met me in the tunnel and held my hand, I remembered it wasn't true anyway, rugby isn't all I have. I tell you, man, having someone you can't live without is everything.'

'What the hell's in that drip?'

'I mean, forget your fucking head, man, and listen to your heart.'

Cassie could hear Ryn slapping something, presumably his chest, for emphasis.

'Fine, since you're sky high, and Heather's conked out here on the bed, I'll admit that losing today isn't the worst thing that I could lose, not by a long way. It's like, the single-minded player I was is gone, there's another layer now. Next time Camford have the psychologist asking what motivates us, I'll be up at the fucking front handing out roses and blurting out the word "love".'

Cassie giggled to herself at the vision.

'Bruh, that's the same for a lot of us, once we've found who we belong with.'

'Yeah? Well, I think I might belong with Cassie.'

Now she could hardly breathe.

'Funny way of showing it, mate. If she means that much to you and you don't want to lose her, why aren't you acting like it?'

'You're right. I just hope it's not too late – that's why I came here. Where is she?'

'What, so you're not here for me then? She's getting coffee, which is also not for me.'

Cassie took a sip of her coffee, only then reminded she'd been holding it.

'Shh, Heather's waking, we'll talk about this another time,' said Danny.

'I heard most of that,' Heather murmured, 'this lighting made me sleepy. When did you get here?'

'A few minutes ago, took my first and last ever motorbike taxi. Half the people in accident and emergency have probably fallen off of one.'

'You big baby. Well apart from enjoying that touching man-to-man conversation, for what it's worth, and before Cassie comes back, you should listen to me. If you have someone is in your life that loves you the way you've always wanted to be loved, hang on to them. Love them back harder.'

'Thanks for the extra serving of relationship advice, am I on the psych ward?'

'Watch it mate, I could still whoop your ass with my good arm. Adjust your tone with my wife.'

'Baby, leave it, we both know that if it's not the right time, you can't force it. But Danny, if it's the right time, you can't stop it either. God, even I know that sounded like something from a romance novel. I wish I'd agreed to that coffee; Cassie must be lost.'

Never one to miss her cue, Cassie loosened her stance, shook her hair and breezed into the room as if walking straight in from the corridor.

Danny bolted upright from the visitor's chair. 'Cassie.'

'Danny.'

'Coffee, thank God,' said Heather, removing Cassie's drink from her hands.

'Where's mine?' asked Ryn.

Memory loss, thought Cassie, it must be his concussion.

'Nope, still none for you, babes.' But Heather mollified him by taking a swig of her coffee then kissing him gently.

'Mmm, more of that please,' he muttered, going in for another kiss.

'Hold that thought for a few days, meantime you'll hopefully have a coffee of your own in the next forty minutes.'

Cassie was aware that Danny's gaze on her hadn't moved throughout Ryn's cute exchange with Heather.

He cleared his throat. 'Would you mind if Cassie and I go for a walk until then? My legs are tight, and there's probably a garden here somewhere.'

'It's freezing and dark outside,' said Heather, 'but there are miles and miles of corridors.'

Danny would prefer the garden, Cassie knew. 'Back in a while, then,' she murmured, following him out.

'And bring more coffee with you.' Ryn called.

Outside of the ward, Cassie gestured to the left. 'The lifts are along that way; they'll at least take us down to the ground floor.'

Danny nodded and walked beside her in silence until they got into an empty lift. Once the doors closed, he turned to her. 'I don't know where to start, or how to. I just know I want to.'

'We're here, together, that's the best place to start. I'm sorry about the match, are you OK?'

'Yes, but I want to talk about us. I haven't tried as hard as you, but I will do from now on, if it's not too late.'

Cassie slipped her hand into his. 'It isn't.'

Danny gripped it hard and exhaled slowly. 'Thank God.'

The doors opened onto the busy ground floor corridor, and they found their way back to the main entrance. To Cassie's dismay, people were shaking off wet outwear, and windows everywhere wore streaks of rain.

Danny tugged her towards the reception desk, apparently undeterred. 'Hello, any chance you have a spare umbrella there, preferably a big one?'

One of the women held up a bucket that held a variety of walking sticks and umbrellas. 'Take your pick, these have all been left behind.'

'Thank you.' He selected a long golf umbrella and turned to Cassie. 'I'm game if you are.'

'Definitely.'

They stepped outside and Danny pulled her tight into his body, his arm protectively around her shoulders, as they set off for the gardens accompanied by the pitter-patter of rain on the umbrella.

Immediately, Cassie raised the subject of her mother and clarified the reasons for having held back on daunting conversations with him about her teenage years. 'I suspect that everyone's different, in how and whether they keep difficult things to themselves. In my case, I wanted to tell you, but gave myself excuses to avoid the pain of it. I'm sorry, that wasn't fair on either of us. With my encouragement, you opened up while I chose the easier option not to, which wasn't an equal exchange. Something good that's come from it, and having been inspired by Josh, is that I think I'll seek out a professional to talk to about what happened.'

Danny drew them to a halt. 'That's a good idea, but I also want you to feel that there's nothing you can't share with me. I'll always believe what you tell me, OK? You can rely on that.'

Cassie nodded, almost too choked to speak. 'Yes, and I will be more protective of your trust. I know what it means that you give it.'

Danny brushed a hand across her cheek. 'I'm sorry I went behind your back to meet your mother. But I'd still like to help you both find a way through what's happened, which would include dealing with

Gethin and anything else you need. But only if those are things you want.'

'He has something on you.'

'I suspect he'll value the pub and his reputation above anything else.'

'You might be right. Let's keep moving, the rain's coming down harder now.'

'At least you've got shoes on, today.'

'I really thought you were going to pick me up and carry me back to the car, that day,' she chuckled.

'I didn't want you to hurt your feet.'

She nodded and urged him to continue along the path. On they walked, finding steps down to a sunken, recently landscaped garden. Unsurprisingly, no one else had braved a wet, cold and dark walk to spend time there. She and Danny took refuge beneath a covered shelter for a few minutes.

'I was gobsmacked that my cousins and Mr Hayes were at the game, I nearly lost it when I saw them.'

'I'm glad, they were very keen to be there for you, too.'

Danny turned to face her and took her hands in his. 'I'd like you with them, next time, if I'm selected to play.'

'I'd love to, although just to be clear, I won't wear an England shirt, in public, but I *might* be persuaded to wear it somewhere in private. I have news about my next Hystar projects, by the way, and you might be interested to know that I'll be exclusively UK-based for the foreseeable future, as one element can be undertaken from anywhere.'

'I *am* very interested to know,' he said, putting up the umbrella again, and angling it in a way that shielded them from any possible viewpoint, 'but first, I want you to know that I still love you, Cassie.' His voice cracked. 'And…I don't want to lose you.'

'You haven't. I love you too.' She wrapped her arms around him as tightly as she could, feeling the solid strength of his banded arms around her back. 'Mmm, I've missed these hugs,' she muttered.

He bent his head towards hers, tipped her chin and kissed her like she meant the world. For more than four minutes. Slowly.

Epilogue

18 months later

Have fun tonight baby, sorry I can't be there. See you at home on Sunday. Love you more than ever, Dx

While Cassie got ready for the Hystar Group summer party that evening, she stopped intermittently to smell the white roses that had accompanied Danny's note. Home. She couldn't have known eighteen months ago how deeply at peace she would feel in the 18th century cottage in Camford, near to Heather and Ryn, that she and Danny now rented together. She thought of their cosy open fire, the bookcases either side of it and how the house had become a sanctuary from their busy lives. His only stipulation had been to have some space for Cassie to write, hers that he'd have a garden to potter in.

    Last weekend they'd finally hung up Danny's framed England caps and his Premiership winning medal from Camford's sensational year. With them were Cassie's teenage writing-competition pieces, and newspaper articles from Stumble Inn's walls. On the sideboard, two industry awards twinkled in the candlelight, recognition for the docuseries, alongside

Danny's cherished photograph of Laura and a recent one that he'd taken of Cassie with her mother, in the garden, when she'd visited their house.

Tonight, Danny was still away on Camford Rugby's pre-season training camp, and she was staying for the final time on the sofa bed in her old Clapham apartment, the lease on which her mother was about to take over.

The newly divorced Gwyn Forde had found herself work in a local restaurant, but would be looking for something nearer to Cassie, once Gethin had finished buying out her share of Stumble Inn, using a carefully worded contract.

At the party's entrance, a young Jamaican DJ spun infectious reggae, setting a chilled Caribbean party vibe that matched colourful flower arrangements and strings of overhead lights. A member of waiting staff immediately approached Cassie, bearing a tray of assorted cocktails. The legacy of having had her drink spiked two Christmas's ago still saw her rely on an abundance of caution. And, in support of her mother, she'd decided not to drink alcohol at all. Her nerves, now significantly more settled thanks to the reduction of live television gigs, also thanked her for it.

'Thank you,' Cassie smiled, picking up what she was assured was a simple, non-alcoholic margarita, then scanned the vast event for sight of anyone familiar.

'Cass, over here,' Fox's unmistakable tone floated over the music, from where he was stood with his fiancée, Livvy.

'Hi guys, you look great.'

Fox curved his arm proudly around Livvy's shoulders. 'Doesn't she? The most beautiful mum-to-be *ever*.'

'Ever,' Cassie agreed, pleased for her friends. If all went well next year, she and Danny had talked about buying a house together. Her projects could become more home-based and Danny, while still having the mental and physical resilience to win another season, anticipated an eventual switch to coaching at The Manor. The subject of future fostering came up frequently.

'You look gorgeous, my friend, shame you're flying solo,' said Fox.

Cassie smiled, pleased that the black, one-shouldered cocktail dress she'd worn complemented her deep chestnut curls, but as she sipped her drink, she grimaced. 'That is not alcohol-free, I need to swap it. Where's the nearest tray of drinks?'

'Hold that thought,' said Fox, 'there's one's coming our way, six feet behind you.'

Cassie turned and met a broad-bodied, dark-eyed and heavenly-smelling rugby player. Stood in an unfamiliar but well-fitting dinner suit, her man had never looked hotter.

'Hello, beautiful,' came Danny's deep rumble, before he kissed her and handed over a luminous-looking fruit cocktail. He tasted of pineapple. 'I had a fruit punch made up for you at the bar, it's delicious.'

She couldn't agree more. 'How are you even here?'

'Coach decided to give us tomorrow off, so we left Cornwall after lunch. I asked to be dropped in

London on the way through, and Fox hired me this dinner suit. Cheers, by the way, mate.'

'Glad it fits,' Fox murmured.

Cassie tucked herself into Danny's side and felt the warmth of his hand rest in the small of her back. Equal parts thrill and security swept through her, and she slid her hand up into the nape of his neck, to reciprocate.

'I loved your book,' Livvy said to her. 'Do Damon the rugby player and Story the physiotherapist have any other adventures coming up? I think a sequel to *Just Try* would be another hit.'

'They don't, but I have another idea I'm working on. It will mean that I can research and write between this season's docuseries production, and I'll be home more nights than not.'

Danny smiled down at her. Both of them were looking forward to that.

'So, what sport are you filming this time?' Livvy asked.

'God help me. It will be cricket, for Essex County.'

'Oof, good luck.'

'I'll do my best. Luckily, Fox will be on hand for some of it, at least.'

'She literally doesn't know her "outs" from her "ins", it's going to be painful,' Fox joked, then drew everyone's attention over Cassie's shoulder. 'Who's that coming this way and waving at you?'

Cassie turned to investigate. 'Oh, that's my editor. I ought to check in with the Hystar Publishing lot, sorry, I'll catch up with you both later.' She air-kissed Fox and Livvy before moving away.

'Alice, hi, you remember my boyfriend, Danny? Danny, you met my editor Alice Cook at Christmas?'

'Good to see you again.' Danny nodded, still stroking Cassie's back.

'And you. Look, I won't keep you, but I wanted to give you the heads up; we've been approached to co-write a sports biography, and you were number one on the subject's list of writers. It's actually your colleague, Danny, Josh Webber? He's a real character and so much good came from him talking about mental health in your docuseries. His work since then with the mental health charities and of course the worst kept secret, that he's tipped for an MBE in the King's birthday honours next June, means that the time is right for a book. He's specifically requested that we approach you first. Have a think and come back to me, see you a bit later.'

After waving off Alice, Danny dropped a kiss onto Cassie's bare shoulder and murmured, 'Before anyone else arrives, you look incredible tonight. That hair, your dress, God, I want to take you home immediately.'

'Don't think I wouldn't let you, either, you know full well that hand on my back is driving me insane. You look mouthwatering in that dinner suit.'

'I think you'd best take a picture of us, for the group chat, while we've still got our clothes on. It'll give everyone a break from pictures of Nathan holding baby Alfie, and the scenery landscapes David shares from his travels. By the way, Jake messaged this afternoon; he's down to the final two for that new musical I told you about. Says it might take him and his friend to Broadway if it's a hit.'

'I saw his original post, let's hope he gets it. That "friend", was she the one he was acting opposite in the Autumn show? They were sensational together, very convincing.'

'I think so. Right, smile.' Danny took a couple of pictures of them and examined the results. 'Or I could share this picture from last weekend?' He showed her the screenshot of the DNA results he'd received, having finally sent off the testing kit.

'I'm not sure anyone will see that coming,' she said, 'Mr I'm 81%—'

But Danny didn't let her finish, and instead kissed her tenderly. 'I love you, baby.'

'I love you too, or maybe I should say, *Je t'aime, mon amour*?'

'Let's go for a walk outside.'

'Alright, but we can't be long, though.' She smiled, sliding her arm through his, as he guided them towards some gardens.

Fire danced in his eyes. 'You know how long we'll be.'

Acknowledgements

To my friends and family who beta-read *Red, White & Cue*, thank you for your time and encouragement. I don't take any of it for granted. Fellow authors Enni Amanda and Lauren Foley, your insightful feedback was invaluable. Ellie Peterson, thank you for your helpful guidance on my use of the Welsh language, and Gemma Rakia for creating a gorgeous book cover. Celia Killen, I consider myself very fortunate to have secured your editorial services, thank you.

Red, White & Cue allowed me to indulge my interest in rugby, to explore the world of broadcast journalism and aim for a genre-appropriate story of the same, if not better standard as my debut, *Fall & Fly*. It has been another fulfilling experience, though I'd be lying if I didn't admit how perceived pressure, a new round of reviews, months of research, writing, editing, publishing and marketing preparation took turns in generating self-doubts. As ever, special thanks go to my darling, Gary. Your patient reassurance, and reminders that I'd survived and learned from my debut, kept me on track. For this, and so many other things, I love you.

This story references various guises of motherhood. I like to think that all mothers want the same thing: for their children to be happy. What I know to be true, is that the joys and challenges of being a mother myself, have enabled deeper appreciation of my own, incredibly lucky childhood. From the bottom of my heart, thank you, Mum.

RED, WHITE & CUE

Coming in 2025

Book 3 in The Captains series

Follow theatre star, Jake Reed's journey from London's West End to New York's Broadway, and his on/off stage relationship with fellow performer, Summer McIntyre.

***

Also by Polly Meek

Book 1 in The Captains series

'Fall & Fly'

Midlife love is in the air for commercial pilots Romilly and Nathan. With front row seats from the flight deck, travel to San Francisco and London, as our pilots navigate an eventful journey to happiness.

Available on Amazon in paperback and Kindle formats

For Polly's latest news visit:

www.thetownhousewriter.co.uk

and follow her on:

Facebook.com/pollymeekwriter
Instagram.com/pollymeek_thetownhousewriter
Twitter.com/pollymeekwriter
Tiktok.com/@pollymeekwriter

RED, WHITE & CUE

Printed in Great Britain
by Amazon

Failed novelist Cassie Forde secures a sports journalism internship, when assigned to assist with televised coverage of a Premier rugby match, predicts a day of running errands and fact-chec Instead, events take her out of her comfort zone and into a whirl connection with one of the players.

Planet Rugby has saved cynical Danny Reed from the legacy broken childhood, and a life that taught him to live without. After y of single-minded training, he makes his overdue debut to a televised, capacity crowd. Facing hidden demons and brutal pla conditions, the game marks a significant milestone, but it is the imp of meeting Cassie that lingers.

In need of respite from her high-pressured job, Cassie grasps the o to produce and film a sports-life docuseries - despite its subject location. To achieve success, she must navigate her history with player who stole her heart.

Now valued by Club and community alike, Danny's fearless playing s and ambition to stake a claim on an England Rugby shirt, are tes when Cassie reappears. As filming of training, home and av matches take place, Cassie and Danny enter each other's world. W trust, and undeniable chemistry steer them through challenges memorable Christmas ball declares Danny as Cassie's last line defence. When a series of shock revelations are made, th relationship is tested and each must ask themselves, what matt most, when you have something to lose?

ISBN 9798343302660

9798343 302660